Abraham Lincoln's Personal Creed:

—I believe . . . in God, the Almighty Ruler of Nations, our great and good and merciful Maker, our Father in Heaven, who notes the fall of a sparrow and numbers the hairs of our heads.

—I believe . . . in His eternal truth and justice. I recognize the sublime truth announced in the Holy Scriptures and proven by all history that those nations are only blest whose God is the Lord.

—I believe . . . that the Bible is the best gift which God has ever given to men. All the good from the Saviour of the world is communicated to us through this book.

—I believe . . . the will of God prevails. Without Him all human reliance is vain. Without the assistance of that Divine Being, I cannot succeed. With that assistance I cannot fail. Being a humble instrument in the hands of our Heavenly Father, I desire that all my works and acts may be according to His will; and that it may be so, I give my thanks to the Almighty, and seek His aid.

—I believe . . . that it is right to recognize and confess the presence of the Almighty Father equally in our triumphs and in those sorrows which we may justly fear are a punishment inflicted upon us for our presumptuous sins to the needful end of our reformation.

I have a solemn oath registered in heaven to finish the work I am in, in full view of my responsibility to my God, with malice toward none; with charity for all; with firmness in the right as God gives me to see the right.

GOD'S LEADER FOR
A NATION

ABRAHAM
LINCOLN

By

David Collins

ILLUSTRATED BY MYRON QUINTON

MOTT
MEDIA

Milford, Michigan 48042

COPYRIGHT © 1976 by Mott Media
Second Printing 1981
Third Printing 1982
Fourth Printing 1983

Norma Cournow Camp, Editor

LIBRARY OF CONGRESS CATALOGING IN PUBLICATION DATA

Collins, David R.
  Abraham Lincoln.

  (The Sowers)
  Bibliography: p. 147
  Includes Index.

  SUMMARY: Abraham Lincoln recounts the story of his life.
  1. Lincoln, Abraham, Pres. U.S., 1809-1865 — Juvenile literature.
[1. Lincoln, Abraham, Pres. U.S., 1809-1865. 2. Presidents] I. Title.

E457.905.C64   973.7'092'4 [B] [92]   76-2456
ISBN 0-915134-93-4 Paperbound
ISBN 0-915134-09-8 Hardbound

FOREWORD

"Scoundrel!"

"Devil Servant!"

"Villain!"

Unbelievable as it seems, these names were once hurled at one of America's greatest heroes. Abraham Lincoln endured much suffering in his lifetime, but he was a true sower of faith and freedom.

The life of Abraham Lincoln is well recorded for history. Thankfully, he provided his own account of many personal experiences. To his own accounting may be added the research of countless other historians.

But sadly enough, the spiritual side of Abraham Lincoln has been seldom reported. Because he held no formal church membership, he has even been labeled "anti-Christian."

There is, however, little doubt that Abraham Lincoln was a most devoted Christian. His entire life reflects a deep personal faith in God. Certainly there were periods of doubt and questioning. But do doubts and questions weaken or strengthen the spiritual faith a person holds? In Lincoln's case, the trying events of his earlier life seem to have provided him with a rich full faith during his final years. This book will attempt to explore the spiritual side of Abraham Lincoln, relying on his own words and the observations of his family, his friends and historians.

To add a more personal dimension to the life of Abraham Lincoln, his story is told as a first person account. Hopefully this means of presentation will allow the reader to become part of the events as they occur.

Dave Collins
Moline, Illinois

To my mother,
whose faith in the Lord
has been the strongest human force
I have ever known.

CONTENTS

A Big Decision

Maybe Pa wasn't coming home.

I wondered if Ma had thought of that. Other folks had left Knob Creek and said they were coming back. Many never did.

I watched Ma standing in the cabin doorway. "A fine figure of a woman" Pa called her when he wanted her to blush and laugh. She raised one hand to shade her eyes from the sunlight. She was watching for Pa, searching for a moving figure on the Kentucky hillside.

"See anything, Ma?" I called out.

Slowly she turned, shaking her head. "No, Abe. Just the breeze stirring the trees a bit."

I knew Ma was worried. Pa had been gone before, but never this long. It had been over a month since he set out for Indiana. What if he didn't come back? If Pa didn't come —

Suddenly I heard a familiar voice outside.

"Ma! Abe! Come out!"

In answer to my sister Sarah's squeal, Ma and I bolted toward the cabin doorway.

"I think it's Pa coming!" Sarah yelled. "Look down the road."

Ma lifted both hands to shield out the sun. I dashed to the road, hoping for a better look. As I squinted westward, I could see a man on a horse approaching.

"What makes you think it's Pa?" I shouted back at Sarah. "It could be any traveler from Louisville going to Nashville."

Sarah made an angry face at me, but Ma stood smiling in the doorway. "Your sister's right, Abe. It is your Pa. Thank the good Lord for bringing him home to us. Now you children get on inside. Your Pa's likely to be tired and needing a warm meal inside him. Sarah, you see if we have some fresh berries. Abe, you ready a good cooking fire."

I dashed back to the cabin with Sarah, while Ma headed on down the road. I knew she wanted to be alone with Pa, but I was eager to hear him tell stories about Indiana.

"Think we'll be moving soon?" Sarah asked inside the cabin. She began plopping berries from a wooden bucket into a bowl.

"Could be," I answered, tossing a few pieces of kindling onto the fire.

Sarah stood a moment, her hands unmoving. "Would you want to move, Abe? Do you want to leave Knob Creek?"

I pointed to the doorway. "We need more berries. And we got more chores waiting. It's not for us to say where we go. Now hurry along. They'll be coming soon."

As I grabbed a small log, I looked into the fire. I thought about what Sarah had said. Did I want to move? Did I want to leave Knob Creek? It was hard to say. I couldn't remember living any other place. Sometimes Pa told me about the little cabin near Hodgenville where I was born. It was only ten miles from Knob Creek.

"February 12, 1809. That was the date, all right!" Pa would smile as he showed me the writing in the front of the family Bible. "And here's your sister's birthdate too. February 10, 1807. Naturally, we was hoping for another girl when you came along. But you take what you get in such matters."

Ma always blushed when Pa talked like that. He would laugh loud and long.

"Well, that's a good welcome home fire!"

I turned around and saw Pa behind me. Quickly he scooped me up and hoisted me to his shoulders. I couldn't stop laughing.

"Such foolishness!" Ma exclaimed. "I might expect such actions from a boy seven years old. But *you*, Thomas Lincoln!"

Pa spun around the floor, bouncing me harder. Soon Sarah begged to be twirled too. As usual, Pa gave in.

"Will you tell us about Indiana?" I asked. "Will you?"

"After we've eaten a few vittles," Pa answered.

Three times Ma had to stop me from gulping my food at supper. Finally, Pa stood by the fireplace while Ma sat peacefully in her rocker. Sarah and I lay before the crackling fire.

"Well, I'm thinking we might be better off over there in Indiana. The land has been surveyed and is selling for two dollars an acre. There would be no trouble with land titles like we've had here in Kentucky. And I could farm there without having old Knob Creek flooding every year and washing away our best crops and topsoil."

Ma rocked slowly, mending a torn trouser Pa had brought back. As I looked back at Pa, I saw his eyes sparkling.

"That Indiana land is open and free too. No
slaves are kept there. I never have liked the idea of
one man keeping another. Goes against the Lord's
teaching."

Ma nodded her agreement. She had been quiet
a long time. I wondered what she was thinking.
Finally, she spoke.

"Thomas, this is a big decision. There are the
children we must think about too. Here there's a
school where Sarah and Abe can get on. And there
are the prayer meetings. Both the children are
getting to know the Lord well, thanks to the
preachers who come to Knob Creek."

"Thanks to you and your Bible, don't you
mean?" Pa answered.

I couldn't help smiling as I saw Ma redden. Pa
never cared much for the Knob Creek School.
"Life is the best teacher," he always said. But he
still let Sarah and me go. When Ma read to us from
the Bible, Pa sometimes shook his head. But I
knew he was listening too.

"Well, woman, I can't go making promises
about schools and preachers in the new place."
Pa stretched his stout body like he was reaching
for the cabin ceiling. "But I'm thinking there will
be other folks settling there talking like you.
They'll be wanting a school and prayer sessions
too."

For the first time I was sure Pa had made up his
mind. Yes, we were going to move. Sarah seemed
to know it too.

"Is there a place we can swim in the summer?"
she blurted.

"Is there anywhere I can catch crawfish?" I
asked.

Pa rubbed his chin.

"The place I'm thinking about is a lot like this
one. It's called Little Pigeon Creek. The creek

flows right beside some hills and through a small woods."

"I'll help you clear the trees," I offered.

"The woods are full of grouse, deer, turkey, berries—"

"I'll pick the berries!" Sarah joined in.

Suddenly I knew what my Pa was doing. Whenever he wanted Ma to think the way he did, he got us on his side. Again the plan worked. I was ready to leave tomorrow. I looked over at Sarah. Her face wore the same ready look.

Slowly Ma stood up. The old rocking chair rolled against the hard dirt floor.

"Well, if we're going to Indiana, there will be a lot for us to do," she said. "I think we had best keep our bodies and souls strong. We can start by getting some rest."

I did not want to go to sleep. I wanted to hear more about Indiana. But a nod from Pa told me he agreed with Ma. Sarah and I prepared for bed. I could not get to sleep that night. I kept thinking about Little Pigeon Creek. I hoped it would have a school. I reached for the shingle and charcoal bit I kept nearby.

"A-b-r-a-h-a-m.

L-i-n-c-o-l-n."

I said the letters aloud as I wrote them in the darkness on the shingle. I liked the sound of my name.

"Vain brings pain!" Sarah always said. "The Lord thinks little of those who think much of themselves."

I set the shingle and charcoal aside. I fell asleep wondering about our new life ahead in Indiana.

Our New Home

There was a lot to do in the weeks that followed. Pa went off to find a buyer for the cabin and our two hundred and thirty acres of Kentucky land. Three times he went back to Indiana to clear land for our future home. On one of the trips he took a wagon full of our belongings.

"A man named Posey will look after our things until we get there," Pa said. "It won't be long now."

I didn't think moving day would ever come. But it did and it was a warm day in the autumn of 1816. Pa brought two big farm horses to the cabin. Sarah and I didn't like horses.

"Must we ride, Pa?" I asked. "Sarah and I could walk along—"

"What foolishness!" Pa exclaimed. "Abe, you'll ride behind me on this roan. Sarah, jump up behind your Ma on that bay mare."

Sarah and I did as Pa told us. Scared as we were, we wanted no whipping. I held on to Pa hard.

"How far is it?" I asked.

"About one hundred miles from here," Pa answered. "It should take us four, maybe five days."

I could always tell when Pa did not want to talk. He was silent as we rode through the woods and meadows, leaving Knob Creek behind.

After an hour my back got tired, and then my arms, and my bottom too. I wanted to ask Pa to stop and rest. But I didn't. I was glad when Ma spoke up.

"Thomas, I think we have gone far enough for one day."

"We'll go a bit farther, Nancy," Pa replied.

It seemed like another hour of riding before we stopped. It felt good to slide off the horse's back and sleep on the soft autumn leaves.

Too soon it was morning. Pa's voice sounded harsh.

"Make haste, you sleepy heads. Move those legs. We still have far to go."

So it started again. This time I tried to sleep, but the rough hillsides made for too many bumps and bounces.

Sometimes I wished we had never left Knob Creek, and I didn't care if we ever got to Indiana. All I did care about was the nighttime when we could rest. Sarah and Ma were tired too, but Ma warned us against complaining.

"The Lord rewards those who suffer in silence."

Finally, we came to the river — the mighty Ohio. It looked so long and smooth. I had never seen a river before.

"We're going to ride across this river?" Sarah asked, her voice trembling a bit.

The question sounded so foolish. "Not on horses," I teased.

Sarah grinned a bit, the first one I had seen since

leaving Knob Creek. Pa got off the horse and reached for an old bell hanging between two hickory posts.

Clang! Clang!

"Watch the river," Pa called to us. "There'll be a ferryboat coming across soon. It's over on the Indiana side. When the captain hears someone ring the bell over here, he brings the boat over."

Pa was right. Soon a flat heavy ferryboat, rolling on a thick cable, crossed the river. The man steering it wore a beard and coonskin clothes.

I was glad to get aboard the ferryboat. As we crossed the river, I felt Sarah slip her hand inside mine.

"Don't tell Pa," she whispered. "The river frightens me."

The ferryboat bobbed up and down. I watched the waves slap against the sides of the ship. Ma came over and stood between us while Pa talked to the man steering the boat.

The ferryboat rolled up against the Indiana shore. As we stepped onto land again, I looked back across the river. I hadn't been afraid at all.

"No time for wasteful dreaming!" Pa snapped, leading the horses.

I had hoped we were close to Little Pigeon Creek. But first we had to go to Mr. Posey's.

"It's about sixteen miles from there," Pa told us. "You'll not mind it riding in the wagon."

Mr. Posey and his wife treated us real friendly. They gave us fried pork and corn pone.

"I hope you'll like your new home," Mrs. Posey said to Ma. "Lots of room for the children. Pretty wild flowers, clear water springs, and all the good wood you'll be needing. Not many folks settled there yet. But I reckon there'll be more coming."

Ma nodded. I knew she was thinking about the prayer meetings and the school. If there weren't people, there would be no preachers or school. But Ma said nothing.

I never saw bigger oxen than the two that pulled our wagon. The road was full of ruts and holes, but those oxen didn't stumble once.

Everywhere we looked we saw trees. For miles and miles the trees shut out the sunlight. There were oaks, maples, elms, and lots more.

The wagon rolled on. Hours passed. I guess I must have fallen asleep. Suddenly I felt a hand shaking me.

"We're here, Abe," Ma said.

Quickly I jumped out of the wagon. It was still afternoon and the sun warmed my skin. I looked around. The land was clear except for a low barrier of tree stumps.

"Don't stand there gawking, boy," Pa said. "I started a shelter the last time I was here. There's more work to be done on it."

I nodded. Turning around, I saw Sarah and Ma standing close together. They were frightened.

"Don't fret, Ma," I said. "We'll take care of things." Ma smiled and put her hand gently on my shoulder.

By nightfall, our three-sided shelter was completed. My arms ached from hauling limbs and dried weeds from the woods.

"Why does the shelter only have three sides?" Sarah asked.

Pa was short with his answer. "We've got to keep a fire going to keep away the bears and wolves."

It was the first time Pa had said anything about bears and wolves. He probably thought Sarah would be afraid. She was, and I was too.

Pa promised to start building a cabin at once. I hoped he would keep his promise. I knew until

Ma and Sarah were sleeping in a cabin, they would fear each night.

Pa did start building our cabin the next day. But he enjoyed hunting more. The woods nearby were full of rabbits, quail, squirrels, and deer.

"Always keep the pot boiling, Nancy!" Pa would laugh. "No Lincoln will starve with me around."

That much was true. We ate well. But good food could not keep out the bad weather. The winter of 1816 was long and bitter. The winds and snow swept into our three-sided shelter. Even the fire we kept burning helped little.

"It gets so cold, Abe," Sarah said one morning. "Won't Pa ever finish the cabin?"

"The Lord rewards those who suffer in silence," I reminded my sister. "Pa will finish the cabin soon."

I wanted Pa to work more on the cabin. But he loved having a rifle in his hand. I knew he was eager for me to hunt with him.

One morning we were working on the cabin. I was helping Pa put mud between the chimney stones. A flock of wild turkey flew over us. Since there was no roof on the cabin, we watched them.

"Here, boy," Pa said. "Shoot us some supper."

He handed me his rifle. I aimed it skyward and fired. A moment later a turkey lay on the ground nearby. Pa was happy.

"Good shooting, Abe. You got the biggest one of them."

I felt sick inside as I looked down at the bird. The red blood stained its rich feathers. I handed Pa his rifle and turned away. My stomach churned. I could feel the tears on my cheeks and I wiped them away with my sleeve.

When I turned around, Pa stood shaking his

head. "You'll never be a hunter, Abe. You got the
eye for it, but not the heart."

I knew Pa was right. A hunter I would never be.
I promised myself I would work harder in other
ways to do my part for the family. Even if Pa
chose not to work on the cabin, I would do what I
could without him.

But a welcome event changed my plans a bit.
Early one morning Ma shook Sarah and me awake
with good news. A school was opening on Pigeon
Creek. It was nine miles to the school, but Ma
wanted us to go.

"But who will do their chores?" Pa protested.
"We'll be planting crops. Sarah and Abe would
have to leave at daybreak and won't be back until
dusk."

Ma stood firm. "They're going to the school.
No more needs to be said about the matter."

So Sarah and I went to the Pigeon Creek School.
It was a lot like the one at Knob Creek in
Kentucky. There were children from six families
in the school. Each of us spoke our lessons aloud,
over and over. The schoolmaster walked among
us, listening. He smiled at me often and I knew he
could hear my loud voice. On special days, we
had spelling contests.

"I think the schoolmaster thinks Abe is the best
pupil in the school," Sarah told Ma and Pa. "He
never gets switched."

The news pleased Ma, but Pa didn't seem to
hear.

When I wasn't doing chores or in school, I
helped Pa work on the cabin. Finally it was
finished. We got it raised just in time too. A few
days later, we had visitors from Kentucky.

Sarah and I were picking berries when we heard
Ma calling. We raced back to the cabin.

There in the cabin doorway stood Ma's Aunt Betsy Sparrow, her husband Tom Sparrow, and Ma's cousin Dennis Hanks.

"Who's this?" Dennis laughed, rubbing his hand through my long black hair. "It must be a bear out of the woods. It couldn't be young Abe, could it?" Pa shook his head. "He's not so young anymore. The lad's ten. Sarah is twelve."

Sarah and I learned that the Sparrows and Dennis had come to stay. Pa gave them our old shelter in the clearing until they could raise a cabin of their own. Dennis slept in the sleeping loft with me.

"I only hope you don't snore, Abe," he teased.

It was fun having new people around. Ma spent much of her time cooking and sewing with Betsy. Pa, of course, took Tom and Dennis hunting.

The first spring they were with us, the Sparrows planted a garden. I enjoyed watching the beans and turnips grow. By summertime they were ready for picking. Sarah and I helped.

One night Tom Sparrow came pounding on our cabin door. Pa talked to Tom outside, then returned to the supper table.

"Tom says Betsy is ailing. She's awful pale and feverish. Tom's wondering if you can come over and tend to her, Nancy."

Ma went right away. She was gone all night. The next morning when she came back, her face looked tired. "Betsy and Tom are both sick. Looks like it might be the milk sickness," she said softly.

"What's that?" I asked.

Ma shook her head. "Nobody seems to know. A lot of folks are getting it around these parts. Animals too. I'll be going back over to tend the Sparrows after we've eaten."

All summer Ma took care of Betsy and Tom. No
cure was known for milk sickness so Pa said there
was no use in going for a doctor.

In August Betsy and Tom both died. Pa and
Dennis buried them on a hillside near the clearing.
It was a lot quieter after that. No one seemed to
talk or laugh as much.

Betsy and Tom had been gone a month or two.
Then Ma started looking awful pale and tired. I
think both Sarah and I knew. Pa probably did too,
but he tried to hide his thoughts.

"I don't think I can get up today," Ma said one
morning. "I must be ailing a bit myself."

I ran to get her some cool, fresh water. Sarah
warmed some broth.

For seven days Ma did not get up. Once, when I
was sitting beside her, she asked me to lean close.

"What is it, Ma?"

She smiled. "Abe. Abe. You're a good boy."

"Can I fetch you something, Ma?" I asked.
"Some cool water maybe? You want your shawl
around your shoulders?"

Slowly she shook her head. "I have the Lord.
He is all I need."

The next day Ma died. We built a coffin and
buried her on the hillside beside Betsy and Tom
Sparrow. Then Pa rode off. When he came back,
he brought a preacher named Reverend Elkin.

"Your Ma would have wanted some prayers,"
Pa said to Sarah and me. "We'll be going out to the
hillside now."

Pa led the way. Reverend Elkin told us he had
known Ma back in Kentucky.

"Nancy Hanks Lincoln was a good woman,"
Reverend Elkin said. His voice sounded deep
and sure.

On the hillside, we stood by Ma's grave. There

was a soft breeze, the kind Ma used to say was "stirring the trees a bit."

Reverend Elkin took out his Bible. " 'The Lord is my shepherd; I shall not want....' "

How often Ma had said those same words. I listened closely as I knelt down with Sarah beside me. How could we ever get along without Ma? I ached to have her back.

" '...and I will dwell in the house of the Lord forever.' "

Somehow I knew Ma *was* in the house of the Lord. She was safe now, with no work or worries.

That night I lay awake a long time. I knew things would be different now. Everything had changed. I wondered what would become of Sarah and me. What would the future years bring to us?

Who could say?

"Mysterious Ways"

For an hour I had listened to the wolf howling. Each night he came to the clearing to moan his sad cry. Sometimes I wished I had learned to shoot and hunt like Pa wanted.

If only Pa was here now. He could take care of that wolf. But ever since Ma died a year ago, Pa had been different. Sarah's tried hard to keep the place clean like Ma had it. She's learned to cook rabbits and squirrels by herself. But it still wasn't the same somehow.

That wolf's got a mean sound to him. I sure do wish Pa was here.

What was that noise? It sounded like a rifle shot!

"Dennis?" I whispered across the sleeping loft. "Did you hear a shot outside?"

There was no answer. I rubbed my eyes, pushed aside my blanket and scrambled down the wall pegs. A lone figure stood trembling near the glowing embers in the fireplace. It was Sarah. She ran quickly to me.

"Oh, Abe, that awful wolf keeps coming back. Did you hear it?" Sarah shivered and grabbed my arm. "And did you hear that rifle shot? Somebody's out there. We've got to do some—" The sound of crunching snow outside turned us both toward the cabin doorway. I moved swiftly to the corner where Dennis kept his rifle. It was gone.

The cabin door flew open. There stood Dennis, his breath frosty white in the cold night air.

"Well, we'll not be listening to that varmint any longer at night," Dennis declared. "Or fearing for our lives in the daytime."

Sarah stepped forward, helping Dennis off with his heavy coonskin coat. "Thank the Lord you're safe," my sister whispered, still shaking.

It was not the first time we thanked the Lord Dennis Hanks was with us. Since Pa had gone to Kentucky a month ago, Dennis had seen to it that we had plenty to eat and the cabin was kept warm. But he never fussed about us washing or cleaning much.

One night at supper Dennis seemed to know what Sarah and I were thinking.

"I bet you two are wondering if your Pa's going to come back from Kentucky," he said. "Well, if he does, we'll all be mighty glad to welcome him back. If he doesn't, then the three of us will just have to be that much closer a family."

Dennis's laugh and happy spirit soothed Sarah's worries. But I found myself still wondering — and worrying too. "The Lord sometimes moves in mysterious ways," Ma used to say. I wondered if the Lord had called my Pa back to Kentucky and was keeping him there.

The answer to my wondering came one December afternoon.

Dennis and I were chopping wood on the

hillside. I had just stacked some kindling when I thought I heard a strange sound.

"Hold your ax, Dennis" I said. "Listen a spell."

"What is it you hear, Abe?"

I listened again. Sure enough, I could hear the sound of horses. It sounded like they were pulling a wagon.

"Come on!" I shouted, racing across the hillside toward the cabin. "Someone's coming!"

My long legs proved useful. Moments later I stood by the cabin looking across the clearing. Sarah stood in the cabin doorway, her bare feet moving up and down in one spot to keep warm.

"Who is it, Abe?"

I couldn't rightly tell at first. There was more than one person in the wagon. But then I could see the driver was my Pa.

"Sarah, it's Pa." I turned to where Dennis was just coming around the cabin. "It's Pa, Dennis. He's bringing some other folks too."

The wagon drew closer. I could see five people in it. There were mounds of bundles and furniture tied to the wagon too.

Pa whoaed the horses and stood up in front of the cabin.

"Abe! Sarah!" Pa was smiling and he waved us forward. "Don't be fearing these new folks. I brought you a new ma, two new sisters, and a new brother."

I couldn't believe my ears. A glance at Sarah told me she was unable to believe what she'd heard either.

As we started unloading, Pa told me about the new lady.

"She's a widow lady, Abe. Sarah Bush Johnston was her name. I knew her before I met your Ma back in Kentucky. Her two girls are Elizabeth and

Matilda. The boy is John. I'm thinking you'll like the lot of them soon."

I was not so sure. The Johnston folks appeared mighty formal and fancy. Pa's new wife swished around in starched skirts. I never saw such fine belongings as we unloaded from the wagon. There were chairs, a clothes-chest, a bureau of drawers, a table, cooking pots and pans, silver forks and knives. There was a big pile of soft and thick quilts. At least, I thought they were quilts.

"Ever seen a feather bed, Abe?" the new lady asked as I lifted the quilts off the wagon.

"I don't think I have, ma'm," I answered.

"Well, you're holding on to three of them. One of them's going to be yours. I've brought you a pillow too, and a blanket I spun myself."

By suppertime we had the wagon unloaded. We ate on the new table and I saw that Sarah looked different. Her hair was combed, her face washed, and she wore a clean calico dress.

"*She* gave me this!" Sarah whispered, pulling me off to the corner. "Elizabeth and Matilda helped comb my hair. I thought I'd scream when they pulled through some of the tangles. How do I look?"

"Mighty fetching," I mumbled, suddenly aware of my dirty hands and soiled clothes. I promised myself that tomorrow I would visit the fresh water spring over the hillside. Cold water or not, I felt like having a good scrub.

Supper tasted good that night. Sarah Bush Johnston Lincoln was a fine cook. The chunks of rabbit meat in the hot broth were rich and salty.

"This is a good sturdy cabin," she nodded as the meal was cleared from the table. "But too much wind sneaks through the walls. Thomas, a little clay will take care of that."

I looked at Pa, expecting him to grumble a bit. He sat quietly, his head nodding agreement.

"And I do want a wood floor. The winter cold will freeze us all if we don't have a wood floor."

Again I looked at Pa. Once more he nodded. I wondered if he was really hearing anything being said.

But the next morning Pa was up early, filling in the cabin cracks with clay mud. The new lady of our house was going to make changes. Somehow I felt they would make our life better.

Soon after our new mother, sisters, and brother arrived, I was called in from working in the clearing. Sarah Johnston Lincoln smiled as she handed me a big quilt.

"Abe, this feels mighty bumpy to me," she said. "Maybe you can help get out the bumps."

It was a heavy bundle. A long piece of blue calico had been wrapped around it. As I pulled the calico strip off, a pile of books spilled over the kitchen table.

"Tarnation!" I blurted, forgetting I was with a lady. "I never saw so many books! Whose books are these?"

My stepmother laughed. "Why, they're mine, Abe. Or rather they *were* mine. Now they're ours."

I looked at some of the titles. There was a book called *Pilgrim's Progress* and another called *Aesop's Fables*. I flipped through the pages of one called *Robinson Crusoe*.

"I can tell you like reading, don't you, Abe?"

"Well, you'll have plenty to read for the time being. Your Pa tells me you do right well with your writing and ciphering too. Maybe you could be helping my brood a bit. Elizabeth and Matilda take to learning right well, but John is a little slow."

"I'll do what I can, ma'm."

I lay awake a long time that night, thinking about Sarah Bush Johnston Lincoln. I was glad Pa had gone back to Kentucky to bring her to us. I liked her. It wasn't just the soft feather bed or the books. I liked the way she made people feel good. I hadn't seen Pa smile at all since Ma died. Now he was laughing and fixing up the cabin. Both Sarah and I had forgotten about staying washed and clean. Now we wanted to. It didn't seem right sitting at the table with soiled clothes and dirty hands. Yes, Sarah Bush Johnston Lincoln had brought good changes to us. I knew I'd never forget my real Ma. But I was thankful to the Lord for the good turn He did us in bringing a new mother into our house.

"You do move in mysterious ways," I whispered, "and I'm telling you now, I'm grateful."

Midnight Attack

Elizabeth, Matilda, and John Johnston soon grew to love the woods as much as Sarah and I did. We swam in the creek and followed our own trails among the trees. We could feel the squirrels and deer watching us. Often we listened to the woodpecker's drumming song and the wood dove's cry. Some of the forest creatures seemed to know us and did not run off when we visited.

"We're all creatures of the Lord!" I'd call out. "We want to be your friends."

Human creatures of the Lord need a place to worship. And that was the reason some families came to see Pa.

"We know you to be good with your hands, a fine carpenter," one man said. "Thomas Lincoln, we'd like you to help us in the building of a meetinghouse. We need a place where we can all get together for prayer meetings and visiting."

Pa agreed to help. I offered to work too.

With the sturdy logs and mud clay the meetinghouse grew slowly. Pa showed the other

men how to do the simpler tasks. But he, himself, carved the cabinets and the pulpit. When the building was finally finished, the people made Pa a trustee of the Little Pigeon Creek Church and Meetinghouse. We were all proud of him.

"Work in the service of the Lord is the best work of all," the preacher told the men. "You have served Him well."

The new church and meetinghouse brought more people to Pigeon Creek. Some settlers came from far away. I liked to listen to their stories. The stories that made me laugh were my favorites. I tried to remember them so I could share them with other families.

I heard one story that gave me the thought for a good joke to play at home. It happened shortly after we had whitewashed the cabin ceiling.

I was standing near the cabin one morning when I saw the two Murphy boys wading in the creek. They were both shouting and carrying on like two bears stomping in honey.

"Hey, you two kings of the mud!" I yelled at them. "Get those feet of yours as muddy as you can. Then hightail it right over here."

The two boys looked puzzled, but they followed my orders. I peeked in the cabin, making sure no one was inside.

Minutes later my stunt was completed. Across the whitewashed ceiling were two sets of muddy footprints. One at a time I'd hoisted the boys up and allowed them to tramp across in double paths.

It seemed forever before my stepmother and the others returned. Sarah Bush Johnston Lincoln dropped the whole basket of berries she had picked.

"Laws of mercy!" she squealed. "What kind of creature has been running loose in our cabin!"

I could not stop laughing. Neither could the

others. It was well worth the scrubbing it took to
get the mudprints off the ceiling.

It wasn't long after that Sarah surprised us with
some news. We had just finished supper when my
sister rose at the table.

"Aaron Grigsby has asked me to be his wife."
Sarah could not control the pride in her voice.
"I am thinking I will agree."

"He'll be getting himself a fine wife," I leaned
down to whisper in my sister's ear as I gave her a
hug. "I'm only hoping he'll not be needing help
with the horses on his farm."

Sarah's eyes twinkled at my teasing,
remembering how we both feared horses. My
sister hugged me back. I knew she was thinking
about all we had shared together.

It was a small wedding in our Pigeon Creek
Church and Meetinghouse. I listened to the
preacher as he spoke.

"Let us ask the Lord to bless this union between
Aaron and Sarah. May their time together be
blessed and joyous."

So Sarah left our cabin. It seemed empty
without her, but she did not live far away and
came back often for visits.

Within a year Sarah brought news that she was
with child.

"So I'm going to be an uncle, am I?" I laughed
aloud. "Uncle Abraham. That has a mighty fine
sound to it."

But it was not to be.

One morning I went over to help Aaron's
brother Reuben. We were putting planks up in the
smokehouse when we heard Aaron yelling. As we
ran outside, Aaron came running up the path.

"She's dead!" Aaron blurted, his voice choking.
"She was feeling pain yesterday and I went for the

doc. He tried to save the baby but couldn't.
Sarah, my Sarah — she's gone."

Gone. The word had such an empty sound to it.
Yet I heard it over and over again. In the days that
followed I did not want to be with anyone. I
walked through the woods, gazing at all Sarah and
I had shared together. I could see her picking
berries, and laughing as I fell off a slick stone into
Pigeon Creek. I remembered how she mended
stockings before the fire and stirred the steaming
pots.

But all that was over now. *Gone.*

Aaron stayed with us a few days. He seemed to
gain strength and comfort with us.

One morning as Aaron and I walked through the
woods, he stopped. He leaned against the oak tree
Sarah and I had played around years before.

"Abe, I've been thinking about what the
preacher said when Sarah and I were wed."
Aaron's eyes had a faraway look in them. "May
their time together be blessed and joyous."

"I remember, Aaron."

"It was, Abe. The Lord gave us little time, but it
was blessed and joyous."

I was glad for that. I thanked the Lord for
making Sarah's final time "blessed and joyous."

After Sarah's death, I found peace and comfort
on the creeks and waterways of the Ohio River. I
even built myself a little flatboat. Pa praised its
sturdiness, and I found myself hauling a passenger
or two out to meet steamboats in the river. I came
to be thought of as fairly able at handling a riverboat.

Master James Gentry, a merchant and farmer
who lived about four miles from Pigeon Creek,
heard I liked working on the river. One afternoon
he came to make a business call.

"I have a boatload of hogs, grain, and tobacco," Master Gentry said. "They'll make a good sale in New Orleans, Abe. I'd like you and my son Allen to take them down river. You're known for being able and honest."

I was very glad to hear Master Gentry's words. Many traders and other folks had spoken of New Orleans as they passed through our lands in southern Indiana. I accepted Master Gentry's offer.

Allen Gentry and I began at once to build a big flatboat. By April of 1828 we were ready to leave. Our cargo loaded, we pushed off from Gentry's Landing into the slow Ohio River current.

It felt good to hold the steering pole, gazing across the water on both sides. We moved at a steady sluggish pace until we met the mighty Mississippi River in Illinois. My task grew greater then, having to keep a keen eye out for sandbars, or logs floating in the river.

Southward we sailed, looking at the giant cotton plantations that sprawled along the shorelines. Cotton bales were stacked high beside plantation wharves.

Each night Allen and I stayed at a different plantation wharf. One such stay I knew I would never forget.

It was midnight. From our place in a wharf shelter, I could hear a church bell in the distance tolling the hour. Suddenly I heard Allen calling my name.

"Abe! Help me!"

Quickly I jumped up and raced to our boat. In the moonlight I saw Allen wrestling two dark strangers. I pulled one of the men off, tossing him into the river. I felt a sudden pain in my back, then another on my forehead. I flung myself around,

knocking two more attackers to the floor of the
flatboat. The night villains hurried off into the
rising river mist.

"Are you all right, Allen?" I asked, my heart
beating fast.

Allen leaned against me for support. "Yes, Abe.
I think they must have been runaway slaves from
some nearby plantation. There are many of them
along the river."

I ran to the ropes that held us to the wharf.
"We'll not risk our lives again," I told Allen. "We'll
be off tonight. The moonlight is enough for travel
in these waters."

I was glad to reach New Orleans where the
dock seemed to stretch for miles. Carefully I held
the steering pole, skirting around the fishing scows
and travelers, the sailing ships, steamers, the
dinghies, and canoes. Finally we found an empty
pier on the water front.

Allen saw to the unloading of our cargo. He had
been to New Orleans before. I am certain I
looked like a fool. I wandered along the crowded
docks, stretching my long neck to view the tall
buildings and strange people.

Never before had I seen such people. Some
wore clothes made of coonskins, others wore rich
velvet and fancy silk. Here and there were
Indians, cloaked in bright colored blankets.
Round caps rested on sailors' heads.

"A far cry from the folks at Pigeon Creek, isn't
it, Abe?" I nodded agreement to Allen's comment.

"I sold the cargo and the flatboat too," Allen
continued. "Got a good price for both. We'll go
home on a fine Yankee steamer. But I've got some
sights I want to show you before we do."

In the next few days we roamed through every
street in New Orleans. I wanted to remember
everything I saw so I could share with people back

home. We ate in gracious inns, visited spice shops and open markets. In amazement I stared at the fancy iron grilles that surrounded balconies along the building walls.

But it was in the New Orleans Square that I saw the sight I could not believe. There, a giant crowd stood shouting to a man on a platform before them.

"Forty dollars. I'll give ya forty dollars!" one man yelled.

Another man called out, "Fifty dollars. I'll pay ya fifty!"

It was an auction block. Negro men, women, boys, and girls were being sold to the highest bidder. I watched the faces of the slaves being sold. Each one seemed to wear the same look, a sad and lonely stare of helplessness.

I felt sudden anger at what I was watching and hearing. Surely the Lord did not mean for one man to own another. And those who had written the Declaration of Independence — was this what they meant in declaring "all men are created equal"?

I turned to Allen, but somehow I could not voice the thoughts in my mind. They were confused, muddled.

Some day I hoped this could be changed.

Some day I might find a voice for my thinking.

Life on the River

Not long after my return from New Orleans, Pa began talking about traveling too. Dennis Hanks's brother John sent glowing reports from Illinois, the land to the west.

"He writes that the land there is fertile and the people friendly," Pa told us. "If I could get a good price for our farmland here, we just might head west."

But everyone, including Pa, knew there was more than money to consider. Dennis Hanks and Elizabeth Johnston had married and were raising a family. Squire John Hall had taken Matilda Johnston as his wife. They had an infant son. We all had become a close family. If there was to be a move, all of us would have to go.

In February of 1830, that is just what we decided to do.

There was new talk of milk sickness in the area. Quickly Pa sold his land, our corn and hogs. Master Charles Grigsby paid Pa the whopping sum of $125. The money went to purchase oxen that would pull the family's wagons.

At twenty-one, I was thought old enough to handle one of the ox-teams. We left early in the morning with the sound of creaky axles weighing beneath our piled wagons.

Slowly we rolled across long stretches of prairie. Each night we were happy to warm ourselves around the evening fire, supping on game and corn pone. It felt good to climb under heavy bearskins and listen to the steady trickle of a nearby stream or a sad hooting owl.

I sensed Pa's eagerness to get into the new land of Illinois. At the same time, Sarah Johnston Lincoln fretted about having left something behind. She didn't know of any one thing for certain, but kept mumbling about being sure she forgot something or other.

While crossing a creek near the Wabash River, we almost *did* forget something. Chunks of ice jammed our wagon wheels. My stepmother took the driver's seat as the menfolks helped push the wagons across.

I was just pulling on my boots on the other side of the creek when I heard an awful yelping. I looked back. On the far shoreline sat my dog, his tail wagging like a cattail in a windstorm.

Pa saw the dog the same time I did. "We can't be slowing down for that little varmint," he said. "There'll be more dogs ahead of us, maybe with more sense than that one."

I didn't say anything. There were some things I don't think Pa could understand. I set my boots back down and waded back across to my dog. He leaped into my arms, his sticky tongue lapping my face.

"Don't go getting me any wetter than I am," I said. Not wasting another minute, I splashed back through the ice.

Pa just shook his head when I caught up with the

wagon. "That was a fool thing to do, Abe," he
scolded me. "You could have found another dog."

"Don't be angry with me, Pa. Don't you
remember that Bible verse from Matthew —
'Inasmuch as ye have done it unto one of the least
of these my brethren, ye have done it unto me'?
I'm thinking we have to look after the Lord's
creatures, man and beast alike, that can't be
looking after themselves."

Pa just shook his head again. But my
stepmother reached out her hand to cover mine.

"I'll not be fretting anymore about leaving
something behind," she whispered. "If it had been
worth bringing, you'd have remembered it, Abe."

A warm and grateful welcome awaited us in
Macon County. John Hanks provided us with a
full table and warm beds. Early the next morning
he took us to a clearing about ten miles from the
village of Decatur. There he had cut the logs for
our new home. With all of us working, we raised a
sturdy cabin by nightfall.

"If we fence the land and plant our corn at
once," Pa said, "we could have a crop by autumn.
But there can be no waste of time."

Indeed, there was not a spare minute wasted.
Trees were plentiful near our cabin. Dennis and I
axed the split rails for fence posts. Pa broke the
tough sod with a bull-tongued plow. By the time
we had fenced ten full acres, Pa had sowed the
seed. Just as he had hoped, in the autumn of 1830
we harvested our first farm crop on Illinois soil.

What time I could find, I used hiring out. There
was always a farmer needing an extra hand to
plow or split rails for fencing. Often the farmers
could not pay in money. It mattered little to me. I
was always in need of homespun jeans-cloth.
Many a farmer's wife turned the cloth into
breeches.

"It takes twice the usual length of cloth to cover those long legs of Abe's," Pa teased. "I would hope these farmers' wives do not stop to notice."

Pa's teasing sometimes made me feel a mite guilty. I always split a few extra rails when a pair of breeches was offered in exchange. Dennis Hanks did some measuring one day and said I stood six feet and four inches tall with my boots off.

"I think you'll be bumping into the clouds soon," Dennis exclaimed. "But that's all right, Abe. Everybody in these parts knows you're the hardest working fellow they could hire out, except when you stop to tell a story."

Dennis smiled and I nodded. I had to admit I enjoyed sharing a story or two while I was working. It made me feel good to hear people laugh. People just don't laugh enough. Lots of tales I tell are about me and the fool things I've done. I wish those stories were all made up. But I have to admit there's more than a speck of truth to most of them.

Maybe the most foolish thing I did happened in the winter of 1830. A farmer on the other side of the Sangamon River, Major Warnick, hired me to split three thousand rails. Pa took sick early in the winter so I stayed home and tended the stock. I built myself a canoe for going back and forth to Major Warnick's as soon as Pa was feeling better.

By the time Pa recovered, the Sangamon River was swollen and filled with ice. The first time I paddled across, a drifting chunk of ice ripped into my canoe. I tumbled into the water, barely managing to hold onto the boat. Somehow I pulled the torn canoe to shore. After tying the boat, I stumbled off toward the Warnick farmhouse. My skin felt raw as the winds slashed across the prairie lowlands. My feet were soaked

inside my boots. But as I made my way through
the thick snowdrifts, I felt the water harden into
ice. Ice! The thought gave me fear. I trudged
forward, falling now and then in the snow. My
feet burned and my eyes watered, the tears
freezing on my cheeks. I longed to rest, to sleep.

Finally I reached the Warnick farmhouse. Mrs.
Warnick met me with a gasp as she opened the
door.

"Oh, Abe! What's happened to you? Here, get
yourself inside!"

The warm fire felt better than anything I could remember. But I could see the worry on Major Warnick and his wife's faces. After they had pulled off my boots, I overheard their mumbled words.

"The lad's feet are frozen," the old man said. "I don't think we can save them."

His wife was not so sure. "We can try."

For hours Mrs. Warnick rubbed my feet with snow mixed with an ointment she had made herself. Then she wrapped my feet with bandages.

"We'll not know for some time," Mrs. Warnick told me, "what good we have done. It is now in the hands of the Lord."

In the two weeks that followed I had much time to ponder Mrs. Warnick's words. The Lord had been good to me before. I prayed that He would not choose to punish my clumsiness. The Major loaned me the family Bible. The good familiar words gave me new hope and helped me endure the pain as the circulation returned to my feet.

I gave thought to my own future if my health would mend. Farming? I had plowed enough sod and planted enough seed. No, I did not choose to spend the rest of my years with the soil. I wanted to be with people, to hear them laugh and share thoughts. I liked talking with folks. And John Hanks told me once he'd rather listen to my stories than feast on a side of venison.

"You got good sense," he would say. "You know how to tie your words together better than anybody I know. You ought to run for some office. You make a heap more sense than some of those yokels who come through these parts with their fancy words and phrases."

I chuckled as I recalled John's words. But I had

to confess — the thought of running in an election
had some appeal to it.

Each day I began feeling better. Soon I was
standing and walking. I was eager to get to work
and start splitting the rails. For the debt of food
and care, I offered to ax an extra thousand rails.

The second day I was working, Major Warnick
called me into the house. He led me into the parlor
where a stout fellow in fancy duds stood puffing a
cigar.

"This is the lad I spoke of," Major Warnick said,
pulling my elbow. "Abe, this here is Mr. Denton
Offutt."

I had scarcely nodded a greeting and shook
hands when Mr. Offutt started talking faster than
a hungry magpie in a treetop. His voice was loud
and he puffed a cigar excitedly. Smoke drifted
above his head.

I'm looking for someone to take my produce to
New Orleans, Mr. Lincoln. Major Warnick tells
me you're a good worker with an honest spirit."

"Well, I always try to —"

"I'll be bringing my goods to Portland's
Landing as soon as the Sangamon River's free of
ice." Mr. Offutt puffed again on his cigar. "Do
you suppose you can find another worker or two?"

I knew my stepbrother John Johnston would
welcome such a chance for travel. "Yes, Mr.
Offutt, I know —"

"Fine, fine. I'll have everything at the landing as
soon as the thaw sets in. I have offices in
Springfield if you need me. You'll be well paid,
Mr. Lincoln. Thank you, Major Warnick. Now
if your kind wife will bring me my hat, I'll be on
my way."

Major Warnick returned shortly, wearing a
wide grin. "He's quite a talker, isn't he, Abe? But

he's a good man of business. You'll not regret hiring out to him on the river."

After rail-splitting for a couple weeks, I returned home. The spring thaws had spread water everywhere. Pa was in a mean temper, promising to move again to "anyplace where there's never a flooding."

But young John Johnston, a burly lad of seventeen, outyelled Pa when I told him we were going to New Orleans. He was ready to leave the next hour.

"Tarnation, Abe! We're going to New Orleans — and getting paid to do it! I'll be a one-legged rooster! New Orleans! Whoop-pee!"

Cousin John Hanks caught the "travelin' fever" too. "It couldn't be this Master Denton Offutt might be needing another man, could it, Abe?"

I rubbed my chin, teasing John on a mite. "Well, now as I recall, Master Offutt did say he might use another man or two."

"You need look no further," John laughed. "We'll all be going together."

As soon as the Sangamon River softened, we headed for Portland Landing at Beardstown. Finding no sign of Denton Offutt or his cargo, we walked the six miles to Springfield.

"Change in plans," Master Offutt told us when we found him. "I'm without craft and cargo. But if you'll agree to build a flatboat on the Sangamon, I'll pay you each twelve dollars a month. By the time you finish, I'll have you a full cargo."

Dennis, John, and I talked the offer over. Finally, we agreed.

Soon we had set up a small camp near the Prairie Creek sawmill. There was plenty of timber close by which could be readied into clean planks at the mill. We shared the camp chores, with myself handling the cooking. I surprised Dennis and John with the good food I set before them.

I must confess that one batch of corndodgers were not up to my usual fine quality. Contrariwise, they seemed to have a mind of their own as they sat baking.

"Be careful not to take one of these corndodgers aboard the flatboat, Abe," Dennis warned. "We'd all just be sitting at the bottom of the Sangamon River."

John joined in the insults. "Why, these can't be corndodgers. Abe must have gone to the Sangamon shore and picked up rocks for a fancy collection. You must have the food and rocks ajumbled, Abe."

But for all their jokes and funning, Dennis and John stayed mighty healthy with my cooking. And I seemed to notice them both filling out their breeches a bit more by the time the flatboat was finished.

The building of the boat took us one month. True to his word, Denton Offutt supplied us with a full cargo. We loaded barrels of corn and pork, plus a lively collection of squealing hogs.

"Sounds a bit like you two at the supper table," I told Dennis and John. "Except these critters smell a mite better."

The launching of our loaded flatboat drew quite a crowd to the river's edge. A big cheer went up as we shoved off into the water.

But the cheering did not last. We had poled but a short distance to the village of New Salem when our boat snagged on a dam.

The pigs started squealing and the barrels rolled back to the stern. When the prow tilted skyward, I thought we were all going to be pitched into the water.

"Get off my dam!" some fella yelled from off to the side. I looked over to the mill where two men were shaking their fists and jumping up and down. "I'd sure like to oblige you," I hollered back. As fast as I could, I looked over the situation. There seemed to be but one thing to do. We needed an auger to drill some holes, and then shift the weight aboard the flatboat.

Looking over to the landside, I discovered we'd drawn quite a crowd. In the water around our boat were young lads in small crafts of their own.

"Can one of you boys fetch me an auger?" I shouted.

One boy's face lit up with a big smile. "My Pa has one. But he'll need it right back. He's the town cooper. If you're needin' good wooden barrels or casks, he'll be glad to —"

The boy reminded me of Master Offutt, and I had no time or good manners to spare. Quickly I sent the boy to fetch the auger with a few of his friends.

"We'll have to unload these varmints," I said, pointing at the hogs. "Maybe these lads in their boats will help us."

"Sure, Mister."

Once we got the pigs off, we moved the barrels forward. Not all, mind you, just a few. When the boy fetched his auger, I waded out by the prow and began boring a hole.

"That fellow's lost his wits!" I heard someone on shore yell out. "Puttin' a hole up there will do no good."

It was no time to argue the matter. Once I had a good-sized hole bored, I yelled to John and the others to push the barrels forward. Taking a moment to ask the Lord for a little help, I then jumped aboard and started pushing the barrels to the front of the boat.

The flatboat creaked. Slowly it slipped forward, sliding off the dam. I raced forward, knowing I had to plug the hole I had drilled with the auger.

The people lining the shore and the bluff let out a rousing cheer. In their boats nearby, the lads helped us reload the hogs. I thanked the Lord for His help and began poling down the river again.

I reckon Master Offutt was right pleased with the way I handled myself. How do I know? He offered to hire me on as a clerk at the store he was planning to build in New Salem.

"It's a right nice place, that Salem," Denton declared. "Already got a good hundred folks settled there, with a mill, two or three stores, a meetinghouse, a cooper's shop. Yep, that's a right fine place to be settling for a spell."

Little persuading was needed. I was already weary of hiring out. I felt a need to meet new people and to hear their ideas. I reckoned there would be books in Salem too. If ever I was going to make something of myself, I figured it was time to get started.

New Salem. That sounded like a good place to start.

FIRST ELECTION

There were no more accidents on our journey to New Orleans. Peacefully the Sangamon joined the Illinois River, then flowed into the Mississippi. I had promised myself that I would not venture into the square. But something seemed to draw me there.

It had been three years since I had watched the selling of people like cattle. Little had changed. The air had a hot and sticky feel to it. It made a person wish for a good hard scrubbing.

Or maybe it wasn't the air at all. Maybe it was what was happening. The auctioneer's voice bellowed out over the crowd.

"Look here, what we have," the man shouted. "Here's a fine piece of woman flesh, just made for pickin' your cotton in the fields — or doing your washing of clothes."

The chains which hung around the young girl's wrists and ankles were heavy and twisted. Still the auctioneer lifted her arms to show "muscles and bone eager to work for her new master."

I tugged at Denton's arm. "I'll not stay here. This is the Devil's place."

Denton nodded, and followed after me.

The cargo sold quickly and Denton paid me sixty dollars for my labor. Never had I had so much money. Before we parted, we made plans to meet in New Salem. I headed home by steamboat. But when I arrived I found that Pa had packed up the family and moved south to Coles County.

When I returned to New Salem, I found no sign of Denton Offutt — or his store either. But I found other reasons for staying around the town. It seemed almost every soul in New Salem had been watching that day our flatboat got stuck. People were friendly, offering to give me board until Denton Offutt appeared.

I accepted the invitation of Billy Greene and his family. They had known Pa back in Kentucky. One of the Greene's cousins, a fellow named Mentor Graham, was the New Salem schoolmaster.

"You ought to think about settling here, Abe," he said. "There's always room for a fellow with good sense. Take a close look at our people and town. I think you may like what you see."

I met a lot of people the next few days. I was glad to be able to thank Henry Onstot, the cooper whose auger I had used on the flatboat. James Rutledge, the man who owned the dam we snagged, bore me no grudge. The conversation was lively, with all the men I met. They talked of politics and issues of the day.

When Denton Offutt arrived, he brought with him goods to sell in a store. There being no store, the next task was to raise one. The chore was quickly done, with thanks to many willing workers in the village.

Carefully we arranged the stock in the cabin. Sugar, calico, coffee, spices, hardware, bonnets — all were put on the shelves. Soon our store was enjoying a steady stream of customers.

Saturdays were the busy days. Men who came to buy also came to talk. Other days gave me time for reading. It seemed like everyone in New Salem knew of my love for books.

"Here is a book of Shakespeare's plays," one woman said, extending a thick volume. "I shall come for it next month."

Before I could nod my thanks, another book was thrust into my hands. "Here, read this one," a tall gentleman said solemnly. "It is a book of language, of grammar. Heed the rules within, and you will be wiser for it."

And so the days and weeks went by. I enjoyed my work, and when Denton Offutt expressed a desire to move on to another town, I shook my head.

"I am learning here," I told him. "Men have taught me how to survey land and how a gristmill is run. I am learning about the law, what people feel is fair and just. This is a good place."

Denton Offutt was convinced, I guess. He did not bother me again about leaving. But his boasts did provide me with trouble among the boys of Clary Grove.

There was always much talk about the Clary Grove boys. Some said the Devil himself lived with them. That was the only thing that could explain their constant drinking, swearing, and fighting. Somehow this band of wild wolves heard tales being spread by Denton Offutt that he had the "strongest, cleverest clerk in these parts." As fine a fellow as Denton Offutt is, I often wished he could keep his tongue from wagging.

The leader of the Clary Grove boys, Jack Armstrong by name, took Denton's boasting as a personal challenge. He told Denton he would fight me.

I knew why Denton picked a Saturday for this event. The fight would bring more men to his store. Begging the Lord's forgiveness, I went out to face my opponent.

We stood in a ring marked in dust near the store. I looked over at Jack Armstrong. He was short, but his muscles bulged from everywhere. His friends stood just outside the ring, yelling and cheering.

"So this is mighty Abe Lincoln," my rugged opponent sneered. "Looks like a starving crow to me."

Armstrong moved forward, thrusting his arms out. His face looked downward as he struck. Quickly I grabbed his head and held him away. I was grateful for my long arms which felt only the breezes from his angry swings.

"Get him, Jack! He's makin' a fool out of you!" This shout from the crowd sent Armstrong into a frenzy. He lifted his right foot and kicked me solidly on my instep. The pain shot through me. Quickly I grabbed Armstrong, lifted him off his feet, shook him soundly, and dropped him.

A few of the Clary Grove boys stepped forward, eager to take on their leader's fight. But Armstrong, who seemed a mite dazed and confused, stood up and raised his hands.

"No-no — this Lincoln is all he's said to be. He's a fair fighter. I'll not have anyone fighting my battles. He knocked me down fairly."

I was grateful for Armstrong's words, but my instep still throbbed from his heavy foot. As I went back inside the store, I told Denton Offutt to say no more about his store clerk. He agreed.

Denton kept his word. Yet there were still other troubles with the store. Somehow it could not seem to bring a profit. By spring of 1832, Denton decided to close the store.

I had no wish to leave New Salem. The folks in town seemed willing to board me. I was glad I had saved the money I'd earned clerking so I could pay for my keep. Since I wouldn't be having to clerk, I would have more time to read and visit. I liked the debating society too. Once a week the menfolks gathered in the meetinghouse. Mentor Graham had been kind enough to take me to a meeting. I suppose some folks might think a collection of fellows sitting around for hours talking about current issues might sound foolish. But it sure wasn't to me. I enjoyed it.

"You have a clear head for thinking," Mentor told me as we walked home one night. "You talk smooth and simple. That's what folks around here like, Abe, not fancy language, but talk that is to the point and makes some sense."

No, I had no yearning to leave New Salem. The people were good to me. And there was Ann to think about too.

I met Ann Rutledge at Mentor Graham's one evening. She was probably the prettiest thing I'd ever seen. But there was more to her than a smiling face and sparkling blonde hair. She had dreams for herself, plans for her future. She was getting herself ready to go to the academy over in Jacksonville. Mentor Graham was helping her. He seemed to think he could help us both a mite — and I could find no objections.

"Ann and Abe, you both got ambition inside you," he told us. "Now just set your goals high and then reach for them. The best way of reaching is by working. I'll help you all I can."

At first my own lack of education bothered me.

All together, I guess I only had about eleven months of schooling back in Kentucky and Indiana. But Mentor Graham said that was of no matter.

"Education is not just sitting in a schoolhouse," he told me. "Education is learning, and that can be done anytime and anywhere — as long as the mind is willing."

I was willing, that much was certain. Some nights Mentor and Ann and I talked about poems, sometimes about language, sometimes about George Washington, or cooking, or just about anything we took a notion to talk about.

"You know an awful lot," Ann said to me as we walked home one night. "But you don't put on any fancy notions like some men would. You're a good man, Abraham Lincoln. I'm glad I know you."

I held Ann's words right kindly. I knew she was spoken for by John McNamar, and they were planning to marry when he got back from the East. But Ann was still something special to me too. She made me feel important and not so clumsy.

One night Ann could not go to Mentor's. I went on by myself and found I was not the only visitor. Three men were seated near the fire, and they welcomed me warmly. I soon discovered they had plans for me.

"We're thinking you might have a notion to run for the state legislature," the tallest man said. "Mentor Graham tells us you know these folks here in Sangamon County and might do them proper service. Think on it, Mister Lincoln."

I did think on it, and talked on it too. The folks in New Salem probably got tired of hearing me ramble. But I had to find out if they thought I'd be a decent candidate for them. Those good folks seemed willing to have me run, so I declared I would.

As was the custom, I had to sit down and put my thoughts and beliefs into words for the local newspaper. There were some folks who knew me, but a barrelful more who didn't. I spoke my piece for the barrelful, and the *Sangamon Journal* in Springfield printed it on March 9, 1832.

The piece looked good, if I do say so myself. First of all, I thought Sangamon County had to find a better way of getting produce to market. Some folks talked about bringing railroads in, but that would cost too much. It was my notion to just deepen and straighten the old Sangamon River. For the new settlers, I suggested having fair rates of interest when they had to borrow money. My Ma would have liked the notion I gave about having better schools for the young ones. Yep, that one would have pleased her, I'm thinking.

Once the piece in the paper was printed, I planned to get out and start meeting some more people. But before I got a chance, there was another job to do.

Some Indians up north on the Mississippi seemed to be causing trouble. The governor asked for some volunteers. There were about twenty-five of us from New Salem who decided to enlist. Mentor Graham feared I might not return before the election. But having no family or work, it seemed only right for me to lend what help I could.

We traveled to Richmond where the men I accompanied did me a big honor. They elected me captain of their company.

"Even if I don't win the election to the state legislature this fall," I told the men, "I sure can't say I didn't win an election this year."

I did my best to get the men ready for whatever
fighting we might have to do. But as it turned out,
we saw not a speck of battle. The Indians, under
their chief Black Hawk, slipped across the
Mississippi into Iowa.

As we walked back to New Salem, I did meet a
fine gentleman from Springfield. His name was
John T. Stuart, and he was running for the state
legislature too. He had even come from
Kentucky, just as I had. But from then on, we had
little background in common. Mr. Stuart had a
good education and was a practicing lawyer. We
shared many hours of conversation. He even
offered to lend me some of his law books. That
was an offer I accepted without hesitation.

By the time I got back to New Salem, the
election was less than two weeks away. There was
talk of a big auction to be held nearby, so I
decided to give a campaign speech there.

I'm afraid I didn't have very good duds to wear.
But Ann said I looked more than a mite handsome
in my coat and pantaloons.

The folks at the auction listened kindly to my
talk. I said much of what I'd written in the
newspaper. I told a few stories too, that the
menfolks seemed to enjoy.

I talked to as many folks as I could before
election day. Then I went to Springfield where
they'd be telling the results after the votes were
counted.

I met John Stuart again. He introduced me to
another lawyer friend of his named Stephen
Logan. I guess it made me feel right important,
knowing two fine attorneys in Springfield.

But the election news was not so good. John
Stuart won one of the four seats that were open. I
placed eighth out of the thirteen who were
running.

"There'll be another time," John told me. "After all, you got all but seven votes of the menfolks in New Salem. Those people must think right highly of you."

I thanked John and wished him well as I left to return home. No, I was not feeling low. Maybe if I'd have had more time, I just might have won. Poor Mentor Graham would be disappointed. Ann, too, perhaps. But as for myself, I felt more than a mite satisfied. The good Lord had brought me to a place where I had friends, and I felt I had a home. As for the election, I kept thinking of John Stuart's words.

And I knew, for certain, there *would* be another time.

New Salem Living

I had expected Mentor Graham and the folks in New Salem to be more than a mite disappointed in me. But by the fancy spread that covered the Rutledge Inn table, you'd have thought I'd won. Roast turkey, dressing, potatoes — each platter was piled high.

"I fear you've not received a proper report of the election," I told my friends. "I was *not* among the winners."

"You showed yourself good and respectable," Ann answered. "The people here in Salem know you. It's those folks in the country who don't know the wise gentleman you are. But they'll soon be finding out."

It was a festive evening, too soon ended. When it was over I knew I had big decisions to make. The New Salem folks had treated me right kindly, but smiles and handshakes would not pay my bills.

I decided to call on James and Rowan Herndon. They ran a store in the village and might be needing another clerk. Sadly enough, James met my offer with a loud guffaw.

"Salem's dying, Abe. The steamboat line's selling out and this place is headed for the graveyard."

Rowan nodded his head. "We'd like to help you, Abe. If it's bed and board you're needing, we can offer you that. But there are no clerking jobs."

I accepted Rowan's offer for bed and board. Having a place to stay would give me time to consider my future.

I spent some time with Josh Miller at his black-smith's shop. It seemed good, honest work.

"You're suited fine to blacksmithing," Josh told me. "You've got the strong arms and back — and the movin' jawbone as well."

I chuckled, knowing Josh meant I could trade stories with the customers. Whether a fellow needed a door hinged or a horse shoed, he always ended up spending an hour talking with Josh.

While doing my thinking, I decided to travel to Springfield. John Stuart had invited me. When I arrived at his law offices, I found Stephen Logan there also.

"Master Logan," I joked, "if you're needing legal help, I advise not taking it from this scoun-drel."

Both my friends laughed. After a hearty meal we talked long into the night. It seemed John and Stephen felt I had a proper head to become a lawyer.

"But I've not been educated," I argued.

John shook his head. "There's book education and people education. You've done a good job on your own of getting people education. And what books you've had, you've done right well with. I'll be loaning you some law books anytime you want them."

I promised to think about our talk. But I had hardly returned to Salem when James and Rowan

Herndon presented a business offer. They
wanted to sell out their store. William Berry, the
preacher's son, wished to purchase a half interest.
The other half was mine, if I be agreeable.

"Your offer is a tempting one," I said. "But I
have no money. I could only promise to pay you
when I am able."

"That's good enough for us," Rowan exclaimed.
"You are known as a right honest man, Abe. Pay us
when you can."

I accepted the offer. Shortly before Christmas
1832, we put up the sign for the Berry-Lincoln
Store. There was a back room in the store where I
lived.

The days passed quickly. Blacksmithing was
not the only business requiring a lively jawbone.
Store tending gave many chances for sharing
stories. When business slowed and the store
emptied, I found time for reading. But one lady
who came to the store cast angry words at me as a
store clerk.

"I've been standing here a full five minutes
waiting for you to tend business," she told me.
"You just sit there with your nose hidden in that
book you're reading. This is not the only store
where I can do business, Mr. Lincoln."

My apology was little noted. She left the store
huffing like a windstorm.

Now and then I slipped down to Springfield. I
always left John Stuart's law offices loaded with
books. At an auction, I paid a handsome sum for
Blackstone's Commentaries. John had spoken
often of the book. I found it most useful.

"Your own law library is now born!" John
laughed. "It will grow swiftly, I am certain."

But as my interest in the law grew, our store
sank deeper into debt. Will Berry disappeared for
days at a time.

"He's a victim of the Devil's brew," Salem folks told me. "His Pa preaches against drinking, while Willy is known as the biggest drinker in these parts."

I was not one to judge Will's deeds. Such duties rest with the Lord.

Will and I struggled through the early months of 1833. But we could do nothing to bring the store back to life. It was gone to the grave, winked out under a pile of debts. Sadly we closed the store.

No sooner had we started to pay off our obligations when Will took sick and died. It was a loss to all of us.

"Let us hope he has settled his debts with God," said Mentor Graham. "He has left many behind in this world."

I felt a special sadness that God had chosen to call Will home when he seemed to be finding his way. I questioned why? If Will had only been given more time. Why couldn't I understand God? I would search for the answer.

Heartbreak was written on the faces of his family. I promised to repay not only my store debts, but Will's also.

"But you have enough to worry with your own," Mentor argued.

I stood firm. "I must pay Will's too. He cannot do it."

"Abe, do not confuse nobleness with foolishness."

I chose not to answer Mentor further. I knew what I must do.

The people of New Salem again showed their kindness. They found work for me building fences. Good fortune smiled when I was hired as village postmaster. I had declared myself a Whig politically and the Democrats controlled such positions. I was surprised at the appointment

but was told it was of little importance to those
granting it.

Since it would keep me from starvation, it
meant much more to me. The position would pay
me over one dollar weekly.

But the money was not the greatest joy to the
position. Once again I could visit with folks.
When the mail came in each Saturday, the
villagers flocked into the store.

"Got me a letter today, Abe?"

"Did my newspaper come?"

Mentor laughed at me. "I never have to read my
Illinois State Register," he told his friends. "I only
have to ask Abe what's in it. He never misses a
word."

In a few months Mentor brought news of still
another position I might enjoy.

"The county surveyor is much in need of help,
Abe. Settlers are arriving every day. Land deeds
are piled high on his desk. He could use a good
assistant."

I thought about it a moment. "Surveying. Yes, it
is a position I could learn to like. But doesn't
surveying require skills in mathematics. My own
such skills I could fit neatly into a squirrel shell,
with much room left over."

Mentor shook his head. "That doesn't mean you
couldn't learn. If you be willing to work at it, I will
teach you."

Eagerly I agreed, once more grateful for
Mentor's confidence in me.

There was much to learn. Laying farm
boundaries, plotting new roads, planning towns
and villages. Mentor was a good teacher, patient
and kind. Often we sat before his fireplace long
hours into the night.

But my time with Mentor was well spent. I
purchased myself a compass and surveyor's chain.

Together Surveyor Calhoun and I rode through
the hazel brush, waded through the marshes and
climbed the wooded bluffs.

For each quarter section, or one hundred sixty
acres, I established with boundaries, I earned two
dollars and fifty cents. I was given two dollars a
day for expenses. The farmers and settlers paid
willingly, at least most of them did. A few balked
at the prices. But there was usually a way of
meeting agreement. When Jack and Hannah
Armstrong needed work done, they found a useful
means of paying their debt.

"We ain't got money for you, Abe," Hannah said
with a sigh. "I am thinking there's something
better we can give you."

"And what would that be, ma'm?"

Hannah turned and went inside the Armstrong
cabin. When she came back, she was carrying fine
buckskins.

"Abe, if you'll be kind enough to slip into a pair
of Jack's breeches, I'll be a-fixing yours. I'm
thinking some of the threads across the seat may
be getting a mite thin."

I smiled. Hannah Armstrong was a wise
woman. Sitting in a saddle tends to wear heavy on
the seat.

"I'm right grateful for your offer, Miss Hannah.
You may be saving me from my death of cold
during the wintertime."

My postmastering and surveying duties gave
me the chance to meet many new people. I
learned to carry letters in my hat, delivering them
to folks near the places my surveying chores took
me. Everybody seemed right glad to get mail. It
was good to see joyful faces.

By the summer of 1834 I felt ready to make
another try for that spot in the state legislature.
Mentor, John Stuart, Stephen Logan — all of them

agreed I'd have a better grab at the barrel this time.

Ann Rutledge was confident too.

"I know you'll win," she told me. "Why, everybody around here knows you now."

"Maybe that's not such a good thing," I teased.

I spent the summer talking to folks. Sometimes I'd help with their harvesting, other times I'd visit their husking bees. If there was a picnic nearby, folks could expect flies, ants and — Abe Lincoln. And folks would have had to shove a melon in my mouth to keep me from talking.

The election was held in August. I knew I'd get the Whig votes, but I didn't know about the Democrats. When the tally was announced, I was at the top of the list.

"You knew you'd win, didn't you?" Ann asked.

I gulped, suddenly realizing that I was beginning a whole new task. It was one thing to talk and ask for votes. But now that I had won, it gave me a funny churning inside.

"I sure hoped I would win," I answered Ann. "Now I'm hoping I can do right by the people."

A Haunting Question

Vandalia, capitol of Illinois. How often I had read of the busy life of Vandalia in the newspapers. Laws being made, speeches in the House of Representatives and on the floor of the Senate. Vandalia. Before it had been but a name, a word. Now, for part of the year, it would be my home.

One thing was certain. My wardrobe of worn breeches, faded shirts and tired shoes needed tending. I wished no disgrace to come to the people of New Salem. I decided to visit Coleman Smoot, a farmer for whom I hired out.

"I'll be going to Vandalia come December," I told Farmer Smoot. "I'd be obliged if you could lend me some money for a few clothes."

Smoot looked me up and down, rubbing his chin during the careful inspection. "I'm thinking that's a wise notion. You appear in Vandalia like you are now and they'll think it's a walking scarecrow from somebody's farm."

The words stung a mite, but good sense grabbed my tongue and kept me silent.

Farmer Smoot continued. "You'll be making decent pay serving there in the legislature?"

I nodded. "Three dollars a day, I've been told."

"A grand sum of money for what good comes from those scoundrels," Master Smoot huffed. "But you'll be cleaning them up, Abe. I'll be giving you two hundred dollars as a loan. That should dress you with the best of them. You can pay me as you are paid."

I agreed and signed a note of promise for the money. The next day I took myself to Springfield. In the company of John Stuart, I visited a tailor. For an hour he measured me, showing me roll after roll of cloth. It seemed to me time could be put to better use.

"You'll face the legislators in style," John told me. "It would be wise to come to the capitol by stagecoach too. It will keep your new suit in fine form."

Mentor Graham agreed with John Stuart's suggestion. "You'll start off showing those folks we people in Salem have good taste and wisdom."

My first session at the state legislature opened December 1, 1834. The moment I stepped from the stagecoach I sensed the busy hustle of Vandalia.

The city rested on a bluff overlooking the Kaskaskia River. Log cabins lined the streets, muddied from November rains. The city's town square sat in the midst of town. I thought back on New Salem, so often quiet and not a soul moving outside. Not so with Vandalia. Movement was everywhere — stagecoaches, men on horses, the ladies gathering for gossip fests, children playing games.

"You'll get used to the commotion," said John Stuart, reading my thoughts. "It's a different life, but it has its rewards."

If there was commotion *outside*, the State
House Building where we held our legislature
meetings was like a chicken house stuffed with
hens. Every fellow sitting in that place had a
barrelful to say. And they all seemed to be saying
it at once. I figured I would add peace to the
situation by resting my own jawbone and listening.

But about the fifth day of listening, I decided to
share my thoughts a bit too. One fellow was
saying he wanted the justices of the peace to be
given more rights. Around New Salem, these
fellows seemed to think they had every right and a
few thousand more. I stood up and suggested we
put some limits on the rights of the justices of the
peace.

"They should be told what authority they have
and don't have," I said aloud. "And we should be
the ones to tell them."

When I sat down, another fellow leaned toward
me.

"You're new here, aren't you, boy? You been a
justice of the peace yourself?"

I didn't like being called "boy." Seemed to me
only a Pa has that right. But John Stuart had
overheard the question and decided to add a dose
of humor.

"No, my friend, Mister Lincoln has been no
justice of the peace," John said. "But he has been a
farmer and a riverboat sailor and a postmaster and
a surveyor and a store owner and — "

The gentleman who had called me "boy" raised
his hand for John to stop speaking.

"I apologize to Mister Lincoln. Anyone who's
done all he has cannot be called 'boy.' More than
likely, he'd be called 'old man.' "

The remark drew laughter from others around

us. I could not help but chuckle myself. I caught John's wink and nodded my thanks.

It was not the first and only time John proved a welcome friend in the legislature. I learned much from him, especially after the daily sessions. He explained many bills and laws to me — and he knew much about the people we were serving with.

"Watch that fellow," he told me one morning. "His name is Stephen Douglas."

The gentleman John pointed to was a short, black-haired fellow. At first I did not think him to be standing, he appeared so small.

John shook his head. "Maybe in size, he's small. But he is respected and making his name known. His future is bright, so they say."

At times I wondered what anyone was saying about *my* future. But such thoughts were quickly forgotten as my duties grew. Before I knew what was happening, I had been placed on three committees. John helped me prepare my first bill. It called for a bridge to be built over Salt Creek.

"The folks from my county don't ask for much from this state legislature," I told the other representatives. "But when they say they need a bridge, they're not just hollering in the wind."

John said I gave a fine speech. When the votes were tallied, the bridge bill had passed.

Money, money, money. Every problem brought up for talk seemed to need money for solving. Money for roads, for schools, for buildings. As we finished our duties and readied ourselves to go home, I felt joy and relief.

The folks in New Salem were eager to hear about the business of the legislature. Work on the Salt Creek Bridge was due to start in late spring. I was grateful the people were satisfied with my efforts.

"We heard good reports," said Mentor Graham. "Now we're hoping you'll be taking over your postmaster and surveyor chores."

I nodded. "I'll be more than a mite happy to get back into my old breeches. I'll never be much for those fancy suits."

"Abe, you haven't changed," Ann said. "And we hope you never will."

I learned that Ann's life had changed little too. Each day she waited to hear from John McNamar, a fellow to whom she considered herself engaged. He had gone East to settle family affairs in 1832. At first he had written. Now Ann heard nothing.

"I may receive a letter tomorrow," she kept saying. "Or maybe John himself will return."

I said nothing. But it did seem that three years was a long time to wait.

One morning as I was surveying in the fields near New Salem, a horseman came galloping toward me. It was Ann's brother, David Rutledge.

"Abe, I've come to fetch you. It's Ann. She's mighty sick."

No more time was wasted talking. In minutes we were at the Rutledge home.

Ann's father sat at a table, staring ahead. He did not see me, nor did we speak. Quietly the doctor motioned toward the door.

"It's this cursed fever," the doctor said bitterly. "I'm afraid she has little time left with us."

I paid little heed to the doctor's words. Ann could not die. She was too full of life. Quickly I slipped past the doctor and entered the room.

Ann lay on the bed, a patchwork quilt pulled neatly up to her chin. She was like a picture, her golden hair framing her face. The pink color of her cheeks was gone. But her eyes flickered and she motioned me forward.

For a long time I sat next to her, gently holding

her hand. Now and then she whispered my name.
I dropped to my knees.

"Help us, O Lord our God, for we rest in thee."

Finally I stood, looking down on the sleeping
girl before me. Sleep. Surely sleep would ease her
suffering and make her well again. I slipped my
hand from hers and quietly left the room.

I have little memory of the days that followed. I
recall a voice saying "Ann's gone, Abe. She's dead
and gone forever."

A knot in my chest wanted to rise up and burst
from my throat. Gone away forever? Dead? Not
Ann. I could see her running across the fields —
sitting beside the river — setting the dishes on her
father's table. I could hear her voice, soft and
smooth as she spoke of her future — merry and
laughing as she told a happy story. Gone forever?
Why? I could change jobs or towns or friends, but
this I could not change. I could not bring Ann
back. Gone! I felt helpless against death.

"It was God's will, Abe. We must accept His
wisdom."

Again the words came from a voice I did not
know. I wanted to shout, to run into the wind, to
feel rain on my face. Why did Ann have to die? If
God be merciful, why did He not show mercy?
What wisdom steals a young girl's life, leaving
emptiness and sorrow in its place? I remembered
standing on a hillside in Kentucky as my mother
was buried. Then there was my sister — good,
kind Sarah. Now it was Ann, who had given us all
such joy and love. Gone forever. Why?

The question haunted me. When and where
would I find the answer? I could not understand
the ways of God. Was there something missing in
my faith in Him?

I knew I would never be the same man I had
been. And New Salem the place I loved so dearly,

would never be the same either. It was gone too.
Gone forever.

"Love is Eternal"

I was grateful that the state legislature began holding special sessions in the fall. Hopefully work would offer some escape from the recent past in New Salem. It was good to leave that town.

The Vandalia State House was a welcome sight, as was John Stuart. He was carrying five large black books when he welcomed me back to work.

"These volumes are yours to study," John said. "They are law books. If they do not broaden your mind, they will surely broaden your shoulders. I believe each one weighs a goodly ton."

Taking the books, I felt John had understated their weight. My hands must have scraped the ground as I carried the books.

The session of the legislature was a lively one. There was talk of relocating the state capital. Some favored Springfield — myself included. Others spoke for Jacksonville, a few for Alton. No vote was taken, but it was a matter sure to come up again.

There was talk about allowing non-landowners to vote. If a fellow pays his taxes and is willing to bear arms for his homeland's defense, he should be able to vote. Such voting rights should be given the ladies as well, some of us thought.

As the session ended, John asked about my future. "You'll run for reelection, won't you, Abe?"

"I am thinking so," I answered. "A fool will stay as long as his hosts allow."

Once more I returned to New Salem and the folks of Sangamon County. They seemed happy with my services, and promised their support. Some of the folks made no secret of their wants.

"Make Springfield the capital city," spoke one businessman. "Vandalia is too far south. People are settling in the north."

"Spend more money on good roads," a farmer said. "We cannot get our crops to the cities."

But Widow Abell of New Salem had the most surprising suggestion of all. "Abe, I want you to do only one thing this next year."

"What is that?" I asked.

"I want you to marry my sister Mary Owens. She's coming back from Kentucky to stay with me. I'm thinking you two would make a right fine couple."

I smiled. "Fellows running for public office make a lot of promises," I told Widow Abell. "But marriage with me would be more likely a threat than a promise."

The folks of Sangamon County decided to send me back to Vandalia for another term. In fact, there were nine of us in all from the fast growing Sangamon County. And a man the size of Stephen Douglas would have been lost among us, we were such a gangly bunch. The nine of us totaled fifty-four feet, an average of six foot a man.

"Long Nine!" someone shouted as we boarded the stage to Vandalia. "Look at the 'Long Nine' from Sangamon County!"

Being the tallest among the nine, I only hoped we were "long" on good sense too.

The Democrats controlled the legislature, but we Whigs were a hearty minority. The others of my party did me the honor of choosing me their leader.

"Don't let those Democrats get by with a thing," friends told me. "We trust you, Abe."

"They'll have to crawl in a barrel and lock the lid to hide from me," I answered.

It was no easy chore. Some days I needed to cut myself in three pieces to be everywhere I was supposed to be. Often I got but a few hours sleep before another early morning meeting was scheduled. Meals were a mite scarce as well.

But the time spent seemed well placed. New canals were planned, railroad lines charted, drawings for bridges accepted. Money was a problem, but what we had was put to good use.

Finally, a vote was taken on a new location for the state capital. Tempers were hot and I believe the State House walls blushed in shame from the fiery words that flew for hours. When the shouts died down, the decision was made — the capital would be moved to Springfield. Naturally, the vote left me well satisfied.

Joy replaced satisfaction the next day. I received word my application to practice law was accepted. Now I was a licensed attorney.

When the session ended, our "Long Nine" journeyed from Vandalia to Springfield. We were met with cheers and smiling faces.

"You have served us well," the people of Sangamon County told us. "You Long Nine are mighty fine!"

Before I could return to New Salem on horseback, I was invited to three grand dinners. The tables were covered with fine food. The speakers praised the work we had done.

"Your future lies here in Springfield," said John Stuart. "What law business will there be in New Salem? Come and be my partner, Abe. Move here to Springfield."

I promised to consider the prospects of moving. But I first wanted to go back to New Salem.

The village had changed since I had been there last. Sadly, the post office had been moved to Petersburg. My old job was gone.

Mary Owens and I had exchanged letters while I was in Vandalia. I called on her, wondering if some deeper feelings than friendship might be held. They were not. She seemed happy with her life as it stood.

Thus, the decision was made. Springfield would be my new home. My belongings fit neatly into two saddlebags. Yes, at twenty-eight years of age, I fit my total belongings into two saddlebags.

"The Lord does not judge us on what we carry outside us," said Mentor Graham. "It is what we carry within."

If there had been time, I would have liked to pursue the matter further with kind Mentor. No longer did I carry the faith, the unquestioning faith, of my early years. I was troubled by doubt. If a Christian always finds life full of joy, of daily peace in mind and spirit, then I am not a Christian. I had many questions about God. I needed answers. Where would I find them?

My farewells in New Salem were swift and few. Although I had enjoyed happy days in the village, they were overshadowed by grey clouds.

Springfield. My new home. It recalled to me the noise and activity of New Orleans. I felt

Springfield was not new to me. At the legislature meetings, had I not listened for hours as men spoke praises of this town. Fifteen hundred people it boasted, most living in sturdy wood homes. Yet log cabins still dotted the streets of the town.

And churches. Six of them, I was told. Two newspapers. Plenty of schools. Even an academy for advanced students. Yes, Springfield was right well suited to be a capital city.

I made my way to the store of Joshua Speed. Master Speed had been one who had spoken to me of leaving New Salem and coming to Springfield. I entered his store wondering if he still had memory of his suggestion.

"Why, if it isn't Abe Lincoln!" Joshua exclaimed.

I nodded. "Yes, that's who it is."

"And how are things in Salem, Abe?"

"Behind me," I answered. "I've come to stay in Springfield. I'm wondering about the cost of a bedstead."

Joshua rubbed his chin. "About seventeen dollars, I'm thinking."

"You're thinking a bit more money than I'm carrying," I answered. "Until I'm settled in with a few legal clients, I'll be sleeping under the open sky. Unless I can find a friendly soul who — "

"You're looking at just such a critter," Joshua interrupted. "I've a big room upstairs with a large double bed. If you could find my company tolerable — "

"I'll go out and fetch my belongings in."

Quickly I took my things upstairs. A minute later I returned.

"Well, Joshua, I'm all moved in."

I left Joshua to look over the town. I no sooner

had crossed the street, when I heard a voice calling
my name.

"Abe. You, Abe Lincoln!"

The owner of the voice was my friend William
Butler. He was the clerk of the Sangamon Circuit
Court and had visited in New Salem more than
once.

By the time William Butler and I had finished
talking, he had invited me for supper. "In fact,
you may eat with me anytime you wish," he
added.

It was a welcome offer. William was good
company, and from his jolly round appearance, a
good eater as well.

As always, John Stuart seemed happy to see me
again. "Abe, my request still stands. If you be
willing to become a partner, we shall practice law
together."

It was kind and generous of John, and I
accepted at once. On April 12, 1837, we posted
official notice of our partnership in the *Sangamon
Journal*.

> *J. T. Stuart and A. Lincoln,
> Attorneys and Counsellors at Law
> will practice conjointly in the courts
> of this Judicial Circuit. Office No. 4,
> Hoffman's Row, upstairs.*

Our law office was a mite drab, perhaps like this
half of the partnership. But its convenient location
provided those requiring our services an easy
place to come. Our set fee of five dollars a client
would be shared evenly.

Soon after our partnership gained some footing,
John announced he was going to run for the
United States Congress. His opponent would be
Stephen Douglas, our former friend from the

legislature. Mr. Douglas often visited Joshua
Speed's Store, and we had held many talks in the
back room. I knew Stephen Douglas would not
be an easy target.

With John campaigning, many of the legal
affairs of our office fell into my hands. The hours
of work were long, but the time was satisfying.

John Stuart seemed pleased with my work.

"Folks around town speak right highly of our
law practice," he said. "Each day we become
better known and better trusted."

I hoped such was the case. But I could not help
but recall the passage from Proverbs: "Boast not
thyself of tomorrow; for thou knowest not what a
day may bring forth."

I felt more and more pulled into the busy life of
Springfield. By invitation, I joined the Young
Men's Lyceum. Each week the group met to
discuss and debate the issues of the day. The
meetings stirred a new interest in me.

Now and then I submitted letters to the city
newspapers, sometimes using a name that fitted
my fancy. "Otis Witherspoon" was one I used,
and "Abner Burrows" was another. I made certain
there were no true folks in Springfield wearing
such labels, but I'm afraid few readers were
fooled by my game.

"You can change your name," said wise John
Stuart, "but the style remains that of Abe Lincoln.
Your thinking is clear and plain, and your words
reflect it. Amuse yourself writing letters, but there
are only a few folks you're fooling."

I decided to seek another term in the
Legislature during the summer of 1838. It
appeared my work had so far pleased the voters,
for they elected me again. Soon after, the Whigs
picked me to lead the party too.

"If those Democrats in the assembly would act

wisely, you'd be our Speaker of the House," one of my friends told me.

Apparently, wisdom did not lie in enough quantity among the Democrats. I was nominated for the Speaker's slot, but promptly rejected.

Legislative business set a quick pace. Always there were plans for new roads and deeper canals. There seemed to be countless ideas from railroad men too.

"I don't think Illinois will have a tree or free open stretch of land left," I told John Stuart. "By the time I die, I'm afraid I'll have to be buried beneath the water or under a railroad track."

If progress had come to Illinois, much of it had landed right in Springfield. In only one week, a bookstore opened, a thespian group was formed, and the great Daniel Webster came to speak.

I found my calendar more and more crowded with meetings, meetings, and more meetings. But in truth, I found time for socializing too. The parties were plentiful. Although my dancing was a mite awkward, the folks I spoke with seemed to enjoy a good story and happy laughs.

It was at such an evening affair I first laid eyes on Miss Mary Todd. I had been told this young lady was visiting her sister Elizabeth Todd Edwards. Ninian and Elizabeth Edwards were known throughout the city for their splendid parties, and this was not the first I had attended. But as I gazed on Mary Todd, I sensed this party would be different from all the others.

She was wearing a white dress, tied behind at the waist with a black sash. Her voice was cheerful, her smile constant and sincere, her eyes sparkling and bright. From a distance I listened to her happy conversation; now and then I nodded to her.

As I watched her whirl gracefully across the

dance floor with Stephen Douglas, I could not help but glance down at my own long clumsy legs. If only I might dance with Mary Todd, and not prove myself a complete bumpkin.

The next thing I knew I was standing before her.

"Miss Todd, I'd like to dance with you in the worst way."

Mary Todd smiled as she stepped forward. "Certainly, Mr. Lincoln, although I usually prefer gentlemen who wish to dance with me in the best way."

The dance ended too soon. But not before I had learned Mary Todd was the most educated and interesting woman I'd ever met. She had little idea I planned to see much more of her in the future.

It was a promise I kept faithfully. In the months that followed, I called on Mary Todd often. Unlike most ladies, she seemed eager to talk of politics and business. I learned much about music, dancing, and drama. Indeed, Mary Todd was well bred and proud. But she was no peacock. I felt most at ease with her.

"It is said about town she hopes to become a President's lady," said John Stuart. "Most folks speak of Stephen Douglas being her choice, although I have heard your name mentioned as well."

I smiled. "If my name be coupled with Mary Todd's, I would be most pleased. However, if she be seeking a President, she'll not be sitting in my corner."

I called on Mary Todd for over a year. Finally I felt I should make clear my intentions. I asked Mary Todd to be my wife.

"I accept your offer," she answered simply.

The engagement was not without ripples in the stream. I came to know Mary's moods and she

came to know mine as well. "No two of the Lord's children are just alike," my mother used to say. At times, Mary and I seemed to fit perfectly. Other times, our future together seemed hopeless.

Our fear of making a mistake by marrying led us to a "disengagement." Joshua Speed, who had become a good friend, was undergoing similar doubts about marriage. His intended, a Miss Fanny Henning, was back in Kentucky. Much of their courtship had been by mail. When it came time for Joshua to bring Fanny to Illinois as his wife, my friend weakened.

"I fear she'll find little happiness with me," Joshua said. "Courting is one thing, marriage is another."

That much was true. But there seemed little doubt to me that Fanny and Joshua were perfectly suited. I agreed to return with him to Kentucky to bring Fanny back. I was able to convince Joshua that he was indeed ripe for marrying. And I found my own thoughts, my own love for Mary to be richer.

Eagerly I returned to Springfield. Would Mary still have me? My hopes and prayers begged for her consent.

Thankfully, God was listening. Mary was willing to become my mate.

The wedding was a small one, Ninian and Elizabeth Edwards hosting the event in their home. It took place November 4, 1842. Debts had taken their toll, and I could afford only a small gold wedding ring. But Mary seemed pleased as she read the inscription inside.

"Love is eternal," she whispered. "It's perfect, Abe. I shall make you the best wife I know how."

I prayed the Lord would make me worthy of Mary's love.

A Question of Faith

Mary and I settled into a life together without fancy flowers and lace. No chest of gold christened our marriage. In truth, a few old debts remained to be paid. But the sweet bride I had picked seemed little worried.

"We have each other," she laughed.

That much was certain. But I still wished I might have provided a short honeymoon journey, or perhaps a better home. We found ourselves rooms in the Globe Tavern near the Square in Springfield. Upon my return home one evening after work at the law office, I found Mary wearing a wide smile.

"This place we are living in is busy indeed!" she said.

"In what way?" I asked.

"Did you know the stagecoach station is on the ground floor? Well, each time a stage arrives, a bell is rung. Then the coach boys bring out fresh horses. Not being accustomed to such noise, I came running out each time the bell sounded. At

first, the driver told me to bring out the horses.
Can you imagine me leading horses?"

I joined Mary in laughter. No, I could not
imagine Mary leading horses. Maybe a donkey
like Abe Lincoln, but not horses!

With John Stuart's election to Congress, it
seemed wise to abandon our law practice together. We had been a successful team, but he felt
guilty being away so often in Washington. I had to
admit the work grew heavy sometimes.

Good fortune stayed with me however. Shortly
after my breaking with John, I found myself
another partner in the person of Stephen Logan.

At times I considered myself more of Stephen's
student than a partner. He took special care with
each of his law cases. I watched him closely and
learned much from his example.

"I can't really believe he's as fine as you say,"
Mary said one night at mealtime. "Why, that mop
of red hair of his floppin' in the breeze makes him
look like a wild rooster. He could tend a bit more
to his appearance."

Having never won very much attention for
appearances myself, I said little. But I was
impressed with Stephen, and felt blessed to have
him as a partner.

My partnership with Mary was equally satisfying. Always she was willing to accompany me to
parties and dinners. Her conversation sparkled
like her eyes, never failing to delight those around
her. I knew our marriage was seed planted in rich
soil.

But like all unions, ours had moments of strain
and some struggle. Only a short time after our
bonds were spoken, Mary suggested we begin
regular church attendance.

"We have visited many fine homes in
Springfield together," she told me. "Let us not

forget the importance of visiting the House of
God."

I shook my head. "The Lord listens to us
wherever we are. We can speak to Him in an
open field, in an attic chamber or in a deep forest.
Must one make a public show of worship?"

Tears came to Mary's eyes. "We agreed to share
our lives together, and our love as well. Will you
not come with me to share worship and love of
God?"

Memories of the past rolled back to me. Much
as I had tried, I could not overcome my doubts
and questions. In my childhood I had listened to
my mother tell stories from the Bible. As soon as I
was able, I took to reading it myself. Indeed, I
prided myself on being able to recite passage after
passage from memory. But knowing words,
remembering passages — surely this was not all
there was in being a Christian. Is not faith, the
faith of good Christians, complete unyielding trust
in God? I could not pretend to possess such an
allegiance.

But Mary did not give up easily.

"You, yourself, claim that the Lord listens to us
wherever we are," she insisted. "Then He will
listen to you just as carefully if you be with me in
church than if you be here at home alone."

"Perhaps you should have been the lawyer of
this household," I laughed.

I gave the matter of church attendance much
consideration. Finally I decided little fault could
be found in hearing the words of the Lord regularly. My consent pleased Mary and we took a pew
at the First Presbyterian Church in Springfield.

I soon learned Mary had decided to make me a
refined gentleman. Such was a foolish notion.
Sadly enough, you cannot turn an oak tree into a
maple tree. But Mary was determined to try.

"Abe, you shouldn't carry law papers in your
stovepipe hat. It's just not respectable."

"You slouch a bit, Abe. Stand up straight."

"Must you read lying on the floor, dear? It looks
so unnatural with your feet propped on that chair
and your book on your chest."

Yes, I did have some peculiar habits. And I'm
afraid each one provided Mary with another
headache.

But as the months of 1843 wore on, good news
entered the Lincoln home. Mary was expecting a
child. Carefully we began tucking away what
money we could. I lived in the hope of someday
having my own home, where a family could live
together in peace and closeness.

"You worry too much about the walls of a home
you provide," said the church preacher. "It is
what we hold within ourselves that is truly important."

"True enough," I agreed. "But I should like to
have both shelter from the rain and security for
my soul."

The preacher nodded.

Our son, Robert Todd Lincoln, was born in
August of 1843. His entry into this world was well
announced by his own hearty squeals. Inwardly, I
joined this chorus.

"He carries your looks," Mary said as she held
our baby in her arms.

"I hope you are mistaken," I answered, "for his
sake."

Christmas brought me special joy. After returning from church, I sat Mary down on the sofa.
Softly she hummed a hymn to our sleeping child.

"Mary, I have found us a house, a home of our
own," I said. "It sits on the corner of Jackson and
Eighth Streets."

"Oh, Abe, when can we move? It will be so

wonderful to have our own place. I hope it has a yard in which Robert can play?"

I nodded and smiled. "That was one of the first things I looked for. There are other children in the neighborhood too. But there is only one thing our new home does not have."

"And what is that, Abe?"

"There is no stagecoach bell which will signal for you to bring out fresh horses."

"Oh, Abraham!" Mary laughed.

Moving to a new home was but one change that my life took in the new year. Stephen Logan began to speak of taking his son as a law partner. It was a natural desire and I wished not to be a hindrance to such a change.

"I have enjoyed our association, Stephen, but you are free to dissolve it at any time. A friendly handshake will be all I ask of you."

With just such a gesture, the partnership of Logan and Lincoln came to its end. I had no wish to practice law without an associate, so I took to pounding the bushes for another partner.

I had heard tell of a lawyer cousin of Rowan Herndon from New Salem — William Herndon by name. It was said he was young, energetic, and well schooled in law. I extended an invitation for the young man to visit me.

I was much taken by William Herndon's appearance. From his patent leather shoes to his spotless silk hat, William was truly a dandy.

"You are highly thought of, Mr. Lincoln," he told me. "I should only hope I might enjoy the respect you have earned."

Only a deaf man would not enjoy such praise. I cannot claim that his words did not have a pleasant effect. Before our first meeting was over, Billy Herndon had agreed to be my junior partner.

My life was changing, for the better I thought.

Although I had enjoyed the time spent in the state legislature, I felt no urge to retrace such footsteps. Since John Stuart declared he would not run for the United States Congress in 1844, I began to think of such a journey myself.

I had little chance to share my intentions among my Whig friends. They chose me to serve as a delegate to vote for Edward Baker for the position John Stuart had left open.

"I should have made my feelings known sooner," I told Mary. "It is a fool who comes to supper an hour late."

"Just be sure you are the first one seated at the table the next time a meal is served," Mary answered.

There was much sense in her thought. The next time I would make known my intentions early and be ready.

Billy Herndon was a big help to me with my plans. He seemed to thrive on the office chores I hated most. He was a tireless worker, always willing to complete the paperwork tasks that I found a nuisance. His youth and lively spirit made him known among many folks of Springfield. He was a worthy friend for one considering election plans.

Work in the law office and traveling around Springfield kept me busy. But when Mary announced she was again with child, I promised to spend more time at home.

Mary badly wanted our second child to be a girl. It mattered little to me, as long as the child be blessed with good health.

In March of 1846, we welcomed Edward, our second son, into the world. Again, he seemed born with true Lincoln lungs.

Within weeks I was tossed into the sea of campaigning and speech making. I realized how much I had missed politics. Meeting new people, listening to ideas, sharing beliefs. It offered excitement and challenge found in no other way.

But my opponent, Peter Cartwright, cast a gloomy shadow into the battle for votes. A circuit-riding preacher, he hurled angry charges at me.

"If you want crude stories and vulgar jokes," said Cartwright, "then vote for Abe Lincoln. He is no Christian. He has no conscience. If you seek such a candidate, he is yours for the asking."

The newspapers and circulars carried Cartwright's words. Mary raged about the house, bitterly denouncing "Preacher Peter."

"Abe, you cannot let his charge be ignored," she shouted. "How dare him claim you are not a Christian. You must answer his speeches with your own."

I disagreed. "The character and religion of Jesus Christ have no place in political speeches. It is the issues of the day that deserve our attention. Each man must find his own place with the Lord."

Mary was unconvinced. Many of my friends sided with her. Finally, I felt obliged to put my thoughts about the matter on paper.

> A charge having got into circulation in some of the neighborhoods of this district, in substance that I am an open scoffer at christianity. That I am not a member of any Christian Church, is true; but I have never denied the truth of the Scriptures; and I have never spoken with intentional disrespect of religion in general, or of any denomination of Christians in particular. It is true that in early life I was inclined to believe in what I understand is called

*the "Doctrine of Necessity" — that
is, that the human mind is impelled
to action, or held in rest by some
power, over which the mind itself
has no control; and I have sometimes
(with one, two or three, but never
publicly) tried to maintain this opinion in argument. The habit of arguing thus, however, I have entirely
left off for more than five years.
And I add here, I have always understood this same opinion to be held
by several of the Christian denom-
inations. The forgoing is the whole
truth, briefly stated, in relation to
myself, upon this subject.
I do not think I could myself, be
brought to support a man for office,
whom I knew to be an open enemy
of, and scoffer at, religion. Leaving
the high matter of eternal conse-
quences between him and his
Maker, I still do not think any man
has the right thus to insult the feelings, and injure the morals, of the
community in which he may live. If
then, I was guilty of such conduct, I
should blame no man who should
condemn me for it: but I do blame
those, whoever they may be, who
falsely put such a charge in circulation against me.*

Mary thought I had stated my feelings as well as
I might. As I gave the statement to the
newspapers, I promised myself it would be the
last time I would allow my faith to be used in a
political arena.

Most folks predicted a close election. To my satisfaction, the tally found me beating Peter Cartwright 6340 to his 4829.

"I am so proud of you," Mary told me. "It will be hard to leave Springfield, but I know our future will be exciting in Washington."

I hoped Mary would not be disappointed.

Trials and Triumphs

We left our home in Springfield on a cheerful autumn day in 1847. After a tiring journey by steamboat and rail, we arrived in Washington. Soon after settling into a boarding house, I took my place as an elected Congressman from Illinois in Congress.

In many ways, Washington was much like Springfield. Rains turned the streets into mudpools, winds lifted the dust and tossed it into faces and house windows. Only Pennsylvania Avenue lay paved with big cobblestones. Buggies and carriages of the rich rolled and rattled across the stones. Needless to say, I was not among those enjoying such transportation.

The city bulged with 40,000 people, a goodly portion of them Negro slaves. Within view of the Capitol Building is the largest slave market in the country. Sometimes I wondered how the devoted members of our nation could daily witness this selling of human life and not suffer with guilt. Just what does a man own when he owns a slave? Does

the owner possess another mind? Or an extra
heart? Surely he could not hope to own the soul
and spirit of another man?

"Why does slavery trouble you so deeply?" my
good wife asked often. "Many fine people own
slaves. Take care when you speak about this issue.
Careless words can bring a quick end to your
future."

Mary meant well, and her advice reflected
some wisdom. But I had always believed every
man should be free. If there be slaves, let the
slaves be those who choose to be — or those who
desire it for others. Whenever I heard people
argue for slavery, I felt those people should be the
first to try such an existence.

The Mexican War was over when I assumed my
duties, but war problems still lingered. It seemed
too bad all the state and territorial boundaries
were not decided and marked when people journeyed westward. Then wars like this one could
have been avoided.

But for any war we must enter, and I pray there
will be no more, it is Congress who must decide to
enter — not the President. No one person should
be left with the power to declare war. Such power
must rest with the people, through a vote of their
elected representatives. President Polk over-
stepped himself when he thrust our country into
conflict with Mexico.

And from all accounts I had heard of this war,
Americans did indeed show aggression. The first
blood shed in this fighting is soaked into *Mexican*
soil.

"Are you calling our soldiers villains?" many of
my fellow Congressmen asked.

I shook my head. "I call no one names. Just
show me the *spot* where there was Mexican agres-
sion!"

The debate continued. Back home in Illinois the newspapers labeled me "Spotty Lincoln." Somehow I became most unpopular — only for seeking the truth.

Mary suffered too. She arrived in Washington eagerly expecting fine parties and exciting times. Sadly, it was not to be. The people in this city were content with themselves. More and more Mary kept to our boarding house rooms, straying out only for meals.

But our two boys constantly lifted our spirits and gave us joy. Once I returned home only to discover my best stovepipe hat crawling across my bed.

"Mary!" I called. "My hat has come alive. Come and see!"

Mary rushed to the doorway. She stood watching and laughing until she could stand it no longer. Then she dashed forward. Underneath my stovepipe hid a smiling two-year-old Eddie.

Robert, too, provided us hearty laughs. One day I took him for a walk. We strolled the streets of Washington, gazing upon the small shacks and giant mansions standing side by side in the city. As we returned to the boarding house, one of our friends called out to us.

"We'll all be crowded indeed, Mr. Lincoln, if you bring your new friends inside!"

I turned around where I knew Robert was following in my path. The boy was there, and he was not alone. Directly behind him waddled four plump ducks, forming a straight line.

"Robert," I said, "unless you plan to pay for these extra boarders, you'll not be bringing them inside."

I thought by Robert's face he planned to make a plea in behalf of his new waterfowl friends, but he decided it would be hopeless. Sadly he turned, clapped his hands and stomped his feet. The quacking parade disbanded at once, running in all directions.

As soon as she could, Mary arranged to leave Washington and take our two fine sons to Kentucky. There she would find comfort among her family and friends. I offered no objection, but I knew the rooms in the boarding house would be empty indeed without my family.

My days in Congress passed slowly. The evenings were worse. I threw myself into the writing of a bill — a bill that would gradually free the slaves in the District of Columbia. I thought if we, in Washington, would set such an example, other states and territories might follow our lead.

But it was a foolish notion. Few looked on my thoughts with favor. My bill shriveled and died.

The hours in the evening passed slowly. I wrote to Mary, telling her how much I hated to stay in the rooms without her. I hoped my blessed fellows would not forget their lonely father.

Letters from Springfield made one point certain — I would not be reelected. Even young Billy Herndon scolded me for my attacks on President Polk and our country's actions in the war. I knew Billy would have felt as I did had he been here. But he was not. Anyway, I looked with pleasure at the thought of returning to Springfield with my beloved family.

I was glad when my term in Congress ended. Surely news that I would not run for election again was well received in Springfield. A crowded henhouse is glad to be rid of a trespassing mole, no matter how helpless he is.

The Lincoln return to Springfield went largely unnoticed. But the house on Jackson Street looked like a castle to us. Even the law office of Lincoln and Herndon, though drab and dingy to many, seemed a welcome sight.

Mary's spirits soon blossomed in our own Springfield. Friends came calling, wanting to hear of our adventures in the East. Bob and Eddie again became a part of neighborhood mischief.

As for me, I gladly became part of the circuit. The "circuit system" had not changed in my absence. Circuit courts were set up in small communities which only occasionally required a judge and lawyers. Most cases concerned boundary disagreements, debt settlements, and will disputes.

Judge David Davis rode the circuit around Springfield. He seemed glad to welcome me back.

"Glad to have an able lawyer like yourself coming with me," he said. "I've got a new buggy we can share."

I was grateful for the judge's kind offer. However, since the judge was of hearty frame, well over three hundred pounds, the space in his buggy was a mite snug. I invested money in a horse which I promptly named Old Buck. The judge and I were surely a laughable sight to the people we approached — the roly-poly and lanky-flanky twosome from Springfield.

Billy Herndon enjoyed the duties in the office. He had no desire to ride the circuit.

"I know the meals you get in those inns along the way," he said. "I want no part of riding horseback in the cold and rain. Enjoy my share of that as well as yours."

I did just that. The countryside of Illinois was changing. Gone were many of the log cabins. In their places stood firm frame houses. Horses replaced oxen for plowing and farm chores. The

tough steel plows of Deere and McCormick dug deep into the rich soil.

But although I liked riding the circuit, it always felt good to return home. The old back stove at Corneau and Diller's Drugstore was a favorite gathering spot. Hours of storytelling were passed in the fine company of Stephen Logan, Stephen Douglas, and Judge Davis.

No times were happier than those at home with Mary and the boys. Sometimes my wife and I spoke of adding another to our family.

"To you, there are only two boys in this house," Mary would say. "But I count three, for when you are with Robert and Edward, you are every bit the boy each of them is."

I knew Mary spoke the truth. Sometimes I sensed a neighbor's disapproving look meant our boys were running too freely. Yet I found myself unable to restrain such spirit. I wished those days might have lasted forever.

But another plan was being followed.

When the time came for Robert to enter school, we had to face a truth we had long ignored — or thought time would change. There was a problem with his eyes. The eyes were slightly crossed. Thankfully, we were able to secure a doctor who performed a brief operation to correct the problem.

No sooner had this situation been met when we received sad news from Kentucky. A dreaded plague had swept the state, killing many in its path, including Mary's beloved father. She returned to her native soil quickly.

Upon her return there was little time for joyful homecomings. Edward became sick, the doctors uttering only a short fearful verdict: "It looks like diphtheria."

For days the dreaded fever raged. Mary and I

took turns at Eddie's bedside, wiping his small hot head and chest with a cool cloth. Often we slept in our clothes, stealing away briefly for sleep and a bite to eat.

Finally the fever broke. But the doctors warned it would be months before we could be certain of the boy's health. The tiny fellow was so brave through it all. At times he could hardly swallow, but still he found a smile within him to brighten our spirits.

Nothing could save our little boy. On February 1, 1850, he slipped away from our world into another. We were left saddened and empty. Only four years did we have him, but who can measure memories in years. Once again death turned my thoughts more to God and His ways.

Mary withdrew, finding comfort by being alone. I honored her wishes, and saw that Robert did also.

I returned to circuit riding. My horse Old Buck had missed me. To lift my own spirits I bought a new buggy. It gave me opportunity to read as I rode, a more difficult chore when I rode on horseback.

The warm spring brought more than soft showers and bright blossoms. Mary learned she was to have another baby.

"If it be another boy," I told our faithful Doctor Wallace, "he shall carry your name next to ours."

The doctor was pleased. "I'll do my best."

No one could have known how much the kind doctor would be tested when the baby arrived. Mary developed an infection, running a fever of 104°. Our new son was sick too.

Doctor Wallace offered constant attention. Both mother and son responded to his care. With much gratitude and heartfelt thanks, we named our new boy William Wallace Lincoln.

With two young boys in the house, Mary and I decided a milking cow would make a sound investment. Such an animal was purchased and joined Old Buck in our meadow near the house.

Happily, the law firm of A. Lincoln and B. Herndon grew. Now and then people asked if I planned a return to politics. The question was usually met with a head-shaking no, but in truth, the dead coals on the outside still sheltered a few sparks of fire beneath.

News of my father's death saddened me. His life had not been an easy one, and I prayed he would find peace with his Maker. When Mary gave birth to another son, in the year 1853, the babe was promptly named "Thomas" after his late grandfather. Our new son squirmed and wiggled so much he resembled a tadpole, so he was promptly nicknamed "Tad."

With more and more settlers arriving, the circuit law duties increased. No boasting intended, I began to feel right at ease with the law. Perhaps it was the Duff Armstrong case that brought me my greatest satisfaction.

Duff was the son of my old friends Jack and Hannah Armstrong. The story was that a certain James Metzker had met his death at a camp meeting. He had been hit on the head by a man named Norris, then finished off with a slingshot by Duff Armstrong. The whole ugly event had been witnessed by a fellow named Charles Allen.

Norris had been tried and found guilty. There seemed little doubt he had indeed committed the foul deed.

But my meetings with Duff Armstrong convinced me he was innocent. Convincing a jury would not be so easy.

Much of the case rested on the testimony of

Charles Allen. It puzzled me how he could be so sure of himself.

"I saw everything that happened," he said in the courtroom. "I was only a hundred feet or so away from it all. Those two, Norris and Armstrong, are both murderers."

"And when did this take place?" I asked. "What time at night?"

Allen did not hesitate a moment. "It was 'bout midnight; that's when it was."

I rubbed my chin. "Isn't that a mite dark out to be seeing so clearly?"

"There was a full moon. You could see everything clear as in sunlight."

I was glad I had done my homework for the case. Reaching for a book on a nearby table, I picked up the volume and flipped through the pages. Allen leaned forward, trying to see what I was reading. Finally, I shared my secret.

"This almanac records but only a first quarter moon on the night we are discussing. By midnight it was gone."

In the background a few whispers could be heard. Allen glanced over at the judge, then at the jury. For the first time he seemed unsure of himself.

The case against Duff Armstrong crumbled a mite more when it was proven the slingshot displayed in court was not his. The jury quickly found Duff innocent.

Hannah Armstrong squeezed me like a bear around a tree full of honey. "You're a good man, Abe, and we're much obliged to you."

There was no fee collected for the case. The debt was one paid in friendship.

It was always good to return to Springfield after riding the circuit. No father should miss the joy of

watching his children play and laugh together.
Indeed, there was much of that around the
Lincoln house.

There was always a good meeting or two in
town every night too. Mary sometimes shook her
head wearily as I came home after midnight. But
I think she knew talking and story-swapping was
as basic to me as food was to others.

There was little doubt what issue concerned
people most — slavery. It was bewildering how
so many good folks could think favorably about a
man owning another. My friend, Stephen
Douglas, who had lifted himself into the United
States Senate, was a champion in support of
slavery.

"Men should be allowed the right to manage
their own property and affairs," said Senator
Douglas. "If he wants to own slaves, that is his
own business."

I could not accept such thinking. Neither could
I believe the country could keep holding together
having some states as free states, others as slave
states.

Many of Douglas's own fellow Democrats
could not accept his pro-slavery views. Joining
with the Whigs who felt the same, a new political
party was begun — the Republican party.

I attended many of the meetings held by the
Republicans. When they held their convention in
June of 1858, they chose me to oppose Senator
Douglas in the next election. In presenting my
acceptance speech, I made clear my feelings
about slavery.

"A house divided against itself cannot stand," I
told the people at the convention. "I believe this
government cannot endure permanently half
slave and half free...It will become all one thing, or
all the other."

The delegates at the meeting clapped and cheered. It was a welcome sound, one that lifted my spirits.

But I knew a long hard battle was just beginning.

"The Little Giant"

It was soon easy to tell who most enjoyed having Stephen Douglas and Abraham Lincoln as political opponents. Newspaper cartoonists took up their pens and had an amusing time drawing our pictures.

It was difficult to say who suffered more. Stephen was always shown in proud peacock clothes, his feet lifting his five foot body high off the ground. Always his mouth was open, looking like a giant cave. As for me, I appeared a scrawny hungry scarecrow. Seldom were my pantaloons touching my boots, and my sloping nose seemed to measure just a mite under ten inches.

"I'm just hoping folks don't vote for the most handsome candidate," I told Mary. "It's for certain I'd run a far back second."

Mary shook her head. "You would still be getting my vote, if I but had one."

That was Mary's way — reminding me not to make the campaign just one issue, that of slavery. I promised her I would do what I could for women if I were elected.

There was much to be admired about Stephen
Douglas. For six years he had served the people
of Illinois in the Senate. He had helped to bring
government aid for building and land development.

If he had only not tampered with the Missouri
Compromise. For over thirty years the
compromise had worked. States entering the
Union north of the Ohio River-Mississippi River
junction would be free. Those states entering
south of the junction would be slave. Then
Senator Douglas decided, in 1854, that people in a
new state should be allowed to vote if they wanted
slavery or not. Of course, the most unfair part of
that thinking was that slaves could not vote!

Douglas was a convincing speaker. His voice
was deep and powerful, the words flowed from
him smoothly.

"Our country was founded on freedom," he told
audiences. "A man should be free to work as he
wishes, own what he wishes, and enjoy life to the
fullest."

Sadly enough, Douglas seemed to think of the
black man, the slave, as a horse or an ox. He was to
be the white man's helper, nothing more. He
talked of slaves as a piece of property like a shed
or a shack.

It would be the state legislators who would
actually be picking between Douglas and me. But
the legislators would vote according to the
feelings of the people. I knew there was much
money behind the Douglas campaign. There was
little chance of matching his funds. Thankfully,
the newspapers gave me a fresh thought.

"It would be a political feast to get Douglas and
Lincoln together," one editor wrote. "Before the
hens pick the best fox, let's see the two foxes in the
same henhouse," suggested another editor.

Such a meeting seemed a worthy notion. Quickly I challenged my opponent to a public debate. At first he hesitated, probably sensing he would be giving me an advantage. Finally, he agreed, and a committee set up seven meeting places in Illinois and made rules for the debates.

The opening speaker would have one hour to speak — then his opponent would speak an hour and a half — with the opening speaker having a final half hour. Douglas was to open the first, third, fifth, and seventh debates. I would open the second, fourth, and sixth meetings.

The newspapers gave the forthcoming debates much space and attention. Small but powerful Stephen had earned himself the nickname "The Little Giant." Reporters made much use of the label. "Abe Hopes To Become Giant Killer" one headline declared. The cartoons reflected the same flavor.

We opened our debating sessions in Ottawa. I traveled by rail, and was met by a handsome collection of men and ladies.

"We're so proud and pleased you picked our town for your first battle, I mean debate," one woman said.

I chuckled at her slip of the tongue. I wondered if Douglas and myself would be led to a debating platform — or a dueling arena.

A platform it was, surrounded by flowers and ferns. Everywhere there were bands and banners. I hoped all the fancy extras would not detract from our true purposes for gathering.

Stephen was in rare form. His eyebrows danced up and down, his voice ranted and quaked with anger.

"My opponent seeks to take your freedoms away," he shouted. "Is this what you want?"

It was not always easy listening to my opponent

twist my words and beliefs. But I knew I would
have my turn to speak too.

"All men are created equal," I told the crowd.
"The color of a man's skin should not make him a
servant."

The people listened. There were cheers and
boos for each of us.

It was impossible to tell who won the first
debate. The Republican newspapers proclaimed:
"LINCOLN TRIUMPHANT! THE GREAT
GIANT SLAIN!"

The Democratic newspapers found a different
verdict: "12,000 PEOPLE WITNESS THE
ROUT OF LINCOLN — DOUGLAS AGAIN
TRIUMPHS!"

The second debate was held at Freeport. The
town was bustling. When I arrived in the morning,
there were sounds like the whole place was ex-
ploding.

"You're mighty important to us folks," one
gentleman said. "We decided to give you a cannon welcome."

It was a generous tribute. "I only hope you'll not
be turning the guns on me while I'm speaking," I
answered.

One fellow at the debate had a rare sense of
humor. "Mr. Lincoln, how long do you figure a
man's legs ought to be?"

The question was off the topic, but not to offer
an answer might appear devious. After glancing
down, I looked my questioner in the face. "Well, I
think a man's legs should reach from his body to
the ground."

The crowd laughed and cheered. It was a good
sound. Even my opponent chuckled.

But most of the questions asked dealt with
slavery directly. As I listened to people talk, I
became more convinced that there was no easy

way of ending slavery in states where it was legal.

"However, we cannot allow it to spread into new states," I told the people. "It must be halted if this country is to survive. Eighty years ago we declared all men equal. Now Mr. Douglas proclaims the sacred right of self-government allows one man the right to enslave another. Those who deny freedom to others deserve it not themselves, and under the rule of a just God, cannot long retain it."

As the autumn leaves turned colors, Douglas and I continued our meetings. Jonesboro. Charleston. Galesburg. On to Quincy, then Alton. The crowds listened, calling out questions from time to time. Finally, it was time for the decision.

"Win or lose, Abe, you have given the Republican party a respected name and position," John Stuart told me. "I'm thinking there will be no more slavery states coming into the Union."

On November 2, 1858, the Illinois state election was held. The Republicans gained, but the Democrats still controlled the houses in the legislature. When the people's representatives met two months later, they elected Stephen Douglas by a vote of 54-46.

"You spoke your piece well," consoled my dear wife. "You can rest easy and proud."

No words could take away the sting of defeat. I felt too old to cry and it hurt too much to laugh.

INTO THE WHITE HOUSE

My Springfield law office was in sorry condition after the debates. Campaigning had cost me a pretty penny. I knew it would take months to pay all the bills.

"Don't fret, Abe," said Billy Herndon. "You've made a right fine name for yourself. People all over the country know who you are."

It always amused me that some folks believed a famous name paid off debts. Somehow I never met a man who said "Forget the money you owe me. I've heard good stories about you."

Judge Davis made me a kindly offer in the spring of 1859. He said he wanted to take a rest from his duties.

"The other lawyers respect you, Abe. They know you'll be fair with them," Judge Davis declared. "Will you take my place as a judge for a spell?"

It was an honor I had not considered, but I was grateful and accepted.

While sitting as judge, I received another most

interesting offer. This one came from a newspaper editor, and it caused me more than a few chuckles. It seems this editor thought I'd be a proper choice running for President in 1860.

"It's not such a foolish notion," Mary scolded me. "Your views on slavery brought you no friends in the South. But the folks in the North would support you."

Perhaps desire clouded Mary's usual wise judgment. Whatever the case, I dashed a quick note off to the newspaper editor — "I must, in candor, say I do not think myself fit for the Presidency."

Mary was not content with my decision. "If you're going to close the door, do not lock it tight," she cautioned.

Good Billy Herndon and Judge Davis offered similar advice. They encouraged me to give speeches often for the Republicans. It was a happy chore. Meeting new folks provided excitement and joy. Politics seemed much like the rabbit stew my Ma would make us back in Kentucky — when one had a taste, he always wanted more.

"I sense the door is opening a crack," teased my wife.

"Maybe," I answered, "but a small crack is all."

The people in the Midwest had offered me kind reception. But if any dreams for national office were to be held, the feelings of other folks would have to be known. Early in 1860, I boarded a train for New York. I had been invited to present a speech. This would test the heat of the water for certain.

If there be any warmth in New York for my arrival, it was not in the weather. Snowflakes big as goosefeathers swirled around the Cooper Union Building where I was to speak.

My host, William Cullen Bryant, the noted

scholar and poet, was most apologetic for the
weather. "It is a shame that we welcome you here
on such a cold night."

"Such an evening will make my own hot air that
much more appreciated," I laughed. "Anyway, I
fear you have as little control over the weather
here as we do in Illinois. Thankfully, such control
rests in greater hands than our own."

Fifteen hundred people had packed into the
building to hear the speech. At first, I could think
of little else besides my tight new shoes and my
crumpled black suit. But once started, the words
came easily.

*Some claim that our country's
Constitution affirms the right of one
man to own another as a slave. A
true inspection of the Constitution
will reveal no such right exists!*

*Wrong as we think slavery is, we
can yet afford to let it alone where it
is, because that much is due to the
necessity arising from its actual presence in the nation; but can we, while
our votes will prevent it, allow it to
spread into the national Territories,
and to overrun us here in these free
States? If our sense of duty forbids
this, then let us stand by our duty
fearlessly and effectively. Let us
have faith that right makes might,
and in that faith let us to the end dare
to do our duty as we understand it.*

The crowd applauded. There were cheers and
whistling.

"Amen, Abe!" a voice called out. Everyone
seemed to jump to his feet at once, yelling and

shouting. Hats went sailing skyward, while Mr.
Bryant shook my hand like a thirsty man pumping
a water handle.

After a few more speeches in the East, I eagerly
returned to Illinois. Billy Herndon was a welcome
sight, and brought cheerful news too.

"You're sure to be the Republican candidate for
President when the party meets in May," he said.
"Everyone is saying so."

If politics be a fever, Billy Herndon had a
mighty dose. In truth, my own head was burning
as well.

Decatur was the setting for the gathering of Republicans. A wolfpack of ten could not have kept
me away. But little did I expect to see my old
cousin, John Hanks, walk into the convention. In
his hands he carried two weather-scarred fence
rails. A banner hanging between the rails read:

ABRAHAM LINCOLN
The Rail Candidate
For President in 1860
Two Rails from About 3000
Made in 1830 by Thomas Hanks
and Abe Lincoln — Whose Father Was
the First Pioneer of Macon County

My friends from Macon County followed John
around the convention floor. They sang and
hollered, pushing the rails up and down. When
they stopped, John called to me.

"Abe Lincoln, look at these rails. They're yours,
ain't they?"

Carefully I looked over the pieces of wood,
then winked at old John. "I cannot say I split these
rails, but I have split a great many better-looking
ones."

John's laughter caught on like rolling thunder.
"Abe, the Rail Splitter!" someone yelled, and the
chant was taken up throughout the place. By

nightfall, the votes were cast. I was the candidate.

But getting the votes of the Illinois delegates was only a small task compared to being nominated at the Republican National Convention. Who was I, when there were such famous men as William Seward of New York and Salmon Chase of Ohio?

A special building had been built in Chicago for the national gathering of Republicans. The flimsy structure of wood was called The Wigwam.

So off to The Wigwam went good Billy Herndon, Judge Davis, and Stephen Logan in May. They urged me to join them, but I felt a little too much a candidate to stay at home and not quite enough a candidate to go.

The waiting in Springfield was not easy. Hours passed slowly. "The hearts of the delegates are with us," wired my friends. Yes, thought I, but what of their votes?

On the night of May 18, 1860, the news arrived — I had been nominated on the third ballot. Quickly I left the newspaper office where I had been waiting. There was little doubt that Mary would welcome the news more than even I had.

Friends were waiting at the house. The news had spread like fire in a parched field.

"How about a drink, Abe?" a neighbor asked. "Surely the occasion demands such refreshment."

I shook my head. "Gentlemen, let us indeed drink to each other's good health and fortune. But let us choose the most healthy beverage God has given to man — pure Adam's ale from the spring."

The cool water tasted extra fine that night. It blended perfectly with the company of friends and family.

How many speeches I wrote in the weeks that followed, I could not guess. Each day there were reporters seeking stories, artists wanting to draw me (a fearful task, for certain!), visitors wishing to share opinions and gossip, and countless business-men with ideas for saving the government. The family schedule of meals and sleep lay hacked and torn. Thankfully, Robert slipped away to finish his studies before entering Harvard University. Willie and Tad seemed to find the busy days a merry party. Mary sparkled too. It seemed only the candidate grew weary and tired.

Across the country Lincoln supporters formed clubs and marched. "Rail Splitters for Abe" one group called itself. Other folks called themselves "Wide-Awakes."

And the mail poured in. Thousands of letters arrived. Some letters were most unfriendly, but the bulk of it came from kind thoughtful people. One young girl of eleven, from New York State, wrote a most honest letter suggesting I grow whiskers! "All the ladies like whiskers," wrote little Grace Bedell, "and they would tease their husbands to vote for you and then you would be President."

At times it seemed Election Day would never come. But finally it did. The November breezes were brisk in Springfield, offering relief on an otherwise hot day.

"When will you be voting?" Mary asked me.

"I'll not vote in this election," I answered. "It would not seem mannerly."

Mary would not accept such thinking. Within minutes she returned with Judge Davis.

"There are other candidates running," the Judge said. "Ignore your own name if you choose, but support the party."

I agreed — and voted.

As first reports of the votes came in, the news was good. Of course, we all knew our greatest support lay in the North — and that's where the

early votes were counted. Hopefully, the total would be large enough to bury the votes against us in the South.

It was. The final tally found us capturing the electoral votes of every free state except New Jersey, which was divided.

"Hooray for my Pa!" Tad shouted, running through the house with a banner. "Cheers for President Lincoln! Now we'll surely have fun!"

Fun. How I wished it would be as Tad wanted it. But troubles lay ahead. Could the country be held together?

The election cheers had hardly died when the problems started. South Carolina wanted no part of a Union where a "slave loving Abraham Lincoln was President." The state was not an orphan long. Soon Georgia, Alabama, Mississippi, Louisiana, Florida, and Texas joined South Carolina in forming their own government — The Confederate States of America. They wasted no time in electing a President, Jefferson Davis.

"Now we'll surely have fun!" Tad's words echoed in my mind. Can there be fun in suffering, in total despair? Was there anyone, in any time, who had faced such hopeless times.

My answer came one night as I sat by a dying fire. Slowly I turned the worn pages of my Bible. Here, this was the story I sought — Jesus in the Garden of Gethsemane. He was betrayed, lost, alone. I slipped to my knees, sharing the sadness of my Savior. And I felt shame for my own self pity.

There was much to do before leaving for Washington. Mary handled the sale of our furniture and found a renter for our home. Carefully she took to packing clothing and our personal items.

As for me, I knew there were final good-byes to be said.

To a small house in Charleston I traveled first. There, in a wooden rocker sat Sarah Bush Johnston Lincoln. More than a stepmother she had been to me. She had given me love, hope, confidence. Her kiss was warm and welcome.

Then to the old law office in Springfield, where Billy Herndon sat smiling. For sixteen years we had been partners, yet never a cross word had come between us.

"Don't be taking down our sign," I told him. "Give our clients to understand the election of a President makes no change in the firm of Lincoln and Herndon. If I live, I'm coming back some time, and then we'll go right on practicing law as if nothing had ever happened."

A goodly crowd of people came to the train to bid farewell. It was not easy to offer parting words, but I did what I could.

My Friends: No one, not in my situation, can appreciate my feeling of sadness at this parting. To this place, and the kindness of these people, I owe everything. Here I have lived a quarter of a century, and have passed from a young to an old man. Here my children have been born, and one is buried. I now leave, not knowing when or whether ever I may return, with a task before me greater than that which rested upon Washington. Without the assistance of that Divine Being who ever attended him, I cannot succeed. With that assistance, I cannot

*fail. Trusting in Him who can go
with me, and remain with you, and
be everywhere for good, let us con-
fidently hope that all will yet be
well. To His care commending you,
as I hope in your prayers you will
commend me, I bid you an affec-
tionate farewell.*

Slowly the train pulled away, leaving the
waving hands and saddened faces. The wheels
clattered along the track. The rhythm sang a song,
so steady and true as we swayed onward. How I
envied the train engine whose pathway snaked so
clearly across the land.

If only my own pathway were so clear to
follow.

14

WAR!

The departure from Springfield cast a cloak of sadness over the journey to Washington. But gloomier news lay ahead. A plot to kill the President was uncovered. An afternoon speech in the city of Baltimore had been planned, shortly before arriving in the capital.

"It is unsafe," Allan Pinkerton told me. A noted detective, Mr. Pinkerton looked worried. "The risk is too great."

Does a President take office hiding? It seemed no time for fear.

"I have been threatened before, Mr. Pinkerton. Let us proceed with the plans as they are."

The detective stood firm. "Sir, in all respect, it is no longer up to you to decide solely about your person. My orders are to protect you. Make certain you consider the fate of all the people of this nation in whatever decision you make. You now belong to them."

It was a moving speech. True, it was not a President's right to make decisions based on his

own comfort and thinking. I promised myself to
never again forget the people.

"You have stated your case well," I told Mr.
Pinkerton. "Give whatever orders you feel necessary."

The President's train slipped through Baltimore
during the night, safely arriving in Washington the
next morning. Soon afterward, a train pulled into
the Washington station — a train carrying
armloads of joy named Mary, Robert, Willie, and
Tad.

The inauguration of a President was usually a
bright moment in Washington. But few plans for
celebration were made in my case. On the
morning of March 4, 1860, a nasty raw wind stung
the hands and faces of the small crowd gathered
for the swearing-in ceremony. Yet the welcome
sight of old Mentor Graham from New Salem
warmed me inside. And it was Stephen Douglas
himself who offered to hold my new stovepipe hat
when I began my acceptance speech.

My words were brief. I told the people there
would be no interference with slavery wherever it
was legal. The government would be used to help
the people, never to meddle into their affairs.
There was no reason to separate, to divide our
country. If a war be fought, the cost would be
senseless.

"Intelligence, patriotism, Christianity, and a
firm reliance on Him who has never forsaken this
favored land, are still competent to adjust in the
best way all our present difficulty..." I concluded.

The Bible was extended and I raised my right
hand. "I do solemnly swear that I will faithfully
execute the office of President of the United
States and will, to the best of my ability, preserve,
protect, and defend the Constitution of the United
States."

In the distance I heard the booming of a cannon.
Hopefully, I thought, there will be no future need
for guns.

In my speech I had called for everyone to share
moments of calm thinking. The words went un-
heard. Within days of the inauguration, representatives of the Confederate States requested
complete independence from the Union. Major
Anderson, commander of Fort Sumter in the
harbor of Charleston, South Carolina, asked for
thousands of soldiers and supplies. Calm thinking
seemed but a foolish notion.

Sadly, Major Anderson's request had come too
late. On April 12, 1861, Confederate guns fired on
Fort Sumter. For thirty-three hours the Union
troops inside held the fort. It was a hopeless task.
Soon the new Confederate flag snapped in the
wind above the fort.

The country was at war.

War. Even the word itself had an evil sound.
Strange how some words are like that. *Sin. Hate.
Greed.* Each carries the sound of its own ugliness.

Action was needed quickly. So it was taken.
Volunteers were called up and our ships called
home. Generals were appointed, provisions of
food and supplies determined.

Memories of General George Washington were
recalled. Surely he felt the suffering of his men,
sickened with the sight of the wounded and dying.
Stories of the Revolutionary War still lived on.

And yet, how much more tragic was this war —
a civil war. Family was against family, brother
against brother. Mothers and fathers were watching young boys leaving home, maybe never to return.

But there was no choice. To allow slavery
within new states entering the Union would be to

discard all public and private principles I had always held. To allow states in the Union to withdraw as they chose — ridiculous! No country could survive with such a loose allegiance. How far could a wagon travel minus one wheel?

Meetings went on and on with Secretary of State Seward and Secretary of War Stanton. Always their faces were grim, grey, and weary. "We need more horses." "Our troops were cut off." Death and blood and the bodies of soldiers appeared in my sleep, haunting my rest.

Only Willie and Tad provided some relief from the heavy days. Their surprises never ended.

One morning a carefully printed note appeared on my desk. "Lincoln Circus" the note read. "In the Attic at 2:00 This Afternoon. Five cents admission."

Promptly at two, I slipped out of my office and walked to the attic. A fair assembly had already gathered. Some kind soul had posted a sign on one chair. "Old Man Lincoln" it read. Indeed, the sign was a good description.

Willie came dancing in, strumming an old banjo and waving at everyone. Sadly, the boy had a mite too much of his father's voice, but his fingers flew across the banjo strings gracefully.

The songfest ended with the entrance of a most unusual creature. Somewhere, hidden beneath his mother's old dress and bonnet and a pair of his father's drooping spectacles, stood eight-year-old Tad Lincoln. He happily joined his older brother in a play, composed I am thinking, as they went along.

It was a welcome delight. When I returned to my office, the solemn face of Secretary Stanton met mine. He found little amusement as I shared the circus experiences.

"Pardon me if I do not join your merriment," Stanton said. "But while soldiers are fighting and dying, I find little to laugh about."

"Laughter does much to comfort the troubled spirit," I answered. "It is times like these when we most need such comfort."

Often I rode into the city, visiting the camps around Washington. Troops were everywhere, gathering their guns and provisions. Tents were crowded with wounded soldiers. Sometimes I would hear boys call "Father Abraham!" It was a kind comparison to the Biblical leader. I only wished I held such wisdom as he displayed.

The time dragged by slowly. Each day brought new casualty reports. I grieved for each family that suffered a lost one.

One winter morning Mary came to the office. Her face wore an expression I had seen often — the tired eyes, the pursed lips.

"Abe, it's Willie. He caught a chill yesterday; I'd hoped the sleep would carry it away. But now he has fever."

Quickly a doctor was sent for. "Rest and care," he told us. "The lad will fight off the sickness."

The past became the present as Mary and I again took turns sitting with our little boy. Tad was forbidden in the sick room, but orders seldom hold when love is concerned. Quietly the lad would open the door a crack, whisper "Get well, Willie!" and then close the door softly.

Like a true soldier in battle, Willie fought bravely. But his thin body and worn spirit could not win. He slipped away quietly in his sleep.

Mary was crushed. "Abe, oh, why to us again? Is it not enough that we are surrounded by death? Could God not have spared us this agony? Why, Abe?"

Why? From the past the question came back to

me. It rang so true. How many times had I asked myself "Why?"

That evening I sat alone. Now and then I heard the sobbing of my dear wife. I wanted to comfort her, to ease her grief. But what words could I find? I took the Bible from beside my chair and began reading. Minutes ticked away as I read.

"He shall gather the lambs with his arm, and carry them to his bosom." The words from Isaiah were soft and gentle. And from Matthew: "But Jesus said, Suffer little children, and forbid them not, to come unto me: for of such is the kingdom of heaven."

Slowly I began to feel an understanding of God's words I had never known. Over and over I read the words in John: "Jesus said unto her, I am the resurrection, and the life; he that believeth in me, though he were dead, yet shall he live."

Faith, love, hope — each one and all lifted the heavy weight of my sorrow. Quietly I joined my wife.

"Mary, we must be strong. God has called our Willie home."

Sadly my wife turned to me. "But I want him home, here with me."

"Dear Mary, Willie was the Lord's to give and he was the Lord's to take. Let us be grateful the Lord chose us to share sweet Willie's life, even for such a short time."

Mary's tears did not stop. My cheeks were wet as well. Yet in grief and sorrow, I knew I had found a rebirth, a reborn faith in my beloved Master. Yes, in the Scriptures He had promised us extra strength in times of greatest suffering. The Lord had lived and died for us, for all of us. How small was our suffering for such love.

Willie, good young Willie. Surely he was at home with the Lord. What joy the boy had given

us. Truly the Lord would welcome such a new
bright spirit.

"The people are praying for you, Mr.
President," a gentle lady told me at Willie's fu-
neral. "We all are."

"I am glad to know that," I answered. "I want
them to pray for me. I need their prayers."

The war, the ugliness and dying, continued.
Some days Stanton seemed a bit more cheerful.
Usually he brought news of a victory, a small
military triumph.

But the death count, that cursed scrap of paper
listing men killed grew larger and larger. Is there
victory when one side loses only 500 while the
other side loses 1000? The Nation is lessened
by fifteen hundred lives. What victory lies in
that?

Yet, the country could not forever consume
itself in war. What of those slaves, those human
creatures who had suffered inhuman treatment?
The time has come for freedom.

In the fall of 1862, I presented my thoughts
about freedom for slaves to the cabinet members.
Often they had met my ideas with argument.
There was none on this issue. My statement, called
the Emancipation Proclamation, was then
released to the newspapers. It was short and clear.

That on the first day of January,
in the year of our Lord one thousand
eight hundred and sixty-three, all
persons held as slaves within any
State, or designated part of a State,
the people whereof shall then be in
rebellion against the United States,
shall be then, thenceforward, and
forever free.

On and on the fighting went. Then, in 1863,
signs of hope appeared. The Union commander,

General Grant, seemed to send the Confederate troops running. Maybe the end was in sight.

In November, I was invited to present a speech at the dedication of a national cemetery in Gettysburg, Pennsylvania. It was no secret the invitation was extended by courtesy, not true feeling. The great orator Edward Everett had been invited to speak also, and there was little doubt he would provide the audience with a fine presentation.

But I accepted anyway. Not for the people who would be attending, rather for the men who had died. Intentionally, my part in the program was kept brief. There were, however, a few thoughts I wished to share. Mainly, that we were not only dedicating a cemetery, but much more. I concluded my remarks:

> *It is rather for us to be here dedicated to the task remaining before us — that from these honored dead we take increased devotion to that cause for which they here gave the last full measure of devotion — that we here highly resolve that these dead shall not have died in vain — that this nation, under God, shall have a new birth of freedom — and that, government of the people, by the people, for the people, shall not perish from the earth.*

My words seemed empty to me, not measuring up to the faith I hoped to instill. Thankfully, Edward Everett disagreed. He felt my speech was far better than his.

But words seemed so empty, so worthless in the face of the fighting. Each night I slipped into bed, hoping and praying the war would soon end.

SUNSET

How refreshing was news not related to the
bloodshed and fighting! A kind letter from the
King of Siam offered gentle relief.

"His majesty wishes to send us pairs of
elephants so that we might begin our own herds," I
told the cabinet members. Those men who still
remembered how to laugh did so.

While the war cannons thundered in the
background, many new laws made their way
through Congress. A uniform rate of mail postage
was passed. The last Thursday in November was
set aside as a national day of Thanksgiving. A Department of Agriculture was added to our cabinet
positions. "In God We Trust" was a phrase added
to each of our minted coins.

One newspaper editor showed himself to be
most generous. "Maybe President Lincoln is not
half the fool we thought him to be. He may be
only a quarter the fool."

But as General Grant continued to claim
victories, the people gained spirit and hope. "The

Lord is on our side!" I overheard a fellow declare.
I shook my head. "I am not so much concerned
that the Lord be on our side, but rather that we
may be on the Lord's."

If sides there were, the Union's grew stronger.
At the beginning of the fighting I had heard myself
called "Scoundrel." "Devil Servant!" Such labels
were forgotten as the war tide turned. When the
Republicans held their convention in the summer
of 1864, I was nominated on the first ballot.

It was not a time for campaigning. All energies
were directed at bringing about the final stages of
the years of war. Thankfully, the people understood. The Lincoln presidential train was
returned to the track once more. We were reelected.

By the early months of 1865 the outcome of the
war was known. The Confederacy was crumbling.
Their armies were gone, their generals defeated,
their rich southern homes destroyed. It was sad
and tragic.

Now, truly, the work began. Unity was needed.
The North and South must be pulled together, re-
joined. We had to make friends of enemies. No
hate, no battlestain could remain, only unity.

My second Inauguration Day, March 4, 1865,
opened with a drizzling rain. But weather could
not diminish the spirit of the people who stood at
the Capitol steps. And nothing, save the power of
God, could crush the joy I felt knowing the long
fighting was almost over. My words came easily.

*With malice toward none; with
charity for all; with firmness in the
right, as God gives us the strength to
see the right, let us strive on to finish
the work that we are in; to bind up
the nation's wounds; to care for him
who shall have borne the battle and*

*for his widow, and his orphan — to
do all which may achieve and cherish a just and lasting peace, among
ourselves, and with all nations.*

A month later news reached Washington —
"Union Army Triumphant!" The President of the
Confederacy, Jefferson Davis, fled at the thought
of being captured.

Surrender — the final act in warfare. Surrender
came on April 9, 1865. Confederate General
Robert E. Lee met with General Grant at the small
Appomattox court house in Virginia. The
Confederate and Union leaders talked quietly. As
ordered, Grant told Lee no Southern citizen
would be punished unless he committed a hostile
act against the government. Indeed, there had
been enough suffering.

Happily I welcomed General Grant back to
Washington. He had served his nation well. I introduced him to all the cabinet members, allowing
him to receive the praise he had so richly earned.
It was April 14, 1865.

The sun was bright. The warm breezes rustled
the new leaves on the trees. "Stirring the trees a
bit" as my Ma in Kentucky had said so long ago.

"Fine afternoon for a carriage ride," I said to
Mary.

My good wife smiled, then hurried to get a
shawl. An hour later we rode through the city.
People were laughing, smiling, waving. Peace,
what a glorious word. Peace.

And that evening, a play at Ford's Theatre.
Laura Keene in *Our American Cousin.* A comedy.
More laughter. How fine to hear people laughing
again. To be with Mary. To think of the years
ahead. Please God, never let people forget the joy
of love, the pleasure of laughter, and the beauty of
peace.

(WASHINGTON, D.C.) — PRESIDENT
ABRAHAM LINCOLN WAS SHOT AT
FORD'S THEATRE SHORTLY AFTER TEN
O'CLOCK LAST EVENING. AT 7:22 THIS
MORNING, APRIL 15, 1865, HE DIED.

BIBLIOGRAPHY

Angle, Paul M. *The Lincoln Reader*. New Brunswick, New Jersey: Rutgers University Press, 1947.

Barton, William E. *The Life of Abraham Lincoln*. 2 vol. New York: Bobbs-Merrill, 1925.

Cary, Barbara. *Meet Abraham Lincoln*. New York: Random House, 1965.

Daugherty, James. *Abraham Lincoln*. New York: The Viking Press, 1943.

Foster, Genevieve. *Abraham Lincoln's World*. New York: Charles Scribner's Sons, 1944.

Herndon, William H. and Weik, Jesse W. *Herndon's Life of Lincoln*. Edited by Paul Angle. New York: World Publishing Company, 1949.

Hill, John Wesley. *Abraham Lincoln, Man of God*. New York: G.P. Putnam's Sons, 1927.

Johnson, William J. *Abraham Lincoln, The Christian*. New York: Eaton and Mains, 1913.

Johnstone, William J. *How Lincoln Prayed*. Nashville, Tennessee: Abingdon Press, 1931.

Lang, H. Jack. *The Wit and Wisdom of Abraham Lincoln*. New York: World Publishing Company, 1941.

Lorant, Stefan. *The Life of Abraham Lincoln*. New York: New American Library, 1954.

Miers, Earl S. *Abraham Lincoln in Peace and War*. New York: Harper, 1964.

Nicolay, John G. and Hay, John. *Complete Works of Abraham Lincoln*. 12 vol. New York: Boy Rangers of America, 1894.

Nolan, Jeanette Covert. *Abraham Lincoln*. New York: Julian Messner, Inc., 1953.

Richards, Kenneth. *Story of the Gettysburg Address*. Chicago: Children's Press, 1969.

Sandburg, Carl. *Abraham Lincoln: The Prairie Years*. 2 vol. New York: Harcourt, Brace and Company, 1926.

Sandburg, Carl. *Abe Lincoln Grows Up*. New York: Harcourt, Brace and Company, 1928.

Sandburg, Carl. *Mary Lincoln, Wife and Widow*. New York: Harcourt, Brace and Company, 1932.

Sandburg, Carl. *Abraham Lincoln: The War Years*. 4 vol. New York: Harcourt, Brace and Company, 1939.

Wilkie, Katharine E. *Mary Todd Lincoln, Girl of the Bluegrass*. New York: Bobbs-Merrill, 1954.

INDEX

SOWER SERIES

ATHLETE
Billy Sunday, Home Run to Heaven
by Robert Allen

BUSINESSMAN
Clinton B. Fisk, Defender of the Downtrodden
by W. F. Pindell

EXPLORERS AND PIONEERS
Christopher Columbus, Adventurer of Faith and Courage
by Bennie Rhodes

HOMEMAKERS
Abigail Adams, First Lady of Faith and Courage
by Evelyn Witter
Susanna Wesley, Mother of John and Charles
by Charles Ludwig

HUMANITARIANS
Jane Addams, Founder of Hull House
by David Collins
Florence Nightingale, God's Servant at the Battlefield
by David Collins
Teresa of Calcutta, Serving the Poorest of the Poor
by D. Jeanene Watson
Clara Barton, God's Soldier of Mercy
by David Collins

MUSICIANS AND POETS
Mahalia Jackson, Singer for God
by Evelyn Witter
Francis Scott Key, God's Courageous Composer
by David Collins

SCIENTISTS
George Washington Carver, Man's Slave Becomes God's
Scientist, by David Collins
Samuel F.B. Morse, Artist with a Message
by John Hudson Tiner
Johannes Kepler, Giant of Faith and Science
by John Hudson Tiner
Isaac Newton, Inventor, Scientist, and Teacher
by John Hudson Tiner
The Wright Brothers, They Gave Us Wings
by Charles Ludwig

STATESMEN
Robert E. Lee, Gallant Christian Soldier
by Lee Roddy
Abraham Lincoln, God's Leader for a Nation
by David Collins
George Washington, Man of Prayer and Courage
by Norma Cournow Camp

STEAL AWAY

STEAL
AWAY

KATHARINE CLARK

Fawcett Books

The Ballantine Publishing Group

New York

A Fawcett Book
Published by The Ballantine Publishing Group

Copyright © 1998 by Katharine Clark

http://www.randomhouse.com/BB/

LIBRARY OF CONGRESS CATALOGING-IN-PUBLICATION DATA
Clark, Katharine.
Steal away / Katharine Clark. — 1st ed.
p.   cm.
ISBN 0-449-00276-4 (alk. paper)
I. Title.
PS3553.L28579S7   1998
813'.54—dc21   98-22694
CIP

Book design by Mary A. Wirth

Manufactured in the United States of America

First Edition: November 1998

10 9 8 7 6 5 4 3 2 1

*To every mother who has gotten up in the night
to listen to her child breathe.*

ACKNOWLEDGMENTS

Thanks go, first of all, to the four people who made this book happen: my huband, Ken Cohen, for encouraging me to write; my friend, Justin Scott, who helped me find the story; and my agents, Robert Levine and Danny Baror, who treated me and the book with such respect and generosity. Mere thanks are inadequate for the gratitude I feel. Thanks to my editor, Leona Nevler, who believed in the book and sent me, gently but firmly, back to rewrite time after time. I'm glad she did. And thanks to all the people who helped along the way with reading, inspiration, advice and expertise: Jack Nevison, Nancy McJennett, Diane Woods Englund, Robert Moll, Susan Pollack, M.D., Sgt. Tom Le Min, Christy Bond, Christy Hawes, Peter W. Rogers, Brad Lovette, Ilse Plume, and my sons, Jake and Max Cohen. I have been well advised. Any mistakes are my own.

I T WASN'T A *long ride from the school to his house, but David had played baseball at recess and after lunch and he was tired. He was ready to kick off his sneakers, take off his socks, and curl up on the window seat in the kitchen while his mom fixed him a snack. She'd promised peanut but-ter cookies today and she'd better not forget. Not that she forgot a lot of things, but sometimes, if she got wrapped up in her work, she'd forget what time it was and just be starting his snack when he got home.*

He lifted his head and sniffed the wind, wondering if he was close enough yet to smell something if she was baking. He hadn't liked what they served at lunch and he was hungry. His front tire hit a pothole. He skidded, nearly fell, and regained his balance, getting off far to the side to let the car behind him pass safely. His mom was always nagging at him to get way off to the side when cars came. It was hard to hear with his helmet on, but he didn't take it off. A lot of the kids did, when they thought they wouldn't get caught, but David had just started taking long rides and he didn't feel safe without it.

The car didn't pass. It slowed down until it came to a stop beside him, and the woman inside rolled down her window and leaned out. David edged farther away from the van. His mother had given him at least a million lec-tures about strangers. "David," the woman said, "something awful has hap-pened to your mother and your father. You're in great danger. You've got to come with us."

David just stared. He'd never seen her before in his life. She was older than his mom and she looked nervous and not very friendly. He looked toward

the front of the van. Was there room to get past it and ride away? No. That was silly. Cars could go a lot faster than bikes, even though he could ride very fast. He'd have to go into the woods. He didn't like the idea. The woods were scary, especially if you were alone, and they were full of mosquitoes.

The sliding door on the van's side slid open. "David," the woman repeated, using his name like she knew him, "I'll explain it all to you once we're on our way. You've got to come with us. You can't go home. A very bad man who didn't like something your daddy did as a lawyer came and hurt your daddy and your mommy and he's waiting at your house to hurt you. Now jump in. Hurry!"

David edged closer to the van. She sounded serious, worried. But she hadn't given him the password and he was never to go with anyone who didn't know the password. He waited.

The woman looked annoyed. "Come on. Hurry up." She looked nervously over her shoulder. David didn't move. "Oh, for heaven's sake, David, rutabaga."

It was okay then, he thought. "What about my bike?"

"We'll take the bike, too. Come on!"

A man in the van reached out his hand. David took it, was lifted off his feet and into the van. The heavy door slammed shut behind him and he heard the click of a lock. The man jumped behind the wheel and the van drove off, the wheels spinning loudly through the gravel as the van turned around and headed back the way David had come.

"Hey. Wait! What about my bike?"

"There was no time. Someone was coming. It might have been him. We'll get you another one, I promise." The woman sounded sad, like she really had wanted to bring the bike.

His new bike. Brand-new. He bit his lip, not wanting to seem like a baby crying over his bike, but he watched it until he could see the shiny red no longer. There was a pebble in his shoe. He untied it, took it off, shook the pebble out. His hands were trembling too much to retie the laces. He left the shoe sitting on the seat beside him. "Is my dad all right?" he asked.

The woman shook her head. "I'm sorry, David," she said. "I didn't want to tell you this way. . . ." She did look sorry.

"Is this the way back to the highway?" the man interrupted.

"Yes," the woman said sharply. "David, your dad and your mom are . . ."

She looked at the man but he wouldn't meet her eye. David filled the silence with all his worst imaginings and then she confirmed them. "Dead, David. They're both dead. I'm so so sorry." She reached back with a wrinkled hand and patted his knee. Carefully, like she was not used to children.

She must be wrong, he thought. In a minute she'd probably explain what she really meant. He distracted himself by thinking about happy things. When he looked out the window, he saw that they were almost to the place where the kid in his mom's stories, Cedric Carville, had thrown all those things out of the car. He picked up his shoe, hefted it. Flexed his arm muscles. As they whirred around the curve, he opened the window and threw his shoe at the sign, watching the red sneaker spin end over end, landing just a few feet short. Not bad! A few more tries and he'd be able to hit the sign.

"Oh, David! That was a stupid thing to do, wasn't it?" the woman said. "Now you've only got one shoe."

David looked down at his foot and back at the woman. She was trying to smile but didn't look very friendly. "Sorry," he muttered, lowering his eyes. "Where are we going? Where are you taking me?"

"Far away from here," she said. "Someplace where you'll be safe. Where no one can find you."

"Will my grandma be there?"

The woman shook her head.

"My aunt Miranda?"

She shook her head again.

"Why not?" David asked. "Why did they send you? I don't know you."

"Because they knew you'd be safe with me." She tried to smile again and he thought she meant to be reassuring. "The bad man will be watching for you. He'll be watching your grandmother and your aunt Miranda."

David didn't feel safe at all, even though the woman had known the password. He thought about jumping out the door but the van was going very fast and he'd heard awful stories about what happens to children who fall out of cars.

"Will my aunt Miranda come and get me, then?"

"Of course she will, when it's safe. Until then, we're going to pretend you're someone else and you mustn't let anyone know who you really are. The bad man will be looking for you. Are you hungry? I have some nice home-made cookies."

David thought he was too scared to eat anything, but when the woman handed him a big chocolate chip cookie and a cup of juice, he found he could get them past the lump in his throat. She seemed pleased to see him eat and smiled the way grown-ups do when children are being good. But David wanted his mother and he wanted to go home. He sat wondering what to do next, but before he could think of anything, his eyes closed and he fell asleep.

Farewell, thou child of my right hand, and joy!
—BEN JONSON, "On My First Son"

CHAPTER ONE

She was going to be late again, Rachel thought, stepping on the gas. She couldn't make peanut butter cookies without peanut butter and brown sugar, and she couldn't be home baking if she was at the store buying supplies. There wasn't even enough time to get the cookies in the oven before David got home. He'd give her one of those looks, both irritated and understanding, that seemed so odd coming from a nine-year-old. Odd unless you knew how much he was like his father. Her husband, Stephen, was always giving her long-suffering looks. A woman who lived on sufferance, that's what she was. Always teetering on the verge of failure, clinging to the cusp of competence.

A shiny red bike lying at the side of the road caught her eye. Someone had a bike just like David's. Some kid biking home from school who'd stopped to explore the woods near the old pine tree. Maybe to climb the pine. It was the kind of tree that invited climbing with its well-spaced, sturdy branches. It took a kind of revenge, though, by daubing its climbers generously with pitch. David had ruined more than one good pair of pants that way. Usually when he

was with his best friend, Tommy. Tommy was the kind of kid the term "daredevil" was made for.

She snapped on the signal and whisked into the yard, grabbing the grocery bag and running for the door. In the distance, she could hear the muted roar of the bus. She hurried into the kitchen, vaguely aware of how silly she looked in her workout wear. She usually took it off the instant she finished class, but today she hadn't had time. They all dressed like this, the women in the suburbs. She didn't feel like one of them, but she knew she looked the same, a peculiarly gnome-shaped creature, body rounded and squared off by the bulky sweatshirt, perched on skinny little black Lycra legs.

She grabbed a bowl and stuck in the beaters. Threw a stick of margarine into the microwave to soften. Pushed the button and hurried to the window as the bus roared around the curve, passed the driveway without stopping, and disappeared into the trees. "Hey, wait a minute," she said aloud, rushing out the door and down the long driveway. Halfway down, feet churning, the arm that wasn't holding a mixing bowl waving, she remembered. David hadn't taken the bus. He'd gone on his bike. The bike she'd seen lying on the roadside.

Something felt wrong. David had just begun to be allowed to ride his bike to school. He wouldn't stop off without permission. He'd come straight home, then go out again after asking her. He was a cautious, methodical child, not a willful one like Tommy. But he and Tommy had planned to ride together. Maybe Tommy had persuaded him to stop. Only she hadn't seen Tommy's bike, just David's. Unbidden, Rachel's feet were moving faster, carrying her down the driveway. She left the mixing bowl by the mailbox and hurried along the road until she reached the bike.

She cupped her hands and called "David" several times, listening each time for an answer. Waiting without breathing. She walked to the base of the tree, cupped her hands again, and called up. She had a soft voice, hard to hear; she had to work at being loud. She circled the tree, staring up into the dark branches. There was no one there. She walked back into the woods, calling as she went, heedless of the damage she was doing to her pristine white aerobic shoes, shoes that

normally never touched ground outside the gym itself. A knot of panic grew in her chest and her footsteps got faster as she plunged deeper into the brush.

This was silly. David didn't like the woods. He might go in with Tommy, just to show how brave he was, but the woods scared him. He didn't like small, enclosed spaces, didn't like the feeling of things closing in on him. She hurried back to the street, walked a few hundred feet in either direction, calling. Crawled down the bank and peered into the culvert, shouting his name. Her voice echoed back to her, hollow and metallic over the gurgling of the water, but no voice answered. Heart pounding, she climbed up the bank and looked up and down the empty road.

Maybe she was panicking over nothing. She didn't know that the bike was David's. His helmet wasn't there. Besides, David loved his new bike; it was the pride of his life. He wouldn't leave it lying in the gravel like that. He'd probably stopped off at Tommy's, so excited by being a big boy who could ride his bike that he'd forgotten to ask for permission. She ran home and called Carole.

"Carole," she gasped, cutting off the drawled hello, "It's Rachel. Did David stop off there on his way home?"

"Nope. I meant to call you and apologize. I forgot they were going to ride their bikes today, and I didn't wake Tommy in time. He took the bus. While I've got you on the phone, can I get your recipe for that cucumber salad? We're having some people from—"

"Can I call you back?" Rachel interrupted.

"Is something wrong?"

"David . . . he didn't come home. I've got to call the school. Talk to you later." Rachel disconnected and called the school. While she fretted on hold, pacing a loop as large as the phone cord would let her, the secretary found a teacher who remembered seeing David set out with all the other riders just before the buses left. "Was he wearing his helmet?" Rachel asked.

"I'll check," the woman said doubtfully, probably immediately consigning Rachel to the realms of the hyperanxious, one of those lunatic mothers who's always calling to keep track of her child's every move.

Rachel waited an eternity before the woman returned and confirmed that David had been wearing his helmet. An eternity during which she began to imagine awful things had happened to him. She thanked the woman, grabbed her keys, and began driving slowly down the street, retracing the route that David would have taken. There was no one. Not a power walker, not a jogger, no in-line skaters swooping gracefully as dragonflies. Where the hell were they? Why wasn't anyone out when she needed to ask if they'd seen David? They were always out when she wanted the road to herself.

She turned around in the schoolyard and drove slowly home again, peering down side streets and into driveways, until she came back to the spot where the bike still lay. Her hands were shaking and she couldn't quite remember how to breathe. She stopped the car and sat there, hands gripping the wheel. He had to be somewhere. There had to be some reasonable explanation for this; she just hadn't thought of it yet. He wouldn't go off somewhere without telling her, not unless someone had made him go. Unless he'd gone with another friend?

She picked up the car phone and called Carole again. "Carole? There's no sign of him. Can you ask Tommy if he might have been riding with someone else? Someone he might have gone home with?"

"Hold on." She heard Carole calling Tommy, heard the snap in Carole's voice that was her own fear being transmitted.

Carole's answer hit her like a gut punch. "He says David was hurrying home because you were going to make cookies. He wants to know what's going on. Should I tell him?"

"Yes. No. I don't know. I just don't know. I don't think so. Ask him if he saw David from the bus."

She waited, straining to hear the mumbled voices, and then Carole was back. "He says they didn't pass David along the way. But they wouldn't, if he set out ahead. The bus has to go all around that loop. . . . He didn't come home?"

"No. There's a bike . . . I'm sure it's his . . . lying by the road near that big pine they like to climb . . . but there's no sign of David."

"You'd better not waste any time, Rach. If he's been taken, the sooner the police get on it, the better."

"Taken?"

"Well, you said he wasn't in the tree or in the woods. And anyway, Mister Know-It-All is standing right here behind me and he says no way would David leave his bike just lying anywhere. . . ."

Rachel thought she might be sick. "Carole, I've got to go."

"Wait, is there anything—"

"Gotta go," Rachel repeated, and broke the connection. Sat shaking in her car with her awful thoughts closing around her like a gray blanket. "Oh my God, oh my God, oh my God. . ." She whispered it over and over like a mantra. "Oh please dear God don't let him be. . ." Her mind skipped over the words she couldn't say, couldn't even bring herself to think. "Oh please God! No!" David was her life.

She picked up the phone again and called Stephen, the red bicycle on the gravel in front of her car gleaming in the gray afternoon light. He grabbed the phone, didn't let her get past an anguished "Stephen" before he interrupted.

"Can't it wait, Rach? I'm right in the middle of—"

"David's missing. He didn't come home from school."

Instantly, she had his attention. "How long?"

"Not long. I thought he was on the bus. . . . He was on his bike. . . . I got home and the bus went by and then I remembered I'd seen a bike down the road. . . ." She was dithering. Stephen hated dithering. She gulped some air, drowning in her panic, and tried to be coherent. "Maybe twenty or thirty minutes."

"Call Carole. He's probably over there." She could sense him turning away, imagined him picking up his pencil and turning to his papers.

"I did, Stephen. I already called her. He's not there and he's not at school and he's nowhere along the route. . . ."

"Did you look in his room? Maybe he got past you and you didn't notice."

"I didn't. How stupid of me. I'll go check right now. I'll bet he's there. He probably came in while I was out looking for him." Relief flowed through her. "I'll call you back."

"I'll hold on while you go check."

"I'm not at home. . . ."

"Then where the hell are you?"

"Down the road . . . by his bike . . . where he left it lying by the road. . . ."

"Lying? Like in the dirt lying? Not on the kickstand?"

"Yes. Lying, like it was dumped there in a hurry."

There was a silence on Stephen's end, disturbed only by the pounding of her heart. "He'd never do that," Stephen said. "Call the police. I'm coming home."

A tidal wave of panic, unleashed by Stephen's confirmation of her worst fears, rolled over her. It took four tries to start the car and then she was so shaky she drove like a drunk the short distance to their driveway. She left the car with the doors open, sprinted for the inside phone, and dialed 911.

"My child . . . my son . . . he's missing," she told the man who answered. Behind her, the microwave beeped to remind her of the forgotten butter.

He asked her name and address, David's name and age, and a few brisk questions. "I wouldn't worry too much, ma'am. He's probably just off exploring. He'll turn up any minute. You'll see."

"But I am worried. You don't know him. He's not the kind of boy who—"

"All boys go wandering," the man said cheerfully. "They just forget about the time and . . ."

Through the fog of her panic, she realized that he was brushing her off, that he wasn't going to help her. "Not my son," she interrupted. "He'd never go off and leave his brand-new bike lying in the dirt like that. Someone has taken him and we need your help right now!"

"Now, ma'am, please, calm down," the man said. "If it will make you feel better, I'll send an officer over to talk to you. . . ."

"It *would* make me feel better," Rachel said, imagining David's frightened face peering at her from some stranger's car, imagining her only child in the grip of some unknown man, snatched off his bike, his helmet still on, "if you would take this seriously. If you would sound a little bit concerned."

"I'll send someone, ma'am," he said in his police dispatcher's

dispassionate voice. "If you'll give me your address . . ." She gave it and he disconnected.

She stood a while, holding the bleeping receiver while the microwave cried at her like an unmilked cow, the mechanical world crying out for attention. The best way to forestall panic was to do something, anything to occupy her mind and keep out the awful thoughts. Call the neighbors. She tried them all. No one had seen anything. Everyone was sorry they couldn't help. And still no Stephen and no police. She'd finish the cookies. She turned on the oven and got out some baking sheets. Wait. She hadn't looked upstairs. Stumbling in her hurry, she rushed up the stairs and into his room, hoping, praying to find him there bent over a book. It was dark and empty, the only sound the bubbling from the fish tank.

She shut the door quickly on the emptiness and hurried downstairs to silence the microwave. She measured out a cup of sugar. Went to dump it into the bowl. Couldn't find the bowl. But she must have gotten out a bowl. Maybe she was losing her mind. Better her mind than her child. She couldn't bear that. Not again. Then she remembered. She'd left the bowl out in the yard. As she rushed to the door, something rustled by her ear, something in her hair. She snatched at it, dashed it to the floor, hoping it wasn't a bug. A leaf. She put a cautious hand up to her head, felt the leaves and sticks, and looked in the mirror.

She looked like a lunatic. Her face and shirt were streaked with mud, her shirt stained green from rushing through the bushes, from crawling around the culvert. Looking down, she saw that her shoes were green and muddy. Stephen would be upset, she thought, and then, who the hell cares. She opened the door and would have raced down the driveway to the mailbox, but there was a big man standing there, a cold-faced, red-haired stranger, holding her missing bowl.

"Lost something?" he asked.

Numbly, she took the bowl and tucked it under her arm. "Yes. My child. I've lost my child." It hurt to say the words.

"Detective Gallagher. May I come in?" His voice was gravelly and cautious. She knew instantly that there would be no comfort coming from this man, no reassurance. Over his shoulder she watched the

Lexus coming up the drive, watched Stephen get out, his face set and terrible. She knew he was holding back the same fears she was feeling, holding them back and determined to master them. Stephen had little patience with weakness, with fear. Except when it was David's. There, through some resource that Rachel had never understood, he always found the patience and gentleness he needed.

She ran toward him, her arms out, seeking some reassurance that things would be all right. He stopped and stared at her, sidestepped, and headed toward Gallagher and the house. "Rachel, for heaven's sake, have you looked in a mirror? Have you seen yourself?"

"I wasn't thinking about me. I was thinking about him," she said, but Stephen wasn't listening. He'd shaken Gallagher's hand and was leading him inside. Rachel turned to follow and ran into an impenetrable truth, hovering like a barrier between herself and the door. This was really happening. This wasn't her vivid imagination or an excess of worry. Not a dream or an irrational fear. While she was at the store buying sugar and peanut butter and listening to an old lady's complaints, someone had come along and snatched her child. Taken her son. Her David. Reality delivered another enormous punch and she collapsed on the step like a puppet whose strings are cut, arms folded tightly around her body to keep the pain from blowing her apart.

Tears poured down her face but she couldn't cry out or even sob. The horror of it stunned her into silence. She could only crouch there like a helpless animal while the realization pierced her like a thousand swords. This was really happening. David was gone.

"Rachel. We're waiting. Hurry up!" Stephen called.

Heavily, gravid with grief, with fear, with awful anticipation, with the burden of a thousand maternal imaginings filling her mind, she pushed herself up and headed not inside, but down the driveway, down the road toward David's bike, toward her last tangible link to her son. She approached it carefully, as though an inanimate conglomeration of metal parts could be sensitive, and stood staring, her hand outstretched, reaching to touch it, to put her hand where David's had been. It shimmered before her blurry eyes, proud and red.

"Don't touch that, please, ma'am." Gallagher stepped between

her and the bike so abruptly, she stumbled backward. She hadn't heard them coming.

Stephen caught her arm roughly and set her on her feet. "What do you think you're doing, Rachel? Come inside. The detective needs to talk to both of us," he said impatiently.

Rachel looked up into his tight, fierce face. "He must be so scared," she said.

Stephen's face softened and she saw the fear that matched her own. He put a supporting arm around her. "He must be. But don't worry, Rachel. We'll find him. We've got to find him." Together they went inside to talk to Gallagher.

She was Rachel,
weeping for her children. . . .
—MELVILLE, *Moby Dick*

CHAPTER TWO

Rachel knelt on the cold spring ground, oblivious of the damp, of the ubiquitous New England pebbles poking her knees, of the harsh wind that tore at her clothes, and stared at Jonah's headstone. She stretched out a thin hand, brushed away the leaves that clustered at its base, and read the words again: Jonah Stark, infant son of Rachel and Stephen, born November 12, 1983, died April 17, 1984. He would have been twelve now. Looking at the world through Stephen's eyes, getting ready for baseball season, for no child of Stephen's would be allowed to grow up without a baseball in his hand.

His hand. She looked down at her own hands, long, slender, bony. On a good day, when she was feeling all right about herself, she might call them artistic. She stared at her fingers and remembered the pressure of Jonah's tiny fingers curling around them, clinging. She closed her eyes and felt it still, after all these years, the surprisingly strong grip of those little fingers. Strong but briefly, before the disease had begun to weaken his muscles and waste him away.

"Werdnig-Hoffman's," the doctor had declared, not meeting her

eyes. Not looking at Stephen. His own pain at the news he was forced to deliver so great, she'd felt an urge to comfort him even as her own heart was breaking. Such a big, cold Teutonic name for something afflicting a little baby. Jonah would not be sick, the doctor had explained. He would go on being a cheerful, social baby. He would smile and interact and want to play. He would not be sick, but he would be dying. Growing gradually weaker until his lungs failed. Jonah hadn't wanted to die. He'd clung to life with astonishing tenacity, fought as valiantly as any hero in the history of the world. It had been his courage, almost more than his dying, that had shattered her heart.

"I've got some sad news for you, baby," Rachel said, patting the place where she thought his little belly might be. "It's more than three weeks now since your brother David disappeared. Vanished without a clue, without a witness, without a trace. Like an alien abduction. Three weeks is twenty-one days. Five hundred and four hours. Thirty thousand two hundred and forty minutes. You know how people in solitary confinement sometimes keep track of time by making notches in things? I'm making notches in my soul. I've got a notch for every one of those minutes. Thirty thousand notches, Jonah. I've got a soul like corrugated cardboard by now. When I rub my mind over it, I can feel all the bumps."

Against her will, for she'd vowed she wouldn't cry, Rachel felt the traitorous tears sneak out and roll hot down her icy face. She dashed them away with the back of her hand. "These tears are for your brother, David, but I've cried a river over you, too, Jonah," she told him. "Not a trickle, a rivulet, or a stream, but a river. You were the best of babies. And I have not let you be forgotten. I've faithfully imagined your life. You would have been musical, I think. Remember how you used to try to wave your arms to Beethoven? And vocalize? Mingling your little baby sounds with his—"

She broke off and looked around, knowing how odd she would seem to an outsider. The look was almost a formality. No one ever came here. To other parts of the graveyard, yes. She'd passed them on her way here, little family groups, talking and tending as she did. But Jonah was tucked away in a lonely corner among people who

hadn't been loved, where no one pulled the weeds and no one planted flowers. She was sorry for them, yet grateful. It meant that this was a place where she could be sure of being alone, a place where she didn't have to pretend, where she still was allowed to be sad when the world believed she should have "gotten over it" by now.

Certainly that's how Stephen felt. He hadn't said so. Not in words. Stephen didn't need to use words. His body language was enough. It was there in the tightening of his lips, in the arch of his eyebrow, in the way he'd spot her teary eyes and trembling lip and sigh and turn away from her, making an elaborate show of finding his place or straightening his paper. When she answered his questions about what she'd done during the day, she always omitted trips to the graveyard from her account. Not that she came here much anymore. Stephen's disapproval—everyone's disapproval—had been too painful. Now it was mostly on the dates of his birth and death, or when a particularly acute pain hit her. Otherwise, she visited him in her head.

It wasn't just visiting Jonah he seemed to disapprove of, either. It was remembering Jonah. So she never mentioned that she'd seen a boy running or laughing or calling to a friend who looked like Jonah would have, or that she had heard his voice. When she woke up with that terrible pain inside her, the pain she knew wasn't a major body system gone wrong but just a knot of pent-up grief, she kept it to herself.

They never mentioned Jonah. In the silence between them, it was as if he'd never been. Sometimes she wondered how Stephen felt, wondered if he ever talked to Jonah or imagined Jonah, as she did, but she was afraid to ask. Whatever Stephen still thought or felt about their dead baby was locked away in a box like Kryptonite.

A clump of daffodils, late here in this dark and shady corner, appeared when she pulled the leaves away. Poet narcissus. They would open soon and spill their perfume over this sad, empty place, like a writer reading to an empty hall. But Rachel would know. She'd come and sit and smell them, and tell Jonah they were blooming. Her mother, who knew that she came here and talked to Jonah, thought it was sick and kept urging Rachel to go get some help.

She patted him again. "This is something you never got to see, in

your little life, but before an egg is laid . . . while it's still inside the chicken, the shell isn't hard, like we're used to. It's thinner and rubbery and translucent and you can almost see the yolk and white inside. My grandmother used to let me hold them sometimes, when she was cleaning a chicken. They're so fragile, like the egg is wrapped in paper." She swept back a strand of the long hair that had blown into her face. "That's how I feel right now, Jonah. Like my outer wrapping is so fragile, people can look through it and see my insides. I've got no hard shell left, baby, and now that David's gone, I'm afraid someone's going to push so hard they'll break right through and the last of me will leak out and I'll be gone."

The tears fell harder. Some busy little internal crew, manning the pumps, was trying to drain her dry and stop this interminable crying. She fumbled in her pocket for a tissue, pulled out a handful of anonymous junk, and stared at it. A bunch of Legos. David left them everywhere. Some Magic cards. A lollipop without its wrapper, coated with pocket fuzz and sand. Some ancient prizes from McDonald's Happy Meals. A chocolate-smeared Dunkin' Donuts napkin. A paper clip. A pocket-sized pencil from a miniature golf range. A tiny silver goblet belonging to a tiny medieval knight. No tissue.

Rachel blew her nose and wiped her eyes on the chocolate-smeared napkin. Shoved it angrily back into her pocket. She held the Legos out toward the headstone. "I don't understand anything anymore. He's here. David is here. In my pockets and in my car and all over the house and in my head and yet they can't find a trace of him anywhere. How can someone simply disappear? How can they? Oh, little baby, Stephen says it's all my fault."

She leaned forward until she was almost lying on the grave, the grass prickly against her cheek, the smell of the earth filling her nose. "All my fault," she repeated. "For not being there. But who ever would have thought . . ." But that was sort of a lie. Mothers worried about their children all the time. Hardly a week went by without at least one heart-stopping moment. And yet. And yet. What good had it done? She leaned back, absently picking up some of last year's leaves, blackened now, and limp, and letting them blow away from her fingers.

She wiped her face with her sleeve, staring in surprise at the muddy streaks her tears had made. She couldn't go back to the house looking like this. Couldn't bear the way they'd stare at her with those prune faces that read as clearly as TelePrompTers, "Poor, crazy Rachel." She searched the other pocket for a tissue, pulled out a pair of David's gloves, and quickly put them away.

"I'm hopeless," she said. "Your mom is hopeless. No good mother ever leaves home without tissues. It's in the rule book somewhere. But tissues . . ." Her voice caught on a sob, staggered, and went on. "Tissues are the least of it, Jonah. Your mother keeps losing children. No good mother does that."

She sat back on her hip, legs curled to one side, arms folded across her chest. "I looked so funny when they arrived. You would have given me one of your big gummy baby smiles. I'd come straight from exercise class and there I was in these black exercise tights and a big gray sweatshirt that didn't come to my knees, my hair in one of those bungee things, sticking up like a plume, and I was all covered with mud and prickles from crawling around searching for your brother. I looked like a nineties version of the Madwoman of Chaillot—at least, that's what I thought when I saw me in the mirror—and when I tried to throw myself into your daddy's arms, he wouldn't take me because I was so dirty. And now I've done it again."

She checked her watch. "That's another sixty notches in my soul. I'd better go back. It's deadly there, Jonah. Someone is always sitting and watching. Cops. Relations. Neighbors. Even your father. Stephen sits and watches me with this look on his face that I can't fathom. I don't know if he blames me or if I'm just blaming myself. He won't tell me. He barely speaks. He fiddles with things and he watches me and he paces. He makes phone calls and takes pages of notes and then he jumps up and goes to work. He never tells me what he's doing. The air is so full of memories and questions and anxiety, it hurts to move through it. Sometimes half an hour will pass and all I've done is count my breaths but I don't dare get far from the phone in case someone calls with news.

"You used to hate the phone. When it would ring, you'd arch your back, open your eyes wide, and scream. I want to do the same.

Every time it rings, it feels like someone has raked me from head to foot with long, sharp nails. I bind up my bleeding wounds, pull myself together, and answer it. It is never news. Never good news. Never any sort of news when there's only one thing I care about hearing—that they've found David. Your brother has vanished. Even though I am connected to him with every shred of my being, just as I was to you, I reach out and I yearn for him and I call to him and I get back cold, hard silence. He doesn't answer me. He used to answer me. I used to know what he was thinking. Used to know he was out there, and now . . . nothing. It can't mean what I'm afraid it means."

Rachel patted the earth and stood up. "You wouldn't recognize me anymore. I never laugh or sing, like we used to do. Do you remember how we laughed? You had a laugh that could stop the world. Sleep well, baby. I'll be back."

In the distance, a small black figure was running toward her, waving and shouting. Rachel couldn't hear the words. The malicious, interfering wind seized them and carried them away. She went to meet the runner. Not running herself. Even though her heart was pounding like a war drum, she had, over the weeks of phone calls at all hours, surprise visits from tense cops, and leads that promised false hope, learned to steel herself against expectation.

"Good God, Rachel! Why didn't you tell us where you were going? I've been everywhere." Miranda, her beautiful sister, broke off, breathless, hugging herself with her arms. "It's freezing out here, you know. Your lips are blue."

"The whole of me is blue," Rachel said. She tried to say it lightly, to stave off comments about how she was muddy and red-eyed and lurking in a cemetery. She knew what they were thinking, knew what they said about her to each other when she was out of the room. That this had just about put poor Rachel over the edge. They feared for her sanity. Sometimes she feared for it herself. But not right now. What she felt most of the time was an overwhelming sense of dislocation. She felt the kind of panicked shutdown she used to get during math tests, when suddenly her brain would refuse to think and she'd be left in utter panic with no way out, locked in an answerless room. These days her whole life was an answerless room.

"You're a sight, you know," her sister said, spitting on a tissue and scrubbing Rachel's face just as she had done when they were children.

"I don't care," Rachel said.

"If you won't think about yourself, think of Stephen. It frightens him when you let yourself go like this. He thinks you're losing your grip."

Rachel held her hands out before her, clenching and unclenching them a few times. "I've still got my grip."

Her sister rolled her eyes. "Think of Stephen," she repeated. "You don't know how lucky—" She broke off. Hesitated. "That policeman called. Detective Gallagher. They've found . . ."

Rachel's heart stopped.

". . . a sneaker they think might be David's. They want you to come and look at it."

Lub dub. Lub dub. The squishy roar was back in Rachel's ears. She was still alive, though weak with a mixture of relief and disappointment. "Did they say what kind of a shoe it was? Did it have a name anywhere?"

Miranda shook her head, her short hair bobbing. "He just said shoe. But you told them what kind of shoes David was wearing, didn't you? I mean, I don't suppose he's going to be bringing a black mid-heel pump for you to look at."

"I guess not," Rachel said. She looped her arm through Miranda's and rested her head briefly on her sister's shoulder. "Thanks for coming to get me."

"Better me than Stephen," Miranda said. "You know how he feels."

Rachel didn't—that was one of their problems—but she nodded anyway and let herself be steered toward the waiting Volvo. It was time to go home and look at a faded red high-top sneaker. Rachel couldn't remember whether she had walked to the cemetery or driven there in her own car, but it didn't matter. She stumbled along beside her sister, following blindly, her thoughts turned inward. "Watch your head," Miranda said. She seized Rachel by the elbow and loaded her into the car. Passively, Rachel obeyed, her entire mind now filled with a single shoe.

Ships that pass in the night, and speak each other in passing,
Only a signal shown and a distant voice in the darkness
—LONGFELLOW, *Tales of a Wayside Inn*

CHAPTER THREE

The shirt button snapped between his hurrying fingers, one half clinging to the shirt by a thread; the other tumbled to the floor and rolled under the bed. No sense in retrieving it, Stephen thought. It couldn't be reattached anyway. He went into the closet to get another shirt. Damn! There was only one left. Dirty shirts destined for the laundry overflowed the laundry bag and lay about the closet floor. Rachel had promised to take them in yesterday. Effusive, abject promises accompanied by humbling hand gestures and downcast eyes. But Rachel's promises had become as ephemeral as the wind. Dust piled up in the corners and dishes mounted beside the sink while she sat and stared at pictures of David.

Twice lately he'd lost control and yelled at her; it gave him no satisfaction. Yelling at Rachel was like kicking a small, helpless animal; she stood and took it like she deserved to be mistreated. The second time, when he'd broken off in frustration, she'd stared at him with those sad, magnificent eyes and he'd felt like she was staring right through his skin and seeing all his little tawdry secrets.

He'd been too ashamed even to apologize, consumed by the help-less, wordless rage that her passivity engendered.

Rachel had always puzzled him. Even when they were falling in love, when they'd been in that brief, intensely intimate stage where people want to know each other and want to be known, when they'd shared their secret selves, she'd been an enigma. Even though they shared a common language, Rachel spoke a different dialect, a strange, obscure dialect he sometimes had trouble comprehending. In the beginning, sex and mutual caring had bridged the gap and he'd found her elusiveness attractive. For a long time now the bridge had been out, washed away on the flood of Rachel's tears. He was still attracted to her, thought he still loved her, but she required so much effort. More and more, he'd found himself drawn to simple, less complicated women.

Stephen had no patience with tears, no sympathy. Crying, and the weakness and self-indulgence it represented, annoyed him. He was impatient with mystery and with ambiguity. He liked to get to the solutions, find the answers, fix things. If he couldn't find the fixes or the answers, he believed the best thing to do was accept it, then buck up and move on. It wasn't that David's disappearance didn't matter to him. No man loses a child without pain, without remorse, without being haunted by uncertainty. But after three weeks, he didn't know what else he could do. He'd talked to all the neighbors. He'd looked under every rock, every bush, every log. Peered in every culvert, stalked through every swamp, walked the roadsides, stared at pictures the police brought until his eyes crossed, and wrung every bit of information out of his soul that he could wring every time that miserable cop came calling.

The uncertainty of it was choking him. Give him a task and he would do it with a will. He would work tirelessly at finding his son. It was when there was nothing to work at, when he was forced to sit helplessly by and wait for something to happen, when the whole thing lay in someone else's hands, that he lost his normal calm. He'd become snappish, disagreeable, could find no place for the burning frustration and anger he felt. Rachel was content to spend forever in a holding pattern, endlessly buzzing and circling like a fly at the din-

```
   25 OCT 2002          SOUTHEASTERN OHIO
REGIONAL LIBRARY              04:39pm
                                Circul
ation                      UV Port 198
                         RECONCILE HOLD

 ALERTED ITEMS


                             FILL HO

LD


                        Enter barcode:

31705002957592
```

Title: Steal away /
Requestor: JACKSON CITY LIBRARY ID#2350
98   phone at: 740-286-4111

Item is on HOLD   Press "H" t
o continue.

ner table. She'd said "I wasn't even late; I got home before the bus" a million times, even though the statement was irrelevant. She could sit for hours with one of David's Lego constructions in her lap as if she were waiting for it to speak to her. Stephen had never been able to sit still.

Even though he'd done his best to be cooperative, Stephen hated the intrusion of the police in his life. He hated the feeling that he and Rachel were under a microscope or being interrogated under those intense lamps they used in old movies. He hated the way suddenly nothing was personal, the way they asked him and Rachel the same questions, over and over, as if they assumed one of them had done away with David and buried him in the flower bed. He resented the suspicious way they looked at him when he couldn't account for some insignificant piece of his time, resented the probing questions about his relationship with David and with Rachel.

It was because of that resentment, and to preserve at least a shred of his privacy, that he hadn't told them about the letter. That and the fact that right now he didn't believe Rachel could handle the letter. Her hold on reality seemed so tenuous at times that its contents might be enough to push her over the edge. The letter, a single sheet of paper with its impersonal, clinical message, cut right to the heart of everything that was deeply private and most painful about their relationship. A letter that could not have been more badly timed, could not have been more devastating if it had been deliberately designed to hurt them both the most. It had arrived the day before David disappeared. Stephen had been looking for a good time to share it with Rachel, and then the bottom had dropped out and there had been no possibility of mentioning it.

He jerked up his arm and glared impatiently at his watch. That cop would be here anytime now. It had been at least half an hour since he'd called and asked if he could come by with the shoe. Stephen hoped Miranda had been able to find Rachel; he didn't know a damned thing about David's shoes, other than that the boy kept outgrowing them at what seemed to him like an absurd rate. It was just like his wife to go off without telling anyone. She drifted around like a wraith these days.

He put on his last clean shirt and threw the defective one down on Rachel's pillow. She could goddamned well mend it for him to wear tomorrow, since it was her fault he had no others. He was meeting new clients, hoping to get chosen as their counsel on a promising new case. He needed to look nice. In his haste, he knocked a picture off the nightstand. He picked it up, brushed the dust off, and stared at it. It was a picture of Miranda and Rachel, taken when they were in college.

In Rachel's family, they always referred to Miranda as "the pretty one." Stephen had never understood why. Miranda was pretty, in a wholesome, all-American cheerleader way. She had a brilliant smile and lively eyes and thick, shiny hair. And Miranda was pleasant, fun-loving, practical, with a sassy, provocative body. But she couldn't hold a candle to Rachel. Not with Rachel's eyes. Rachel's miraculous, mesmerizing eyes. The rest of Rachel's face was nice—great bones, her funny, generous mouth, her slightly prominent nose. But it was her eyes that had captured him. Large, luminous, compelling eyes, slightly exotic. A changeable shade of greenish blue. Eyes that reflected her passion, her joy, her enthusiasm, her sorrow. Eyes that seemed to look into your soul. Lately he'd been unable to meet them, had prayed for the habitual, demure lowering of her lids. He didn't want her to see his secrets, to gauge his dissatisfaction and start asking questions.

The doorbell chimed into the silence downstairs. Damn! Where was Miranda? Where was Rachel? He tossed the picture onto the bed, tucking his shirt in as he dashed for the stairs. The chimes again, arrogant. Impatient. Demanding. Just like that bastard Gallagher. He pulled the door open, noticing that it was sticking slightly, that the knob could use some tightening. Miranda and Rachel were on the step, Rachel looking muddy and wilted, her nose red from the cold. "Forgot my key," she murmured, eyes lowered, and glided past him into the house. "I'll go upstairs and change." Placating him again. Rachel never locked the house, never needed a key. Stephen was the compulsive door locker.

"I left a shirt on your pillow," he said. "My last shirt. It needs a button so I can wear it tomorrow." It wasn't what he'd meant to say.

Through the still open door, he saw the detective's nondescript gray car pull in and creep slowly up the drive, come to an easy, effortless stop behind Miranda's Volvo. The door opened and the tall policeman got out, a shoe box under his arm. Stephen wrinkled his nose. Gallagher smelled like he ate in cheap diners. He always looked around like he was sure David was under the floorboards and either Stephen or Rachel had put him there.

"I'll make some coffee, shall I?" Miranda said behind him. "You want decaf?"

"Regular would be better," he said. "I've got a lot of work to do tonight."

"You work too hard, Stephen," she said. He often wished Rachel would say that, but she never seemed to notice whether he was working hard or not. For all the interest she showed, he might have been a ditch digger instead of one of the hottest plaintiff's personal injury lawyers in the area. It had been Miranda, not Rachel, who'd danced around the kitchen with delight when he won his last case, and Miranda who had snatched the cold bottle of champagne from the refrigerator.

But it had been Rachel who'd bought the bottle and put it in to chill. And later, as they were getting ready for bed, she'd stepped out of her closet wearing nothing but a bright red bow and said, "I'm so proud of you, Stephen. You did a wonderful thing for that woman and her two children," and the glow in her eyes had made him breathless.

He realized he was still holding the door open as a few of last fall's leaves, dancing in the wind, skittered past his feet and into the front hall. It was too late to close it now; the cop was starting up the walk, a curious look on his face.

"Sorry to bother you again, sir," the cop said, thrusting out his hand. Stephen took it, trying to return just the right amount of macho pressure. The cop had a grip like an unpegged lobster, but Stephen doubted that he shook Rachel's hand the same way.

"No trouble," he said. "My wife is upstairs changing. She's the one who'll know about David's shoes, of course. She'll be down directly." Shit, he thought. Why had he said "of course," as though he,

a mere father, couldn't be expected to know about his son's shoes? These people pounced on any indication of weakness like a cat on a mouse, and to them, not knowing your child's dentist or doctor or being able to identify their shoes was a sign that you didn't care. It was a short leap from there to assuming that you'd hurt your child.

There was a crash upstairs, a door hitting the wall. Stephen cringed. Their house was ancient, a partially restored farmhouse, and the fragile doors swung wildly on their old hinges at any but the gentlest touch. A second later, a step on the stairs, and Rachel appeared, long and lean, her bare feet emerging from tight jeans, her long neck emerging from a midnight blue velour ballet top, too tight over her gently bouncing, braless breasts. Stephen swallowed painfully as the cop watched Rachel's chest descend the stairs.

She stopped two steps from the bottom, where she was still taller than the cop, swept the man with her suffering saint's eyes, and held out a hand. "You've found something," she said, her voice slightly husky. It was not a question but a statement that held a world of hope.

T HE WOMAN KEPT *telling him to hold still, to stop wiggling, that it wouldn't take long. She wasn't mean or angry, just firm and matter-of-fact, the way she always seemed to be when she wasn't making a special effort to be nice. Then she would smile at him and tell him how glad she was that he was living with them and talk about all the fun things they were going to do. She seemed to be hoping that would make him happy, make him forget about his mom and dad and his aunt Miranda. It made him squirmy, though. She was like one of those grown-ups who don't know much about kids so they put on a high-pitched voice and an extra cheerful manner.*

He tried to be nice back, but his heart wasn't in it. He missed his parents too much and his life was too strange and scary. The woman wanted him to like her, but he couldn't. When she wasn't being that kind of nervous, forced cheerful, she was so calm that it was frightening. Calm with a dead kind of coldness. None of the people he was used to were calm, not even his mom. She was faraway and dreamy sometimes—she said it was because in her mind she was picturing her work—but not calm. David didn't think he was a calm person, either.

Right now he couldn't be calm. The stuff the woman was putting on his hair smelled horrible, worse than anything his doctor or his dentist had ever used, though it had a similar chemical smell. It stung his eyes and made them water and it felt like his scalp was burning. "I hate this!" he said, trying to wriggle free. "It hurts. My eyes sting."

"It won't be much longer," the woman said, clamping her legs more firmly around his waist. "You just have to be patient."

"I'm not patient," David argued. "I hate this. Why are you doing this to me?"

The woman looked at the man across the room, who only shrugged. The man rarely said much. He didn't seem well and he always looked sad. There was a lot of work to do around the place and when he wasn't working he spent most of his time sitting and staring out the window. Sometimes he smiled at David, though, and it wasn't a forced smile.

"You remember what I told you about your mother and your father?" she asked. "About why your mother sent us to pick you up so you wouldn't go home, because it was dangerous? About the bad man who was mad at your father? The bad man who came and killed them?" David was silent. He tried not to think about his parents being dead. He knew his brother was dead. He'd been to the cemetery with his mother. Dead wasn't something he understood very well. "Well," the woman continued, having grown used to David's silences, "that same bad man wants to find you and kill you, too. So we have to be very careful never to mention anything to anyone about your real name or your real family or where you came from. We're changing the color of your hair so you won't look the same."

"I like the way I look," David said stubbornly. "I look like my mother." But he was scared by the idea of someone wanting to find him, wanting to kill him. Everything was scary now. These people. This place, so big and empty and far from everything. The cows, with their big, snorting bodies. The sheep with their eerie eyes. The woman tried to give him things, but they weren't his things. And she scared him most of all, with her stiff hugs and painful smiles. He always had a pain in his stomach and trouble breathing, but he never told her.

The woman didn't respond. She didn't like it when he talked about his mother and father. She looked at her watch and then at the timer, the shape and color of a green apple, sitting on the counter. As if she'd willed it, it gave a small, grating ring. "You're done," she announced. "After we've rinsed you, we're going to go into town and buy a baseball glove. My nephew Charley is coming over this afternoon to play ball with you."

"I don't want to play ball," David said. "I hate baseball." It was a lie. He loved baseball more than anything in the world, except his parents. Had

loved his parents. David didn't know how to think about all that. It made him sad and he didn't want to cry in front of this woman.

"Maybe you could do it to be nice to Charley," the woman said. "He loves to play baseball, and living so far out in the country, he doesn't have any other kids around to play with." David thought about how strange that would be, not to have other kids around. This must be an awful place to live. He hoped he wouldn't have to stay here too long, hoped that soon things would be safe and his aunt Miranda would come and get him. He missed Tommy and his school and his baseball team. Probably Will was getting to be the pitcher now, just like he'd always wanted. He wasn't as good. The tears welled up and he couldn't hold them back.

The woman patted him roughly on the shoulder. "Don't cry. Boys your age don't cry," she said. "Let's get you rinsed. Bend over, close your eyes tight, and hold your breath. Keep your mouth shut so none of this stuff gets in it." David did as he was told. The water was too cold, but he couldn't open his mouth to complain. "That's it." She wrapped a towel around his head. "Go in the bathroom, comb your hair, and put on a dry shirt."

When he came out, his dark brown hair now an ugly blondish brown, she was standing by the door, jiggling her keys. "Can we take the truck?" he asked.

The woman shrugged, then nodded. "Father," she called to the brooding figure by the window, "we're not taking the van; we're taking your truck." The man looked up at them uncertainly, as if he wasn't sure he knew them, then nodded, and David and the woman went out.

She slammed the door, hard and angry, different from her creepy calm, and shoved the lever that made the truck go. "We had a boy once. He died." That was all she said.

They sat silent, two stiff figures as far apart on the bench seat as possible, as the truck bumped along. For a while, David enjoyed the feeling of being up high and the carnival-ride jouncing as they rode the bumps, until he summoned his courage and asked, "Am I going to go to school here?" He asked not because he wanted to stay but because he needed something to do, something to fill all those long scary hours when he imagined awful things about his mother and father and what might happen to him.

She turned on him, too quick and eager, with her awful stiff smile. "Would you like to? We've got a nice school here."

"I should go to school," he said. "I don't want to get behind."

"I'd like to let you," she said, "but there's a problem."

David waited for her to explain the problem but she didn't. Now that he'd said it, he liked the idea of going to school. It worried him, being with new kids, but it was something he knew. And it would get him out of her gloomy house, away from her staring eyes. In his short time with her, he'd learned the woman didn't like questions, usually didn't answer them, but he wanted to know. "What problem?" he asked.

He thought she wasn't going to answer, the way she gripped the wheel and stared straight ahead. Finally she said, "Keeping you a secret." That was all until they were parked at Wal-Mart. Then she said, "Well, maybe. But you'd have to keep your mouth shut, see. And be more careful than maybe a nine-year-old boy can be. If he finds you, he'll kill you, you know, with no more remorse than a man swatting a fly. Come on, now."

As he slid out of the truck and reached up to shut the door, she studied him. He tried not to let her see his tears or his shaking hands. "We better get you a haircut," was all she said.

And we are here as on a darkling plain
Swept with confused alarms of struggle and flight . . .
— MATTHEW ARNOLD, "Dover Beach"

CHAPTER FOUR

Rachel led the way into the living room, waited until Stephen and the policeman were seated, and held her hands out for the box. She tried to keep her eagerness from showing, tried to still the shaking of her hands, though she was desperate to hold the shoe. Instead of giving it to her, Detective Gallagher took the lid off and, keeping it close to his body, tipped the box so she could look in. "Is this Dave's sneaker?" he asked.

"David," Stephen said. "We never called . . . call . . . him Dave."

Rachel bent forward to stare at the shoe and then at the detective's face. "May I pick it up?" She held out her hand. From the kitchen came the clattering of cups and saucers as Miranda got ready to serve the coffee.

"Why?" asked the detective.

Stung, Rachel dropped her hand and forced a smile—a smile that said he was being silly. Then she gave the correct answer. "So I can see if it's his. He used to write his name in funny places . . . and then, the lace on the right side of his left shoe had lost that little cap

on the end . . . I don't know what they're called . . . and the . . .
grommet, I think they're called . . . on the bottom near the sole . . .
you know what I mean, those little vent holes . . . well, one of those is
missing. They're the first thing to go, every pair." She held her hands
out again, both of them this time, feeling like a supplicant. Feeling
foolish and exposed. Angry with him for forcing her to beg for this
remnant of her child.

"May I?" She waited for permission, watching Stephen out of the
corner of her eye. Normally Stephen would have grabbed it by now.
She admired his patience. Detective Gallagher tried even her patience, and she had the patience of Job.

While she waited for the detective's response, she thought of the
real reason she wanted to hold it. Not to identify it. She wanted to
hold it because she knew that it was David's sneaker and it had been
with him nearly a whole day longer than she had. A whole day that
she somehow thought she could feel if only she could have it
in her hands. It was another connection, a closer connection. She
thought the shoe might be able to tell her something. It was the kind
of thought that, if she voiced it aloud, would have everyone in the
room giving her funny looks. She'd grown weary of funny looks. And
it wasn't as if all the logical people with all their sensible approaches
were getting anywhere.

Her family had always treated it as odd, as sort of a joke. When
she was given presents, someone was bound to say, "Okay, Rach,
close your eyes and tell us what's in the box." Of course, it didn't
work like that. She wasn't psychic, didn't possess mystical powers.
Sometimes she sensed things before they happened. A heightened
perception, that's all. Maybe she was just more attuned. Whatever it
was, she'd learned to hide it, stifle it. Until David.

She studied Gallagher as he indulged in his absurdly long hesitation. Watched him and thought how much she hated him for the
way he tortured them. An overgrown altar boy, she decided. She
could see him in his angelic cassock, his pale, freckled face arranged
in an attitude of piety, his saucy red curls making a halo around his
face. She could even imagine the fatuous approval on his mother's
face as he followed the priest through the motions of the mass. She

pictured him growing, like Alice in Wonderland, suddenly taller and wider, his broad shoulders straining against the gathered fabric, his long, gangly wrists protruding from the sleeves, a vast expanse of pant leg showing between the hem and the floor, the angelic, boyish face growing wider, harder, handsomer.

"Give her the shoe, goddammit," Stephen snapped, grabbing the box out of Gallagher's surprised hands and thrusting it at her. "This isn't some kind of a game, you know. It's not your child who's lost. If you were worried about tainting the evidence, you should have brought it here in a plastic bag or something or not brought it at all." He maneuvered his body between Rachel and the detective, shielding her from Gallagher's green-eyed scrutiny, and put a supportive hand on her shoulder. "What do you think, Skee? Is it his?"

Skee. He never called her that anymore. Skee, from her maiden name, Filipovsky, was a nickname belonging to an easier, happier time, from a time when Stephen had been Vee, and Rachel had been Skee, and they had both laughed together a lot and grown tender at the use of their own private nicknames. Then Skee had lost her baby and retreated into a more defended world, and Vee had become a workaholic and a cautious, undemonstrative grown-up.

Rachel took the shoe from the box and cradled it in her hands as she squeezed her eyes shut and opened her mind. "Where are you, David?" she wondered. "Please talk to me." She waited for an answer, trying to keep herself open and receptive, knowing that Stephen and Gallagher were staring at her. She wished she could take the shoe upstairs to David's room and sit there with it alone, but while they didn't understand a thing about her connection to her child, she understood a great deal about convention and the necessity of not being considered crazy. She waited, but nothing came. She opened her eyes and studied the shoe. The missing grommet, the missing lace tip, and there, on the edge of the sole, nearly worn away, David's initials. Sadness sliced through her like a knife.

She dropped the shoe back in the box and held it out to Gallagher. "It's his. Where did you find it?" There was no magic. It was just a worn red shoe. But she could keep hoping for a miracle.

"Yes, where did you find it?" Stephen said. "It can't have been

anywhere near the bike. We searched that area with a fine-toothed comb. We couldn't have missed a red sneaker."

"No. You didn't miss it. It wasn't there," Gallagher agreed.

Rachel stared at the impassive face, wondering what it was in the man's makeup that compelled him to torture them this way. Then she looked at her husband. A working muscle in his jaw was the only sign of his rage, but she knew. She could see Stephen's anger singing in every line of his body. If she reached out and touched him, she'd feel the sparks of it under his skin, but she didn't think Gallagher knew. Didn't think Gallagher, police detective or not, paid enough attention to actually see them as people.

The door, propelled by the force of Miranda's tray, flew open and crashed into the wall, the hardware clacking. Miranda gave them an embarrassed smile and bent gracefully to slide the tray onto the coffee table. "It's caffeinated, Detective. I hope that's all right?"

"It's fine. Thank you," Gallagher said, manufacturing a perfunctory smile.

Miranda poured him a cup. "Cream or sugar?"

He shook his head. "Black." He shifted his eyes to Rachel. "It's called a tag," he said. "The thing on the end of a shoelace."

If it was an attempt at reconciliation, Rachel wasn't buying it. "Where did you find the shoe?" she asked again.

"Nowhere near the place where we found the bike," he said.

"Coffee, Rachel?" Miranda asked.

Rachel shook her head. More stimulation was the last thing she needed. She was already so keyed up from seeing the sneaker, from Gallagher's insane games, that she was practically jumping out of her skin. Even though she had a hand on it to keep it still, her knee vibrated like an anxious greyhound.

"Listen, Gallagher," Stephen said, "this may be a game to you but it isn't a game to us. We want to know where you found the sneaker."

Gallagher sipped his coffee and didn't answer.

"Detective, please." Rachel tried to keep her voice matter-of-fact, but she couldn't keep the pleading out. She stood up, took a step toward him. There was something hard beneath her foot, stabbing the tenderest part of her instep. She bent down, lifted her foot,

picked up a small red Lego piece. "I don't know what you can possibly be thinking. Maybe you're not telling us so that you can go park around the corner and when you leave you think we're going to go rushing out and drive to the spot where you found David's shoe to see if there's anything else we forgot to hide." Damn! She could hear the tears trembling in her voice. "But we don't know where David is and all you're doing is torturing us. If you don't want to tell me, then don't tell me. You can blindfold me or I'll ride in your car or whatever you want, but please, will you take me there? Now? Today?"

Stephen and Miranda moved in closer to her, one on either side, and put their arms around her. Rachel could feel the difference between them, feel Stephen's big hard arm around her shoulders, Miranda's soft, warm arm around her waist. Both hugging her to show their solidarity. Suddenly, Stephen dropped his arm and strode out of the room. "We've been cooperative long enough," he said, slamming the door behind him.

"If you won't take her there, Detective," Miranda said, "can you at least explain why? My sister likes to understand things."

I have not been long in your country, Rachel thought, and I do not speak the language well, but my sister Miranda speaks good English. Maybe she can make you understand. There was a roaring in her brain, like something was trying to take over her head. Grief, a big, black wave of it, threatened to wash over her. She wanted to sit like a bereaved peasant woman, with her head in her hands, while she rocked and wailed. "I don't understand," she said. "Someone has taken my child. My son." Unconsciously, she had folded her hands over her abdomen. "You won't help me and you won't let me help you. You can't imagine how that feels.

"I say I want to go there, to the place where you found the shoe, and you say why?" She scanned his face for some sign of humanity, for some sign that talking to him made any difference. She didn't see any. "Shall I tell you why?" She waited. He said nothing. "That was a question, Detective!"

Miranda laid a cautionary hand on her arm, but Rachel shook it off. "Do you have any children, Detective Gallagher?" Gallagher shook his head. Rachel's throat was choked with the rush of things she

wanted to tell him, about carrying a child inside you and about holding a newborn and looking into his eerily wise eyes, and about the
bond you have, right from the start. She could have spoken volumes
about the empty days and the footsteps in the night that weren't
there and about the reminders that were everywhere. About rushing
home to meet a child who didn't come home anymore, and weeping at the sight of a school bus. She could have told him about the
incredible, indescribable pain inside that grew and grew and was
crushing her other organs and sometimes felt like it was going to rip
her open and leap, screaming, into their midst. But all she said was,
"The place might mean something to me that wouldn't be obvious
to you."

Before Gallagher could reply, Stephen was back, banging the
door again. He held out a portable phone. "The chief wants to talk
to you," and as Gallagher reached out to take the phone, Stephen
gave Rachel a thumbs-up sign. When pleading and reason failed,
there was always the old boys' network.

Gallagher mumbled something, listened intently, and disconnected, dropping the phone on the coffee table with an angry thump.
"Get your shoes on. I'll take you. I'll be in the car." He was almost to
the door before a veneer of manners returned and he gave Miranda
a perfunctory smile. "Thanks for the coffee." Stephen he ignored
completely.

Rachel paused on her way out. Reached out and touched Stephen's arm as he stood staring after Gallagher. His body was rigid
beneath the silky cotton of his shirt and he jumped at her touch.
"Thank you," she said.

"I'd like to kill that bastard," he said. He turned and went into
his study, closing the door behind him.

Gallagher was behind the wheel, hands at two o'clock and eleven
o'clock, glaring straight ahead through the streaky windshield. He
didn't bother to turn or acknowledge her when she got in. She shut
the door and folded her hands quietly in her lap like a penitent. She
didn't say anything either. There were still two bright patches of red
staining his cheeks and his shoulders were tight with anger. His entire rigid body and furious demeanor were not unlike Stephen's

when she passed him in the entry just now. Two big angry men. They reminded her of rutting bulls in the way they jockeyed for the privilege of pushing her around, of defining what she might know and do.

No. That wasn't fair. Stephen had been trying to help her.

Gallagher put the car in reverse and backed smoothly down the driveway. Rachel admired the way he did it, with such ease and confidence. When she had to back up any distance, it was with a decidedly uncertain waver. She wasn't even sure she liked cars. They always seemed to her to be on the verge of going out of control. Because cars scared her and because keeping David safe was so important, she'd devised a series of games to keep him distracted while she drove, so he wouldn't do anything to startle her.

They'd played word games and geography games naming local hills and streams and roads. Number games. Memory games. Color games. And when all else failed, she'd told stories. Long, elaborate related stories telling the ongoing adventures of a series of intriguing characters, like the giant, mutant rabbits who escaped from a local farm, or the kangaroo who loved to skateboard, or the boy who was so determined to be the world's best baseball player that he was always throwing things, sometimes with unexpected results.

Rachel wasn't surprised when they headed toward the highway access ramp. If someone was going to take David away . . . She had to believe that he'd been taken by someone who wanted him, that he was still alive, not just driven down a deserted road, assaulted, and murdered. "Oh no," she said, clutching her stomach. She rushed to push the scary thoughts out of her mind.

She hadn't realized she'd spoken aloud until Gallagher responded. "What's wrong? Are you all right?"

"I was just thinking about David," she said. "About things we used to do together."

"But you said 'oh no.' " To her surprise, he pulled over to the side of the road and stopped. "Why?"

Why, why, why, Rachel thought. The man was like a child, having to ask why about everything. But the rage and anguish she'd felt back at the house had exhausted her. She'd barely slept since David's

disappearance, and she didn't have the strength to fight with him again. "I was thinking about the people who took him, how they must be people who wanted him, and not someone who wanted him for sex or wanted him dead, and then the idea of him dead just kind of hit me, and I must have spoken, though I didn't mean to."

She stopped, having said all she had to say, and waited for Gallagher to respond. He didn't. The detective made her stoic, self-contained Stephen seem garrulous. "I'm all right," she said into the heavy, uncompanionable silence. "I'm not going to cry or get hysterical or anything. We can go on."

"We're there," he said, opening his door and stepping out. When he was seated he seemed normal, but standing he was massive. He watched her as she got out, his eyes too intrusive, too personal. An undefinable shade of green that made her momentarily long for her colored pencils. In her rush, she'd forgotten to bring a coat, and he noticed her absence of a bra, she knew. Rachel wasn't used to being assessed and it made her uncomfortable.

"Where?" she asked, aware she was imitating his terse style. They were parked on the grass verge of an island created by a highway entrance ramp. About thirty feet away, a green road sign, abandoned and neglected, leaned against the base of a tall light pole. Rachel looked at the patch of faded yellow grass, not yet renewed by spring, desolate except for litter, hubcaps, and the foam cups that bloomed like mushrooms. "Where?" she repeated. "Show me."

She followed Gallagher's long strides toward the pathetic sign. Half the reflective white letters were missing, rendering the remaining message gibberish. Gallagher stopped so abruptly, she bumped into him. He caught her handily and set her back on her feet. "There," he said, pointing at a small orange stake.

Rachel stared at the stake, at the sign, and back to where the car was parked. "I forgot the shoe," she said, turning back toward the car. As she turned, a truck came cruising briskly along the ramp toward the highway. As it passed Gallagher's car, a hand came out the window and flung a beer bottle toward the sign. Automatically, she put up her hands to protect herself. The bottle hit the sign and shattered. Looking down, Rachel saw the ground was littered with glass.

"Well?" Gallagher towered above her, hands on his hips. "What can you tell me that I might not otherwise have known?"

He was mocking her now. Rachel looked up at him, then down at the ground. She'd been so sure that something would come to her if she could only see the place. She stared down at her hands, embarrassed. A sliver of glass from the bottle had pierced the full part of her hand, below the thumb. She grasped it, pulled it out, and watched helplessly as blood began to well out and drip onto the ground. She didn't like the sight of blood, especially not now. She closed her eyes and tried to open her mind. And then it came to her.

She and David were riding in the car. David was restless, didn't want to stay in his seat. Kept undoing his belt. She'd yelled at him four times, was losing patience. Finally, she'd pulled over and said, "What am I going to do with you?"

"Tell me a story, Mom," he'd said.

"About the kangaroo?"

"That's baby stuff," he'd said. "Tell me a story about a baseball player. Tell me about a boy who wants to be the best baseball player in the world, just like me." That's how the stories began, the stories of Cedric Carville, soon to be the world's best pitcher. And Cedric Carville had taken them on many a drive, gotten them through many a hard day. Including the day that Cedric Carville, trying to hit passing road signs, had thrown a dozen eggs, five oranges, four lemons, three cupcakes, two containers of yogurt, and both of his sneakers out the car window before his mother could stop him.

Rachel brought her hands to her face, rocking back and forth, as she remembered. She felt the flow of blood against her lips, tasted the hot salt. She closed her eyes and rocked, oblivious of the puzzled form of Gallagher, looming beside her. She relaxed her mind and let the memories come, heard David's voice in her ear. "So what do you think, Mom; shall I throw my sneakers out?"

And her voice, answering. "No way, Jose. Do you know how much those things cost?"

"Can I throw something else, then? A Coke can or something?"

"That would be littering and you know it."

And then, with an impish gleam in his eyes, David held up an apple. "This, then. It's organic. Biodegradable." Lowering the car

window, and, as they sped past the sign, his arm shot out, and there was a faint, answering *bonk* from the sad old sign.

"Oh, God, David!" she whispered, dropping to her knees. "Speak to me. Are you alive? Are you all right?" Above the traffic noise, beyond the roaring in her head, fainter than the sound of her own breathing, Rachel thought she heard an answer. David's own faint voice, coming at her from far, far away. A single word. "Yes."

Was it a vision, or a waking dream?
Fled is the music—Do I wake or sleep?
—KEATS, "Ode to a Nightingale"

CHAPTER FIVE

She was cold. Cold and scared and confused and bleeding but she couldn't get up. The emotional impact of what had just happened was too great. She couldn't summon any strength. It was as if a high wind had blown through her head and scattered her senses all over the dull brown field, leaving her helpless and incoherent. She clenched and unclenched her fists experimentally, thinking she'd use her hands to push herself up. She had to get up before Gallagher concluded that she was a total nutcase.

She could hear him beside her, stomping like an angry bull. He was even breathing through his nose. She disliked him intensely—he was a terrible choice for a sensitive job—but he was all she had in her quest to find David. Stephen wanted to bring in a group that specialized in finding missing children, but Rachel was resisting. The thought of all those people swarming about, with their sympathy and their intrusion, made her cringe. So did the idea of seeing David's face everywhere she went, a constant, unrelenting reminder of their loss. But she was beginning to wonder if Stephen was right. The

police weren't getting anywhere. One part of her was ready to back down, to agree that they should call in help. Another part resisted for a reason more important than her privacy. What if broadcasting David's picture frightened his kidnappers into killing him? What if their desire to possess him was overwhelmed by their fear of being caught?

She tipped her head back and looked up at Gallagher, even larger now that she was down at ground level. His faraway face was as cold and unyielding as ever. Why couldn't he ever smile at her, ever show even the faintest glimmer of humanity? She gathered her stumbling wits together enough to say, "Could you help me up?"

He thrust two big hands under her armpits and hauled her to her feet, managing, in the process, to grab both breasts. He set her roughly on her shaky feet and backed away, the two color spots back in his cheeks. "I'm sorry," he muttered, turning from her so she could barely hear. "It was an accident."

"It was no accident." Rachel was astonished to hear her own voice, sounding strong, when she felt so weak. "You've been wanting to do that all along."

"An accident," he repeated sullenly. "Come on back to the car. I'll drive you home."

Rachel was suspended outside her body, watching her progress, an exhausted, almost drunken stagger back to the car. She wished the man would disappear in a puff of smoke and leave her alone. Then she'd sit back down by the sign and try to reach David again. She couldn't do that with him around. He was too distracting, too physical. Gallagher opened her door, pushed her roughly in, and got in himself, slamming his door unnecessarily hard. Rachel leaned her head back against the seat and closed her eyes. "Would you have a handkerchief you could give me? For the blood?" She held up her injured hand. "It was a piece of broken glass."

He pulled one out, holding it suspended for a minute like he was surrendering, then gave it to her. She wrapped it around her hand. The pain was the only thing about this whole afternoon that seemed real. "So, do you want to know what I remembered going to the spot, or don't you care?"

He shrugged. "If you think it might be useful . . ."

"It's not my job to decide what might be useful. It's yours, Gallagher. Even though you act like you don't give a damn whether David ever gets found. Do you? Give a damn, I mean."

"Of course."

"There's no of course about it, Detective. Except for an occasional glimmer of your secret hope that you can nail me or Stephen, I haven't seen any sign you care about the fact that a nine-year-old boy has been abruptly snatched from everything and everyone he knows. I'm being shredded with the agony of it while you're completely indifferent. How can you hope to do your job when you don't care about people?"

"I'm not indifferent," he growled, slapping his hands onto the wheel at two and eleven and gripping it tightly.

Rachel stared at his hands. Big, wide, competent hands, with freckles and tufts of reddish hair at the ends of arms too long for his sleeves. His naked white wrists were the only vulnerable thing about him. The rest of him was as stiff and hard as a starched shirt. David had arms and legs like sticks, though he was developing some muscles from baseball, and long, thin hands like hers. Stephen's hands were blunt and square and hairless.

"No, you're right," she said. "You're not completely indifferent. You have shown an interest in my chest. I wish you wouldn't. It distracts me. I'm not used to being stared at and it makes me uncomfortable. Are you lonely? Are you unsatisfied? Isn't there a woman in your life? Look . . ." Rachel pulled up her top and bared her breasts. "Two perfectly ordinary, medium-sized, middle-aged female breasts. Nothing to write home about. Now you've seen them, so maybe you can stop staring. Or maybe looking isn't enough?" She arched her chest and tightened her muscles so they rose and stood out toward Gallagher. "Maybe you'd like to touch them again? Would that help? Then could you get your mind back on this investigation?"

Gallagher stared at her in astonishment. His face was flaming and he seemed incapable of speech. Overwhelmed with shame, she pulled her top down, turned her back on him, and started to cry. "I'm sorry. I don't know what came over me. I've never done anything

like that in my life," she stammered. "I can't believe I did that. . . . God . . . maybe I am losing my mind." She opened the door, got out, and started walking away. Anything to get away from him. From what she'd just done.

There was the gritty roar of tires on gravel and the car accelerated, shot toward her, and braked to a rocking stop beside her. "Get back in the car," Gallagher ordered. "I'm taking you home."

She got in the car, curled up into the smallest ball possible, and sat staring straight ahead. Neither of them spoke until she was almost home. Then Rachel broke the silence. She might have just done something ineffably, unimaginably stupid, but that didn't erase the reason they were here—to find David. "I'm going to tell you the story of Cedric Carville, the boy who wanted to be the greatest baseball player in the world." Gallagher gave no sign that he'd heard her, and certainly none that he cared, but Rachel told him the whole story anyway, finishing with David and the apple. "So I know that the sneaker was a message. He was trying to tell us where he was going. And I expect that, if he had the chance to throw it, somewhere out there is another shoe, waiting to be found . . . and a store where they bought him more sneakers. . . ."

No reaction from Gallagher. Not an acknowledgment, not a "good thinking," not any sign that he cared in the slightest about a desperate little kidnapped boy throwing sneakers out a car window. She wanted to grab him by the arm and shake him until his teeth rattled, but she'd already done a lifetime's worth of stupid, impulsive things today. She had to exercise some self-control, even if she didn't feel she had any.

He pulled into the drive, rolled up to the house, and stopped without a word. Rachel got out and tottered up the walk. She'd done some stupid things in her time when she let her passions rule her head, but this one took the prize. She wanted to crawl into bed, pull the covers over her head, and stay there for a month. If she didn't have a mission here, she'd vanish off the face of the earth.

Stephen was waiting in the entry, an anxious look on his face. "Well?" he asked before she was even through the door. "You learn anything?"

She leaned against the door jamb for support. "You remember about Cedric Carville?"

He looked puzzled. "Those stupid baseball stories?"

She nodded. "They were pretty awful, but he liked them. Anyway, there was one where Cedric Carville throws his shoes out the car window, trying to hit a sign. That's what David was doing. He threw the shoe at that abandoned road sign out by the highway."

She watched recognition dawn. "You told Gallagher?" he asked. She nodded. "What did he say?"

"He didn't say anything."

"What do you mean, he didn't say anything? He didn't understand that David was trying to send us a message? Or he didn't care?"

"I don't know," Rachel said. "He never says anything. I don't think he cares. Can we sit down? I'm awfully tired."

Stephen seized her hand. "You're frozen, Skee," he said. "Where's your coat?"

"I forgot it."

"You need a keeper," he said.

"I have a keeper. You." She leaned against him, grateful for his presence, his support. Sometimes she felt so alienated that she might have been on a different planet. She knew she scared and confused him. Sometimes his distance, and his attempts to control her, made her furious. But she loved Stephen. She only wished she could make him happy without changing who she was, without always feeling that she wasn't normal and seeing his disappointment whenever he looked at her. He should have married Miranda. She was totally normal.

"Right now your keeper thinks you need a warm bath and a drink."

It sounded heavenly. "Thanks, Stephen. I think my keeper is right. I'd love a bath." She hesitated. "About Gallagher. He keeps staring at me without expression. It makes me crazy. I never know where we stand with him. I don't know if he cares at all about David. I'm afraid I lost my temper with him. I yelled at him. . . ." Could she really tell Stephen what she'd done? Not the truth, the whole truth, and nothing but the truth, but she'd feel better if she told him

a corner of the story. It was as much as he could handle, and as much as she could bear to tell. "I told him I wanted him to stop staring at my chest and pay attention to the important things. . . ."

"It would help if you'd wear a bra," Stephen said sharply.

She lowered her eyes. "I know. I'll be more careful from now on. I was in a hurry and they were all in the wash. It didn't seem important."

"Sometimes we have to do things because they're important to other people, Rachel," he said wearily. She heard the sigh in his voice, knew he got tired of trying to conform his feckless wife to the realities of other people's opinions.

"I said I'd try to do better. Has Miranda gone?"

"She had a date. She left us some dinner, though. Some sort of vegetarian slop, I think."

Rachel sighed. Her sister was recently divorced and determined to reenter the singles scene. So far, her dates had all been disasters. "I hope this one turns out better. Don't you know any nice single men you could introduce her to?"

"I like your sister a lot. You know I do. But her expectations are completely unrealistic. She's still looking for Prince Charming and he doesn't exist. And since she went on this health food kick, she's become the world's worst cook. I'm not going to expose a friend of mine to that." He got up and went to the bar. "Bourbon or Scotch?"

"Vermouth. Red. With a twist." She turned sideways, swung her feet up over the arm, and kicked off her shoes. Her body felt leaden, pressed into the soft cushions by the inexorable force of gravity. She cradled her wounded hand on her chest. Her breasts felt heavy and sore. Sleeplessness and stress playing havoc with her hormones again. She closed her eyes, listening to the familiar sounds of drinks being made. The clink of ice in the glasses. The slosh of pouring liquor. The *tunk* of the knife as he cut the lemon. The tinkle and swirl as he crossed the room and held out her glass.

"What happened to your hand?"

"I cut it on a piece of glass. The whole place was covered with glass from people pitching bottles at the sign. I wonder who found the sneaker."

"Maybe someone collecting cans? Here, let me see." He knelt beside her and took her hand in his, gently unwrapping the handkerchief. "Ugly," he murmured, "but not deep. You shouldn't need stitches. Better wash it, though, and put iodine on it. You wouldn't want to catch anything. . . . Rachel . . ." There was an abrupt change in his tone. "There's something we need to talk about. . . . No . . . never mind . . . not now."

Rachel opened her eyes and looked at him. He was staring intently at the hand, a peculiar expression on his face. "What is it?" she asked.

He swallowed, hesitated, and told her a lie. She didn't have any idea what the truth was, but she knew his answer was a lie. No, not a lie, just not what he'd been going to tell her. Another truth instead. "I miss him. I miss David. The house . . . the days . . . time . . . it all seems so empty. I keep expecting him to walk around the corner. Thunder around upstairs. Ask me to play catch. Go into one of those infuriating series of yells for you when you're out of earshot. God! I'd give anything to have him here irritating me right now. Anything!"

"I know," she said. She reached out and pulled his head down onto her chest, wrapping her arms around him and holding him there. Burying her chin in his clean, soft hair. The light shining through his ear made it a translucent pink. He had elegant ears, beautifully formed. She'd always wanted to draw them. Once she'd asked him if he'd let her, once when she was holding him like this. He'd jumped away like he'd been burned, a horrified expression on his face as though there was something obscene about drawing ears. She'd never suggested it again.

She didn't know what his family had been like—he claimed not to remember—but when she met Stephen, he'd been so stiff and touchy, a public embrace made him jump like a kangaroo and the possibility of a kiss would have sent him scurrying for cover. She'd had to coax him toward ease and intimacy step by cautious step, not an easy task for a girl as shy as she had been. But Rachel had known from the first that she wanted to sleep with Stephen, long before she knew she wanted to marry him, and even though she'd never slept with any man before.

Under our civilized veneer, we're all just animals, she thought, and the mating instinct is strong. Stephen put his hand underneath her jersey and touched her breast, his usual sign that he wanted to have sex. It was the right thing to do. It would comfort him, and it would put something normal and natural between her and her memories of that awful scene in Gallagher's car. "Let's go upstairs," she said. She took him by the hand and led him out of the room.

Oh, what a tangled web we weave,
When first we practice to deceive!
—SIR WALTER SCOTT, "Marmion"

CHAPTER SIX

Stephen was an early riser. He always had been, even as a teenager when his peers were sleeping until noon. He liked the feeling of being up when no one else was, of having the world to himself. When they were first married, he'd gotten up and fixed coffee for Rachel, who always had trouble waking. Lately, though, she'd had trouble sleeping. Ever since David had disappeared, he might wake up at any time of the night and find her sitting in the old rocker, staring out the window. If she wasn't there, she was by David's bed or just sitting in the middle of his rug, often clutching a toy or a stuffed animal. So this morning, when he found her sleeping, he'd crept quietly out of bed and tried not to disturb her.

Halfway to the door, his clothes clutched under his arm, he turned back and looked at her. She was curled up on her side, one fist pressed under her cheek, the other hand lying on the blanket, her thin, graceful fingers stretched out toward him. Asleep, she looked just like David—they had the same nose and mouth, and her eyes, which were very different, were closed. A strand of dark

hair draped across her cheek. One shoulder was bare. He wanted to go back and cover it—the room was cold—but was afraid he'd wake her.

He felt almost normal this morning, a rare experience these days when their house seemed to be full of the constant comings and goings of cops and technicians and detectives and reporters and neighbors and friends and the curious. The sex had helped. He noticed that he was humming as he shaved. Rachel was strange about lovemaking. Often reserved and undemonstrative. Often sad and unreachable. Sometimes too disjointed and disinterested to approach. Or too tired. Rachel tired easily. The only times Rachel had been open and greedy about sex were when she was pregnant. As a result, Stephen sometimes went hungry, sexually speaking, since he wasn't the type of man to force himself on his wife, or he picked up snacks somewhere else. So last night had been especially satisfying, with Rachel initiating things, and their common need had connected them in a way that they hadn't been connected lately.

He stripped off his underwear—he hated pajamas—and studied himself in the mirror. Women he'd slept with often told him he had a nice body. He wasn't a big man, though he almost topped six feet, and he lacked the burly chest and arms of a jock, but he kept himself in shape. His shoulders were wide and his waist was still narrow and he'd recently overheard a temporary secretary in the office remark that he had nice buns. He turned and looked over his shoulder. He couldn't see it, but at least they didn't wobble when he walked. He'd never let that happen. A courtroom lawyer has to look good from the back.

Rachel came into the bathroom just as he was stepping out of the shower. With her tousled hair, sleep-pink cheeks, and blue wisp of a nightgown, she looked incredibly young and fragile. She grinned at him, a sweet, lopsided grin, and stared openly at his naked body. "Lookin' good, Vee," she said. "Turn around so I can see the rest." Obediently, he turned his back. She put her arms around his waist and pressed against him. "You're all wet," she whispered, taking liberties.

"Skee . . . Rachel . . . we can't. I haven't got time. I've got a meet-

ing." Darn her. Three hundred and sixty four days a year he would have been happy to get down and roll around on the bathroom floor with her, but today's meeting was important. Mucho important. He needed some quiet time in his office to prepare, and making love to Rachel required time and attention. "Can I get a rain check?"

She dropped her arms and stepped away. He turned toward her but he couldn't tell what the expression on her face meant. She left the room without speaking and suddenly the bathroom was cold. Irritated and vaguely aroused, Stephen hurried into his clothes, brushed his hair and teeth, and went into the bedroom to look for shoes. Rachel was sitting in the rocking chair, staring out at the yard. "He's alive," she said.

Hope flared up, then died. "How do you know?" Stupid question. Obviously she hadn't heard anything he hadn't heard. They'd been together all weekend. She must have been on the psychic hot line.

She looked at him nervously, lowered her eyes. "I could feel him yesterday when we were out by the sign. In my mind. I heard him speaking. I think he's far away, though."

"You know I don't believe in that stuff, Rachel."

"I know. I wouldn't believe myself if it didn't happen to me. But it does. Life isn't all logical and linear, like you expect it to be. There are dimensions of the mind that we shut ourselves off to because they scare us. Besides, I'm more connected to him than you are. . . ." She hadn't meant to say it, and bit off her words as soon as they crept out, but it was too late.

"Thanks for reminding me." Stephen turned on the heel of his shiny black wingtips and walked out, the sting, coupled with his frustration at the timing of her advances, turning to anger at Rachel. She couldn't let him forget, could she?

Miranda was in the kitchen, bending over to get something from the fridge, the hem of her skimpy nightshirt rising to reveal a teeny black thong between the cheeks of her nicely shaped rear. He coughed politely and she did a little Betty Boop jump as she turned to greet him, grinning without shame as she tugged at the inadequate hem. "How was the date?" he asked.

She rolled her eyes. "They're all alike, Stephen. I think they make 'em in some factory in Illinois. They talk about their work, like how important they are and how much responsibility they have and their cars and their personal trainers and microbreweries and cigars, not necessarily in that order. And sports teams and computers."

He poured himself a glass of juice and slid a bagel into the toaster. "What do you want to talk about?" he said.

She shrugged and her breasts bounced. "Myself? Relationships. Real estate. The new septic system regulations. Great food. Roller-blading. Vacation spots. Movies where no one gets blown up. Good books. Nutritional supplements. Whether the *Cosmo* cover girl is really man's ideal. How many times an hour they think about sex." She reached for the pot. "Coffee's ready. You want some?"

"Are you working today?" he asked, watching the T-shirt ride up again so he could admire the smooth line of her hip.

"Does the pope shit in the woods?" she asked. "Why?"

He shrugged. "I don't know. I thought it might be nice if Rachel had someone around today. . . ." He opened the paper and started reading the headlines. Miranda's nearly bare bottom kept intruding.

"Is she awake?" Miranda asked.

"Sitting in that damned rocking chair, staring out the window."

"Did she sleep?"

"For once. At least, she was sleeping when I got up."

Miranda came around to his side of the island, set down his coffee, and sidled toward him until her breast was resting on his arm. "I thought maybe *you* needed someone to be around today. . . ."

He folded the paper and regarded her. "You've got a rotten sense of timing," he said.

"Nothing ventured, nothing gained," she retorted. "All those hours in the company of pumped-up morons makes me horny. They may be brainless but there's brawn aplenty. Never mind, Stevie. I'd hate to muss your suit." She picked one of his hands off the paper and placed it on her breast. "You can have a rain check."

He pushed her up against the sink, tugged the thong aside, and slipped his hand between her legs. Unlike Rachel, Miranda didn't

take a lot of priming. "Rain check. Twelve-thirty at the motel," he said.

Miranda pouted. "Why not now?"

"With Rachel in the house? I don't think so."

"It wouldn't be the first time."

He shrugged. "It doesn't feel right. Not now. Not with all that's going on."

She raised her eyebrows. "A sudden attack of conscience?"

"Just, as we say in the law, a change of venue. I guarantee you'll get more than you'd get from those pumped-up morons you date."

"Since I can't have you," she shrugged, "you might at least say something nice."

Stephen looked at his watch. "Another time, when I'm not in a hurry, I'll think of a dozen nice things to say." He pulled her to him, sliding a finger inside her, resting his chin on her sweet-smelling hair. Then he withdrew the finger and held it up. "My secret weapon," he said. "I'll sit there in my meeting, tapping this finger thoughtfully against my lips, and they'll all think I'm planning some killer strategy when all the time I'm smelling you."

Miranda turned her back on him. "You're bad, Stephen."

"Am I?" He went into his office, to his desk, and took out the letter. He brought it back to the kitchen and gave it to her. "What do you think I should do about this? Is she strong enough to handle it right now?"

Miranda read, little concentration lines forming in her forehead as she went down the page. When she'd finished, her hand fell limply to her side and she looked over at Stephen, her eyes wide. "This is horrible! Good God! How could they just send a letter like this, out of the blue, with news like that?" She shook her head vigorously. "No, of course you can't tell Rachel. Not right now. There's no way she could handle this. Not after Jonah . . . not with David . . . no. She feels so guilty and helpless already. Don't tell her." Then, as she stared at him, a realization about her own situation came into her face. She flushed red and glared at him. "What about you? Jesus, Stephen. We've been . . . Have you been tested?"

Stephen glared at her. Miranda was irritatingly literal and she

always had to talk about things. No wonder she was having trouble on dates. She couldn't just sit there and look interested; she had to challenge everything. Besides, he hated having his honesty questioned. It irked him like few things did, and people these days were always questioning the honesty of lawyers. He could remember a time, before he began to practice, but he could remember it, when society looked up to lawyers. When it had been an honorable profession. In his mind, it still was. He was proud of what he did. "You're perfectly safe," he said. "I've been tested. It was negative."

"Thank goodness for small favors," she said. "Though I would point out that no woman who has been screwing her sister's husband while her sister is in the house can be called 'perfectly safe.' What about Rachel? Is she okay? She hasn't seemed very well lately . . . and she does get tired so easily. I mean, what are the risks here? I know woman-to-man transmission is harder, but could she still have it? Or David?"

Stephen set his briefcase on the counter, a little heavily to show his irritation, and took the letter from Miranda's hand. "The chances of getting AIDS are slight. There have only been a few cases, so I'm not worried. The doctors said we didn't need to worry. I just had the test to be doubly certain. . . ."

"But she should be checked!" Miranda said. "Suppose she's sick. . . . There are some things they can do, aren't there? To prolong life, I mean?"

Miranda could be such a moron. "I can't very well have her tested without telling her why, can I?" he said. "And, as you agreed, just weeks after her only child has been abducted is hardly the time to tell Rachel that the sperm donor who fathered that child is dying of AIDS and she and the child should be tested to see whether the virus has been transmitted. A child conceived by artificial insemination because her husband carries a poison in his genes that kills the children that he fathers. Christ, Miranda. Use your brain. And don't say anything about this to Rachel." He shoved the letter in the briefcase and snapped it shut.

"You guys aren't sleeping together these days, are you?" Miranda asked.

"Not since last night." He tapped his finger against his lips. "Catch you later. Starlight Motel. Twelve-thirty." He picked up the briefcase and left.

Miranda picked up his coffee cup and hurled it against the wall. "Bastard!" she said. Ignoring the brown stream cascading down the white paint, she went into the bathroom, got her robe, and took some coffee up to Rachel.

Every journey begins with a single step.

CHAPTER SEVEN

Rachel was sitting in the chair, staring out at the basketball hoop, imagining David racing around, laughing and shooting baskets, when Miranda came in. Miranda set down the cup and immediately started fussing over her. "Rachel, look at you. You're barely dressed and it's cold in here. Do you want to get sick? Where's your robe?" She jerked open the closet and pawed among the clothes, her voice coming muffled through the door. "It looks like a bomb went off in here. When's the last time you took in Stephen's shirts? I can't find the damned robe. . . ." She emerged with Stephen's robe and gave it to Rachel. "Put this on and come downstairs. I'll fix you some breakfast."

Mechanically, Rachel took the robe and put it on. She wasn't hungry and she wanted to be alone, but if she humored her sister, Miranda would check her off the chore list and move on to the other details of her day. "Are you working today?" she asked.

Miranda nodded. "Meeting a couple out at the Sears place. This is their second time back. I think they're very interested." She waved her arms wide, an elaborate gesture of dismissal. "They'd be stupid

not to buy it. After the mess she got herself into, messing around with Alan's boss and getting caught by his wife, Lena Sears is hot to get out of here and go where people don't stare when she walks down the street. She's what we call in the business a motivated seller. I have to be out there by nine, but I've got time to fix you something."

"I'm not completely helpless," Rachel said, staring at Miranda's costume revealed by the open robe. The areas of pale shaved skin where pubic hair should have been looked naked and vulnerable and curiously obscene. "Cute outfit," she said. "Did you see Stephen before he left?"

The quick look Miranda gave her suggested something Rachel really didn't want to think about, but maybe she was just being paranoid. People seemed to be giving her funny looks all the time lately, and her own ability to perceive and order her universe wasn't exactly in working order. Look at what she'd done yesterday. Her cheeks burned just thinking about it. If she never saw Gallagher again, it would be soon enough for her.

Miranda didn't seem to have noticed; she'd started folding a basket of laundry. "They'd better buy it. I wasted a ton of time on that other couple . . . the older couple I told you about, the ones who were so interested in the community and the schools because their daughter and grandson might be coming to live with them. I spent a gazillion hours taking them around and showing them the town, the post office, town offices, schools, police station, and what seemed like every damned house in a twenty-mile radius and what do they do? One morning they up and check out of the hotel without so much as a word, leaving me with six expectant sellers and nothing to tell them. I hope it wasn't something I said or did." She paused for breath.

"If I had my way, people would have to pay for the privilege of looking at houses. That would keep them from wasting my time. What happened with you and Gallagher yesterday? Was it helpful?"

Helpful? Rachel thought. To pull up my shirt and bare my breasts like a teenager at a rock concert? She took a deep breath, trying to dissipate the knot of shame in her chest. "I'll trade the whole story for two poached eggs on toast," she said.

Miranda, clutching her robe shut, headed for the door. "See you downstairs in five," she said. "I've got some great granola. . . ."

Rachel shook her head. "Eggs. Granola takes too much energy to chew."

When she'd gone, Rachel went into the closet to dress and stopped, paralyzed, staring at the mess. Miranda might be a bit too forthright, but she was right this time. It was a massive, depressing mess. Poor Stephen was a saint to put up with her. As she pulled on her jeans and a bra—maybe she should wear two to make up for yesterday?—she remembered Stephen coming out of the shower and felt a little surge of lust. If there was any bright spot in the whole dismal landscape of their lives, it was that this awful time was drawing them closer together. Not that he understood her any better; she didn't believe he ever would, but they were each being kinder.

She paused in the door of David's room and looked around. She hadn't changed a thing but the police, going through it, had moved things so that it didn't quite feel like David. He was boyish in his passion for collection, but strangely tidy for a child, at least in his own room. He liked things organized in certain ways, and when they weren't, he had to set things right before he could go on with homework or a game or anything else he wanted to do. Stephen's passion for order. Stephen adored David. He'd worked so hard to make David his that David was more like his father than most biological children are. When they were together, she'd sometimes watched in astonishment. Their gestures, their inflection, the way they moved their bodies, were uncannily alike. She blotted her tears on her sleeve and went downstairs.

Brilliant spring sunshine was streaming into the kitchen through the skylights. The kitchen was new. It and the sprawling family room beyond were an add-on, the one part of the house that didn't creak and groan and send drafts down your neck and across your feet. Miranda was standing at the stove, breaking eggs into a poaching pan, a frilly white bib apron over her business clothes. Miranda maintained, and everything in Rachel's experience confirmed, that to dress like a realtor all you needed to do was think you were your mother. For work, Miranda wore tailored, fashionless country club clothes, clunky gold costume jewelry, and low-heeled pumps. Skirts and low-heeled

pumps to lead clients through stifling attics, dank musty cellars, through barns and garages, and to walk property lines. It might be silly, but if you were good at it, it paid well.

Rachel had never had a job that paid well. She illustrated children's books. People were always saying how exciting and glamorous her job must be. She'd heard starry-eyed gushing about combining art and literature until she wanted to puke, especially from Stephen's colleagues and their spouses. The truth was that she did love her work and couldn't imagine a better job, but the reality of the business was that it paid poorly and got little respect. It was darned hard sometimes to read people's minds and produce what they imagined, and equally difficult some days to force yourself to be creative. Not to mention the times when you'd read one editor's mind and then they changed editors. Lately her mind had been as dry and unfertile as an African desert and she had a deadline racing at her with the speed of an express train.

She loved the book, *Emily's Horse,* the gentle story of how a three-year-old gets what she wants for her birthday; she just couldn't stand thinking about happy families and other people's children. The last time she'd tried to work she'd drawn a picture that reminded her of David and ended up in the bathroom being violently sick; the time before that she'd drawn an Emily so cute, Rachel had cried until she stabbed the drawing with her pencil, ripped it to shreds, and went out into the garden. Today she'd have to try harder. The people in New York didn't care if she'd lost her child; they cared about losing a publishing slot. The only people who truly cared about David were she and Stephen and their immediate families.

Miranda set a plate down in front of her. "I want you to eat it all," she ordered. "You're getting much too thin. Are you feeling all right?"

"A little sick and dizzy. But I always get like that when I haven't slept." She picked up her fork and stuck the egg. The bright yellow yolk oozed out and flowed over the plate. Her stomach did a flip-flop and she quickly bit off a piece of dry toast, chewing slowly and wondering if she could eat her egg without looking at it. "How was your date last night?"

"Great," Miranda said.

"Who was he?"

"Banker," her sister mumbled over a mouthful of toast. "Up and coming. He took me to this place where they do line dancing. I learned the tush push. Well, learned it enough to keep up. I've forgotten it now. But you'd get a kick out of the place. They've all got their costumes and cowboy boots, the whole kit and caboodle." Miranda jumped up, plunked David's cowboy hat on her head, and hooked her fingers into the belt loops of her tailored navy slacks. "So what do you think? Do I make a good cowgirl? He wants me to go again on Thursday."

"I'd skip the hat, I think. But one of those short bias-cut skirts that really swings when you dance would be good. With a pair of decent underpants."

Miranda flipped the hat back toward its peg, missed, and made a face. "Decent? You're such a Victorian. The show's the thing. If you've got it, flaunt it."

"I wouldn't know," she said, feeling a blush steal up her neck. "That all you did, go line dancing?"

Miranda grinned wickedly and tossed her hair. "Wouldn't you like to know."

Rachel sighed. She wouldn't, really; she was only asking to be polite. Miranda liked to live her personal life close to the edge. That was what had finally ended her marriage. Her husband, Jeff, had wanted a traditional suburban thing with kids and station wagon, while Miranda had wanted a Miata, swimming pool, vacations to adults-only resorts, and the possibility of an open marriage. By the time Miranda had started wanting what Jeff wanted, he didn't want it anymore. He'd become the one who wanted to be a swinging single.

She cut off some egg with the edge of her fork and raised it gingerly to her lips. Her stomach stayed calm. She ate another bite. Doing pretty well. It wasn't until the fifth bite that she lost her appetite. She was like this most days, and it seemed to get worse, not better, as time went on. Maybe because in the beginning she'd been more hopeful. Although today she did feel hopeful again, now that she was certain David was alive. "Thanks for making me breakfast," she said. "Aren't you going to be late?"

Miranda looked at her watch. "Oops. You're right. I've got to run." She pulled off the apron, tossed it over a chair, and grabbed her purse. "We went back to his place," she said. "Had champagne and made whoopee. I think this one's got potential. He even says he likes kids."

That's what they all say these days, Rachel thought. They've learned from articles in men's magazines that that's what women want to hear. And men will say anything if it may lead to sex. Some men, anyway. "Great," she said aloud, clasping her hands over her stomach and hoping her sister would leave before she had to go throw up the breakfast Miranda had so kindly made. Miranda would tell Stephen and she didn't want him fretting over her any more than he already did. She managed to wait until the door had finally shut. Then she jumped up and sprinted for the bathroom.

When she emerged, feeling green and shaky, she made herself a piece of toast and cup of tea, carried them into her workroom, and reread the story. She studied the first drawing, the one of Emily and her mother in the kitchen, talking about Emily's birthday present, made a few changes, and pulled out a fresh sheet of paper. She was illustrating the part where Emily and her mother go to the toy store to look for the horse that Emily wants, and the sales clerk is showing them a variety of horses, each of which Emily rejects. Rachel wanted to show Emily astride a broomstick hobbyhorse, galloping around the store. She had the photographs of the little girl she was using as a model pinned up on the board, but she couldn't quite picture the horse. She had made and discarded about eight sketches before she remembered that there was one in David's closet. She went upstairs to get it.

His closet was as orderly as the rest of the room and she found the horse easily. She hurried out, trying to escape before her memories caught her and trapped her there. She'd spent too much of the last three weeks sitting on the floor, agonizing. It didn't help. She was determined not to do it anymore. "Fat chance," said a voice in her head. "Remember when David got that horse?"

She sank down into the chair, the stick between her knees, holding the horse upright by its reins. Closed her eyes. The room was

silent except for the fish tank. She remembered David, not much older than the fictional three-year-old Emily, standing in the toy store, pointing at the horse and asking if he could ride it. Unlike the helpful clerk in the story, a woman had snapped immediately that David could not ride it in the store because he might knock something over. Incensed, Rachel had wanted to storm out without giving them any business, but David had refused to leave without the horse, so they'd bought it, and he'd gleefully galloped off down the street to their car.

In her mind's eye, David on the horse became David on a bike. She watched him ride. He wasn't anyplace that she recognized. It looked like here, yet different. Somewhere where spring wasn't so far advanced, the leaves on the bushes still embryonic, and the tar on the road was a different color. It didn't look like any place she'd ever been before. He turned and looked at her and waved.

A chill rippled her skin. "David, my darling," she whispered. "Where are you? Tell me where you are."

The little boy in her mind gave her a look both sad and confused. "Are you dead, Mommy?" is what she thought she heard him say, but before she could ask again, he turned and rode away and the whole image disappeared.

She was brought from her reverie by the insistent ringing of the doorbell downstairs. She got up, still clutching the hobbyhorse, hurried down the stairs, and opened the door. Gallagher was standing on the steps. He didn't look delighted to see her. He stared at the horse, her face, and her chest. Rachel wished she had worn two bras. "What is it, Detective?" she asked. Cool, careful, nerves clenched. She was learning not to get hopeful at his appearances.

"Do you know anyone who owns a gray or silver van?" he asked. "Someone David might have been willing to go with?"

She shook her head. "No. None that I recall. Anyway, David wasn't supposed to go with anyone who didn't know the password."

"The password?"

"Yes. Because of all the kidnappings in the news. You should know about this, Detective. They tell us parents should give our children a password, so that if we ever do have to send a stranger . . . or

a person unknown to the child . . . the child knows not to go with that person unless the person knows the password. We'd discussed it many times with David." She forced herself to look at him. How could anyone's face be so blank? "I'm sure I've told you this before. He never would have gone with a stranger."

"He went with somebody," Gallagher said.

Belatedly, Rachel remembered her manners. She didn't feel friendly toward the detective and couldn't imagine that she ever would, even if he found David, but he was supposedly her ally. "Would you like to come in?" she asked, gesturing toward the kitchen with the hobbyhorse. "I could make some coffee."

But Gallagher was staring at the hobbyhorse. "Oh, excuse me," he said. "I missed that."

"Would you like some coffee?" Rachel said it as slowly and carefully as if she were talking to her ancient aunt Rose, who was in a home. Rose was slow and deaf. Gallagher was only slow.

"That would be fine," he agreed. "What's with the horse? You aren't cleaning out David's room. . . ."

He had an infuriating way of pushing her buttons. "I'm working," she said coldly. "I needed it for an illustration."

"Nice horse," he said, following her into the kitchen. He pulled out a stool and made himself comfortable at the island, staring with disapproval at the cold egg on her plate.

"Thank you." She found she was clutching the horse protectively to her chest. Looked at Gallagher's detestable face. Briefly pondered the headline: POLICE DETECTIVE BEATEN TO DEATH WITH HOBBY-HORSE. "I'll just put this in my workroom."

"Decaf?" she asked as she rinsed out the pot.

"No sense in drinking coffee if it doesn't give you any kick." She put in a filter, spooned in coffee, and pressed the button. "It helps if you put water in," he said.

Since waking, Rachel had been feeling like she was carrying a fifty-pound bundle on her head. Her temples ached and her neck ached and her whole body was almost too exhausted to stand. As he watched, she put water in the pot and poured it in, rewarded by the machine's satisfied hiss and throaty gurgle. "I think I hate you,

Detective Gallagher," she said. "I can't stand the way you keep coming and pecking at me like a big mean bird."

Gallagher looked surprised. "I'm sorry you feel that way," he said. "I'm only trying to help. In fact, I came today to . . ."

Rachel squeezed her hands together so tightly, her knuckles hurt. "Sorry? Trying to help? How can you help when you treat us so badly you make it impossible to talk to you? Not . . ." She turned suddenly toward him, caught her foot in the rug, put a hand out to keep herself from falling, and knocked a glass onto the tile floor. It exploded into fragments with an astonishingly loud noise. "Not that we know anything that can help you . . . anything we're aware of, anyway. We have no enemies. . . . David had no enemies. We're just a boringly regular family. David was . . . is . . . a delightfully normal child. . . ."

". . . came to apologize for being so difficult. And for yesterday," Gallagher finished. He slid off his stool and came around to her side of the island. Put a hand under her elbow and raised her carefully from the pool of glass, his glittering eyes searching her for signs of damage. "Here, you sit down. I'll clean that up."

Stunned by the change in the man, Rachel let herself be led to the stool and directed Gallagher to the broom closet, watching in a slightly dazed way as he cleaned up the broken glass and poured them both coffee. The change was difficult to believe in. It was probably just another ploy to lower her guard. Why not try being nice to the dippy little broad and maybe then she'll confess. "Why did you ask about the gray van?" she said.

"After I went back to the office yesterday . . . after you told me the story about Cedric Carville . . . I read through the file to see if I'd missed anything." He shrugged. "There wasn't anything but I was . . ." He hesitated. "I was disturbed by what had happened out there and restless. . . . Frankly, I didn't want to leave the office until I'd made something happen . . . until I could prove to you that I didn't keep coming back to talk to you just so I could stare at your chest." He swallowed. "And by the way, it looks neither middle-aged nor perfectly ordinary." He barely got the sentence out before the blush, so unexpected in a man of his years and a cop, flamed in his face. Maybe the agony of those blushes had made him so impassive?

"After I ran out of all the other possibilities, I was going through the daily police logs, looking for anything out of the ordinary, and that's where I found it. Not much. But without you, I would never have known it was significant."

"What is *it*?" Rachel interrupted, leaning forward, clutching her coffee cup, hope unfolding like a paper flower. "What did you find?"

"We have a chronic complainer, a Mrs. Gardiner, who calls several times a week to be sure we're doing our jobs. Her most frequent complaints are about litter. It was in one of them. She'd called again to complain about litter, saying that now it wasn't just the adults with their lottery tickets, beer bottles, and foam cups; now people were letting their children throw things out car windows. Just that day she'd seen a kid throw a shoe out. It was like getting hit with a sledgehammer. For me, I mean, not her," he explained in response to Rachel's confused look.

"I went out this morning to talk with her. In an hour of conversation, I was able to ascertain three potentially useful things. The shoe was thrown on the entrance ramp. She thinks she saw it on the day David disappeared and she thinks it was thrown from a gray or silver van with out-of-state plates, but she has no idea what state. A special plate. One with an animal or something on it."

Rachel found she had been holding her breath. She let it out slowly, staring at Gallagher. The hope and expectation in her eyes was painful. "It's something," she said, an exhalation barely above a whisper. "It's more than we ever had before. What do we do now?"

HE LAY BACK *on the awful bedspread and looked up at the ceiling. The bedspread had cowboys on it, cowboys on black horses and cowboys on tan horses. All the cowboys had bandannas around their necks and wore hats and most of them had plaid shirts. The cowboys had guns in their hands and were shooting at Indians. It was faded and stained and looked like something from a picture book his dad had had when he was a boy. He didn't know why the woman had it and he didn't dare ask her. He wanted to roll it up and put it away in the closet, but he didn't dare ask if he could do that, either. He was too afraid of her.*

David was trying to be good because his mom had sent this woman to rescue him so that he would be safe, but he was very unhappy. He was lonely. The man mostly sat and stared out the window and hardly ever spoke. When he did, he mumbled so it was hard to understand him. The woman worked all the time; she was never still. Cleaning, cooking, folding, sorting, dusting, digging, planting. David thought she was the busiest person he'd ever seen in his life. She never smiled the way his mom used to smile, just because the world made her happy, just those forced, tight hopeful smiles that made his stomach ache. Mostly, when she looked at him, she sighed, like his dad did, and shook her head and went back to her work, like he was doing everything wrong though he had no idea how to make it right. The kids at school stared at him, but no one ever spoke, and he didn't bother because they made him nervous. Anyway, he didn't expect to be here very long.

The house wasn't nice like his house. He didn't think it was because the people were poor. They'd bought him a new bike as soon as they could, and they hadn't fussed at all about the cost. Even his dad fussed more about money. Maybe they just didn't know how to make things nice. It was something he and his mom talked about sometimes, how people liked to make their houses a certain way. He liked the way his mom made things—bright and comfortable and pretty. Once or twice he'd said something, not meaning to be critical but just because it was what he'd been thinking. The woman always frowned and said, "We believe in making do. If there's something you need . . ."

But he couldn't ask because then she'd probably give it to him, along with more of those cold, hard hugs and those long, sad looks. Disappointed looks. She wanted him to be happy, to want to stay with her, to smile and act like her kid. The one who had died. And he couldn't do it. He was too sad.

He tried not to think about his mom. Remembering her gave him a huge lump in his throat. He never even said the word "dead" to himself because he was hoping that the woman was wrong and someday soon his mom would show up and take him home. When he did think about it, he wondered why his mom had sent this woman—these people—to get him. Sometimes he wondered if she actually had sent them. But they'd known the password.

It was mostly at night that things were hard. When he would lie in bed and remember her coming to tuck him in. They'd had a ritual. He'd say he couldn't sleep and she'd offer to tell him a story. That was the loneliest part of the day, going to sleep without stories. Without Cedric Carville and the giant rabbits and the kangaroo with the third roller skate for its tail. Without the quiet burble of the fish tank. Maybe things would be safe soon and his aunt could come and get him. He hoped someone was feeding the fish.

When he thought about his mom and his dad and his friend Tommy, he couldn't keep from crying. He cried only late at night, after he'd heard the woman and the man come upstairs and go to bed. He knew she wouldn't approve of crying. She was always talking about wimps and weaklings and perverts and people that lacked gumption. From the tone of her voice, David could tell she hated them. He was afraid of having her hate him. He didn't like her, but she was all he had.

CHAPTER EIGHT

Stephen emerged from his meeting feeling victorious. It was a ridiculous reaction, since all he'd done was secure the client. The hard work was yet to come. Still, after weeks of everything going wrong and what felt like an endless series of blows to his ego and his competence, it felt good. The clients really liked him, really wanted him; he could tell. Before he shut the door, he looked back at the conference room. A good-sized, well-proportioned room, nicely furnished, the walnut table gleaming, the paintings genuine. It was an impressive place to conduct business. He'd had to force himself to spend the money on a room that wasn't used daily—it had seemed like an extravagance for a small practitioner with just a few associates—but seeing it now, when he was feeling successful, he congratulated himself on his wisdom in spending the extra money. You have to spend money to make money, he thought.

He dumped the stack of papers his new clients had given him on his secretary's desk. "Copies of all of these, and open a file for Larsen," he said. He checked his watch. "I'm going to lunch."

When he got back, he looked at the stacks of papers on the desk, dumped himself into his chair, closed his eyes, and let his mind drift. It drifted to sex. He hadn't meant to think about sex. He thought he'd gotten all that out of his system at the motel. He had scads of work waiting and had planned to plunge right in, but he was momentarily weary and when he closed his eyes, there it was. Somewhere he'd read that men think about sex six times an hour, while women rarely think about it. That was just about right. He thought about it whenever a sight or sound or smell or memory stirred him, which was often. On the other hand, he couldn't imagine Rachel, bent gracefully over her drawing table making her wonderful illustrations, thinking of anything but her work. Indeed, the idea that she might think of sex unless he was in the house was vaguely disturbing. He didn't suffer from a Madonna/whore complex, but if he had, Rachel would have been his Madonna. And Miranda his whore.

He licked his lips and remembered that morning in the kitchen. Miranda had prepared her ambush well, but it's hard to ambush someone who's expecting you. Perhaps it was best termed a mutual ambush. Things had gotten a little out of hand since Miranda came to live with them. She was always so glad to see him, so generous, so supportive. So unlike Rachel. But they were taking too many chances. Begging to get caught. It would hurt Rachel and this was no time for that. That's why he'd suggested the motel. It was probably time to suggest that Miranda move out. What had been intended as a brief, transitional stay while she found a place to live had been going on for nearly four months.

He wondered if he'd made a mistake telling her about the letter. His relationship with David was no secret within the family, but he and Rachel hadn't told the police, and while he expected Miranda would be discreet, she was such a pea brain, there was always the risk of something slipping out. As for the AIDS business, she wasn't going to talk about that. Even Miranda had some discretion. The only risk there was that she'd decide they couldn't have sex anymore. She might. Miranda could be as cold and calculating as anybody he knew, but she had an irrational side like any woman. In a case like this,

even though he'd assured her she was safe, either side, irrational or cold, could decide to shut him out. At least for today, she hadn't.

After he'd taken a mental inventory of Miranda's body, he took a deep breath, let it slowly out, and reached for his stack of messages, sorting them into three piles: discard, respond, and urgent. When he was done, all the ones that proclaimed themselves urgent were from the same person: John Robinson. John Robinson from the Lost Child Foundation who wanted to help him locate David. Rachel was adamant that she didn't want Robinson and his people involved, but Stephen was thoroughly disgusted and frustrated with the lack of success of the police and ready to turn to other sources—sources he could exert some control over—for help.

They'd lost enough time already because of Rachel's stubbornness. Whether she agreed or not, it was time to get the news out. David was his child, too. The pain was his pain, too. Just because he didn't go around vacant-eyed and weeping didn't mean he didn't ache every time he passed his son's room, every time he noticed the baseball shaping the pocket of David's glove, every time he stepped on a Lego in his bare feet. He reached for the phone and dialed Robinson's number.

When he hung up, he felt back in control. He'd asked for Robinson's help, explaining that the delay was due to Rachel's reluctance, and Robinson had been completely understanding. Lost Child had volunteers and computer experts ready to go to work, broadcasting David's picture nationally, now that Stephen had given the word. They already had a photograph of David, which they would begin faxing and putting on-line immediately. Robinson himself would be available to meet with them this evening, to explain more about how he could help and to gather details.

Stephen raised his fist and shook it. "So there, Gallagher," he said aloud. "You can take your suspicions and your intrusive questions and your sidelong looks and shove them all where the sun don't shine!" He knew that Gallagher hated him more than ever since he'd made that call to the chief, but he'd had to do it to protect Rachel. She wasn't strong and Gallagher's game playing was agony to a woman without guile or defenses.

The protective way he wanted to insert himself between Gal-

lagher and Rachel reminded him of how he'd met her. He was doing a night of bar hopping with some out-of-town buddies, showing them the city. Rachel had been at the next table with a date, a flabby artist type with red hair like Gallagher's. Noisy as his group was, he'd been able to overhear their conversation. Mostly one-sided and mostly a loud and vulgar critique of Rachel and her unwillingness to "put out." Stephen was no prude about language, but even he found the man profoundly offensive. Occasionally Rachel would gently ask him to talk more quietly. Finally, she got up to leave and the lout grabbed her arm and slammed her back into her seat.

Stephen had been bigger then, still carrying some of his football bulk, and the guys he was with were bigger still. He'd shoved back his chair, stood up, and told the guy to let her go. That's when he'd seen her eyes. Staring up at him with that mixture of hope and fear that was her characteristic way of viewing the world.

Before he even knew her name, he'd felt a profound blow, a rocking combination of protectiveness and desire. I want her, he'd thought. Then she'd lowered her eyes, lashes trembling, and just like a character in a novel, Stephen had fallen. Hard. And set out to take the fear out of those eyes. He was still trying, but over the years, his adoration had become increasingly tinged with irritation.

Rachel could be so stupid sometimes. It offended him when she suggested, as she occasionally did, that her connection to David was closer than his because David was her biological child. The nature/nurture debate didn't enter into it. David was his son. David was just like him. They thought alike and they moved alike and they were certainly both compulsive neatniks. And look at the baseball. David pitched just like he had at that age, and with the same fierce delight. The story about the shoe made him proud. Of course David wouldn't let himself be taken without putting up a fight. It was just like something Stephen would have done, leaving that shoe behind. And Stephen could appreciate the whole incident without getting absurd and mystical, as Rachel had, imagining that she was communicating with David.

Not that he didn't want to believe that David was alive. You didn't have to be a mystic to want that, or even to have a certainty that your

child was alive. It was just something that parents had. It was normal to insist on believing that your child was alive, even if the statistics were against it. Hope was what kept you going. Hope, and in Stephen's case, anger. It had taken him years to get over Jonah's death, years when he'd kept his sorrow and shame hidden from Rachel and tried to be strong for her, years when he'd struggled with the idea that David was not his biological child—that he couldn't have a biological child—until he was totally caught up in being David's father and it didn't matter anymore. He was David's father and he blazed with anger at the idea that someone was trying to take that away from him. That was another difference between him and Rachel. She got sad and passive; he got mad and active.

"Excuse me?" His secretary stuck her head around the door. "Good heavens, Mr. Stark, what's the matter? You look mad enough to eat your desk. I thought the meeting went well this morning."

Stephen was disconcerted, like someone had just jerked a line and hauled him off his feet. He sat up straighter and rearranged his already impeccable tie. "Nothing is the matter, Charlotte," he said too sharply. "What did you want?"

Charlotte looked crushed. She hadn't been with him very long and she wasn't used to his ways. His last secretary, Sandra, had stood up to him like a trouper and he'd been delighted with her. She'd also been supremely competent. But she'd left to have a baby, and he'd hired Charlotte, who was cute as a button and not much brighter, from the best of a bad lot of applicants. "I was going across the street to get a sandwich and one of those good coffees and I wondered if you wanted anything?"

He looked at his watch. Already after two. He'd better eat or he'd get grouchy, but he was supposed to have eaten already. He pulled a ten from his wallet and passed it across the desk. "Chinese for lunch," he said. "It never stays with you. Coffee and a smoked turkey on whole wheat. Use the rest to treat yourself. And thanks for asking." She took the ten and backed out like she was leaving the presence of royalty, and Stephen, staring after her, thought about how much he missed Sandra. They'd had a brief affair, but what he was really going to miss was her ability to anticipate his needs.

The afternoon passed by in a blur and the next time he looked at his watch it was after five. Time to go home and prepare Rachel for their meeting with John Robinson. It wasn't going to be easy. She was sure to give him that awful betrayed look and then cry. She just wouldn't understand that they had no choice. He threw some papers into his briefcase, grabbed his jacket off the back of the chair, and headed for the car. As he was going out the door, Charlotte came running after him.

"Mr. Stark, Mr. Stark, wait! Your sister-in-law is on the phone and she says it's an emergency."

Time stopped. Stephen didn't even dare breathe as he turned back to face her. David. They'd found David. Alive? Dead? What? He felt his knees grow weak and threaten to buckle as a giant hand seized his guts and squeezed. He clung to the door frame for support, sweat springing out all over his body. He stared down the endless room toward the phone, panting as he took step after stumbling step back toward Charlotte's desk. The adrenaline rush of dread sent the pounding blood through his head and created a choking sensation in his throat as David's high-pitched voice echoed in his ears, "Daddy. Daddy." Was this the call that they'd been dreading? When he got there, would Miranda tell him it was over? That David was dead? That his poor little boy had been found?

He took the phone from a staring Charlotte and uttered a faint "Hello?"

"I'm afraid it's hit the fan this time, Stevie," his sister-in-law said. "You'd better get home pronto."

With a fury born of fear he roared, "Goddammit, Miranda, don't play games with me! What's happened? Did they find him? Is he dead?"

"No! This isn't about David. I told your stupid bimbo secretary that. . . ."

"Then what the hell is the emergency?" he yelled, not giving her time to finish.

"Calm down, Stevie," Miranda said, sounding uncertain. "It's the sperm bank. They sent another one of those damned letters because you didn't respond to the first. And this time, Rachel opened it."

When sorrows come, they come not single spies,
But in battalions.

—SHAKESPEARE, *Hamlet*

CHAPTER NINE

Over coffee, Rachel and Gallagher found themselves relaxing, or at least coming closer to relaxing than they'd ever come before. To preserve the détente, she tried not to think about the stuff that stood between them—his cruelty, her stupidity. They sat on stools on either side of the broad granite island. Rachel perched delicately on hers, the toes of her bare feet clinging to the crosspiece. Gallagher dwarfed his as he leaned toward her eagerly, trying to make something more of their meager clue.

Rachel tried not to let herself feel hopeful, but she had waited so long for hope that she rose to the meager bait like a trout to a fly. "What about people?" she asked. "Who was in the van? How many? And what kind was it? Ford, Chevy, Dodge, Chrysler, Toyota, Nissan?"

Gallagher shook his head. "Who knows? I said Mrs. Gardiner was a complainer. I didn't say she was observant."

"But you did ask her, didn't you?" Rachel couldn't keep the eagerness out of her voice. "She must have noticed something. . . ."

"I'm sorry," he said. "I asked the question a hundred different

ways. The bottom line is that she wouldn't have noticed anything at all if it hadn't been for the littering. . . ."

"You'd think, in her zeal to catch litterers, that she would have written down the license number," Rachel said. It was absurd, given the smallness and probably the uselessness of the information Gallagher had brought, to be so excited, but she was. She lowered her eyes to her cup, wanting to tell Gallagher about her feeling yesterday that David was alive. Was there any chance he'd believe her, that he wouldn't shut down, abruptly end this hopeful détente, and return to his certainty that she was a crank?

She looked up at his face, trying to decide what to do. He was handsome in a hard, ultra-masculine way, the nose aggressive, a little too thin, the mouth a narrow, sharply defined line, the cheekbones jutting under the pale skin, the jawline blunt and belligerent, ending in a slightly clefted chin. The greenish eyes were glittering and dangerous. Not a welcoming face, but one that might be reassuring if you were in trouble and he was on your side. Rachel still didn't know if he was on her side. There was a gentleness about his confession of embarrassment, about the way he'd felt challenged to prove himself to her, that made her wonder. But Rachel, the receiver of many disappointments, never let herself hope too much, except about finding David.

She noticed that his cup was empty. "More coffee?"

He shook his head. "I drink too much of the stuff. It's good, though. You wouldn't believe the stuff some people serve. They must make a pound last at least a year. You could read through it."

Oh, she'd believe it, all right. Rachel liked her coffee with some kick. "I could make us some sandwiches or something. Are you hungry?" It was hours since she'd thrown up her breakfast, though she didn't feel the least bit hungry, but she believed—had learned at her mother's knee—that men must be fed early and often.

He shook his head again. "Had lunch before I came." He checked his watch. "I've got to go. I'll keep you posted, let you know if anything else turns up." He winced at the awkwardness of his own words.

"Now that you know about the van, maybe you can find more witnesses," she suggested.

He shrugged. "Maybe." She wanted to reach out and shake him. Why couldn't he be more hopeful?

Rachel didn't want him to go. She somehow felt that if he stayed, if they could have a civilized talk instead of an antagonistic one, they might be able to discover something useful, something important, in their common body of information. Her hand crept out toward him but she willed it down into her lap, forced back the words "Don't go" before they could escape, lowered her lids over the pleading in her eyes. The world already thought she was unstable and nutty. Much as she wanted to share her intuition, she didn't think Gallagher was ready to hear it. She slid off the stool, her bare toes curling as they hit the cold terra-cotta tiles.

"Thanks for coming." She walked him to the door, her lowered eyes focused on his freshly shined shoes. As she was closing the door behind him, impulse overcame her. "He's alive," she said.

Gallagher whirled to face her so swiftly, it was frightening, and took a step toward her. "Have you heard from him?" he demanded. "Is there something you aren't telling me? Has someone contacted you?"

Rachel stared back, her own eyes raised to meet his. If she was going to make a fool of herself, she might as well not hold back. "Only the kind of thing you wouldn't believe in," she said. "The kind of thing most people don't believe in. Only a mother's intuition. I could feel him. His voice." She touched her head. "In here. His voice was very far away and faint. I asked him if he was alive and he said yes. And then he wanted to know if I was. But I lost him before I got a chance to answer."

He took another step toward her, his looming body filling the doorway. "What are you talking about?" he demanded. "ESP? Mental telepathy? Some sort of psychic communication?"

"You don't believe me," Rachel said. "I knew you wouldn't. Please. Forget I ever . . ." He scared her suddenly, with his loud voice and angry face. He was too close and too intense. She wanted to turn and run away, run to her workroom, shut the door, and lock it behind her. "Please," she said, taking a step backward as he stood there, bristling with an anger she didn't understand. "Please. You

frighten me. Go away. Go find someone else who saw that van. Go find David." She couldn't talk to him about this. She turned and hurried away from him. Toward her workroom. Where she felt safe. He could let himself out.

It was strange, really, how they all perceived it. Stephen was absolutely frank in his opinion of Rachel's ability to communicate with David. He considered it total bullshit. Ridiculous hokum. Miranda smiled at her and nodded when she spoke of it, like an adult humoring a child. Rachel herself was surprised and intimidated by it. Only David was unsurprised. To him, it seemed perfectly natural that a mother and son could each know what the other was thinking without speech. He was only surprised that other families couldn't do it. He didn't find it odd that he might be doing something with fish at school and come home to find Rachel doodling identical fish at her worktable. Or that when he would wake up in the night, Rachel would be there before he could call for her, or that if he was afraid, she would get a choking sensation in her throat. It wasn't big stuff. She couldn't read his mind, though sometimes she saw his pictures. They didn't regularly communicate across the miles. She didn't beam him the answers to tests and he couldn't remotely read the cards in her hand. It was just something that happened between them sometimes. Often enough to be more than coincidence and not much more than that. Often enough to disconcert her and delight David.

She'd always had a touch of it, especially when she was younger and would let it happen instead of forcing herself to be rational, as she did now. But it wasn't the crazy stuff of psychics. She didn't commune with the dead or imagine she could solve murders. She just occasionally had an unusual sensitivity to the people she was close to. Once or twice it had even happened with Stephen, but it scared the heck out of him, so now, if it happened, she'd never tell him. It probably wouldn't happen, though. The gulf between them these days was too great. He no longer jumped away from her physically, as he'd once done, but mentally he dashed away whenever she got too close.

The sound of scuffling feet and a muffled curse behind her told

her that Gallagher was following, that he'd tripped on one of their uneven doorsills. It was a house that took some getting used to. "Come on. Slow down, will you? Relax. I'm not some kind of an ogre," Gallagher complained. Ignoring him, Rachel continued her flight. Hurrying into her workroom, she dashed behind the table, seated herself on her stool, folded her arms, waiting in her sanctuary. Gallagher came in and stopped, surprised, staring around at the drawings on all the walls, at the blown-up sections of text, at the multicolored array of markers and pencils. He'd been in here before but seemed to be seeing it for the first time. His scrutiny ended at the picture of David at bat.

"Cedric Carville?" he asked.

Rachel nodded. "The boy who wanted to be the greatest baseball player of all time. David wanted us to do a book together. He was writing the text and I was doing the pictures. We did that one the day before . . . the day before he disappeared." Tears choked her, though she fought them fiercely.

"It's all right to cry, you know," Gallagher said, holding out his handkerchief.

"Don't be nice to me," she said. "It only makes things worse."

"How can being nice make things worse?" he asked.

She answered his question with a question. "Does this mean you've stopped assuming that we—Stephen and I—did something to David?"

"I never assumed . . ."

"I wasn't born yesterday, Detective," Rachel snapped. "I may be naive and trusting but I'm not an idiot. I can tell when someone doesn't believe what I'm saying."

"Tell me about you and David. About the communication," he ordered, ignoring what she'd said.

"It's nothing," she said, staring down at the drawing of Emily in the toy shop. The little girl was adorable. Rachel had often wished she had a daughter, but after what they'd gone through with Jonah and David, more children were out of the question.

"Are you saying that because you believe it's nothing, or because you don't expect me to believe you?"

"Because I don't expect you to believe me. I'm not sure I'd trust you anymore if you did believe me. . . . It's not how cops are supposed to act."

"People have a lot of funny notions about how cops are supposed to act," Gallagher said. "But you believe?" She nodded. "And you trust me?"

She hesitated, not wanting to offend him, but she had never been able to keep from telling the truth. "I don't know. I don't like you. I think you're mean . . . deliberately, unnecessarily cruel . . . but I think you're honest."

"Ouch! That hurts." Gallagher sat down in the only other chair in the room, a tall, roomy wing chair she sometimes sat in when she was reading the stories she illustrated. It was also where David sat when he wanted her company. He'd been trained not to bother her while she was working, but they often sat quite companionably, Rachel drawing and David reading, for hours at a time. It was only in the car that he got wiggly.

"Ouch!" Gallagher frowned, plunged his hands down beside the cushion, and pulled out a small pewter dragon, holding it out toward her on his palm. "It attacked me."

"Megrim," Rachel said, reaching for it. "We thought he was lost forever." Gallagher dropped the little dragon into her palm and she closed her fingers around it. She believed in signs and omens even less than she believed in ESP, but she couldn't help thinking about how they'd come to buy Megrim. It was after David had come with her to the cemetery once, to visit Jonah's grave. Rachel didn't usually take him, but on this occasion, he'd insisted, and she hadn't the will to argue. Coming back, David had been worried about Jonah and death and how sad she was, and Rachel had jokingly suggested they get him a guardian angel. David had responded that he wasn't sure he believed in angels, but he did believe in dragons, so why didn't they get a guardian dragon. The next time they were at the mall, they'd bought Megrim at one of the little stands.

"Tell me about the day you did the Cedric Carville picture," Gallagher said. "What did you talk about?"

Rachel thought it was a funny question, but she answered it

anyway. Gallagher was so strange today. "We went down to the playground at the school. In the afternoon, after he got home. He'd just gotten the uniform. It's his Little League uniform. He couldn't wait to try it on." She reached down and brought up a portfolio that was leaning against the edge of the table, pulled out some other drawings, and laid them out facing Gallagher. "David and his best friend, Tommy. They were so cute. So grown-up and so silly. You've talked to Tommy, haven't you? Poor kid. He thinks it's all his fault because he was supposed to ride with David that day and he forgot and went on the bus in the morning."

She let her mind drift back to the playground, to the easy pleasure of sitting on the bench beside the ball field, the sun warm on her back, sketching and watching the two boys gamboling like lambs around the diamond. She heard their boyish banter, their high laughs, heard the scrunch of dirt kicked up by their cleats. Heard David's voice, suddenly serious, asking her, "Mom, why would someone sit by the road and watch kids on the playground through binoculars?" Heard her own stupid reply, "Maybe they were talent scouts, looking for Cedric Carville. Were they in a big black limo?" David had replied, "No, just a van," and then he was off again, throwing the ball an incredibly long distance across the field to Tommy.

"My God!" she said. "Oh, Gallagher . . . David mentioned a van . . . the day before he disappeared . . . and I didn't pay any attention."

"Tell me about it. The whole conversation. Don't leave anything out," Gallagher ordered.

Rachel told him everything she could remember, but it wasn't much. "Maybe Tommy was with him on the playground. Maybe he noticed something, or one of the teachers. Even if, like me, they didn't think anything of it, they might have noticed the license plate or the color or make of the van, or who was in it."

Gallagher was making some notes on a pad. He looked up at her and nodded. "Tell me everything you can remember about your communication with David," he said.

Rachel tried to remember. She closed her eyes and imagined herself back in the dirty brown island, surrounded by broken glass. She saw herself pulling the glass shard out of her hand, watched the

blood welling out, tried to open her mind again and get back the image of David speaking. Had she seen anything or only heard his voice? She tried as hard as she could, a concentration of breath and force and labor that reminded her of childbirth, but she couldn't get the moment back. She opened her eyes. "Sorry," she said. "I can't get it back. The only thing I can tell you is that wherever he is, spring isn't as far advanced as it is here. The trees have only tiny buds."

She rubbed her forehead wearily and thought about how good it would feel to lie down. She'd never had a lot of energy and lately she seemed to have even less. "It's like we're doing one of those jigsaw puzzles where all the pieces are the same color. We can only fit things in when the shape seems right. It's such a big puzzle and we have so few pieces. . . ."

"We have more pieces than we had yesterday," Gallagher said.

From the other end of the house came the muffled sound of the doorbell. "Excuse me," Rachel said. "I have no idea who that could be. I'm not expecting anyone except Miranda, and she doesn't need to ring the bell. The door's not locked. Stephen always locks it. He's the security freak. I think a locked door is unfriendly. Besides, I'd always be locking myself out." She tapped her temple. "Scatterbrained, you see." She got up and made her way through the dark, quiet house with Gallagher trailing behind her.

Bill Pottle, the mailman, was waiting impatiently on the step, shifting restlessly from one foot to the other. The story in town was that Bill was so impatient, he'd been six weeks premature because he just couldn't wait any longer. "I'd about given up on you," he said, tearing a card off the letter he was holding. "Another minute and you'd have had to come down to the post office for this." He held out the card and pointed at an *X*. "You sign right there. Doesn't say where it's from, just a street number and city there in the corner, but it's probably important since they want proof that you got it." He handed her the envelope and strode rapidly away.

Rachel held the envelope gingerly in her hands. "You don't suppose it could be a ransom demand after all this time, do you?"

Gallagher shook his head. "They don't usually send them registered mail. Aren't you going to open it?"

"Should I?"

"Why not?"

As it turned out, there were a million reasons why not, but Rachel didn't know that. Under Gallagher's watchful eyes, she tore the envelope open, removed the letter, and started to read. And Gallagher's watchful eyes saw her eyes widen and fill with tears and her pale skin turn gray as paste. Saw the letter fall from her limp fingers, float to the floor, and drift across the tile to come to rest beneath the radiator. Saw her straight, slim body begin to sway, lose its balance, so that she would have fallen if he hadn't put an arm around her and pulled her limp, stunned body against him.

At that moment, the door banged open and Miranda strode in, eyes shining, about to report her latest real estate coup to her sister, and found them. "Detective Gallagher," she said, "what on earth is going on here? What's happened to my sister?"

"She had a letter . . . that one there on the floor . . . that's upset her," Gallagher said. He took Rachel by both shoulders, turned her, and propelled her into Miranda's arms. "Take her upstairs and put her to bed."

Rachel stood unmoving in Miranda's embrace, unwilling to be led anywhere. She watched helplessly as he bent and picked up the letter, reading the dreadful news that she had just received. The last thing on earth that she wanted anyone else to see. She held out her hand and asked for it back, her voice, even to her, feeble and unassertive.

"Miranda," she said, "Stephen will kill me. Make him give it back!" But Miranda was too wrapped up in her perceived job of soothing her sister to listen, let alone act. Rachel was buffeted by a riptide of confusion, coming at her from all sides—fear of Stephen's reaction, fury at the pabulum Miranda was ladling out, shock at what she'd read. She tried to shake Miranda off and couldn't. "Gallagher," she said.

Gallagher ignored her, turning away from her pleading face. The letter, from the Center for Human Fertility, referring to their

failure to respond to an earlier letter, once again informed Mr. Stephen Stark and Mrs. Rachel Stark that the donor of sperm that had been used in several artificial insemination procedures with Mrs. Stark had tested positive for the AIDS virus. That the sperm had been donated and/or the procedures, or some of them, had been performed prior to the clinic's adoption of a program to test donors, and that although the risk was slight, Mr. and Mrs. Stark were advised to have themselves and their child tested.

"Dammit, Miranda, let me go!" she said, finally breaking free and surging toward Gallagher. "Give me that letter. This is not your business!"

Gallagher turned to face her, holding the letter out of her reach, like a bigger child taunting a smaller one. "I'm sorry about this, Rachel," he said, "for your sake. But I think it is my business. Why didn't you tell me about this?"

"How could I tell you?" she said, stunned at the question, "when I didn't know myself?"

"Not about the letter," he said angrily. "I mean why didn't you tell me or any of the police involved in this investigation the facts about David's parentage? Maybe it won't matter, but it's an important fact, and we have to start with all the facts, even secret or embarrassing ones. Don't you understand that?"

"I don't see how . . ." But she couldn't continue. She felt the strength of his anger like physical blows, as though the letter had knocked her off her feet and now he was standing there kicking her. She wanted to curl up in a little ball to protect herself. She might as well have been stripped naked, having these most intimate, devastating revelations shared publicly with Miranda and Gallagher like this. And Stephen was going to be furious.

For the first time in her life, she thought she was going to faint, standing there before his angry face and Miranda's prattling concern, a million accusations against herself roaring in her head. She'd lost both her children. Now had she killed them all? She couldn't think with the two of them staring at her, talking at her. "Excuse me!" she said, pushing past Gallagher and opening the door.

"Rachel, wait!" Gallagher said.

She hesitated for a moment in the doorway, wanting to explain, to excuse herself, but there weren't enough words in the world and she couldn't stay any longer before their pitying, accusing eyes. She turned and ran.

Miranda rushed after her, calling, "Rachel, wait! I'll call Stephen," but she ran on, her privacy, her dignity, and her hope hanging around her in shreds.

Grief fills the room up of my absent child,
Lies in his bed, walks up and down with me . . .
—SHAKESPEARE, *King John*

CHAPTER TEN

Ignoring the sticks and stones and brambles that stabbed her feet and tore at her ankles, Rachel ran. She ran breathless and panting along the path through the woods that led away from Gallagher's angry astonishment and Miranda's exasperated caring, bringing her finally to the back gate of the cemetery. She raised the catch and pushed open the rusting black iron, planning to take the path to Jonah's quiet corner, where she could sit, away from all their pressing expectations, and think calmly about the contents of the letter.

Not that running away would do her any good. Sooner or later they would find her, drag her home, and lecture her about the folly of running around barefoot and without a coat. She hoped that first they would take the time to hold a council, which they couldn't hold without Stephen, and that ought to guarantee her some time alone. Miranda didn't like to act without consulting Stephen. Although they were sisters and had known each other all their lives, Miranda was sometimes as bad as Stephen, treating her like she was fragile, unpredictable, and unstable, though Rachel didn't think she was any of those things.

Gallagher wouldn't know what to do, though from what she knew of him, she expected he'd be seething because they hadn't told him the true circumstances of David's birth. And Stephen would be in a rage both because Gallagher now knew one of his most private secrets and because he thought he'd protected her from the contents of the letter and the bastards had gotten to her anyway. She was sure Stephen had received the first letter. All that anger. All that testosterone. All that seething emotion. She couldn't think, couldn't process, in its presence.

She didn't go through the gate. Instead, she stood there, holding one post, the rusting black paint flaking beneath her fingers, and caught her breath. She went to the cemetery not because she was a grief-racked lunatic but because it was an undisturbed place where she could be alone with her thoughts. She didn't have to go there. She could go sit in her car, but they'd quickly find her there and start trying to "deal" with her. She wasn't ready to be dealt with, to be fussed over and griped at. She wanted to be left alone.

More slowly than she'd come, she turned and retraced her steps to the house, slipping quietly in the back way, going into her workroom and shutting the door behind her. She climbed onto her stool, closed her eyes, and let the feelings come.

A day that had seemed to finally be bringing her some good news had just nailed her with a sledgehammer full of grief. It never stopped, did it? She shook her head, thinking how this latest dilemma had come to be. Because of Jonah. Jonah, with his precious little button nose and huge, spontaneous smile. Smiling even as the illness was wasting his little body. Smiling until he no longer could. Until his body betrayed the proud little spirit and he faded away. Breathed his last breath in her arms. Beginning and ending with her. Leaving her stunned with sorrow.

And now the letter. She felt like something had exploded inside of her and her body was being invaded by sharp, piercing bits that stabbed in dozens of places. This was all her fault. She was a wicked, selfish person. Having known the pure joy of having a child, she had to have another. Stephen hadn't wanted to. He wouldn't father another, of course, because of the disease that killed Jonah, even though

the doctors had said they might have a healthy child, and he didn't want to adopt. He didn't want a child that wasn't his and he couldn't have a child that was his. He said they could live without children.

Maybe Stephen could have, though his love for David made her doubt it, but she couldn't. She'd tried to let go, go on, get on, resume a normal life, but the inside of her head was a giant bulletin board, plastered with pictures of children. Every day, going out into the world where it seemed like everyone had a baby, she walked the walk and talked the talk of a normal person and died a thousand tiny agonizing deaths.

In the end, she had had her way. Everyone, Stephen, Miranda, her mother, even her friend Carole, said that for someone so meek and passive, she sure was good at getting her way. It took a lot of talking—no, nagging, begging, pleading, and tears—to get him to agree to artificial insemination, where it would look like they were having another child and no one would know it wasn't his. Now it looked like through her stubbornness she might have killed them all. She wouldn't know until she had the test, of course, and Stephen would have to be tested. And David, when they found him. Could fate be so cruel as to strike them all down for her willfulness?

Rachel opened her eyes and gazed down at the clenched fists in her lap. There was a blue pencil in her hand. She had automatically picked it up when she sat down. She bowed her head, bent under the weight of life's irony. It would be the ultimate in cruelty if they should find David again and then lose him to a terrible disease. Was it some fatal attraction she had, that having married a man who carried a genetic defect, she should then seek out a sperm donor with excellent credentials as to health, heredity, intelligence, and education, who carried a lethal virus? Maybe she should have died with Jonah, be down there under the cool earth where she couldn't cause any more trouble.

Absently, she pushed back the hair that had straggled across her face, unwittingly leaving a blue streak on her cheek. Could she have seen herself, sitting with hands in her lap, lower lip thrust out, red-eyed and disheveled and looking about twelve years old, she would have been touched. But all Rachel could see was the folly that her

stubbornness had sown. That having lost one beloved child, she might now have harmed them all, when all she'd ever wanted was to be a mother. She would have given her own life to save Jonah, if it would have helped. She would do the same for David. Her gentle, sensitive, methodical, dark-eyed David. Her storyteller. Stephen's baseball player. Their son. The word "son" shimmered in her brain. Her sons, from their first moments, infinitely tiny, had embedded themselves in her soul.

She moved the day's drawings aside so her tears wouldn't smudge them. She mustn't lose sight of the fact that there had been some good news, even if some of it had been only in her head. Just the faintest little faraway voice, but it meant she knew he was okay. And she and Gallagher finally had some clues. A silver van and a smelly red sneaker.

Jonah had never had smelly sneakers. He hadn't lived long enough to walk. But she still had a pair of tiny blue sneakers that he'd worn, tucked away in the back of her closet.

Absently, she doodled with her pencil on a blank sheet of paper, wondering how much time she had before they came and made her leave this room and act civilized and as though life hadn't just delivered another enormous gut punch. As though life hadn't found another dramatic way to tell her what a failure she was. People couldn't stand it—the hurt in her eyes, the way sadness pulled her skin tight against her bones and made her lips tremble. Maybe she was too graphic a reminder of everyone's sorrow. Maybe that's why people were always at her to "snap out of it," as though feelings turned on and off like a lamp.

They'd be at her to wash her face and eat something and have a drink and have some tea and put on socks and someone would hand her a sweater and then they'd sit and stare at her sadly until she wanted to scream. Miranda and Stephen. Her mother and father. Stephen's mother. Even her good friend Carole, from the village, they all fretted over her, refused to listen when she explained that she wasn't depressed, she was just quiet, that she wasn't suicidal, she was just sad, and that she wasn't losing touch with reality, she was just living inside her head instead of spewing it all out the way other peo-

ple did. She didn't want a drink or a Valium or some Prozac. She wanted to feel what she felt. Society might be too busy or want to put a neater gloss on it, but it was normal, in her book, to be sad if you lost your much-loved children.

She thought about the clinic in Chicago, where she'd gone to get inseminated, and shivered. A horrible, depersonalizing place. She wondered about her donor, the man who was now dying. If David's father—no, that was just not the right word—a father was someone like Stephen, someone who loved his kids and cared for them, not someone who ejaculated into a bottle and sold it. Not someone who gave his sperm away as a humanitarian gesture, never expecting or wanting to know the children he'd produced. Her own venom amazed her. Was it unfair? If there weren't donors, people like her couldn't have children. If David's donor knew that he had AIDS, knew that he was going to die, then he must be as sad as she was. She wondered what he was like.

She sat and hugged her body and tried to pull herself together. The news in the letter had left her feeling shattered, as though pieces of herself were scattered around inside her skin, the rough edges rubbing against each other when she moved. Though she loved her independence, the freedom to do her work, her family was the center of her life. It was her life. The idea that she might have destroyed it in creating it was too awful to consider. A flurry of emotions, foremost among them anger at herself, at the sperm bank, and at David's father, rushed through her.

She wanted to find the man and shake him and yell into his face, "How could you do this to us? How could you be so careless? How could you not know you were infected?" The man she imagined was featureless except for David's eyes, the eyes that were so distinct and so clearly not her own, and those eyes stared back at her in dismay as she vented her wrath.

But what if he was as innocent as they were? What if he had no reason to suspect? What if the poor man got it from a blood transfusion, or he accidentally got stuck with a needle? He was a doctor. They knew that much. And really, when you came right down to it, what did it matter how he got AIDS? Maybe he got it from someone

he loved very much and didn't even know about it until recently. No matter how he got it, it was going to kill him. And no matter how he got it, no one was thinking too carefully back then about the fact that along with their donated sperm, donors might be sharing their HIV status, were they? It was just a few months later—months, that was like minutes, no, seconds, in the great scheme of things— that they started testing donors. And then how likely was it that they went back and tested existing stock?

She raised her fists heavenward, shook them, and dropped them back down to her sides. "The gods must hate me. Why else would life keep hurting me and my children?"

Rachel thought of the story of Job. She identified with Job, in all his trials and tribulations, though she lacked Job's faith. If God was testing her, then he would find her wanting. She didn't want to place herself in His hands. What had she done that was so bad she deserved to lose both her children? Blasphemous though it might be, she wanted to be mistress of her own destiny. She wanted to loom up like a giant and move everything on heaven and earth until she found her child. Thinking about it, she felt anger coursing through her, as though her heart were pumping not blood but sheer liquid rage. If she ever found the person or persons who had done this, she'd pull them apart with her bare hands.

But what good did it do to get angry? Her children had been afraid of anger, Jonah especially. When people around him raised their voices, he shivered and cried. David just lowered his lovely dark eyes—those stranger's eyes—and turned away. David. Her beautiful David. The people who took him were watching him. Sitting outside the school with binoculars. It was an odd thing because it was so creepy, but it gave her hope, because whoever took him, it wasn't some random snatching. They didn't want just any kid. They wanted David. The tail of her shirt had come untucked and she twisted it nervously in her hands. She wished she knew why they wanted him. Maybe it would help to get him back.

She heard the clatter of someone coming down the hall. She closed her eyes and listened, trying to identify the person by their footsteps. Light, not heavy, and therefore probably a woman, but slow and steady, not Miranda's perpetual eager rush. She listened

harder. One foot hit the ground harder than the other, and now she could also hear the panting of someone out of breath, so it wasn't Carole, who was the fittest person she knew. "Hello, Mom," she said without turning, "Isn't this a lovely day."

"I'd have enjoyed it more if I hadn't just tramped all over hell and gone, including out to that wretched cemetery, looking for you," her mother said. "Good heavens, you should see yourself, Rachel. You look like a lunatic!" Her mother ended on a note of complaint, as she always did. Rachel's mother had been put on the earth to lament, and as time passed and she grew older, she did more of it, as if she had a quota to meet before she died and she'd fallen way behind. At first glance, she didn't look unhappy. She was a tall, slender woman, well-preserved, beautifully dressed, with thick, well-cut silver hair and young-looking skin. But closer inspection revealed the lines of discontent in her face, long, deep brackets from the edges of her nostrils, past the downturned corners of her mouth, and on down toward her chin.

"Did they call you or did you just happen to stop by?" Rachel asked.

Her mother shrugged. "I stopped by to see if one or both of my daughters might want to have dinner with me—your father has some boring dinner meeting tonight—and found Stephen having a hissy fit over something that awful policeman said and Miranda sulking in the kitchen over something Stephen had said to her. I asked where you were and she said you'd run off to the cemetery again and that it wasn't her turn to go and get you." She ran a distracted hand, gleaming with jewels, through the shock of silver hair that had fallen over her eye. "I've got to get this stuff cut. I look like a hay mound."

"You couldn't look like a hay mound if you tried," Rachel said, getting up and wiping her hands down the sides of her jeans. "Anyway, I think you mean haystack."

"Mound, stack, what's the difference?" Her mother stared with distaste at Rachel's dirty face. "You're covered with blue streaks. You certainly didn't learn that from me."

"No," Rachel agreed, shaking her head. "You did your best with me, but then my true nature came out. By nature I am solitary, grungy, and peculiar."

Irene Filipovsky rolled her eyes and shook her head. "Well, I certainly didn't bring you up to sit around graveyards talking to dead babies."

"This isn't a graveyard and I wasn't talking to anyone. I was just thinking." She looked down at the paper, at what she'd drawn. Jonah's little face, staring out of his crib like a prisoner through bars. David's eyes. Rows and rows of them. Her mother glanced down and clucked with disapproval.

"Like I said. It's my true nature. Peculiar," Rachel said. "Did they tell you what's going on?"

"Who?"

"My sister and my husband."

Her mother gave her a queer look. It matched other queer looks she'd been getting lately when she mentioned Stephen and Miranda in the same breath. There was a rolling sensation as the tumblers in her brain, like the workings of a combination lock, fell into place, and a door she'd been trying to keep shut opened, giving her a glimpse of the knowledge she didn't want. What the hell. If everything else in her life was falling apart, going awry, breaking down, why not this as well? She wasn't naive and she hadn't been born yesterday. She knew that Stephen's sexual needs were greater than hers and that he felt entitled to satisfy them.

"So you know about them?" Rachel said.

Her mother was suddenly staring out the window, very interested in the trees. "We're having an awfully late spring this year, aren't we?"

She should have known better. Even as a tiny child, Rachel couldn't be dissuaded when she wanted an answer to a question. "Did you know about them?" she asked again.

"About . . . ?"

"Stephen and Miranda."

"I don't know anything about Stephen and Miranda."

"Stephen is my husband and Miranda is my sister, who is currently living with us. Your other daughter. The two of them like to screw in the kitchen when they think I'm upstairs in a catatonic state."

"I can't believe you said that!"

"Said what? Catatonic? Or screw? It's true, isn't it? If there had been any doubt in my mind, your reaction dispelled it."

"I didn't say anything," her mother insisted. "Now come along. Everyone is in the kitchen waiting for you. They're worried."

"I'm not surprised," Rachel said.

Her mother gave her one of those arching maternal looks, the kind that are supposed to quell rebellion and shut children's mouths. Rachel, climbing off her stool, was suddenly tired, almost too tired to move her shuffling feet. She lost interest in trying to get her mother to acknowledge the affair and started looking out at the trees herself. If she was HIV positive, how many more springs might she have? Was that why she'd been feeling so sick and exhausted lately? And if David never came back, would she even care?

"So they didn't tell you about the letter?" she said.

"Letter?" her mother said with a sharp intake of breath. "Has there been a ransom note, then?"

Rachel shook her head. "No, no, nothing like that, but we've had a letter from the sperm bank. About David's father . . . uh . . . donor."

"He doesn't want some sort of contact with the child!" her mother burst out, horrified.

"He has AIDS."

"How odd that they should write and tell you that. Did they expect you'd care? What were you supposed to do, take David and go running to his bedside or something?" Her mother was working up a pretty good dudgeon at the imagined outrage.

"It's not that, Mother. The virus is transmitted through sexual contact, as you know—"

"But good gracious, Rachel," her mother interrupted. "You never had sex with the man."

"No. But I did receive his semen, his sperm. And that's where the virus is."

Her mother stopped, hand on the doorknob, and turned to stare at her. "Rachel, you aren't telling me that you've got . . . no, of course not, you couldn't have . . . couldn't be . . . and if you are . . .

then Stephen . . . and David . . . No! Certainly not. It's much too aw-ful to even think about."

"Then don't think about it," Rachel said grimly. "Think about the late spring we're having or how the deer have eaten all the buds off the rhododendrons. Because I could be HIV-positive, and so could Stephen and David. It's not likely. That's what the letter says. That it's not likely but that it has happened before, in the litera-ture." She broke off and made a face. "What am I saying? In the lit-erature? It hasn't happened to books; it's happened to actual human beings who wanted to have children and tried artificial insemina-tion. I feel like that Al Capp character, Joe what's-his-name, the one with his own personal cloud over his head."

"It's not that bad," her mother said stupidly. Her mother was al-ways saying things that didn't make any sense. When she wasn't com-plaining, or nagging at Rachel's father, she was often idiotic. Her problem was that she saw the world through the lens of her own ex-perience, and she didn't have any experience. Anything she didn't understand, she dismissed. "Now come along. You go upstairs and get yourself some socks and I'll make you a nice cup of tea while you wash your face."

Rachel waited a minute for her mother to also offer the sweater and a sandwich, but those would have to come from someone else. Rachel winced as she walked toward the door, realizing how sore and bruised her feet were. It was dumb to have run out without shoes. Her mother, walking beside her, talked steadily. Rachel didn't listen but knew it was local gossip, scandals, how she'd been cheated at the market, how insufferable the bank tellers were these days, how lazy the man who did her gardens had become, and how her father grew more useless and absentminded every day.

Rachel let the sounds wash over her, background noise, like waves on a beach. Something that her mother had said, in one of her babbling comments, was nagging at her brain. Oh yes. Her mother had said, "What did they expect you to do, take David and go run-ning to his bedside or something?"

No. Of course not. No one had expected that. The sperm bank had been very secretive. Rachel and Stephen had known so much

about their donor, and yet so little, and nothing that might have allowed them to locate him. She assumed that confidentiality worked both ways. But suppose a man discovers that he's dying, or at least that he has an illness from which, at present, all are expected to die. Might he not want to find his child, have his child with him, grasp, through his own child, one last chance at posterity?

Wasn't it just possible that David had been taken by his biological father?

A T SCHOOL, DAVID *was beginning to make a friend. His name was Andy and he lived about a mile down the road. They were in the same grade and rode on the same bus and Andy liked to play baseball. He was even on a Little League team, like David had been. His dad was the coach and he said he'd see if maybe David could get on the team, too. As he was getting off the bus, he'd called back to David, "Maybe you could come play later. Call me." Gave his phone number and asked, "What's yours?"*

David didn't know. When he got inside, the woman was baking. She brushed her flour-covered hands against her apron as she asked, "How was your day? They teach you anything?" She came toward him, meaning to hug him, but he darted away, putting the table between them. Her face got sad, and he was sorry, but her hugs only made him miss his mother's great warm hugs that much more, and he couldn't bear so much sadness.

David told her they were learning about Indian tribes, including local ones whose territories had been shown on a map, and finally got up the courage to ask about the bedspread. "Why do you have it? I think it would be offensive to anyone who was a Native American, don't you?"

The woman—Marion—shook her head angrily. "If white people hadn't been stronger and better, they wouldn't have been able to defeat the Indians, David. Anyways, I've had that spread for a lot of years and it's a perfectly good one for a boy's room."

"Did it used to belong to your boy?" David asked.

"You ask too many questions," she said, swiping at the already clean counter with a rag. "You hungry?" David nodded. "At least you've got yourself a decent appetite. Too many kids these days are picky eaters."

David didn't tell her that he ate what she served not because he liked it—she couldn't cook like his mom—but because he was afraid of her. She wasn't the type you told things to. He was getting so full of bottled-up things, some days he thought he might burst. Some days the questions and the worries and the things he was afraid of pressed against his chest until he couldn't breathe. He always thought of her as "the woman." Once, she'd said he ought to call her something, and suggested Nana or Auntie. Without thinking, he'd said, "But you aren't my grandma or my aunt." She'd gotten that tight-lipped, hurt look and changed the subject, but he knew he'd gotten it wrong again. Nothing he did seemed to please her.

"What's our phone number?" he asked.

She looked at him with narrowed eyes and he was afraid she was going to yell at him. "Why're you asking?"

"There's a kid at school. He's on my bus. Lives just down the road . . ." He was so scared, he was stammering. "He thought we might be able to play. He gave me his number and asked for mine, and I didn't know it."

"I don't want you using the phone," she said. "You know. Because of the man. What's his number? I'll make the call."

It was strange. At home, David and Tommy had spent hours on the phone. Talking while they did their homework. Talking while they played computer games. Just talking. "I'd like to play with him," he said, and gave her the number.

Later, when she was in the bathroom, he sneaked a look at the phone, but there was no number on it. It was then that he got the idea of calling his old house to see if anyone was there.

All that most maddens and torments; all that stirs up the lees of things;
all truth with malice in it; all that cracks the sinews and cakes the brain . . .
— MELVILLE, *Moby Dick*

CHAPTER ELEVEN

All three of them were waiting in the kitchen when Rachel and her mother entered, spaced around the island like the points of an equilateral triangle, shimmers of hostility hanging in the air between them. Rachel was eager to share her new idea with all of them but forced herself through the motions of civility—greetings, expressions of concern about whether they had adequate food and drink—then excused herself to go wash her face and put on socks, noticing that when her mother joined the group the arrangement shifted to a square, still with no one willing to stand close to anyone else.

When she saw her face in the mirror, she almost laughed out loud. Ridiculous blue streaks. No wonder her family was embarrassed by her. The girl who refused to grow up. Too bad there was no female equivalent of Peter Pan. She wasn't about to identify with Wendy, a prissy little twit with a strong maternal streak. And the closest thing she could think of in the language generally was "tomboy," and that wasn't quite right, either. "Childlike" had come to mean simple and childish, to not act your age. What did that leave? Now

that she was grown up, she'd settled in her own mind for what she'd told her mother earlier—that she was peculiar. Perhaps she should have said unconventional. But wasn't she really more conventional than the rest of them? All she wanted was marriage, a family, and some fulfilling work.

Marriage. Odd how, when she'd looked at Stephen just now, he'd seemed exactly the same. She'd expected things would be different, that when she looked at him, having finally admitted to herself what she'd known for some time, he'd have horns or an expression of extreme guilt or his eyes would suddenly have become shifty. But none of that had happened. He'd still been handsome, well-built, edgy, and trying to dominate the conversation.

Impulsively, she picked up the phone and called her friend Carole, mother of David's best friend, Tommy. Though Carole was a small, sprightly redhead, she had an incredible whiskey-and-cigarettes voice, a voice that created a real dissonance between her appearance and her sound. People who'd only spoken to her by phone always walked right past her when they were supposed to meet her because they were looking for a statuesque brunette. Carole thought it was hilarious; it would have driven Rachel crazy. Maybe that was because Carole was so comfortable with who she was, and Rachel was not.

As soon as Carole had drawled her titillating "hello" into the phone, Rachel asked her question. "Did you know that Stephen and Miranda were having an affair?" Into the silence that followed, Rachel said, "Just the truth, Carole. I'm not looking for the right answer or the perfect answer."

"Yes."

"Is everyone in town going around shaking their heads and clucking their tongues and muttering 'poor Rachel' under their breaths?"

"I wouldn't say that."

"Then how did you know?"

"They try too hard not to look at each other. And the way Miranda doesn't flirt with other men when he's around. You know how she is."

"This is why I love you, Carole. Because you'll tell me the truth."

"Are you okay, Rachel?"

"I'm upright, conscious, and occasionally taking nourishment, but I don't think you could say I'm okay. Would you be, if it was Tommy who was missing?"

"I'd be screaming from a mountaintop."

"Well, that's what I've been doing. . . ."

"At the cemetery again?" Carole interrupted.

"It's not my home away from home, you know," Rachel said. "I do my screaming inside my head. I was just hiding out in my office. Not my fault they couldn't find me."

"You don't care what people think about you, do you?"

"I care," Rachel said. "That is, I'm aware of their scrutiny and disapproval. I just don't seem to be able to conform my behavior to others' expectations."

"It's not a question of ability, Rachel, it's a matter of will. You don't want to conform your behavior."

"You know me too well," Rachel said. "Listen, something's come up. A bunch of things, actually. Could you come over later?"

"What? And miss the PTG meeting and Ron's promised lecture about our taxes? I hardly think I could pass those up just because a friend who's undergoing severe personal trauma needs my company, do you?"

"Anytime you can get here. I'd hate for you to miss the taxes. I know how much Ron likes to give that lecture. The last time I gave a dinner party, he whispered about depreciation and offsetting gains and carry-forward and home office deductions in my shell-pink ear until I'm sure everyone at the table, except you, thought I was receiving the most delicious proposition of my life."

"I'll overlook a lot for a guy who's a good provider, competent in bed, and faithful," Carole said, then caught herself. "Oops, sorry about that last. I really do like Stephen, you know. All that edgy intensity is incredibly sexy. Too bad he couldn't channel it. Like they say about half the kids in this country, I guess he's got a problem with impulse control. Excuse me, I've got to go. Tommy just came through the door holding a snake. If I don't head him off, Susan will find it later in her bed, and then we'll be in for twenty-four hours of

tears and recrimination. See you in a bit." She reminded Rachel of a machine gun, bursts of rapid-fire words followed by long periods of complete silence.

"Wait! Call before you come. We might eat out. There's nothing here except vegetable purees." She put on socks, wincing as she drew them over her battered feet. Sometime soon, when she wasn't busy, she'd soak them and tend them and apologize for the abuse, but not now. She paused on her way to the stairs to grab a sweater, wishing that when she arrived downstairs, someone would have prepared some sort of a meal. She couldn't remember eating lunch; she'd been working and then got distracted by her conversation with Gallagher, and breakfast had bounced back up. No wonder she felt so light-headed and shaky.

The group had moved from the kitchen out to the terrace and seemed to be doing drinks and cheese or drinks and something. Gallagher was no longer with them. That was okay. Otherwise he and Stephen would still have been circling like wary dogs, sniffing disdainfully at each other.

"Is that food?" she asked eagerly as she came through the door.

"You're limping," Stephen said accusingly.

"Thank you," Rachel said. "A glass of white wine is exactly what I'd like. How kind of you to offer." Stephen gave her an irritated look as he went to get her drink. Rachel bent and scooped up a handful of what she thought were nuts. They tasted vaguely nutty but had the texture of dry pet food. "Miranda, what are these things?"

"Wheat nuts. Low fat, low cholesterol, high fiber . . ."

"Not to be ungrateful, but I think I liked it better when we didn't have to eat imitations of everything."

"No wonder you're always tired."

"I'm tired because I have lots on my mind. Because I don't sleep well," Rachel said. "It has nothing to do with my diet."

Miranda planted her hands on her hips and tossed her hair. "Tell me what you've eaten today."

"You know what I had for breakfast, and for lunch . . . I forget . . . I was wrapped up in a conversation with Gallagher. Something. And it's just now dinnertime. Thanks, Stephen." She took the

glass from his hand and tasted the wine. Chardonnay. A delicate green gold. A slightly sweet vanilla. "Mom, do you still want to go out somewhere?"

Her mother studied them all nervously. "Whatever the rest of you want to do. I was thinking of that new Mexican place over on the river. I've heard the food is good. . . ."

"I don't know about the rest of you, but I'm starved," Rachel said. "We could all go in the Lexus, couldn't we, Stephen? You haven't got the backseat full of your briefs or anything?"

Miranda choked on her wine, clasped a hand to her mouth, and said, through a sputtering laugh, "Can you imagine a whole seat filled with Stephen's briefs?"

"No," Rachel said, "but I expect you can. I'll get my purse. And I'd better change these jeans. It's not quite a blue jean kind of place." She left them all staring after her and went upstairs to change.

Miranda and Mrs. Filipovsky sat in the back, Stephen in the passenger seat, and Rachel drove, feeling a little dizzy from drinking on an empty stomach and trying not to show it. It was so like her mother to forget that they'd all eaten at Sol Azteca the night before David disappeared. Normally Rachel would have refused to return there because of the memories, but the wine had made her strangely bold and reckless. She felt like going there might stir her up and help her connect with David again. If Stephen knew what she was thinking, he'd jump out the window and head for home.

Unfortunately, the host recognized them, asking, as he led them to their table, "You don't have your little boy with you tonight?"

Stephen looked ready to eat the man, but Rachel said, "No. He couldn't come," and quickly ordered a pitcher of margaritas, a platter of nachos grande, and some guacamole. Stephen gave her a curious look. He wasn't used to having her take charge. Or maybe he was still puzzling over her comment about his briefs.

"I'm sorry," she responded to Miranda's mental fat counting. "I couldn't help myself. I'm starved."

"They do have salads," her sister snapped.

"And you can order one." The margaritas came in a flash. As she licked the salt off the rim of her glass, Rachel glanced around the ta-

ble. "Everyone knows about the letter, right?" Miranda and Stephen nodded vigorous assents, while her mother looked confused. "Stephen, if you could explain it to Mother. I tried earlier but I don't think I did a very good job."

Stephen launched into an explanation that involved lots of numbers, including the fact that sixty thousand to eighty thousand women try artificial insemination every year and that a total of seven women are known to have contracted the virus, all through inseminations before 1985, when testing of donors began at some clinics. He then went on to discuss issues of regulation and the woeful lack of regulation of most clinics. The fact that a person could be asymptomatic for as long as ten years, that the risk, based on the statistics provided by the clinic, was slight. And that of course tomorrow Rachel would see their doctor, be tested, and put everyone's mind at rest.

"But could David be infected, even if the two of you are not?" her mother wanted to know. Stephen said he didn't know. "And how could you be infected anyway, Stephen? You didn't have the insemination; Rachel did."

"I could only be infected if Rachel is," he said.

"Do we have to talk about this anymore?" Miranda asked. "We are here for dinner, after all. . . ."

"You're not eating sperm, for heaven's sake!" Stephen said, then flushed a deep crimson.

"Before we drop the subject, I had a thought this afternoon I'd like to discuss," Rachel said. "About the donor. David's biological father." Stephen winced at the word father. "Are all of you up-to-date on the latest developments? The sneaker?" Everyone nodded. "The van?" A table full of blank looks. "Okay, when Gallagher came today, he said he'd been going over old police logs and found an entry of a woman complaining about a child throwing a shoe out the window of a silver van. The day that David disappeared. The place where his sneaker was found. He went to talk with her, but all she could tell him was that the van had out-of-state plates."

"So what does all this have to do with some anonymous sperm donor?" Miranda asked, just as the waiter set down the plate of nachos.

"Let me finish. After he told me that, I remembered something that happened the day before the kidnapping. We were at the playground, David and Tommy and I. They were in their new Little League uniforms, running around, and I was sketching, and suddenly David asked me why anyone would sit by a school playground and watch kids through binoculars. I said something dumb about them wanting to watch birds or they liked kids, and I didn't think any more about it until today, when I realized two things: that the abduction was planned, and that it meant the person who took David wasn't just looking for any random kid but looking particularly for him. And I asked myself, 'Why?' But I didn't know why until I got the letter."

She waited for their reactions and all she saw were blank faces. "Don't you see? The man who fathered David has a fatal disease. It means he may not have long to live, though, of course, it doesn't necessarily mean that, and it means he won't have any children if he doesn't already have them. So isn't it reasonable to think that he might have reached out for his one chance at posterity . . . and taken his son?"

She studied their faces. Where she'd expected agreement and affirmation, she saw doubt and confusion. "Look," she argued, "all we have to do is get Gallagher to make the clinic tell him who the donor is, then go find him and see if he has David. What's so hard about that?"

She looked eagerly around the table, expecting to find them nodding in agreement. That wasn't what she found. Rachel had been the recipient of people's queer looks long enough to recognize when she was getting them, and right now she was getting queer looks from the three other people in the world who ought to be on her wavelength. "What's the matter with you people?" she burst out. "Don't you get it? Don't you want to find David? It's perfect, don't you think? Who else would have taken him?"

"You're shouting, Rachel," Stephen said in a warning voice. "Do you want the whole world to know our business?"

"You know I don't," she hissed back. "That's why I didn't want you bringing in that guy Robinson. If he got his people involved, we

wouldn't be able to move without stepping on one of them. And once the word got out, with David's picture on every telephone pole and milk carton in the country, whoever had him would be frightened into getting rid of him."

"Oh no!" Stephen jumped up so suddenly, he knocked his chair over with a resounding crash. Everyone in the restaurant turned and stared at them.

"What is it?" Rachel said. "What's the matter?"

"Robinson," Stephen replied, looking at his watch. "I totally forgot. I asked him to come to the house tonight. He's supposed to be there in fifteen minutes."

"Robinson!" Rachel was on her feet, too. "You called him? You invited him to our house? Stephen, I thought we'd agreed . . ."

"Rachel, you're shouting again," he said, running a distracted hand through his hair. "Look, I couldn't stand it anymore, okay? We weren't getting anywhere. It's been three weeks and the police have nothing! Maybe Robinson can change that. I'm sorry if you don't agree, but I've got to do this. You guys go ahead and eat. You can get a cab home."

"Stephen, no! Wait! Tell him you've changed your mind." Rachel felt as though a gap as wide as the Grand Canyon had opened in the floor between them. Her words, fragile as fortune cookies, hung suspended over it.

"I haven't changed my mind. And he's already gotten started. He started this afternoon." His words, like a giant's hand, crushed the fortune cookie. Rachel stared in disbelief as the fragile crumbs tumbled down into the vast rift and disappeared into darkness. She dropped into her chair and reached for her margarita.

You purchase pain with all that joy can give . . .
—P O P E, *Moral Essays*

C H A P T E R   T W E L V E

Robinson came very late. Stephen had paced the floors of the empty house, frowning at dust in the corners and on the baseboards, at a vase full of dead flowers, at three of Rachel's sweaters tossed carelessly over the backs of chairs. He'd fetched his briefcase from the car and tried to do some work, but hadn't been able to concentrate. Finally he'd poured himself some Scotch, hoping it might calm him down. He'd just finished it when the doorbell rang.

"I'm sorry I'm so late," Robinson said, ducking to avoid the top of the door and again to avoid the rather low chandelier. "One of our volunteers who is a computer expert had some unexpected free time, so I was working with him, trying to get some preliminary information out over the Internet." Robinson was an extremely tall, skinny man, with a thin, bony face, a reedy voice, and a prominent Adam's apple. His hands were large and gnarly, and thin wrists protruded from the sleeves of his too-short coat. Stephen couldn't help thinking that someone ought to tell the man to buy long jackets instead of regular.

"No problem," he said. "I'm grateful that you could come at all on such short notice." He directed Robinson into the study.

Robinson looked around the empty room curiously. "Your wife isn't here?"

"She's having dinner with her mother and her sister. She should be along any minute now."

Stephen hadn't been talking with John Robinson very long when he heard the taxi arrive with Rachel and Miranda and their mother. Heard the murmur of women's voices as the daughters said good night, the firm tromp of Irene's feet on the gravel, and the departure of her car. Stephen had hoped he could make Rachel see the reasonableness of what he was doing, but when she came in she stalked right past the study door and refused to pause or even glance his way when he spoke to her.

"Rachel," he called as she started up the stairs, "please join us?" She shook her head, her back firmly toward him. "Carole called," he added, "Tommy's got some stomach thing. Throwing up every fifteen minutes. She'll call you tomorrow."

"Okay," she said, and continued up the stairs.

Irritated, Stephen went back into the study. That was Rachel to a T. Expecting to be supported and understood, even expecting him to read her mind, but unwilling to reciprocate. Even as he thought it, he knew he was being unfair. Rachel hated surprises. Liked to prepare herself for things. He might have brought her around if he'd taken some time, given her some warning. But dammit, they didn't have time. They'd already let weeks—endless, precious weeks—slip through their fingers while they waited for the police. Waited for the police to do nothing. Well, Rachel's waiting and hoping had gotten them nowhere. It was time to act.

"Your wife isn't planning to join us?" Robinson asked, staring pointedly at the empty space behind Stephen.

"She's tired. Ever since this happened, she hasn't been sleeping." He watched Robinson's face. There was something in the man's eyes. Disbelief. Stephen had the uncomfortable feeling that Robinson could see right through him. It was weak, he had to admit, claiming that a woman who had the energy to go out to dinner was too tired to concern herself with searching for her son.

"Your wife doesn't approve of our involvement?" Robinson asked. The man, Stephen realized, was a lot sharper than he looked.

Stephen shook his head. "I'm afraid ever since this happened, she's
been a bit irrational. She believes the abduction was her fault because she wasn't home to meet David. Not that it would have made
any difference. He was taken before he ever reached home. She just
would have known sooner. It's only a mile to the school. . . ." There
was a curious look on Robinson's face, and Stephen wondered if, despite his carefully chosen words, the man knew that he blamed
Rachel for being so careless. He hurried on with his explanation of
her absence. "My wife doesn't want you involved in this. She thinks
that whoever took David chose him specifically. She's got a whole
theory of the case based on her damned . . ." He shut his mouth,
took a breath, and said instead, ". . . and she believes that a lot of
publicity will put David in danger."

Robinson nodded. "That risk is always there, of course," he said.
"That's why one of the things we concentrate on is letting the kidnappers know that there is a loving, devastated family waiting for the
return of their child. To humanize the situation. If your son is alive,
we want the people who've taken him to recognize him as a loved
and valued child."

"What do you mean, if?" Stephen interrupted. "If you don't
think he's still alive, why bother to do this?"

"We have to hope, don't we?" Robinson said. "Some of the children who disappear are never found. It's a fact of life. A cruel one,
but one we have to face. On the other hand, Mr. Stark, the alternative is to assume that they're all irretrievable and do nothing. I . . .
my organization . . . we don't . . . can't accept that. We believe by
putting the word out, by keeping up the pressure and the publicity,
we can help to find our missing children."

Robinson's calm statement of the possibility that David might
well be dead grated across Stephen's raw nerves like fingernails on a
blackboard. He shivered, then glanced quickly at Robinson to see if
the man had noticed. It didn't appear that he had; he was continu-
ing to talk. "As to the issue of putting David in danger, we find that
generally people believe they won't be caught. They aren't expecting
to be found out. If they took a child because they wanted a child,
why would they harm him? And then, also, one of the effects of pub-

licity is to make the kidnapper aware that he or she is being watched, which might, in fact, deter them from harming the child."

It was just what Stephen thought, what he'd tried to tell Rachel. He nodded vigorously. "I appreciate your willingness to help us. I've been going out of my mind with frustration, watching the pace of the police investigation. They've behaved throughout as though they think one of us did away with him"—Stephen couldn't bring himself to say "killed"—"and buried him in the garden. And while they're screwing around questioning us and the neighbors, valuable time and probably vital information is being lost because the word isn't out about the abduction. Who knows what someone may have seen and never known was important because they didn't know. . . ." His voice failed him. Shamed, he turned his face away. A trial lawyer who couldn't even get out a complete sentence.

"You're absolutely right, of course," Robinson said. "People who might have seen something unusual or significant three weeks ago may have forgotten it by now. The trail is cold. Still, three weeks is better than a month, or three months." He pulled out a little tape recorder and set it on the table. "I hope you don't mind. . . . It helps me to keep track of things. . . ." Stephen shook his head. "Now," Robinson continued, "I'm sure you've been over all of this with the police until you were ready to scream, but we never know what may be important. Why don't you begin by telling me generally about David, what he was like. Before I leave, of course, I'll need a recent picture, and then please tell me everything you know about the day David disappeared. . . ."

Stephen sat in the dimly lit room—his favorite room in the house, with its dark brick-red walls and comfortable deep green furniture— and talked about his son. About David's neatness. About his baseball. All the things they did together. How much alike they were. How, though he hadn't meant to say this, Rachel's spaciness sometimes drove them both crazy. He was talking about how particular David was about the arrangement of his room when Robinson interrupted.

"I notice a certain tension when you talk about your wife. Are the two of you having problems dealing with this together?"

Stephen stared at him, trying to formulate a reply. He wasn't

accustomed to being at a loss for words, but then, he wasn't used to having his mind read, either.

"It's quite common, you know, for a terrible loss like this to act as a wedge between the parents," Robinson said. "It's hard to know what do with your feelings when something like this occurs, when suddenly your whole life seems out of control. People tend to lash out at each other, since the spouse is often the only safe person they can talk to. It usually gets better, as time passes, as people get involved with us and feel like they're getting some measure of control back."

"Yes, that's it exactly," Stephen muttered around the lump in his throat, relieved he didn't have to figure out how not to tell Robinson that his wife was upset because she'd just learned she needed to get an AIDS test because they'd used artificial insemination to conceive their child. He didn't know how much Robinson would respect their privacy. He recounted the day of the abduction, beginning with Rachel's frantic phone call. It wasn't a pleasant experience. He wasn't dreamy or imaginative like Rachel, but he found himself reliving the experience vividly as he told it, complete with the growing knot of fear and anxiety in his stomach as the certainty that David had been taken became clearer with each passing hour.

"This isn't a major highway," he said, "but it still amazes me that no one saw anything. No one drove by and noticed David talking to a stranger. No one appears to have noticed the bike by the side of the road. Nothing. His disappearance is as complete as if aliens had beamed him up into a spaceship and carried him off." He realized he was using Rachel's words. "Not that I believe in any of that stuff, no matter what some Harvard professor may say."

"Well, if he was taken by aliens, it will be a first," Robinson said lightly. "And I don't know how we'd go about reaching them. So there are no witnesses? No clues? No bits of clothing? Nothing at the scene?"

"Oh, but there are," Stephen said. "I mean there weren't, at first. For the first three weeks. The only useful things we've learned have been in the past few days, and then only because we've started forcing them to do their job."

"Which are?" Robinson prompted, leaning forward curiously.

"The shoe and the gray van."

Robinson leaned back in his chair and folded his arms across his chest. "Why don't you tell me about them?"

Stephen told him about Gallagher coming with the shoe, unable to resist adding details about how he'd had to force the detective to let Rachel touch the shoe. He told about Rachel and Gallagher going to the site where the shoe had been found, and how they'd practically had to force Gallagher to cooperate. And then, reluctantly, because he thought it made Rachel look silly, he told about Cedric Carville and why the shoe was thrown out the window. "And Rachel said that while she was there, on the spot with the shoe, she suddenly knew that . . ." He hesitated, not wanting to sound foolish.

"What is it?" Robinson asked. "Something you don't want to tell me? Something about your wife?" Stephen shot him a quick look. "This isn't the time to hold things back, Mr. Stark. Especially if it's something that might help us find David. Protecting your wife's privacy has no place here. We're all on the same side, you know. We're all in this together."

Yes. Robinson was sharper than he looked. Sharper and something else. Skeptical. Or cynical. Or just too analytical. There was a touch of Gallagher about him. Something infuriating in his detachment, in his ability to require that Stephen bare his soul, expose himself and Rachel to the scrutiny of another stranger. Your child gets stolen and suddenly it's like you live in a doll house and anyone can come along anytime, lift off the top, and stare in at you. Pick you up, examine you, manipulate you, rearrange you, and then put you down and walk away, leaving you weary, worn, exposed, and vulnerable. God how he hated to be dependent on the goodwill of others! He picked up his glass and headed for the door. "I'm going to get myself another one of these. Would you like anything?"

Robinson shook his head. "Thanks, but no. Alcohol dulls my mind. I find I need all my wits about me on these cases, listening for the clues behind the words, the unimportant bits of information that turn out to be important. When you come back, you will tell me about what your wife was thinking, out there by the highway?"

"If you think it's important."

"I can't decide that until I hear what it is, can I?"

"Of course not." Stephen stalked out of the room without offering alternatives such as coffee, tea, or seltzer. In his annoyance, he poured himself too much Scotch, and then, defiantly, drank enough to bring the glass down to a discreet level.

He turned at the soft sound of footsteps in the hallway, wondering if Robinson had followed him, seen him gulping liquor. It was Miranda, a bewildered, anxious expression on her face. "We need to talk," she said.

"Not now," he snapped. "Can't you see I'm busy?"

"Later, then. But tonight," she snapped back. "Rachel knows."

"How could she know? We've been careful."

"Don't be a booby," she said. "If that's your idea of careful, I'd hate to see what you consider dangerous. We've been anything but. We've all but begged her to walk in on us. That was part of the excitement. No, I don't think she's seen anything. It's just that damned intuition of hers. The intuition you're always making fun of? I saw it in her face this morning, when I took her some coffee. She knows. Maybe . . ." Miranda tapped herself with two fingers and lifted them to her nose. "Maybe she can smell us."

"Don't be vulgar," he said. "It doesn't suit you."

"And having an affair with my sister's husband does?"

"Apparently. Okay. We'll talk. As soon as this guy leaves."

"Knock on my door," she said, tossing her hair. "I'll be doing my nails."

All the sensitivity in that family had gone to Rachel, leaving Miranda free to be utterly self-centered and narcissistic. Sometimes he wondered if she even cared about what was happening. He carried his drink back to the study, feeling overburdened and cranky. Sat down and met Robinson's expectant gaze. "It's not that big a deal," he said. "Rachel has . . . claims to have . . . some sort of psychic connection with David. I don't mean she thinks she's some kind of a psychic or anything like that. Just that sometimes they seem to communicate without speaking. Just little stuff. He'll be at school thinking about chocolate chip cookies and she'll be at home and

suddenly have to start baking. Or she'll be sitting at her desk, doodling fish—Rachel is an artist, you know. She illustrates children's
books. Anyway, David will come home with doodles of the same fish
all over his papers. It's that level of stuff. I don't know if I believe in it
or not . . ."

"It sounds like you don't," Robinson observed.

". . . but when she was out there, on the spot where the shoe was
found, she claims she heard David's voice in her head, telling her
that he was okay."

"And you didn't want to tell me about it because you're afraid I'll
think your wife is some sort of nut case?" Stephen nodded. "Do you
believe that David is alive?" Stephen nodded again. "Because of what
your wife told you?"

"No. Because it's what I have to believe." Stephen choked on the
words, felt his eyes fill with tears. Goddammit, he thought, gritting
his teeth, I am not going to sit here and cry in front of this guy.

"I guess I'm with you," Robinson said. "But the world is full of
things I don't understand. Tell me about the gray van."

Stephen told him about Rachel and the two boys at the playground, and David asking about people who wanted to watch children, and then about how Gallagher, challenged by Rachel's anger,
had gone back through old daily logs and found the reference about
the van and the shoe. "No one noticed the license plate?" Robinson
asked.

Stephen shrugged. "Gallagher says no. The only thing his witness noticed was that the plate had some sort of an animal on it."

"That certainly narrows the field," Robinson snorted.

"It's not much, is it?"

Robinson's answer surprised him. "It might be more than you
think once we get a whole country full of people thinking about a
gray van with a special license plate and matching it up with a child
who looks like David. That's the advantage of working with us . . . the
reason we get involved. The police have neither the resources nor
the time to broadcast information across the country the way we do.
Nor would it necessarily do that much good to try and find David
and a gray van by alerting police departments."

He caught Stephen's look. "Oh, yeah, they communicate with each other. And maybe with the local news media, so sometimes it gets some national press. I'm talking about something different. I'm talking saturation. An unrelenting media blitz. A few police departments may be paying attention, that's one thing, but when you've got his name and face and the story everywhere, when you've got thousands of people out there looking for something unusual . . . that's when you get results."

He rose to his feet, a gawky unfolding of skinny limbs, and stuck out his hand. "I appreciate the call and all your time. There's more we could do, but you're tired. I think we'd better quit for tonight. I hope I may come back again, if I have questions? Or call you?"

Stephen nodded. "Of course. Of course. Or call me. You have my number at work?"

This time Robinson nodded. "You were going to give me a picture?"

"Oh yes. In here. In the living room. We've got lots of them. Rachel also likes to take pictures. You can choose the one you want." Stephen really didn't want to go in there and look at David's pictures. It hurt.

Robinson's eyes were on him, and he thought, somehow, that Robinson knew that. "I'll pick one out, one that will transfer well on the fax machines." He put a hand on Stephen's shoulder. "I know how exhausting this is, believe me. I lost a child once. That's how I got involved in this."

"Did you . . . did he? She?" Stephen found he couldn't ask the question.

Robinson shook his head. "It's just like you said. She vanished so completely, she might have been taken by aliens. But I've never given up hope."

Stephen saw him to the door and walked down the long back corridor to Miranda's room. Suddenly, he was so weary he could hardly raise his hand to knock. Right now the whole affair, which initially had seemed so tantalizing and revitalizing, seemed sordid and unnecessary. He was about to knock when the phone rang. He almost didn't answer it, geared up as he was to face Miranda, but in

these circumstances, no late-night call could be ignored. It might be news. He hurried to Rachel's office, grabbed the phone, and barked a brusque hello.

"Dad? Mom? Is anyone there? Are you alive?" Unmistakably David's voice. Smaller, timider, but David. Before he could respond, there was a crash and then silence. He stood there paralyzed as the operator repeated her "if you'd like to make a call" message endlessly into his ear. There was no longer any doubt. Even as his heart was breaking, he was filled with a sudden, fierce hope. His son was alive.

In the long, sleepless watches of the night."
—LONGFELLOW, "The Cross of Snow"

CHAPTER THIRTEEN

She dreamed that a man and a woman had stolen David away from a family picnic. She was chasing them across a lake, swimming with huge, powerful strokes against the waves churned up by a rising wind. Ahead she could see the three of them in a small yellow-and-blue rubber dinghy, David leaning out toward her, arms extended, looking helpless and terrified. His fear gave power to her arms and she flew through the water, reached the side of the boat, clinging to it as it bobbed and rocked on the tossing waves, and held out her hand to David. The woman snatched him away while the man picked up an oar, reared back, and brought it crashing down toward her. She let go of the side of the boat and dove to safety, deep through the dark, bubbling water, finally surfacing, breathless, into Stephen's strong arms. He was holding her, rocking her, and his face was wet with tears.

She reached out a tentative finger, touched his cheek, and tasted the salty tear. Then she realized she was no longer dreaming. "Stephen, what's the matter? What happened? What did Robinson do?"

"It wasn't Robinson," Stephen said, his voice oddly small and shaken. "On the phone. Just now. David."

Suddenly Rachel had never been more awake. "You talked to him? To David?"

"Yes. No. I only . . . he just . . . I heard his voice. Oh, God, Rachel, he's alive!"

She reached for the phone. "We've got to call Gallagher. Maybe there's some way we can trace it."

"It was too short. There's no way they can trace it."

"I don't believe that," Rachel said. "There's got to be some way. . . ." But Stephen wasn't listening. He was sitting on the edge of the bed, his head in his hands, the picture of despair. And still talking.

"I didn't even get to say anything. He didn't get to hear my voice. Someone pulled him away from the phone. I think I heard someone say something like 'what are you doing?' and then there was a click. All he said was, 'Dad? Mom? Are you there? Are you alive?'"

"Man or woman?"

"Woman, I think. I really couldn't tell."

"Why would he ask if we're alive?"

Stephen lifted his head and stared at her, his eyes dark with pain. In the lamplight, the shadowy bedroom seemed vast and unfamiliar. Rachel felt like she'd gone to sleep in her own home and woken in some foreign place. "Why?" she repeated.

"I don't know." Stephen kneaded his forehead as though it pained him. He was still fully dressed and smelled like he'd been drinking. "I don't know." Then, in his more normal, lawyerly voice, he said, "Let's consider. Why would he ask that?"

Rachel stared at the picture of the three of them on her bedstand. "Oh, I know."

He looked at her curiously. "You know?"

She nodded. "If you were going to take a child . . . a child you wanted to keep, wanted to make your own . . . how would you get him to go with you in the first place? That's what we've been wondering about all along . . . never mind the password. He could have forgotten about that, even though we must have reminded him a million times. . . . I mean, what would you say once you had him

talking to you, something that would make him trust you enough to go away with you? And once you had him, how would you keep him from constantly asking to go home?" She pulled her knees up and wrapped her arms around them, resting her chin on her knee. "I've been thinking about this a lot, Stephen."

"And?" He didn't even know he sounded inquisitorial. Hadn't meant to sound harsh. She could see in the set of his face and the lines of his body how hope and anguish were at war, how traumatic this was. Stephen was a man of action, and now he had a fact, a certainty, and couldn't do anything with it.

"Well, if I was going to take a child . . ." She was surprised to hear her own voice break. She felt as jittery and unstable as if someone had put her in a giant shaker and tossed her around. "I'd make it seem like an emergency . . . so the child wouldn't have time to think. I'd say that the child was in danger . . . and probably the parents, too . . . and that the child had to come with me right away in order to be safe, that his parents wanted him to come and be safe with me. . . ." She hugged her knees tighter. The trouble was that with every word she could picture David, standing uncertainly by the roadside with his bike, and the faceless strangers leaning out of the van. She could feel the lure of their words, the urgency, his fear and indecision.

"And then, once I'd gotten him away, I'd probably tell him . . . tell him . . ." The awfulness of what she was about to say flooded over her, thick as tar. The ugliness of it, and the realness of sitting here explaining how someone had stolen their child. "I'd tell him that his parents were dead. Killed by someone evil who would kill him, too, if he didn't stay safely hidden with me."

Stephen was horrified. "Did all this . . . come to you?" he asked hesitantly.

"Come to me?" Rachel didn't understand the question.

"From David."

"No. No. Of course not. I was just imagining what someone might say . . . what might work with David. That's all. The communication thing . . . look, I know it makes you uncomfortable, but you asked. It's not something that happens very often. I can never make it happen and I can never continue it on my own when there's more

I want to know. It doesn't work like that. It's not like a tool or a phone line. It's more like a static shock. Now, shouldn't we call Gallagher?"

"Why bother? There's not going to be anything he can do, Rachel. I think we should call Robinson."

Robinson. Damn it. Damn it all! Stephen was hooked already. Pretty soon he'd have Robinson's people camped out by the phones, waiting for the next call. There'd be no place she could go and even have a minute's peace. She said none of this. "Gallagher's going to be mighty pissed if you tell Robinson something before you tell him."

"What do you care? I thought you didn't like the guy."

"It's not a matter of like, Stephen. I don't like either of them. It doesn't matter how I feel about him. Gallagher's our link to finding David."

"So's Robinson."

"He certainly seems to have charmed you."

"Not really," Stephen said. "There's something about him that spooks me. He sees too much. But I think that's what makes him good at what he does. He's not just some guy seeking glory by finding lost children. He lost a child of his own, he told me."

"And?"

"And what?"

"Did he ever find him?"

"Her," Stephen said. "No, they never did. But he said the process made him realize the limits of police procedure and showed him how he might be able to help. By getting lots of people involved in looking for the child. Just in noticing things. It's like having thousands of people helping out."

Rachel wasn't convinced. "You know how I feel," she said. "You know I'm afraid they may be driven to kill him."

"Robinson says it works the other way. That their goal is to convince the kidnappers that the child is loved and wanted, to make the kidnapper more reluctant to hurt the child, while at the same time creating a huge network of watchful eyes to keep the child from being harmed."

"These are desperate people," she said stubbornly. "They wanted

him enough to stalk him and take him. But I don't think they want trouble. If they believe they're about to get caught . . . well, I don't have to draw you a picture. These are ruthless people, Stephen. Willful people. Or one willful person. People who, if they want a child, just snatch him up and carry him away. If it was David's father who took him, he took him because he wanted David to be his future, but if people start closing in . . . asking intrusive questions, what's he going to do? He'll get rid of David so he won't have some messy legal proceedings ruining the rest of his miserable, limited little life."

"Get a grip, Rachel," Stephen said. "You've invented this straw man . . . this desperate father seeking posterity . . . and now, already, you've started hating him. You've invented a whole story to explain David's disappearance without a single fact to support it."

"I have facts," she retorted. "I have that damned AIDS letter, haven't I? And tomorrow you're going to call them and make them tell you who the father is."

"I have a snowball's chance in hell. . . ." he began.

"You're the best plaintiff's personal injury lawyer around," she said. She didn't understand why they were arguing, why they weren't in this together. David's brave attempt to contact them made her heart ache and renewed her determination to move heaven and earth, if necessary, to find him. It was like magic, but it was also a two-edged sword. On the one hand, it confirmed that he was alive. Cut through the bullshit and uncertainty, right to the heart of things. And yet. And yet. To do it, David had gotten caught, putting himself in greater jeopardy, increasing the necessity for her and Stephen to act fast.

"You make your living . . . a terrific living . . . making people tell you what you want to hear when that's not what they want to do. So don't tell me you can't get some functionary at some sperm bank that thinks it may have given us AIDS to tell you who the donor is. We have a right to know! Don't you want to find our son?"

"I don't know how you can even ask me that," he said. "You know me better than that. You know how I feel."

She stared at him, holding back the words that leapt to her lips. Words to the effect that she wasn't at all sure she knew him, that she couldn't know him very well if he respected her so little he was will-

ing to make love to her sister here in their own home; if he refused to share essential information with the police because he and the investigating detective were locked in a bigger dick contest; if he was willing to ignore unilaterally their mutual decision and bring in Robinson; if he regarded himself as a completely independent operator. Instead, she said, "Tomorrow you will call them and find out who the man is."

"I'll try," he said reluctantly, "but don't get your hopes up."

"What have I got, except hope?" Rachel picked up the phone and dialed the police station. "Detective Gallagher, please? He's not? Is there some way we can reach him? There's not? Can't be disturbed? But you'll take a message for him? How kind of you. Yes, there is a message. Um hum. Would you tell him that Rachel Stark called. S-T-A-R-K. We're the ones with the kidnapped child. Would you tell him our son tried to call us tonight. What's that? Now you're interested? Well, that's the message. Just ask Gallagher to give us a call sometime when it's convenient for him." She threw the phone at its cradle. It missed, clattering to the floor and taking a book and some photographs with it.

"He's not in. Can't be reached," she told Stephen. "They'll have him call us." She curled up against the headboard, arms wrapped around her knees. Shaken and angry. Frightened and incoherent. It had been a day of revelations. Revelations of biblical proportions. Maybe the hope of heaven—finding David—maybe the hell of finding that through her willfulness she'd infected them all with a deadly disease. Her husband had betrayed her with her sister, and betrayed her again with John Robinson. And then, after all her steadfast and confident loving, after standing here like a beacon of hope while everyone else blundered about, David's call had come to Stephen. Oh, God! She was mean and miserable and petty. Miserable, miserable, miserable.

Stephen ran a nervous hand through his hair. A shaking hand. "Look, about the letter . . ." he began.

"Old business," she said. "Right now we—"

"I was just trying to protect you, just now, with so much—"

"You would have kept that one from me, too, wouldn't you? Just

like the first one? I'm not a child, you know. I'm not feeble-minded. You don't have to treat me with kid gloves," she said loudly. She felt like yelling. Like screaming. Like tearing her hair and running out into the night. Her skin seethed with so much impacted anger, fear, and misery.

"You don't have to yell, Rachel, I'm only a few feet away," he said. He picked up the receiver, the book, and the pictures. "Let's behave like mature adults."

"You're a million miles away, Stephen. You've been far away for years. You've been far away ever since Jonah died. Close to David, but far, far away from me. You're closer to Miranda than you are to me. You've locked me out. What I say, what I feel, what I think, none of that matters to you at all. You're as bad as the rest of them, Stephen. You give me that look that always seems to have a sigh built into it and I know you're thinking 'poor me, to have a wife who is so peculiar!' " She ran out of the room, and feeling absurdly like a cliché in a bad novel, slammed the bathroom door and locked it behind her.

"You're wrong, Rachel!" he called through the door. "What you say, what you feel, what you think. All of it matters to me. I love you."

"Then why are you having an affair with my sister?" she screamed. "Why?" She poured an overdose of lavender bath salts into the tub. According to the label, they would provide soothing, stress-relieving aromatherapy.

"I'm a horny prick," he yelled through the door. "Sometimes, I don't know . . . I lose control. I've just got to have sex and I don't want to bother you. Look, let me in. I can explain better than this."

She got in the tub, immersing herself until only her face stuck out. The noise of the tap drowned out whatever Stephen's better explanation was for his affair with Miranda. Rachel didn't care. She didn't want to hear it. Her head was filled with the roar of the water as she tried to drown out all feeling, all sensation. It didn't work. Through the roar of the water, David's small, distant voice came to her as clearly as if he was right beside her. "Mom, Dad, are you there? Are you alive?"

She closed her eyes and concentrated on the voice. "Yes, David.

Yes, darling. We're both alive. Alive and here waiting for you. Tell us where you are. Call us again. Tell us how to find you and we'll come." She ran the words through her brain in an endless loop, sending it out into the night with no hope that it would be received. Over and over as the water grew cold and the room got cold and her body got cold. Finally, teeth chattering, she pulled herself out with weary arms, wrapped herself in a towel, and went back in the bedroom.

Stephen, still fully dressed, was sprawled across the bed, snoring. An empty glass, smelling of Scotch and still containing a few vestigial ice cubes, rested on the quilt near his hand. Rachel scooped it up, set it on the bureau, and pulled on her warmest nightgown. When she came out of the closet, she saw Miranda standing in the doorway, staring angrily at Stephen.

"You were expecting him and he didn't come?" she asked. Miranda looked confused. "I'm sure he meant to, but David called, and I'm afraid he got a bit distracted."

Miranda, eyes wide, came into the room and sank onto a chair heaped high with clothes. "David called?"

Angry as she was at her sister, Rachel couldn't make herself be unkind. Miranda loved David, too. "It was only a few words. They pulled him away from the phone before Stephen could say anything. Just his voice. He said, 'Mom, Dad, are you there? Are you alive?' "

Miranda jumped up and held out her arms. Rachel met her halfway across the room, and they embraced, the anger between them temporarily suspended. "He's alive!" Miranda whispered exultantly in her ear. "Alive!"

"Yes," Rachel agreed. "He's alive." Miranda's hair was wet with Rachel's tears, and Rachel's nightgown wet with Miranda's, as they circled in the slow, celebratory dance-hug of desperate people who have been given a glimmer of hope.

WHEN DAVID WAS *sure everyone was asleep, he slipped downstairs as quietly as he could and went to the phone. It was so dark in the kitchen that he couldn't see the numbers, but they kept a flashlight on the table by the door, and he crossed the room, grabbed it, and held it in one shaking hand while he dialed his own number. It rang several times, and he was about to quit when he heard a man's voice, a voice that sounded kind of like his dad. Eagerly, he cried out the question he'd wanted to ask for weeks. "Mom? Dad? Are you there? Are you alive?"*

He hadn't heard the woman come in. Suddenly her hand fell on his shoulder. Her grating voice cut the night, "What do you think you're doing?" Strong hands wrenched the phone away, seized his shoulder, and sent him spinning. "Do you want to get yourself killed? Don't you know they can trace phone calls?"

After she snatched the phone out of his hands, the woman hit him. She hit him hard enough so she knocked him down, and then she stood over him, hitting him again and again, and all the time she kept yelling at him, "Why did you do that? I told you not to do that. You're just like our boy. God-damned willful, single-minded little brat. Why can't you do what you're told? Why can't you do what's right? Do you want them to find you?"

David tried to curl up in a ball so she couldn't hurt him, but he was scared. More scared than he'd ever been in his life. No one had ever hit him before. He had never been hurt like this or yelled at like this and he'd never,

ever seen anyone so mad as the woman was. Her yelling got louder and louder until he stopped trying to protect his body and used his hands to cover his ears, and even then, through the protective hands, he could hear her voice.

"I've tried," she said. "God knows I've tried. I had such high hopes for you, David. You were going to be safe here. Be the boy we lost. We were going to be a family again. I dreamed of it, David. I dreamed of it. Of taking you in my arms. Of bringing you up to be a good Christian boy. Of Father teaching you to fish and hunt and how to care for the animals. . . ." She slapped him hard with her hand.

"All I asked in return was obedience. Asking a child for obedience is not so much to ask. It's not! Learning self-control. Learning to curb your will. David, I thought you'd promised me you wouldn't. I'm risking everything to keep you alive and happy. . . ." Another blow fell, and another. "And when I look in your eyes, all I see is your cold, cold gaze. And fear! I never would have hurt you if you'd loved me. I never wanted to hurt you. You have to believe that. I never did. I just wanted us to be a family. And you betrayed me."

After a while, she started screaming at him about sin and disobedience and God's will and evil and his father and his mother and other things he didn't understand and she started kicking him as well as hitting him. David curled up tighter and tried to find a place inside himself where he could hide from her and then suddenly the man was there, too, talking to her, and he could tell that she'd started to cry, but David didn't dare uncurl or uncover his ears.

He heard her go away, loud, slamming footsteps on the stairs, and then felt the man kneeling beside him. The light was on now and the room was painfully bright. The man talked to him gently, maybe explaining about the woman. David didn't know because he wasn't listening; he was still huddled up inside himself, too scared to come out. The man was touching him all over, murmuring sympathetically. Then David felt himself being lifted, and the man carried him upstairs to bed.

Circumstances rule men; men do not rule circumstances.
—HERODOTUS

CHAPTER FOURTEEN

Eventually Miranda returned to bed, and Rachel sat in the sleeping house and rocked, occasionally hearing, over Stephen's drugged snores and the creaks and groans of an old house, the sounds she was used to hearing that weren't there anymore: David tossing and murmuring in his sleep, the creak of his bed boards as he moved, the squeak of the floorboards as he got up to go to the bathroom, his heavy, naked feet on the wood. David wasn't a very big boy, but he had an elephant's tread. She rocked with her arms wrapped tightly around her body and she ached with the pain of knowing he was out there somewhere, alone and scared, and she was unable to reach him.

Dawn found her in her workroom, intent on her illustration of Emily galloping around the toy store on the red calico hobbyhorse. The drawing was going so well, it was as though it had always been embedded in the page and all Rachel had to do was bring it out. She corrected a few lines, added a bit of brighter gold to Emily's hair, and set the drawing aside. She was reaching for a fresh sheet to illus-

trate Emily sadly rejecting all the proffered horses when a movement outside the window caught her eye. Gallagher was standing there, watching her.

She crossed the room and opened the window, a finger to her lips. "Come around to the kitchen door," she whispered. "I'll make you some coffee." He nodded and disappeared around the corner of the house. She headed for the kitchen, but the peaceful morning was shattered by a shriek and the pounding of feet as Miranda came dashing out of her room. Miranda at midnight; Miranda at dawn. She'd be so glad when her sister moved out.

"Rachel! There's a man out there!"

"Go back to sleep," Rachel said. "It's only Gallagher." Miranda stared at her stupidly and would have said something, but the words became an enormous yawn. She turned and stumbled back to her room.

"Top o' the mornin' to you," Gallagher said as he stepped past her into the kitchen. He took in her nightgown, her shawl, her drawn face. "You haven't slept."

"How could I?" She set about making the coffee.

"There's some that can sleep through anything."

"You've got a bit of a brogue this morning, Detective."

"Yes," he agreed, rubbing his throat. "I'm seeing the doctor about it later. And you'll be seeing your doctor as well?"

She nodded. "How long were you out there watching?"

"Not long. I thought you might be up, but when I saw how intent you were on your work, I didn't want to disturb you."

"That's kind," she said.

"I can be, you know. Tell me about the phone call."

"I didn't answer it. That was Stephen."

"He's sleeping?"

"I don't know. I could see. He was very tired. Yesterday was hard for him."

"What about you? It wasn't hard for you?"

"Every day is like walking the gantlet, Detective. You keep getting whacked by things on all sides and you just try to stay on your feet and keep on going."

He nodded, held out a big, freckled hand for the coffee she offered. "Tell me about the call."

Rachel told him the little there was to tell. Gallagher asked some questions, all of which she answered no. She didn't know any more, didn't think there was any more to know, but there was something else she wanted to discuss. "I have an idea about what might have happened." Gallagher didn't say anything; he just waited. "I suppose, now that you know about the letter, I can talk openly about . . . about David's conception?"

He started to say something, caught himself, and nodded. "Please." She was standing in front of the window, and while her nightgown was floor length and long-sleeved, it was a fine, sheer cotton, and her body was outlined against the light. He tried not to look, studying instead the oily patterns in his coffee.

"I was only thinking that since whoever took David targeted him specifically . . . and since his biological father has a fatal disease . . . isn't it possible that his father took him?" Her voice was full of hope; he knew that if he looked at her face, it would also be alight with hope. "You could find out, couldn't you?" she went on eagerly. "Get them to tell you who the father is and then you go and talk to him and see if he took David? You could do that, couldn't you?"

Reluctantly, he looked again at the lovely woman. Her hope, her eagerness, the expectant way she looked at him, were even more painful than her sadness had been. "I doubt it."

"You doubt it?" He might as well have hit her. "Why not?" She had to push the words past the lump in her throat.

"Well, first of all, I doubt that they'd let me look at their records without a warrant. Medical facilities are very protective of patient's records. . . ."

"But he wasn't the patient. I was!"

"And in order to get a warrant," he went on doggedly, refusing to look at her, "we'd have to have some reason to believe David's biological father was involved . . . which we haven't."

"But we have!" she insisted. "Who else would come looking for him? Specifically for him?"

"Children are taken all the time by unrelated people."

"Opportunistic snatchings, Detective. David was stalked. Targeted. They wanted him in particular."

"It's not enough."

Rachel ran to him and seized his arm. "Don't you see, Gallagher? Don't you see? David represents life. Hope. Posterity. Through him, his father gets to live on!" She realized she was talking about herself as well. She could as easily have said "I get to live on." She tried to meet his eyes, to read what he was thinking. He deliberately looked away. "You could at least try, couldn't you? Why won't you look at me? Don't you want to find him?"

Stephen appeared, unshaven and wearing a grim, hungover face. He wasn't overjoyed to see Gallagher in his kitchen and not particularly happy about an interview so early in the morning. His bleak eyes took in Rachel's sheer nightgown, her proximity to Gallagher. "You should get dressed," he told her sharply, and to Gallagher, "Why don't you just move in with us? We've got another spare room."

"I see you had a visit from John Robinson last night," Gallagher said.

"If you don't mind, I'll leave you two to butt heads," Rachel said. "I'm in the middle of something. Drawing something." What she was in the middle of was a long, drawn-out, agonizing crisis.

"Get dressed first," Stephen said sourly.

She started up the stairs. "You won't forget to call Chicago?"

"How could I?" he sighed.

The woman in the mirror had circles under her eyes bluer than the eyes themselves. And a nightgown much too sheer to be worn in front of strangers. She felt a blush start at her toes and sweep the whole of her body when she saw how she'd appeared before Gallagher. They were right, as usual. She did need a keeper. She was going from peculiar to perverted without even noticing it was happening. Driven in her distraught state to becoming an exhibitionist. Next she'd be dancing naked on the lawn.

She heard a deep, drawling "yoo hoo," accompanied by footsteps on the stairs, and her friend Carole marched in. "Nice nightgown," she said. "You weren't just modeling that for the hunk down in the kitchen, were you?" She nodded at Rachel's startled reaction. "I

thought so. You are just so innocent it's a hoot. Your husband's down there making like Perry Mason with his shorts wedged, so I figured there must have been some sort of nudge to his masculinity." She threw herself down on the unmade bed. "Men are such simple creatures, aren't they?"

"Simple?" Rachel found some clean underwear, pulled off the nightgown, and put on a sturdy blue chambray dress.

"Simple. All their moods, the stuff they do, it's just about sex and food. Give 'em a blow job and a sandwich and they're happy as pigs in—Oops! Listen to me. Ron's taken to calling me 'toilet tongue.' I think I'm losing all those ladylike qualities my mother worked so hard to instill. Or install. It takes concentration to be a lady and I'm so busy wiping noses, wiping counters, wiping handprints off the walls, I'm afraid my manners are just about wiped out. Excuse me. I think allergy season is starting early this year." Carole grabbed a tissue and blew her nose.

"That's a nice prim little dress, Rach. The detective is going to be disappointed. Sorry about last night. Tommy seems to have had one of the nastiest and shortest-lived flus on record. Spewing from both ends with hurricane force. I was three hours cleaning the bathroom after I finally got him settled. Then this morning he jumps up right as rain, gobbles his breakfast, and is out the door before I can even lay a concerned hand on his forehead. They hardly need me anymore, except for the three *L*'s."

"The three *L*'s?"

"Laundry, lunches, and Lysol."

"You underestimate your worth."

Carole patted her glorious red hair and batted her eyes. "Ah do? Well now, dahlin', tell me what I can do for you."

Rachel leaned against the door frame. "Well, when I called, I wanted you to come over and commiserate with me about Stephen and Miranda, but I've gotten over that and now I need—"

"You've gotten over your husband having an affair with your sister in less than twelve hours and while they're both still under the same roof? You amaze me."

"That's not what I meant. When I have the time to think about it, I'll probably want to murder both of them. But I have another pri-

ority right now—finding David. He's alive, Carole. He tried to call us last night."

"Alive?" Carole bounced up from the bed and threw herself into Rachel's arms. "So what do you want me to do? Anything? Break into the Pentagon? Invade Fort Knox? Interrogate every citizen of New York City? You name it and I'm your gal. I'd be so happy if I could do something besides saying I'm sorry and trying to convince Tommy this isn't all his fault."

"The day before he disappeared, there was a gray van parked by the school—gray or silver—and someone in it was watching the kids through binoculars. I want to know if Tommy noticed anything . . . and I want to know if any of the teachers noticed it. Teachers, staff, playground aides, anyone. They might have seen something the boys would have missed. The make. Who was in the van. Something about the license plate. I'd go myself . . . I should . . . but I can't. . . . I can't bear to go there . . . and see all those other children . . . everyone else's children . . . going on as though nothing has happened. . . ."

Carole hugged her again. "You're the bravest person I've ever known, Rachel. If I'd had all the sorrow you've had, I'd slope around with my nose dragging on the ground while you go on being creative and fun and wonderful." She looked at her watch. "In half an hour they'll be gathering in the teacher's room while the kids have recess. A perfect time to begin my career as Carole Nancy Drew. Did you know my middle name was Nancy? All I lack are Bess, George, and the ever-faithful Ned. Or was it Ted?" She shrugged. "Well, it has been about a thousand years since I read those books and Susan wouldn't touch 'em with a ten-foot pole. What can I say? It's her loss. I never expected to produce a child who reads only nonfiction. We know whose genes those are, don't we?"

"So she becomes a second-generation tax attorney. It could be worse. At least this way she'll be able to support you in your old age. If Irene has to depend on what I make, she'll have to switch from Talbots to Kmart. Come down and have some coffee; we can see how the rams are doing."

"Ooh! You're almost as irreverent as I am this morning. I assume Miranda is still in residence?"

Rachel nodded. "As far as I know. I haven't had time to give her

the boot yet. You know me . . . crazy, soggy old disorganized me. Why would I be so mean as to throw my sister out just 'cuz she's having an affair . . ." Her forced gaiety, inspired by Carole's, failed her. She lowered her eyes. ". . . with Stephen." It hurt. Even in her numb, distracted state, it hurt. She tried again for cheerful. "She's probably stirring tofu and sprouts into the Egg Beaters. She tries so hard to keep us healthy. I suppose it's stubborn and wrong-headed of me, but I hate having all my foods be substitutes for the real thing."

"I know. Give me a nice, juicy cheeseburger with bacon, lettuce, tomato, and loads of mayo any day." Carole bounced to her feet. "Race you to the stairs."

"It is not seemly to race to the stairs in a house of sorrow," Rachel intoned, following her demurely down to the kitchen, where they did find Miranda, in a cloyingly cute denim romper, stirring up a batch of synthetic eggs.

Carole grabbed up a cup, fixed herself some coffee, and carried it to the table, where Stephen and Gallagher were sitting in glum silence. "Morning, guys," she drawled in her dangerous voice. Rachel watched Gallagher's eyebrows go up. It never failed. People stared openly. Sometimes their jaws dropped. Sometimes you could literally see them looking around for the real source of the voice. Carole caught Gallagher's eye and gave him a big grin. "I had a voice transplant," she said. She tipped her cup, drained it, and shoved back her chair. "Sorry I can't stick around, but duty calls. Catch you later, Rach. Bye, Miranda. Sell any houses lately?"

"Yesterday," Miranda said. "A big-bucks house, too."

"Great. Now you can afford to get a place of your own. You must be so sick of camping out here. Bye, Stevie. Ron wants to know if you can free up some time for some golf. You'd be doing me a big favor if you pried him away from that desk for a while. Man's as pale as a toad's belly." She whirled and was out the door before anyone could respond.

Stephen shook his head. "She always leaves me feeling like I've been hit by a tornado. I wonder how Ron stands it."

"Without her, Ron wouldn't have a life."

Next Gallagher pushed away from the table, leaving half his synthetic eggs uneaten. "I've got to get rolling. Thanks for the breakfast."

"Are you sure there's no way to trace that call?" Stephen asked.

Gallagher shook his head. "If the phone company knows of one, they aren't sharing it with us."

Rachel sat and played with some toast, reducing it to a rubble of crumbs on her plate. She wished they'd all go away and leave her alone. She had things to do. Pictures to draw. And she needed some quiet time to gather her strength before she called her doctor and arranged to go in for the test. Even though Dr. Barker was the nicest man in the world, and even though he'd been through Jonah's birth and death with her as well as David's birth, it was an awfully private and painful matter that was bringing her there. Just thinking the words to herself, "I need to have an AIDS test," made her insides cringe. How would she manage to say them aloud?

"I called Dr. Barker," Stephen said as he, too, pushed back from the table. "They're expecting you at ten-thirty."

She glanced at him, startled, grateful. "Thank you, Stephen."

He didn't answer, only looked at his watch, sighed, and said, "I'm going to be so late. Don't expect me early tonight. I've got a million things to do today. I'll never get them done if I don't stay late."

"And you won't forget . . ."

"I won't forget to call Chicago. Don't worry." He picked up his briefcase and followed the others out the door.

Miranda was next. Once she found herself alone with Rachel, she began exhibiting such a litany of nervous, guilty mannerisms that after ten minutes Rachel said, "I hate to seem unfriendly, but I really need to be alone this morning. Is there somewhere you could go?"

Miranda immediately shouldered her purse, jingled her keys, and headed out, saying, as she left, "I'm thinking it's about time I found my own place. There's a great little town house over by the lake. . . ."

Rachel put the dishes in the sink to soak, wiped the table and the counters, and returned to her work, but the test, and David, were too much on her mind and she couldn't concentrate. She'd probably be better off if she started going to aerobics again—at least if she got some exercise she might sleep better—but she couldn't

go. She'd tried it once, but she couldn't take the covert looks, the murmurings, everyone's curiosity. She couldn't even take the sympathy, the feeling that the whole world held its breath around her. She didn't know what to do with them and they didn't know what to do with her.

Damn Gallagher. If he hadn't interrupted her, she'd be more than half done by now. She forced herself to stay at the drawing board, making easy sketches, until it was time to leave. As she went out the door, she looked back longingly at the phone, wishing she didn't have to leave it. If he'd called once, he might try again.

She couldn't leave the house without passing the spot where she'd found David's bike. Every time, she slowed down and stared at the spot as if something might have changed, some new clue appeared, or even, as she hoped in her secret heart, that the next time she looked, David would be standing there, wondering where his bike had gone. She supposed it was what they called "magical thinking," but why not? Rational thinking only depressed her.

Today, the route to Dr. Barker's office also took her past the school, something she'd avoided since David disappeared. As she drove past, she couldn't help seeing a huge banner, strung between the building and a light pole, that said: PLEASE LET DAVID GO! WE MISS HIM.

Dr. Barker's nurse, a new one Rachel didn't know, seized her by the elbow the minute she came through the door, and practically dragged her out of the waiting area and into the doctor's office. She'd barely settled into a chair when he bustled through the door and stopped, looking at her sadly. "We're all so sorry, Rachel," he said. "This must be terrible for you. But I'm sure we'll get him back." He picked up her wrist, checked her pulse, and peered intently into her face. "You're not taking care of yourself. Stand up." He circled her slowly, humphing to himself as he did so. "Much too thin." He opened the door and called in the strange nurse. "Find Mrs. Stark a gown and put her in an examining room, would you?"

"I'm just here for a blood test," she protested.

"You're just here to let this cranky old doctor, who has known you for many years, make sure you're going to stay healthy through this

ordeal. You don't do David any good if he comes home to a mother who's collapsed from stress, exhaustion, and malnutrition, do you?"

"No."

"Then humor me."

As if she could do anything else. Dr. Barker often made her feel about ten years old. A great, gruff, bearlike man with a heart of gold. He bullied all his patients for their own good. Even Stephen did as he was told. Meekly she followed the nurse, changed into the ridiculous paper gown, and perched on the edge of the table. While she waited, the nurse came and swabbed her arm with alcohol and drew enough blood to send a vampire into ecstasy.

"Well, if I do have AIDS, you've pretty much depleted my remaining immune system," Rachel quipped. The nurse just gave her a strange look, removed her gloves with elaborate care, and departed with the tray of test tubes. Then she returned with Dr. Barker and they proceeded to poke, prod, and question Rachel until she felt both her mind and her body had been turned inside out.

"Get dressed and come back in my office," Dr. Barker said. When she'd done so, he clucked at her like a father hen. "You're not eating, you're not sleeping. You're losing far too much weight, you're severely anemic, and if you continue to throw up most of what you eat, your condition will only get worse." He pushed a stack of prescriptions toward her. "I want you to fill these first two, and I want you to take the medications. Don't fill them to please me and then stick them in a drawer. That won't do either of us any good. Something for your anemia and something to settle your stomach. Now this one here"—he handed her another one—"is an antidepressant. I think you need it and I know you don't, but just remember . . ."

He waved a hand to stop what she was about to say. "Let me finish, Rachel. Just remember that I'm not saying you shouldn't be feeling depressed, after all that's happened, I'm just saying that this stuff could help you roll with the punches and keep on functioning, which you may decide . . . now or sometime in the future . . . that you want to do. Don't fill it without calling me first. I want to take a look at your test results. And this"—he dangled a last paper between his fingers—"is something to help you sleep. Don't fill this one until

you've tried the others and find you still can't sleep. I know how you feel about pills."

"Yet you're sending me home with half a pharmacy."

"There are millions of people walking around out there who take many more pills than this."

"Did Stephen ask you to do this?"

"To medicate you?" He shook his head. "Stephen asked me to do the AIDS test, and he said he was worried about you. That you weren't eating or sleeping. That's all. You ought to know better than to ask me that. I'm not paternalistic and I don't play God. Nor am I in the business of providing cranky husbands with subdued and passive wives." He took her small cold hand between his two massive ones. "You're my patient and I'm trying to take care of you. That's all, Rachel. Been trying for a long time, though you don't make it easy."

She wanted to lay her head against his wide chest and sob out all her sorrows. Instead, she said, "About the test . . . when will you know?"

"It varies. Sometimes the lab is fast, sometimes slow. We'll call you as soon as we know. I don't think you have anything to worry about."

"Anything more," she corrected. "I have plenty to worry about."

This is the bitterest pain among men,
to have much knowledge but no power.
—HERODOTUS

CHAPTER FIFTEEN

Stephen stared down at the mass of papers on his desk. The stuff of his everyday life, source of his livelihood and much of his satisfaction, today it all looked as unappetizing as boiled cabbage. His day was not going well. Painkillers were finally beginning to take the edge off the pounding headache brought on by too much Scotch, but nothing else seemed to be going right. Charlotte had left her little shred of brain at home. No matter how simple he made his instructions or how carefully he gave them, she couldn't manage the work. If she used an old case as a model, she typed that docket number onto the new case, prepared copies for the wrong parties, addressed originals to the wrong courts. By eleven, the time he'd decided would be good to call Chicago, he could barely manage a civil word and knew they were buzzing about him in the coffee room.

Swallowing hard, he composed himself and made the call, moving through a series of sawdust heads until he reached the director, Dr. Saul Isaacson. "Dr. Isaacson? Stephen Stark. My wife Rachel and I recently received one of your letters. . . ." He trailed off, waiting for Isaacson's response.

"Letters?"

Come on, bozo, he thought, the letters did say we were supposed to call. "Concerning possible exposure to HIV as a result of artificial insemination?"

"Oh yes. We tried to make it very clear in the letter. Both you and your wife should be tested. And, of course, your child, if there is a child."

Isaacson's stiff and cautious reply told Stephen a lot. Among other things, that Isaacson was nervous about the contents of the letter and that enough such letters had been sent so that Isaacson didn't recognize their names. "Your letter asked that we contact you. In fact, you sent us a second letter. What was it that you wanted to know?"

He heard an agitated rustling of papers. "Excuse me a moment." He could hear Isaacson speaking to someone else, snatches of their conversation: ". . . is that damned list. It was right here. There must be another one on Allegra's desk. Go look there. Or maybe Candy has one. And hurry up!" Then he was back with Stephen. "Our concern is for the patients, Mr., uh . . ."

"Stark."

"Of course. Thank you. Mr. Stark. We wanted to be sure that you'd been notified . . . to be sure that you get tested. Some people are reluctant to have the test, of course, and we want to be there . . . to encourage them . . . you . . . to do so . . . for your own safety and peace of mind, of course. So of course we're following up the letters, to be sure everyone is taking the proper steps. Not that we believe there's a significant risk . . ."

Stephen thought he saw the specter of a regulatory agency behind the clinic's concern. "Of course," he agreed, mimicking Isaacson, though he didn't think the man noticed. "How have the results been so far?"

"I'm afraid I can't tell you that. Patient confidentiality, you understand."

"I *don't* understand. You can't violate anyone's confidentiality by stating whether or not you've had patients whose tests were positive."

"Our concern is for *you* and *your family*, Mr. Stark," Isaacson intoned. "Have you been tested?"

Your concern is for your ass and your potential liability, Stephen thought. "Certainly," he answered sharply. He was calling to get information, not to give it.

"And your wife?"

"Yes."

"Is there a child?"

"You don't know whether there was a child?" All Stephen wanted to do was get his information and get off the phone before he blew up at Isaacson. He couldn't get a handle on what the man was trying to do—for that matter, on what the clinic was trying to do—with this information they were gathering. If they were gathering information. Despite the urgent tone of the letters and the fact that they'd sent not one but two, Stephen didn't sense much interest.

"Oh, I see your confusion." Isaacson gave a nervous little laugh. "Not all the inseminations from the . . . uh . . . donor sperm were done here at our . . . uh . . . clinic. In addition to being a fertility clinic ourselves, we also serve as a . . . uh . . . source for many other clinics and private physicians who perform artificial inseminations, so that while we're coordinating the notification, we often don't have any information other than the patient's names and addresses."

"My wife was one of *your* patients."

"Oh. Yes. I see. Was there a child?"

"Yes. A son."

"Congratulations," Isaacson choked on the word, hesitated, then said, "It's always good when these procedures are successful. . . ." He broke off and fell silent for a minute. He obviously didn't possess the facility for making a successful transition between the ritual enthusiasm for success in creating pregnancies and the appropriate response to a parent whose self, spouse, and child may all have been given a terminal illness as a result of that procedure. "Has your child been tested?"

"My child is . . ."

Stephen didn't get any further before Isaacson interrupted him with another abrupt "excuse me." Again Stephen overheard the conversation: "What do you mean she can't find it? We're not going through this again, are we? Those things are supposed to be locked up. Well, what about Candy's copy? A coffee break? That ninny is

always on a break. She's permanently broken." He sniggered. No other word for it. Stephen pictured a Woody Allen head on a scrawny neck and wanted to wrap his hands around that neck and squeeze. Like wringing a chicken's neck. "There must be one in the files," he heard Isaacson whine. "Well, you look and see, don't you? Tell Allegra I'm sending the guy to her." Then he was back on the line. "Look, it's not me you want. You should be speaking with my assistant, Allegra O'Grady. She's actually the one who's coordinating this thing. I'll just switch you. . . ."

"Hold on," Stephen said. "Before you shuffle me off to some assistant, I called to get some information. Vital information. My son . . . our son . . . has been kidnapped. We have reason to believe that David was not a random victim but was specifically targeted by someone who wanted him. The most likely person is, of course, his biological donor. We need information from your files in order to locate him and retrieve our son. . . ." Stephen was annoyed with himself. He'd meant to be more subtle, use more finesse.

"Impossible. Naturally. Impossible. We must preserve the anonymity of our donors or we won't get donors. They expect that we will protect their privacy absolutely."

"What about the interests of your patients? Do you protect them absolutely?"

"Of course."

Stephen could have predicted the response. "So that you've carefully restricted access to your patients' files?"

"Of course. No one has seen our files except the staff person who compiled the list."

"About this potential AIDS transmission. Was there only one donor?"

"As far as we know."

Meaning no other donors had notified him yet that they also had AIDS? Jesus, this was a Mickey Mouse operation. It was scary to think they'd ever put their trust in such a place. "If my wife and I test negative, is there any chance that our son could still be HIV positive?"

"What were his test results?"

"He hasn't been tested."

"Well, let's just see what his test results are, shall we?"

Meaning that Isaacson didn't know the answer. Surely it was a very basic question, one that all the parents were asking. "He can't be tested, goddammit," Stephen said. "I told you. He's been kidnapped. How many people were exposed as a result of this donor?"

"I'm afraid I can't tell you that."

"Why not?"

"Well, frankly, Mr. Stark, because it's none of your business."

Stephen lost the tenuous hold he was keeping on his temper. "Do you keep records of the dates upon which sperm was donated? Will my wife's file tell me when the sperm used in each attempt was donated?" Isaacson made a choking sound. "I'm sure it's no secret, since the information will appear in Rachel's records, so I'll just tell you up front, Doctor, that I'm an attorney. And I'm requesting that a complete copy of Rachel Stark's medical records be made and sent to me at once." He gave his address. "Are you writing this down?" he asked.

"Of course."

"Then read it back to me, please, so I can be sure you've got it right."

There was a long silence. Then Isaacson said, "Maybe you'd better give it to me again."

Stephen repeated his name and address. "And the patient's name?"

"Rachel. Rachel Stark."

"Umhum. You know, Mr. Stark, I'm not sure we still have those records," Isaacson said.

"Don't try that with me, Doctor," Stephen said. "You agreed not five minutes ago that you did have them, remember? And were zealously guarding them. You can't have the files one minute and not have them the next. . . ."

This was far worse than he'd imagined. The clinic wasn't notifying people on its own; someone was making them do it, and it was clear that that was all they were going to do. Just keep hounding people until they called and then check their names off on some list. They weren't interested in helping the patients, offering support,

or sharing information. Even if there wasn't that much they could do, he'd been in the client-getting business long enough to know approach and attitude were everything. He was incredibly frustrated, already reviewing in his mind lawyers he might know in the Chicago area.

Still no response from Isaacson. "Dr. Isaacson, let me ask you this, which you can easily answer without violating anyone's confidentiality. How many people are in the same boat with me and Rachel? Is it ten or twenty? Fifty? A hundred?"

There was another strangled sound followed by another silence. Then Isaacson said, "Quite a few."

"I know the guy was a medical student. What did he do, finance his entire medical education by jerking off in a bottle over a copy of *Penthouse?*"

"There's no need to be vulgar," Isaacson began. "I'm transferring you to Ms. O'Grady. Maybe she can be more helpful."

"Because she knows exactly how many squirts?" Stephen said rudely. "Just one question. When and how did you find out that the donor was HIV positive?"

"About nine months ago. He sent us a letter. I'm transferring you." Isaacson cut him off before Stephen could ask anything more. In Stephen's mind, the question of why it had taken them nine months to act echoed.

Allegra O'Grady had a sugar-sweet voice, a pleasant, accommodating manner, and an absolute unwillingness to reveal another shred of information. She appreciated his frustration, sympathized with the anxious position their letter had put him in, generously forgave him for swearing at her and losing his temper; she could completely understand how he felt. Was aghast at the kidnapping of his child and most sincerely hoped that things would turn out for the best and was sincerely sorry that there wasn't anything she, personally, could do to help. Stephen hung up the phone torn between wanting to tear her throat out and wanting to offer her a job. He had never encountered a more successfully opaque person. The woman could have a real future in the legal business.

The rest of the afternoon was a bust. He was way behind but he couldn't concentrate on his work and couldn't bring himself to be

civil to anyone. Finally he gave up, stuffed some work in his briefcase, and left early, stopping on the way to pick up shirts. But there
was no respite at home, either. He hadn't gotten more than a few
steps through the door when Rachel pounced. "Did you call them?"

He lowered his briefcase to the floor, slowly and carefully, as if it
weighed hundreds of pounds. "Let me get out of this suit and I'll tell
you all about it."

"Just tell me if it's good news or bad news."

"Bad news," he said, reluctantly meeting her eyes. Steeling himself against the electric tingle they gave him, against his desire to
protect her, indulge her, give her anything she wanted. She had to
learn to accept the world the way it was. "They won't tell me. I spoke
with the director, a Dr. Isaacson. He said it was against clinic policy to
ever reveal the identity of donors."

"Then sue them and make them tell you."

He shook his head. "We've got no grounds."

"You can make up some grounds," she said. Stephen just shook
his head. "But you're a lawyer. There must be some way to make
them tell you. . . ."

"There isn't."

Her look said, more eloquently than any words could, that she
didn't believe him. "Well, then, I'll go there and I'll make them tell
me. You can fend for yourself for a few days around here, can't you,
as long as you have Miranda to look after you?" She didn't bother to
wait for a reply. "I hope so, because tomorrow, as soon as I finish the
illustrations for that damned book, I'm going to Chicago and I'm
not coming home until they tell me what I want to know."

"Rachel, you can't. You'll only end up frustrated and embarrassed.
Believe me, I know. I've been trying to deal with these people. . . ."

"Avoiding frustration and embarrassment has a higher priority
than finding David?"

Stephen twitched angrily. "You know that's not what I meant. . . ."

"Then what did you mean?"

"I meant just what I said. That from my efforts to work with these
people, I can tell that you won't be able to get anywhere with them.
It's just one of those intractable systems. . . ."

Rachel just stared at him, betrayal in her eyes. He lowered his

own, unable to face her disappointment. "I thought . . ." she said softly, so softly he had to lean forward to hear, ". . . that that was what lawyers were good at. Persuading people to cooperate when they don't want to be cooperative. I thought that's what your work was all about . . . about using the law to make things right when people don't want to do the right thing."

"It is, Rachel. But you have to have grounds . . . you have to have a reasonable basis for any lawsuit. . . . You can't . . . you shouldn't . . . just bring a lawsuit because you aren't getting your own way. . . ."

"You make it sound like my need to find David's father is some sort of whim, some willfulness on my part, Stephen. It's not. I know David's father is the vital link here. . . ."

"You don't know that," he stated flatly. "You just assume it."

During the course of their conversation, Rachel had been slipping slowly down the wall until now she was perched on the bottom step, staring up at him. "I know it," she said stubbornly. "And I know that if you believed me, if you didn't think my theory was stupid and far-fetched, you'd be as willing as I am to do whatever needs to be done to get the information about David's father. You'd be willing to call some lawyer friend out in Chicago and sic them onto the clinic. And you wouldn't be standing here lecturing me about subverting the purposes of your goddamned sacred law."

"I'm just trying to do what's right, Rachel."

"What's right is finding our son." From the rasp in Rachel's voice, he could tell she was about to cry. He couldn't face tears right now. He was too frustrated with his own problems—unable to work, unable to face Miranda, unable to save his son. He'd only blow up and yell at her, something he was determined to avoid. "What's right is doing what we have to do to find him," she said. "I don't give a tinker's damn how ethical or unethical it is."

"Did you see the doctor today?"

"Yes, I did. And don't try to change the subject." Tears were running down her face now.

He handed her his handkerchief. "I'm going to get out of this suit," he said. "Tomorrow, I'll call a friend in Chicago and see if there's anything we can do."

"Don't bother, Stephen. I'll take care of it myself."

"You can't . . . you shouldn't . . . you're not . . . Rachel, you haven't been well. Rushing off to Chicago, where you'll only be frustrated, can only make things worse."

She stood up and moved aside so he could go up the stairs. "You just don't get it, do you? Things couldn't be worse."

"Of course they could . . ." he began, and found himself at a loss for words. He hated being trapped like this. "I said you shouldn't go." He marched up the stairs and slammed the bedroom door shut behind him.

I have walked and prayed for this young child an hour . . .
—YEATS, "A Prayer for My Daughter"

CHAPTER SIXTEEN

Spurred on by her determination to finish the job and leave for Chicago, Rachel dried her tears, went to her workroom, and spent an hour on the first yard sale illustration for *Emily's Horse*. Just as it had in the morning, the drawing was working for her now, and pictures seemed to flow smoothly under her pen that a few days ago had demanded she concentrate on every agonizing stroke. After an hour, feeling guilty and sorry for having been so difficult, for not having taken a gentler approach, she went looking for Stephen to see what he wanted for dinner. After she'd looked through the whole house without finding him, she looked in the yard and discovered his car was gone. She found a note on the kitchen table: "Went to play some golf with Ron. We'll have dinner out. Don't wait up for me. Stephen."

Relieved that he'd gone to do something he enjoyed, and piqued that he hadn't bothered to come and tell her himself, Rachel made herself a cup of tea and went back to work. An hour later, with the best part of the drawing finished, she heard a door bang and Mi-

randa came down the hall and popped her head in the door. "Hi," she said, shiny hair bobbing. "I've got news. Come find me when you're ready to take a break."

"Will do." Rachel had meant to stop soon and hear Miranda's news, which she hoped involved an alternative place to live, but she got wrapped up in the pictures. This was when it was good, when she finally engaged with the story and the pictures seemed to flow from the text right through her and onto the paper. She finished the picture of Emily and her mother entering the yard sale and started the one where Emily crawls under a table and discovers the old painted rocking horse. She had a clear picture of the delight on Emily's face that she was struggling to capture. On her third try, she finally got it right, and had just sketched in the soft, round happy features when Miranda came in again.

"Do you know what time it is? Did you have any dinner?"

"No and no," she said, laying down her pen and massaging the back of her neck. "What time is it?"

"Almost ten."

"Ten? You're kidding."

Miranda shook her head. "Nope. Look at your watch."

"I'm sorry. I guess I lost track. What time did you come in?"

"Little after seven. Come in the kitchen and I'll fix us something. You can hear all about the properties I looked at today. For me, I mean. It's funny, you know. I'm great at telling other people what they ought to buy, and hopeless about deciding for myself."

Miranda bounced out the door and Rachel climbed down off her stool, amazed at how stiff and awkward she was after so many hours bending over the drawing table. One of her legs was numb and it felt like someone had drawn a tight elastic cord across the tops of her shoulders. "I'm stiff," she said, limping into the kitchen and stamping her foot to try and wake it up. "And famished. What's on the menu?"

"Soup."

"Just soup? I feel like I could eat a whale."

"Healthy soup. Black beans with rice and veggies and low-fat yogurt."

"It sounds too healthy. . . ."

"Wait until you taste it. You'll be pleasantly surprised, I bet." Miranda ladled soup into two big stoneware bowls and put them on the table next to a loaf of dense, brownish bread.

Rachel sat down and picked up her spoon, nagged by the uncomfortable feeling she was forgetting something. She discovered that the soup, unlike some of Miranda's experiments, was delicious. "Did Stephen come back yet?"

Miranda shrugged. "I haven't seen him. Was he working late?"

"Golf," Rachel muttered through a mouthful of soup.

"Well, you know how the guys are. He'll be at the club till all hours, networking and sharing stories. I wouldn't look for him for a few hours yet. So. Shall I tell you about the houses?"

"Of course. Did you see anything you liked?"

"That's the problem, really. I liked three of them, but for different reasons. The first one was a condo, one of those nice new ones out by the lake. Really nice. They've all got private patios and little lawns going down to the water, ending in these sort of sea-wall things. And balconies off the second-floor bedrooms, also with water views. Good kitchens, smallish living/dining areas, and a little second room that could be a guest room or office."

"And the problem is?"

"They're expensive. I'd really have to hustle to pay the rent."

"What about your present house? It's worth something. Can't you use the money from that?"

Miranda shrugged. "Jeff wants to keep it. He doesn't have the money to buy me out right now, but I don't want to put him out. He loves that house. In terms of sweat equity, he's literally drenched the place."

"That's graphic," Rachel said, getting up to serve herself more soup. She was hungry again, just like yesterday. Maybe she was getting her appetite back. Maybe she wouldn't need Dr. Barker's pills. "What about the other places?"

"There's a cute little house in the village. Walk to everything but there's a nice, quiet feel to the yard. Only problem is that it needs everything. New kitchen. Updated bathroom. Floors sanded. Wall-

paper stripped. Price is good, though. I could afford to do all that. The trouble is, I don't enjoy renovating and redecorating."

Rachel wanted the cottage for herself. Some days, even though Stephen was neat and David was quiet, she longed for a place of her own, where no one would appear at her elbow when she was concentrating and interrupt her, looking for food or clean socks. "So what's the third one? Is there a third one?"

"Yep. A nice, boring house in the same subdivision where I used to live. Maybe half a mile away. Good shape. Well kept up. Price is right. A great little family house—"

"Well," Rachel said, interrupting her, "if you want my opinion, it sounds like the village house is the most appealing and affordable, if you can stand to do the work, and you want the slick, pricy condo out by the lake."

"Exactly," her sister sighed.

"I could help you with the renovations. You know I like that sort of thing." Rachel banged at her head with the side of her hand.

"What's the matter? Got a headache?" Miranda asked.

"No. I just have this nagging feeling I'm forgetting something. I was trying to jar it loose." Why aren't you gone, Rachel wondered? How can we each of us have so little pride that we can sit here and be polite like a pair of little old ladies, when I ought to be screaming and tearing your hair and you ought to be hiding your shameful red face? Maybe it was Miranda's presence that kept her from remembering by splitting her concentration. She raised her eyes and stared at her sister, and suddenly Miranda found the surface of her soup fascinating.

They finished eating in silence and Rachel went back to drawing, but she'd lost her momentum. After half an hour she quit and took her tired body upstairs. A hot bath seemed like a good idea to soak out the stiffness. By the time she climbed out of the tub, it was almost midnight. She went downstairs to look for Stephen. He wasn't anywhere in the dark, quiet house. Rachel turned on a few lights to guide his returning feet, and was on her way up the stairs when she heard his key in the door. She paused and waited for him.

"Hello, stranger. How was the golf?"

"Fine." His words were slurred and he lurched unsteadily from foot to foot as he searched his pockets for something. "Here," he said defiantly. He held out a crumpled piece of paper. "You see this yet?"

Rachel's heart skipped as she stared down at David's face, looking back at her from the flyer. It announced that David Stark, age nine, was a missing child, last seen on April 30th in Forest Valley, New York. There were other details, including a physical description, the place he was last seen, and a phone number to call with information. "Where did you get this?"

"It was on a telephone pole. They're all over the place. That guy Robinson is really doing his job. Gimme tha . . ." He reached for the flyer, stumbled, staggered, and grabbed Rachel's arm for support. "I must have seen a hundred. All over town. And I'll bet it's not just here."

She pulled her arm away and he nearly fell. "Do you know what this means?" she asked, waving the flyer. "Do you?"

"Yeah," he answered loudly. "It means maybe now someone will come forward with some information and we'll finally have a chance to get him back."

"Or that whoever has him will have to kill him to keep from being found out." Rachel felt a roaring in her head and a wave of dizziness as bad as Stephen's. She sat down on the bottom step, a place she seemed to be sitting a lot lately, her head in her hands. As the whirling passed and the dizziness cleared, she could see David's face, deathly white and fearful, and his arms reaching out toward her. "Mommy. Mommy. Why doesn't somebody come and get me? I'm scared."

She closed her eyes tightly, clenched her fists, tried to clear her mind, to open herself up to him. "Where are you, darling? I'll come get you. Just tell me where you are." She waited, holding her breath, saw David's face, watched him in her mind, yearning toward him, as he took a deep breath, looked nervously around, and opened his mouth to speak. Stephen, trying to go past her up the stairs, missed a tread, slipped, and half fell on top of her.

"Jesus! Sorry. Drunker than I thought. Help me upstairs, will you?"

David's face vanished as Rachel tried to get Stephen's body righted again, trying to be gentle even though she was burning with frustration and anger. David had been about to tell her something. She was sure of it. She put Stephen's hand on the railing, wrapped his other arm around herself, and tucked her body under his armpit. "Okay, now right foot first, up we go." Even with the railing and herself, Stephen nearly didn't make it. She'd never, in all their years together, seen him so utterly incapacitated by drink.

She got him as far as the edge of the bed and dumped him there. "Do you need help getting undressed?"

"Sure." His grin was loose and lecherous. He patted the bed beside him. "Sssit down and help."

"You're in an awfully good mood."

"Why not? Thish flyer makes me feel lots more confident about finding David. I know you don't like the idea, Rach, but you'll see." He grabbed her and rolled over on top of her, pinning her to the bed, pelting her with wet kisses that reeked of alcohol.

When Stephen finally fell asleep, Rachel got up, put on her robe, and went into David's room. Gathering up a few of his favorite things, she knelt quietly on the floor and tried to reach him again. It was something she didn't know about, this deliberate attempt at communication. Always before things had just come to her. That had been scary enough. Now, trying to force it, she found she was shaking as if she had chills. What scared her even more was that it almost worked. In her mind she could see David, dimly, as if she were looking through smoke, but he was sleeping. Finally, her knees aching and her neck stiff from such intense concentration, she gave up, put his things back on the bed, and left the room.

Downstairs in her workroom, she snapped on the lights and went to work. She had to get this done so she could go to Chicago. There was no more time. David was in danger. She could tell. She had to find his father—and before it was too late. The dark outside got darker, and Rachel worked on. Then, as she began the next-to-last drawing, the dark began to lighten and a cacophony of birds erupted in the bushes outside to greet the approaching day.

She was putting the finishing touches on the last drawing, Emily in the station wagon, falling asleep in her car seat, with the wooden

rocking horse in the back, as Stephen came into the room, gray-skinned and embarrassed. "You're up early," he said.

She smiled and pointed to the pile of drawings. "I had to get this done. This is the last one." She raised her hands high above her head and stretched. Odd. She didn't feel the spacy exhaustion of a night without sleep. She felt energized, like she'd just come back from a brisk walk. "Boy, does it feel good to have this finished. It looked like I was going to be working on this book for the rest of my life."

"May I see?" Stephen reached for the pile of finished drawings and began sorting through them. "She's so cute. It would have been nice to have a daughter . . . but that's stupid, isn't it? Who knows how many tries it might have taken to get a healthy child, and even then . . . would we ever have felt sure . . ." He put the drawings down and turned away so she couldn't see his face.

It still surprised her, these flashes of longing that showed through Stephen's coldness. Yet she knew they were there from his tenderness with David. "Let's not talk about it." Rachel got off the stool. "You want some breakfast?"

"A big breakfast is the best hangover cure I know."

"Over toast and eggs and bacon and home fries," Rachel said. "As soon as I get this stuff in the mail, I'm going to Chicago."

"I don't want you to go," he said.

"I know. But I'm going."

"You'll only be . . ."

"I know. I'll only be disappointed. So I'll be disappointed. You know how you've been feeling these past few weeks, how frustrated you've been because you haven't been able to do anything? Well, that's how I feel, too. Going to Chicago, going to that clinic and confronting them . . . maybe it will work and maybe it won't, but at least I will have tried. . . ."

Stephen shrugged, tried for a smile. "I could drive you to the airport."

She reached across the table and took his hand. "I'd like that."

There is no animal more invincible than a woman,
nor fire either, nor any wildcat so ruthless.
— ARISTOPHANES, *Lysistrata*

CHAPTER SEVENTEEN

Rachel was in the front hall, stuffing her raincoat into her suitcase, when the doorbell rang. She looked to see if it was the taxi—the local guy sometimes came to the door—but it was an unfamiliar car. She was taking a taxi because she and Stephen had both sensibly recognized that the cautious truce achieved over breakfast might not withstand a trip to the airport together, so Stephen had gone to work. When Rachel opened the door, she found a strange woman on the step who instantly and irrationally reminded her of Mary Poppins.

Maybe it was the high-necked, flowered blouse and the long gray skirt, or maybe it was the plain face and the gray hair secured in a bun. And the woman's voice, low and gentle, matched her exterior perfectly. She fixed her bright blue eyes on Rachel and said, "Hello, Rachel. I'm Norah Proust, and John Robinson sent me. May I come in?"

"I'm sorry," Rachel said, thinking she probably wasn't sorry at all, "I'm afraid I don't have time for company right now. I have a

plane to catch." She looked over the woman's shoulder through the still open door. "There's my taxi now."

"Oh dear," the woman said, rubbing her forehead in a vexed way. "I should have known that. How unfortunate. I was so hoping . . . We really do need to talk. When do you expect to be back?"

"I don't know."

The woman's eyes fell on Rachel's suitcase. "You aren't running away, are you, dear?"

"Running away? Why should I . . ." She stopped, thinking it was an odd thing to suggest, and realized that this woman didn't need to know her business.

"No. I'm going to Chicago. I don't know when I'll be back."

"Oh." The woman nodded.

"Is there something I can do for you before I go?"

"Oh, no. I don't think so. I'm here to see you, Rachel. John thought I might be able to help."

Out in the yard, the taxi honked. "I'll be right there," Rachel called. "Help me how?"

"He didn't call you?"

"I'm afraid not." Rachel wondered if this was the beginning of the invasion. Was Norah Proust a keeper, sent to follow her about through her day and support her through these difficult times?

"Here's my card," the woman said, holding out a small rectangle of black cardboard with silver writing. "I'm a psychic. John says you've been hearing from your son David. Sometimes, when a person is getting messages, it helps to work with a professional. You may get better information that way. Call me when you get back." She turned without another word and walked away down the path, leaving Rachel openmouthed and staring. Rachel pulled herself together, grabbed her suitcase and her purse, and hurried out to the waiting taxi.

Chicago. The Windy City. Rachel didn't know anything about it, even though she'd been there several times. Been there only in the sense of flying into O'Hare, taking a cab to a hotel, walking from the hotel to the clinic, submitting to their embarrassing ministrations, taking a cab back to the airport, and flying home. The trips

had all had an unreal quality, a sense of stepping out of her normal life. At the time, she had been distraught, so torn by the conflict between her urgent need to have a child and Stephen's pained and grudging acquiescence to the situation that she had imagined the whole thing as taking place in another dimension. The trips to Chicago were alien abductions and the procedures their weird scientific experiments.

It had all been so awful and degrading and intrusive, and the tension between them at home had been so great that once she'd become pregnant with David, she'd put the whole experience out of her mind and tried never to think about it again. Stephen had never asked anything about it, never shown the slightest interest. She had been isolated, with no one to tell what she was going through, so she had turned to Jonah. Increased her trips to the cemetery, until the open scorn, disapproval, and criticism from her family had forced her to stop, driven her underground. A sad, wacky lady who talked to dead babies in her head.

Now, sitting in the tiny, cramped airplane seat that barely had room enough for a dwarf, memories of those other times came back. Beginning with the fact that she hated to fly. Taking off and landing both occasionally gave her chills, nausea, a terrifying, displaced, dead feeling, and a deep-seated certainty that she was going to die. She didn't let it keep her from taking planes. She and Stephen both liked to visit new places, and Stephen and David loved to go to Caribbean beaches in the winter. But it meant that flying always made her sick with anticipation, as well as sometimes just plain sick.

Today, as she took her "easy to escape from" aisle seat, she felt the familiar deadly chill creep over her, and steeled herself for the arrival of the nausea and the dizziness. This was not going to be a good flight. Had she been Stephen, she would have determinedly distracted herself by planning exactly what she was going to do when she got there. But Rachel wasn't a planner. She could plan her art, and she could plan her days, but both sorts of planning were overlays that she'd achieved in order to be a functioning grown-up. Mostly, she functioned by instinct and intuition. Her mother, half-sarcastically, referred to it as her "artistic temperament." That was in

Irene's kinder moments. It wasn't that Irene Filipovsky didn't want her daughter to be artistic—she genuinely admired Rachel's talent—she just didn't want it to show.

Okay, Rachel, she thought to herself, what does your instinct have to say about Norah Proust, the middle-aged Mary Poppins of psychics? She considered. No answers came. It seemed that neither her instinct nor her logical mind was able to furnish a coherent reaction to the appearance of Norah Proust nor any conclusions about how she should proceed when she got home. She only knew that despite her communications with David, she was almost as skeptical about psychics as Stephen was. She had no interest in engaging in the psychic's games.

Before she could ponder further, the captain announced that they were next in line for takeoff, and Rachel closed her eyes, gritted her teeth, and concentrated on survival.

"Would you like something to drink?" a cheery voice asked.

Rachel unclenched her eyes, unclenched her hands, and looked up. "Ginger ale, please." A minute plastic cup overflowing with ice and underflowing with ginger ale was placed before her along with an impenetrable package of fifteen carefully rationed peanuts. The airline didn't want Rachel or the others to get any fatter or they wouldn't fit in their seats. She closed her eyes and sipped ginger ale and practiced breathing. After an eternity, she began to feel better. This time when she opened her eyes, she noticed the man beside her watching her nervously.

"You look like you're going to be sick," he said accusingly. "Are you?"

"I'm not qualified to answer that question," she said. "But I assure you that I'll do my best not to be." It sounded like bad grammar.

"Well, certainly," he said, with a nervous flutter of his hands. "I mean, I certainly hope not. I'm rather sensitive."

Rather insensitive, Rachel thought. Jerk. It would serve him right if she did throw up on him.

"Newspaper?" asked the attendant's cheery voice.

"Sure." Rachel took one, eager to be distracted. There on the inside page she found David's picture, along with a story about his ab-

duction. "Goddamned John Robinson," she muttered as her stom-ach gave one unsettling lurch and then another. She bolted from her seat and down the aisle. Halfway down, trapped by a serving cart, she stopped, waiting for a chance to get by. The woman beside her was reading the story of David's disappearance. So was the man across the aisle and the woman behind her.

This was a nightmare from which she couldn't wake up. Like a baby seal, ruthlessly clubbed by hunters, she was battered from all sides by the pictures, the words, the devouring eyes. I am a volcano, she thought, as her stomach twitched unsteadily. Ready to blow. "If you don't let me pass," Rachel gasped to the startled attendant, "I'm going to be sick right here."

"You've got an airsickness bag at your seat. . . ."

"Yes. And if I use it, my seat mate will get sick, and perhaps his seat mate, and you'll have an epidemic on your hands. Is that what you want?" Seconds later, Rachel was in the lavatory ejecting her gin-ger ale and her fifteen peanuts. The shock of being surrounded by David's picture was so great, she felt like she'd endured a violent physical assault. She washed her face, waited for the worst of the trembling to subside, and went back to her seat. She spent the rest of the trip with her eyes closed. She didn't even open them when the attendants offered her a meal, just shook her head. She couldn't look. The smell of food was enough.

It was just as bad going through the airport. There seemed to be pictures of David everywhere she looked, taped to walls and posters and cash registers, all asking: HAVE YOU SEEN ME? Was this really what Stephen had wanted? By the time she was through the airport and in a taxi, she was having trouble breathing. If she'd been at home, she would have run to the cemetery, but here there was nowhere to run. She was trapped inside her own skin and inside her own head.

"Are you okay?" the driver asked, turning around to stare at her.

Rachel looked at David's picture, taped on the Plexiglas shield in front of her. "I can't . . ." she cried, getting out of the taxi and walk-ing back to the next one in line.

"Hey, lady," the driver called after her. "You're supposed to take the first one. You can't go with him."

Rachel got into the taxi and slammed the door. There was no picture of David. "Get me out of here," she ordered. The driver pulled deftly around the still yelling man and into the stream of traffic.

"Where to, lady?"

Rachel gave the address and slumped back against the seat. Everything was so much harder than it needed to be. Was it just her? That black cloud she was always joking about? Maybe she was just wrongheaded. Maybe, as Stephen suggested, she ought to be grateful to John Robinson. She ought to be glad that David's picture was everywhere. Maybe it really did mean they had a better chance of finding him. But she didn't think so. She thought it was only a matter of time—a very short time—before those flyers found their way to wherever David was being held, and the people who had him panicked. She closed her eyes, clenched her fists, and breathed, trying not to think about what might happen then.

At the hotel, she rushed inside without looking in either direction, to avoid any more signs of David, checked in, and went upstairs to her room, having refused the offer of a bellboy to assist her. She needed to get away from people for a while. She sat on the edge of the bed, kicked off her shoes, and lay back against the pillows.

"Jonah, baby, we're going to war," she said, and then, very deliberately, reminded herself that people didn't talk to lost babies. Get real. Live in the now, Rachel. Get real? Reality wasn't just the mundane. It was the personal, the intense, the immediate. Doing her illustrations, she didn't look for the bland, the everyday; she looked for the special, stand-out details that would connect readers with the story. Emily's stubborn chin as well as her endearing face. The merry Pennsylvania Dutch detailing on the wooden horse. The natural instinct of the small child to crawl under a table in the confusing jumble of a yard sale. Yes. Rachel shared that child's instinct to crawl under a table. But she hadn't, had she?

Get real. How many times had Stephen and Miranda said that to her. What could be more real than this crazy, disjointed real life that was hers? What more immediate than her looming sense of danger to David?

She looked at her watch. It was 3:30. Still time to get to the clinic today. There was no sense in putting it off. Sitting here and waiting would just be agony. She might as well know how they were going to react. She felt as thin-skinned and fragile as an unlaid egg. And eggs don't do too well in combat. But that's what this egg had to do. Go to battle for David. For her children she could find courage she never had for herself.

Dressing for action, she thought, as she changed her black sweater for a soft greenish blue that matched her eyes, released her hair from its neat ponytail, and put on demure pearl earrings and a matching necklace. She brushed her hair and checked her image in the mirror. "A touch of lip gloss," she murmured. The face in the mirror agreed. In the end, she looked sweet, innocent, and vulnerable. She practiced looking slightly confused and smiled at the result. Doing what comes naturally.

Her plan, though it glorified it to call it that, was to be so innocently outrageous, they'd give her whatever she wanted to make her go away. She'd done some acting in college. Been pretty good at it, too. It was easier for her to be someone else than to be herself. So she was off to be someone battier, loonier than herself, to be the person they all—Stephen, Miranda, her mother—feared she might become. Loon for a day. She tucked her key into her purse and headed out.

The sidewalks were crowded and Rachel felt buffeted by bodies as she walked the few short blocks to the clinic. Just as it had been when she was going there for treatment, as they called it, she and the other women waiting for the elevator didn't meet each other's eyes. No one wanted anyone else to see the anticipation, guilt, and embarrassment that they felt. She got onto the elevator with three other women, and all of them looked diligently down at their feet, just as they'd done at age six when wearing black patent leather shoes.

She held back while the other three conducted their transactions with the receptionist, then stepped up to the window. "Rachel Stark to see Dr. Isaacson," she said.

"Dr. Isaacson doesn't usually . . ." the receptionist began, looking confused. "Do you have an appointment?"

"I'm here to pick up some medical records, and I had some questions I needed to ask him," Rachel said, deliberately not answering.

"I don't think . . ." Frowning, the receptionist consulted her book as though it held the answer she needed. "Perhaps you could see his assistant, Ms. O'Grady. Dr. Isaacson never sees anyone without an appointment. I'll see if she's available. May I tell her what this is about?" She picked up her phone and pressed some buttons.

Rachel took two steps backward and said, in a louder voice, "I'm one of your artificial insemination patients who was exposed to the AIDS virus." The three women in the waiting room all turned and stared at her in alarm.

The receptionist's face turned red. "Mrs., uh . . . please lower your voice. You're upsetting our patients."

"I know what you mean." She put on her confused face. "I'm one of your patients and I'm pretty upset myself." She neglected to lower her voice.

"Please! You must speak more quietly. Everyone is staring."

"Well, that's rude," Rachel said with a shrug. "I've got nothing to be embarrassed about. I was only trying to have a child, like I suppose they are. Dr. Isaacson was perfectly willing to see me when his purpose was to inseminate me with untested sperm. Why won't he see me now?" She was pleased by the note of aggrieved confusion she'd managed to get into her voice.

"Is there a problem here?" The speaker was a honey-haired woman with a supercilious face, a fitted scarlet suit, and stiletto heels, moving with the arrogant overconfidence of the young and pretty. Her look suggested Rachel had a turd on her sleeve.

"I don't think I have a problem," Rachel said, tugging nervously at her pearls and widening her eyes. "I'm just waiting to see Dr. Isaacson. I don't think she's told him I'm here yet." She looked hopefully at the receptionist.

"I told her she should see you instead," said the flustered receptionist.

"That's right," said the woman, holding out a thin hand with glistening scarlet nails. "His assistant. Allegra O'Grady."

"Oh, I'm sorry. I can't. I'm severely allergic to nail polish,"

Rachel said, staring at the outstretched hand. "My eyes swell up and I get these giant hives."

The woman dropped her hand like she'd been burned. "If you'll just come this way to my office."

"But you're not Dr. Isaacson," Rachel said, doing her best to sound confused. "It's Dr. Isaacson I need to see."

"I'm his executive assistant," the woman said, putting a hand on Rachel's shoulder to urge her away from the alarmed faces in the waiting room.

"Please! Don't! Your nails," Rachel wailed, jumping violently away. "It's the formaldehyde, you see. I'd appreciate it if you didn't come any closer." Her friend Carole was allergic to polish and she'd told Rachel horror stories about what kept happening to her before her doctor finally figured it out. She headed for the waiting room. "I'll just sit here and wait until he can see me. I'm in no big hurry. I've come all the way from New York, once I got your letter." She smiled at the three staring women. "I'm sure you've got some nice magazines for me to read. You always did when I was here before. I mean, with the news in that letter and all, I might not have that much time left to read magazines."

She marched past the tongue-tied Allegra O'Grady and dropped into the nearest seat, fanning herself with her hand. "It sure feels good to be sitting. I seem to get awfully tired these days." She picked up a *People* magazine and started thumbing through it, watching out of the corner of her eye as Allegra O'Grady hurried off down the hall and knocked on an unmarked door.

As soon as Allegra was gone, the nearest woman turned to her and whispered, "Did you say you were exposed to AIDS at this clinic?"

Rachel nodded. "That's what they say. We got this letter. . . ." She pulled it out of her pocket and was about to hand it to the woman when she heard a discreet cough behind her and a voice said, "Mrs. Stark? Could you come down to my office, please?"

She smiled sweetly up at him and pulled the letter back. "Oh, you didn't really want to read it anyway. It would only upset you. You're not supposed to be upset when you're trying to conceive, you

know." Then, as a carefully calculated afterthought, she called back, "Good luck." Dr. Isaacson put a polish-free hand on her shoulder and propelled her down the hall to his office.

As soon as the door shut behind them, he wheeled on her. "Just what in hell do you think you're doing?"

"Excuse me? I was waiting to see you. Is something wrong, Dr. Isaacson?"

"The things you were saying, out there in front of the patients . . ."

"Nothing but the truth, Doctor, was it? As far as that goes, I'm just as much of a patient as they are. This isn't a 7-Eleven, you know. It's a medical practice." She tilted her head to one side and looked up at him. "Don't you have to take some kind of an oath when you're admitted to practice medicine, to do no harm?"

"Yes, yes. The Hippocratic oath," he said impatiently. "What is it that you want?"

"I want my records."

"I already told your husband that we'd make a copy and send it to him. There was no need for you to fly all the way to Chicago. . . ."

Rachel looked over at his desk and saw that her file lay on top of a pile of files. She walked over and picked it up. "Here it is now. I'll just take it with me. . . ."

"You can't do that," he interrupted. "Those are all the original documents. We'll need to keep those. We'll send you copies."

"I can wait while you make them," she said. "I'm not in any hurry." She was enjoying acting peculiar and difficult. After a lifetime of being accused of it, it was fun to wallow in eccentricity.

"I'm afraid that's impossible. I haven't had time to . . ."

"Time to do what? Review the file? It doesn't matter, does it? They're all my records. There can't be anything there that I'm not entitled to see. If your staff doesn't have time, I'll just run it down to a copy shop—I noticed one down the street—and get them to do it." One advantage of spending so many years with a lawyer like Stephen—it had taught her not to back down when someone tells you a thing can't be done. Usually laziness, and not rules, was the underlying reason, and if it was rules, well, they were made to be folded, mutilated, spindled, and bent. Wisdom timid Rachel had

learned at Stephen's knee—or, more accurately, off the tip of his sharp tongue. She relished the anguish on Dr. Isaacson's face.

"I don't think you understand, Mrs. Stark. These are confidential medical records. . . ."

"Not from me, Doctor," she said brightly. "Though I must say, your reaction makes me wonder. Is there something in there you think I shouldn't see?" Isaacson looked like he wanted to kill her. His hands, age-spotted and hairy, scampered in and out of his pockets like mangy mice. "I don't think I'm going to let them out of my sight until the copies are made and I have a full set for myself." Rachel hadn't meant to make such an issue out of the records, they were just of secondary importance, but the reaction of everyone at the clinic was so offensive, she felt driven to be as difficult as possible, even if that hadn't been her strategy.

She got up, hands clasped, looking as demure as possible. "Is that something we can take care of now?"

"You only came for the records?"

"Stephen says we should have them," she answered unresponsively.

"Well, all right." He picked up the phone and spoke into it briefly. "Ms. O'Grady will make a copy and bring it out to you, if you'll just wait in our reception—" He caught himself. "If you'll just wait in Ms. O'Grady's office."

Rachel wanted to follow the file. She didn't trust any of them one bit, but she also liked the idea of being alone in Allegra O'Grady's office. She just might be able to pick up the donor's name without the major fuss she was anticipating. "That would be fine," she agreed.

Isaacson escorted her to the office and led Allegra into the hall to discuss the file. While they were whispering together, something else occurred to Rachel. It might be that the information she wanted was in the file itself, and that's why they were being so protective. Now she was torn. If she stayed in the office, they'd have an opportunity to remove whatever they wanted from the file. If she followed Allegra to monitor the copying, she wouldn't have a chance to search the office.

She nibbled at a nail and tried to think what Stephen would do.

Then it came to her. "Excuse me," she said, sticking her head out the door. "There's just one thing . . . before you make the copies . . . I'd just like to see the file for a minute." She smiled sweetly and held out her hand. In response to the fury in their looks, she made her smile sweeter. "Please?"

Finally, with an angry flounce, Allegra O'Grady handed it to her. "Only for a minute," she said. "I've got to hurry if I'm going to get the copies made by the end of the day. Otherwise, you'll have to wait until tomorrow. In fact . . ." Rachel saw her catch on to and grow pleased with the idea of putting this off to another day.

"Oh, I won't be but a minute." Rachel sat down in the nearest chair, pulled out her pen, and started numbering the pages, putting her initials and a number in the upper right-hand corner. On pages that had information both front and back, she put a separate number on each side.

"Wait a minute," Allegra said. "You can't write on those. They are our permanent records. . . ." Dr. Isaacson seemed to have fled to the security of his office.

"Oh, they're just page numbers. You know how it is when you're copying a whole lot of papers; it's so easy to forget a page or two, or to forget to copy both sides. This way we can keep track."

Allegra seemed to be at a loss for words. She glared at Rachel, as if that might make a difference, then paced back and forth the length of the small office a few times. Ignoring her, Rachel went on numbering the pages as quickly as she could. Suddenly Allegra swung around, hands on her hips, and said, "I'm sorry. I can't let you do that."

"Why not?" Rachel asked to buy time.

"It's just not appropriate."

Only a few pages to go. "Why is it inappropriate?" She reminded herself of Gallagher, the man who always had to ask why.

"It just is." Allegra reminded her of a toddler's mother. Do it because Mommy says so.

"That's all right," she said, putting the cap back on her pen. "I'm done. Sorry if it inconvenienced you, but I have to do what my husband tells me, and he said I should keep track of the pages. You

know how men are. So fussy about having the details done their way." She handed the file back to Allegra and tugged at her sweater, trying to pull it away from her skin. A present from Stephen, it might match her eyes and make her look young and sweet, but it itched like crazy. "Should I go back to the waiting room?"

"You can wait here." Allegra huffed out of the office, her well-toned rump pumping beneath the tight fabric of her skirt.

As soon as she was gone, Rachel was out of her chair and searching through the desk. At the bottom of the same pile where she'd found her own file, she found one marked NOTIFICATION. Quickly, she thumbed through it, aghast at the number of names on the list. There was a copy of a letter from the state health department, informing the clinic of their obligation, without further delay, to notify potentially infected recipients of the donor's sperm. And a master list of all the donees of donor number 02013, including the woman's name, spouse, if any, and the names of any children, if known, followed by a checklist with spaces for notification, response, and test results, if known.

There were surprisingly few known children. In the space underneath the donor number was a large whited-out patch that might once have held the donor's name and address. She held it up to the light, and then to a window, but couldn't see a thing. If only she'd had a knife, she might have scraped the stuff off. She tried a fingernail, but it slid harmlessly across the surface. Damn! Not knowing quite why she did it, Rachel folded the list and put it in her purse.

Damn. She searched the rest of the desk but didn't find anything else useful, and the filing cabinet was locked. If she couldn't do any more here, she might as well go and keep Allegra honest.

. . . it was the triumph of hope over experience . . .
—SAMUEL JOHNSON

CHAPTER EIGHTEEN

To her dismay, when she found the copy machine she also found Allegra O'Grady bent over the file with erasing fluid, deleting parts of the record. She reached over Allegra's shoulder and snatched the paper away. "Hey! What do you think you're doing?" Allegra cried, staring with dismay at a white streak across the sleeve of her red suit. The only other person in the room, a small Hispanic woman in a nurse's uniform, stared at them curiously.

"The more important question is what do you think you're doing?" Rachel responded. "I never should have let you and this file out of my sight." She grabbed the rest of the file from under the astonished executive assistant's nose and hastily thumbed through the pages. Luckily, Allegra hadn't gotten far. Still, she had already blotted out several sections. "I can't believe you did this. You know you're just inviting a closer look at your activities, asking for a lawsuit. You know that my husband is a lawyer." She closed the file, tucked it under her arm, and walked out of the room, back toward the waiting room, where there would be more witnesses. Allegra

O'Grady, alternating between anguished glances at her damaged sleeve and furious ones at Rachel, followed, looking like she was about to attack.

"You give that back," she cried, rushing after Rachel and tugging roughly on her arm. "You have no right. . . ."

Now there were four women in the waiting room and they all turned astonished eyes on Rachel and Allegra O'Grady. "What are you going to do? Call the police?" Rachel asked, stepping into the middle of the waiting room so that she was surrounded by patients. She unzipped her purse and thrust the file in, carefully zipping it back up. "I wouldn't mind that."

She spoke slowly and deliberately, wanting these women to hear her. She wanted them to share her growing horror at the attitude of this clinic, wanted them to have second thoughts about submitting their bodies and their futures to a place that placed so little value on patients and took so little responsibility for the psychic harm it had inflicted on her and on so many others. She imagined the other people on the waiting list receiving their letters. The soul-searing shock, couples clinging to each other for support, looking with breathless fear at their children, and even though this wasn't why she had come, anger made her speak.

"It might be very useful to have a police report documenting the fact that when I came to pick up a copy of my medical records, after having learned that as a result of treatment here I may have been exposed to the AIDS virus, the office attempted to destroy portions of the record. I don't see how that could possibly hurt me. But it could hurt you." Allegra O'Grady's artificially enhanced eyes widened and she took a step backward.

"Indeed," Rachel continued, "I wouldn't be surprised to learn that under Illinois law, the records legally belong to me and you were destroying my property." She was talking through her hat, but she didn't think Allegra knew that. It sounded plausible enough.

Usually, Rachel felt small and timid and helpless. Now she felt big and fierce and furious. "Or maybe you're going to attack me and try to take the records away? Then *I'd* have to call the police. . . ." Behind Allegra, Rachel saw that the nurse had followed them and was

finding the conversation fascinating. "But there is one other thing I came for, and if you'll give it to me, I'll go away quietly and never bother you again." She reached in her pocket and pulled out the crumpled flyer Stephen had brought home. She straightened it out and showed it to Allegra and then, turning, to the four watching women.

She felt eerily disconnected from herself, as if she, like the others, were watching Rachel Stark in a dramatic solo performance. Under the itchy sweater, perspiration was running down her arms. This was so desperately important and she was so totally at sea. She glanced down at the picture, pierced once again by the sight of David's face.

"Maybe you've seen this picture." It hung at the end of a trembling arm, fluttering like a banner in the wind. Her throat was closing, choking off her voice. "This is my son, David, who was conceived at this clinic. He's been kidnapped by his biological father. I need to know the father's name and address so that I can get my son back." As she stood there holding out the flyer, all pretense fell away, and Rachel was no longer an actress, she was only a grieving mother. She held the flyer out to Allegra. "Please," she said, "please help me find his father so that I can get my child back. I've already lost one child. I can't bear to lose another."

Allegra O'Grady looked down at the crumpled black-and-white picture and sniffed. "I wouldn't help you if my life depended on it." She turned on her heel and walked away. "Wait!" Rachel said. "I'll trade you the file . . . and a written promise not to sue . . . just give me the information." Allegra O'Grady never even looked back. She walked to her office, went inside, and shut the door.

Rachel stood in the center of those staring eyes, cloaked in despair. So much for playacting. It hadn't gone at all as she had planned. When her big scene came, she'd blown it. She just wasn't any good at things, except drawing and raising children. And was she any good at raising children, she who had lost both of hers? She felt like going out and walking in front of the first bus she saw. Her brave boast to Stephen that she was going to come to Chicago and make them tell her what she wanted to know looked terribly naïve and foolish now.

"You're really the mother of that poor kidnapped boy?" one of the women asked. Rachel nodded. She was beyond polite speech.

"And you were exposed to AIDS here at this clinic?" asked another.

Rachel nodded. "All three of us. We just found out. . . . A letter came . . . after David was taken. . . . I can't even have him tested to be sure. . . ."

"Maybe if you put it out that he is HIV-positive, the kidnapper might let him go," a woman suggested.

"No. They'd kill him to avoid being caught," the first woman asserted. "No one wants an HIV-infected child."

"I would," Rachel said softly. "He'd still be my son." She couldn't meet their eyes, their pitying gazes, or stand their blunt and hurtful opinions. Her own eyes swimming with tears, she made her way blindly to the door and down the hall to wait for the elevator.

"Excuse me?" said a voice behind her. She turned to find the Hispanic nurse beckoning from the shadow of a doorway. "Please, I don't want anyone to see me talking to you. Here." She thrust a folded sheet of paper into Rachel's hand. "This is the father. I am very unhappy with how they are treating you . . . all the patients . . . about this, but I cannot say so because I need my job. I wouldn't do this, only that you are looking for your child . . . and I, too, have lost a child . . . stolen by my husband and taken out of the country." She hesitated, as if she needed to explain something and didn't know how.

"Sometimes, other people have come here, looking for information about the fathers. I understand why we do not give it out. It would make things very confusing, mixing up all the families and maybe invading the privacy of people who don't want to be known. We've had grandparents—even a grandmother once, looking for her grandchildren. She said she wanted to leave them her money. I felt sorry for her, but not enough to help. I'm not sure, but I think she may have tried to bribe the receptionist. And fathers—donors who wanted to know if they had any children. But your situation is different. For you, I try to help."

She looked nervously up and down the hall. "You go now. I must

get back to my patient. Don't ever say to anyone that it was me, okay?"

Rachel hugged her. She was too choked up for speech. "Thank you," she whispered. All the way down in the elevator, she looked at her feet, so no one could see the tears in her eyes. All the way back to the hotel she stared at the blurry pavement and the passing masses of feet. Finally, she was back in her room. She sat down, unfolded the paper, and stared at the name of David's father.

Long is the way
And hard, that out of hell leads up to light.
— MILTON, *Paradise Lost*

CHAPTER NINETEEN

Stephen put in a long day—a productive one—and came home at nine to find the house dark and empty. No sign of Miranda or her car. Rachel presumably still in Chicago. He dropped his suit coat and briefcase in the hall and went into the kitchen. The light on the answering machine was dancing and the counter indicated that there were six messages waiting. He reached out automatically to press the button, then pulled back his hand, suddenly less certain that he wanted to hear the messages, at least not until he was sitting down and fortified with drink. He was still shaken by the memory of David's voice, trying to reach them and abruptly cut off. He was desperately eager to hear it again and at the same time, afraid.

There was a note from Miranda on the counter: "Gone to look at a house, then got a date. I left you some dinner in the oven."

Stephen opened the oven and peeked in cautiously. Some of the things she cooked these days scared him. Tomatoes stuffed with rice and tofu. Curried tofu and cauliflower. Marinated tofu on a bed of lettuce. Tofu, as far as he could tell, was the culinary equivalent of

white noise or the color beige. The stuff in the oven didn't appear to be tofu; it looked like a normal sort of casserole. Smelled like a normal sort of casserole. Smelled good enough to make him realize he was ravenous. He grabbed a plate and scooped up an enormous helping.

While it cooled, he went to the bar and poured a glass of Scotch. A small, gentlemanly Scotch. After the last few nights, he wanted to be very careful of his head. He carried his glass back to the kitchen, sat down, pulled his plate toward him, and took a bite. It even tasted like a normal casserole. Some normalcy germ must have invaded Miranda's body, reasserting itself as it overpowered the health-food virus. He was about to push the button on the machine when the phone rang.

"Stephen? It's Dr. Barker. May I speak with Rachel, please."

Something in the doctor's voice said bad news. "She's not here," he said. "She's in Chicago. She'll probably call in later. Can I give her a message?"

"I need to speak with her myself," Barker said. "Can you give me a number where I can reach her?"

"She'll be back tomorrow," he said, not wanting her any more upset than her self-appointed mission was already going to make her. All day he'd experienced chivalrous flashes that made him want to hop on a plane himself, to go out there and protect her.

"I'd like to talk to her tonight." Stephen, who questioned everything, didn't question Dr. Barker, whose authority was derived not from some Godlike posture but from his consistent refusal to play God. Barker also didn't believe in withholding information from his patients; if he had bad news, they heard it gently, but directly, from him.

"I'll find the number." Stephen's hands were shaking as he took out his appointment book and found the page where he'd written the number of Rachel's hotel. He carried it back to the phone and read it off. "Is it the test, Doctor? Is there bad news?"

"Stephen, much as I'd like to set your mind at ease, you know I can't talk to you about Rachel's medical condition until I've spoken with her." He sounded gruff, the way he always did when he had to

say something he didn't want to say. Unfortunately, with Stephen and Rachel, that occasion had occurred too often. Stephen was familiar with the tone. "I understand. I'll let you go now so you can call her." He hung up the phone before he yielded to the temptation to try and pry more information out of the doctor. Even knowing that it wouldn't do any good, he could hardly resist trying.

He ate the rest of the food before it got cold, and reached for the machine again. Wasn't it a little stuffy in the kitchen? Maybe the house needed a little air. It had a closed and musty feeling he didn't usually notice. He opened the sliders, pulled screens into place, and lingered there, letting currents of cool air wash over him, listening to the night sounds in the yard, the distant sound of baseball on a radio, the pulsing thud of a passing car with the sound turned up. Somewhere in the night a woman laughed, three short, rising bursts, and fell as abruptly silent as if she'd been strangled.

He turned back toward the bright, empty kitchen. Though he thought of himself as an independent person, Stephen didn't like being alone in the house at night. It made him uneasy. He didn't need to be with Rachel, often didn't even want to be with her, but he needed the touchstone of her presence in the house. Needed to know that she was there if he wanted her. Not necessarily sexually. It was more of a comfort thing, like having money in your pocket not because you want to spend it, but just to have the security of knowing it's there.

Quickly, before he changed his mind again, he hurried to the machine and pushed the button, scooping up the pen that was always nearby in case he needed to write something down. The first message purred out in Carole's inimitable voice. "Rach? Guess you aren't there. Hey, listen, I made like Jessica what's-her-name and snooped around at school. Everyone was so anxious to help! I could see they wanted to make stuff up, just to please me. No one knew much. You know how it is there . . . a whole community going around with their eyes on the ground like they were hoping to find scattered twenty-dollar bills. Those who don't, have their eyes on the kids. So few witnesses to a van full of child-napping perverts. Doesn't exactly inspire confidence, let me tell you. Here's the sum total—can you

tell I'm married to a tax attorney?—of my research. It was a van, and I'm quoting here, 'like all the mothers drive,' which I assume means Voyager or Caravan, but I might be wrong. I'd hate to have Mr. Toyota mad at me, not to mention Mr. Ford or Mr. Chevrolet. GMC? You could send Gallagher with pictures. At least two occupants, probably a man and a woman, and they were watching the children through binoculars, though it was hard to see because the windows were tinted. But no one thought to approach them. Or call the police. No one saw the harm in it or wanted to get involved or thought it was any of their business. Those last were all quotes."

There was a silence and Stephen thought the message was over but then Carole went on. "Dammit, Rach, isn't this a no-brainer? Shouldn't alarm bells have been going off in all their pointy little heads? I'm afraid I lost my temper, thinking about how careless they'd been. Despite my mother's lifelong admonitions, I did not mind my manners or keep my hot little temper. I actually yelled at people." There was a little snort of laughter. "Ron says he wished he'd seen it. He, of course, has never seen me lose my temper.

"Oh. I forgot something. The van was there at least twice. The person who gave me that tidbit was a janitor. The Asian one? And I doubt if he's passed that gem along to your friend Gallagher, since no one seems to have considered him important enough to talk to. The janitor, I mean, not the hunk. We've got children being stalked in a school yard here and no one at the whole damn school considers it to be a serious matter, despite that stupid banner they've put up. God! You'd think they'd be searching and interrogating anyone who comes within a thousand yards of the place, but no! I parked and walked in and wandered all around and no one even bothered to ask what I was doing there."

Another pause, some rustling, the more distant sound of Carole talking to someone. "That's when I got mad. Went to the principal and gave him the most vicious tongue-lashing I have ever delivered in my not altogether unconfrontational life. I believe he sported blisters on every inch of unprotected skin. Then I left in a huff. Ron thinks we're going to have to move. I told him no way. Other places are even worse. So call me when you get this, okay?"

Stephen pressed save and moved on to the next one, a gruff, brisk grunt from Gallagher, wanting to come by and talk. What had Carole called him? The hunk? Stephen couldn't see it. He looked at his own reflection in the mirror across the room and stroked some wayward hairs into place. Gallagher was mean, ugly, and monosyllabic. Carole probably just liked him because of his red hair. No need to save that message.

Next he heard John Robinson's quiet voice, telling Rachel that he'd like to talk with her and asking if she could give him a call. He pressed save again, wondering how he could persuade Rachel to talk to the man. When she was set against something, she could be as unmovable as stone. The next message was from Robinson again, this time for him, wanting to know if they could get together to discuss an idea he'd had for finding the van. Stephen wrote "Call Robinson" on his paper and listened for the next message. He never got to number six.

A deep, muffled male voice, difficult to understand. He turned up the sound and played it again. This time he got a few words: "your son," "back alive," and "later with ransom money." Shaken, he pressed save and called Gallagher and Robinson.

He paced impatiently back and forth in the kitchen, then in the entry, and finally outside in the driveway as he waited for them. The night was loud with spring eruptions of insects and amphibians and the sky a deep, clear blue-black. He noticed these things from all the years of having Rachel grab his arm and say look at this or listen to that. He wasn't a nature person; he was a fact person, an idea person, a personality person, while Rachel was visual, earthy in a rather ethereal way, and tuned in to emotions. He didn't need any pop psychology books to tell him how different they were, nor to tell him that he needed to listen in different ways to hear what Rachel was saying. He just didn't always act on what he knew.

While he felt a sense of satisfaction, or at least relief, that something was finally happening, mostly he felt himself in the grip of an enormous fear. If this was it, it was crucial that things be handled properly, and he didn't have much respect for the people who were going to be involved. This might be Robinson's doing. Unsettled by

all the flyers and the risk of discovery, David's kidnappers had grown nervous, and were willing to trade him for a price.

He heard the cars long before he could see them, and before they came into sight, he could see the strobelike flashes of red and blue through the trees. Then they burst into the open, turned off the road, and came racing up the driveway toward him. Gallagher's unmarked gray and a regular police car. As they leapt out of the cars and ran toward him, Stephen had a sense of how it would feel to be pursued, experienced a momentary urge to flee.

He led them into the kitchen, observing, as Gallagher moved past him toward the machine, that the man was too familiar in his house. Without asking for directions or permission, Gallagher punched the button and got the sixth message that Stephen hadn't played yet.

Happy and exhausted, the pace of her speech quickened by excitement, Rachel's words came tumbling off the tape. "Stephen! I did it! I got it! I got the name and address of David's father. I didn't think I would. They were horrible and wouldn't see me at all at first and then they tried to destroy my records and throw me out so I wouldn't upset the other patients. I finally had to grab the file and run and then I was standing by the elevator feeling hopelessly discouraged and wondering if I should go back there with a weapon or something when this kind nurse slipped out a side door and handed me a little slip of paper with the information I wanted."

She hesitated. "Stephen? I wish you were there. I'll try your office, too. Maybe I'll catch you somewhere. His name is Coffin. Isn't that awful? Peter Coffin. And he's in New York. Downstate, in the city. It's too late to get a good flight tonight, and I'm exhausted. I'll be home in the morning and then we've got to go and find this man. I love you."

Gallagher stared at him, sullen, disdainful. "You called us out here for this?"

"Of course not." Swearing inwardly, Stephen forced himself to respond in a calm voice. "I saved it. I'm afraid you'll have to listen to the other messages I saved first. It won't take long." He pushed the button that would retrieve the saved messages, watching with satisfaction as Carole's description brought a blush to Gallagher's pale face.

"Not that one, either," he said with satisfaction. "There are two brief ones, and then the one I called about." Two messages from Robinson. Gallagher looked at him and raised his eyebrows, but Stephen ignored him, listening intently for the message that was coming. A chill ran down his spine as the gruff voice spoke out again. Gallagher and the two uniformed cops leaned forward as they strained to decipher the garbled words.

"I have your son," Gallagher repeated. "If you want him back alive, you'll have to pay ten thousand dollars. I will be calling you again to let you know how to pay the ransom money." Stephen, listening with a giant, agonizing pain inside, wondered absurdly how they could value his son so little.

THE NEXT DAY, *David didn't go to school. He got up, the same as always, and did all the usual morning things like wash up and brush his teeth, even though every time he moved his whole body hurt. He got dressed before he went down to breakfast because the woman yelled at him if he didn't, but he couldn't tie his shoes. It just hurt too much. He would have stayed in bed; he felt just the same as he'd felt when he had the flu last winter, but she scared him so much he didn't dare. He was afraid she'd come upstairs and hit him again.*

On his way downstairs, he stopped, and closed his eyes, and tried to send a message to his mother. Of course if she was dead, like the woman said, it wouldn't do any good, but he didn't believe the woman anymore. Maybe, like those times when he was at school and he'd say inside his mind, "Look at what we're doing today, Mom," she'd get the message and she'd know he needed her help. He held his breath and he concentrated on trying to tell her that he was okay, but she had to come and get him soon. He repeated the message several times over and waited, but he couldn't feel anything coming back. That was all right; he'd never been able to feel her answer.

"Just what in tarnation do you think you're doing, lurking around up there on the stairs. Get down here and eat your breakfast. You're going to be late for the bus."

Reluctantly, David got up again and, using the railing, helped himself down the rest of the stairs and limped slowly across the kitchen. He climbed

onto his chair, looked at the bowl of steaming gray oatmeal, and put a hand over his mouth. Even the toast, usually his favorite part of breakfast, looked awful this morning.

"Well, come on. Eat it up. We don't waste food in this family." She looked awful today. Different. Angrier, as though before she'd been putting on an act and now she wasn't anymore. She didn't give him any of her stiff smiles or awkward pats.

David wanted to tell her that he wasn't a part of this family; he was part of a family that would understand if a boy didn't feel like eating once in a while. Reluctantly, he stuck in a spoon and started to raise a tiny bite toward his lips. The spoon shook and the tears in his eyes blurred the sight. The spoon fell from his fingers and landed in his lap, smearing his pants and shirt with oatmeal.

"Now look what you've done. . . ." the woman thundered. "March up there and get changed this instant! Play clothes, David, not your school clothes. There's no way I can let you go to school looking like that." She slammed a pot onto the stovetop and another one into the sink. "May be no way I can ever let you go back to school, when you can't be trusted. You've really let me down, son. You know that? I had such hopes for you. . . ."

As he fumbled his way out of the chair, he heard springs squeak as the old man got up. Heard the shuffling of old, tired feet. "Leave him be, Mother," the man said in his soft voice. "The boy's not feeling well. Let him rest awhile. I was thinkin' that later I might take him fishin'."

The weariness, the fever, and the fret,
Here, where men sit and hear each other groan . . .
—KEATS, "Ode to a Nightingale"

CHAPTER TWENTY

From Gallagher's reaction, Stephen could see that John Robinson was about as welcome as a skunk at a wedding, but from the minute he entered the kitchen, Stephen felt better. The balance immediately shifted, in his mind, from intimidated, unrespected victim's father versus the police to the high-tech national team of himself and Robinson versus the incompetent local team of Gallagher and the cops. He took a deep breath and his chest didn't feel like it was being crushed.

"Thanks for coming," he said, holding out his hand. "I want you to listen to a message." This time he fast-forwarded directly to the relevant message, grimacing as the gruff voice came on. Thanks to Gallagher's translation, Stephen was able to make out the words—even more wrenching now that he knew what they said—but Robinson craned forward with a strained look on his face.

"What did he say?" he asked in the silence that followed.

Stephen repeated the message. Robinson nodded thoughtfully. "It sounds like a hoax to me."

"Why do you think so, John?" Gallagher asked. Stephen was surprised by the use of a first name. He couldn't imagine Gallagher calling him Stephen.

Robinson smiled. "You won't like this . . . intuition, Joe."

So even Gallagher had a first name. Mrs. Gallagher hadn't looked at her newborn, red-faced, red-haired baby and simply dubbed him Gallagher, to be supplied with a first name, Detective, when he became an adult. It lent an oddly human quality to the situation that no interchange with Gallagher had ever had before.

"Intuition?" Stephen and Gallagher said together. The uniformed cops stared at them.

"Sure. No serious kidnapper is going to snatch a kid, wait three weeks, and then only ask for ten thousand. What do you think?"

Gallagher wasn't used to being asked to share his opinions. Stephen already knew how reluctantly he divulged any information, so he was surprised when Gallagher responded. "He could be running scared. Way you've papered the world with pictures, he might be ready to dump the kid and cut his losses."

"Ten thousand is chump change. It barely covers expenses."

"So maybe the kidnapper isn't smart. . . ."

"He's smart enough to snatch the kid without being seen and keep him out of sight for almost a month. And what about this stalking business . . . if they were after just any kid, why stake out the school yard? And why take such a risk for such a small return? Nah. This isn't the kidnapper. This is someone looking to cash in on the situation and make a quick ten grand."

"I don't agree with you, John," Gallagher said, and Stephen had the feeling he'd said it before.

"I know you don't and I don't expect I can persuade you. My main fear is that you'll get sidetracked by this and put the rest of your investigation on hold. Not follow up on vital things, like the information that woman on the phone picked up. I don't know about you, but I'd sure like to know what make of van it was, and whether anyone noticed anything about the license, or has some description of the occupants to offer. And purely from a public safety viewpoint, shouldn't the school administration be being more vigilant?"

"Come on, John. You really didn't think we weren't going to follow up on that . . . ?"

"What I think is that the boy's been gone for nearly a month and
you've missed an opportunity to gather important information from
people who knew a lot about him."

"Why don't you leave the gathering of information to us, Robinson," Gallagher's cheeks were flaming.

"My only interest is in finding the boy. . . ."

"Your only interest is keeping your name and the name of your
organization in the paper."

"So what do we do now?" Stephen said loudly, interrupting their
tedious sparring.

"Wait and see if he calls again," Gallagher told him. "We'll keep
an officer here, just in case, and put a tap on the line. Does Rachel
know about this?"

So it was Rachel and not Mrs. Stark. Everyone was on a first-
name basis here except him, even people who hated each other.
Stephen felt like the kid who is picked last for the team. "What do
you think, John?"

Robinson looked at him curiously, and once again Stephen had
the feeling Robinson was seeing the things that weren't being said,
was aware of why Stephen was using his first name. "Does your machine record the time that calls come in?" Stephen nodded. "What
time did that one come, then?"

Stephen checked the machine. "Quarter of eight."

Robinson considered. "And it's quarter of ten now. So he should
be calling in the next half hour."

"You've added psychic powers to your repertoire?" Gallagher said.

"You know me, Joe. I'll try anything if I think it may help find
missing children. . . ."

"You'll do anything if you think it will keep your . . ."

"Keep my name in the paper. Yes, yes. You already said that." He
took out his wallet, extracted a twenty-dollar bill, and laid it on the
counter. "I'll bet you twenty dollars that he calls in the next half
hour."

Gallagher whipped out his wallet, took out his own twenty, and

laid it next to Robinson's. "You're on." Addressing Stephen, he said, "That woman on the phone, Carole. She's a friend of Rachel's?"

"Best friend. And her son, Tommy, was David's closest friend. I know you've talked with both of them."

"Since I can't leave for a while—I assume I have to be present to win this bet—do you suppose she'd be willing to come over and talk to me here? You wouldn't mind, would you?" The bet was just an excuse, Stephen knew. Gallagher had no plans to go anywhere for a while, no matter what.

What if he did mind, Stephen thought. Fat lot of good it would do. Gallagher appeared to have been sired by a bulldozer. Unless it was just a bull. "Not at all," he said, rattling off Carole's number. "Just don't tie up the phone for long. We don't have call waiting. Rachel doesn't believe in it. She thinks it's impolite."

"It is impolite," Robinson said. "Convenient, but damned impolite."

"Can I get any of you gentlemen something to drink? I could make some coffee," Stephen offered.

"Sounds good to me," Gallagher agreed, and the other cops nodded. Robinson asked for tea. While Stephen made coffee and filled the tea kettle, Gallagher called Carole, who was happy to come right over, and sent one of the uniformed cops out to the cruiser to make some calls arranging for the phone tap. Fifteen minutes crept slowly by as the coffee finished and got served, Stephen found a package of gourmet cookies, and a pot of Earl Gray tea was brewed. Every minute or so, at least one member of the group cast a surreptitious glance at the clock.

At minute sixteen, the door slammed and Carole came flying into the kitchen, a screwy vision in black-and-white cow-spotted leggings and an oversized scarlet shirt, her rusty hair standing out from her head like an outgrown Afro. The men all stood and Stephen noted that she barely reached Gallagher's chest. He'd never realized she was so small. "I know I look like hell," she said, and both uniformed cops stared at her in astonishment, looking for the source of the voice. "I was cleaning the refrigerator. That's how I calm down when I'm really mad. There's nothing like a succession of black and

green molds to dampen one's ardor. I would have changed but I didn't want to keep you waiting." She planted her hands on her hips and tipped back slightly to stare up at Gallagher. "How can I help?"

"Maybe we could all go in the living room," Stephen suggested. "It's more comfortable in there." The kitchen was a pleasant room, but with so many lights on, it seemed all brightness and hard, flat surfaces. Not comforting or inviting, especially without Rachel. Besides, he couldn't keep his eyes off the clock. There was no clock in the living room.

Gallagher looked like he was going to tell them to leave him alone with Carole, but then he shrugged and without a word led Carole out of the room, leaving the rest of them to follow if they chose. He didn't even make an effort to exclude Robinson.

The living room was all dark wood, oversize, superbly comfortable pieces of furniture and small warm pools of light. Carole chose a big green chair and curled up in it, her feet tucked underneath her, her shoes left behind on the floor. Gallagher sat across from her, in Rachel's rocking chair, an ancient, venerable piece, with the shape of generations of bottoms worn into the seat and the arms worn thin. It creaked under his weight and Stephen tried not to look alarmed. If Rachel came home and found Rustylocks had broken her chair, she wouldn't be pleased. It was the chair in which she'd rocked her babies.

Gallagher began his questions, following up on her telephone message, and Carole answered as best she could. The rest of them pretended to listen, holding their collective breath and waiting for the phone to ring. The silence of the phone almost drowned out Gallagher's big voice and Carole's rich one.

It was like waiting for a jury to come back. Stephen couldn't have explained why, but he was sure that Robinson was right and as the minutes ticked by he began to make up reasons why Robinson's half hour should reasonably be construed to include the following thirty minutes as well. Twenty-six minutes into the bet, he took a cold, hard look at what was happening to him and to all of them and suddenly a streak of anger shot through him like a bolt of lightning.

"This is sick!" he announced, standing up. "We're all treating

this like some great big game. Making a contest out of whether the kidnapper will call. What this is about is a little boy's life, goddammit! I don't care who wins or loses. I just want my son back alive. I just want to see David again."

He left them staring and strode into the empty kitchen, kicking angrily at a stool that was in his way. It toppled over and fell with a loud crash onto the tile floor. He stepped around it and headed for the back door. He was choking on anger, suffocating with anxiety. He needed some air.

Twenty-seven minutes into the bet, the phone rang. Gallagher and Carole fell silent; everyone else's heads came up like startled deer. Alone in the kitchen, Stephen reached out a shaking hand and picked it up.

There is a panther caged within my breast . . .
—WHEELOCK, "The Black Panther"

CHAPTER TWENTY-ONE

Rachel sat on the bed in the impersonal hotel room in Chicago and tried to still the chaos in her soul. In her hand, the unnoticed receiver repeated the endless, grating voice of the operator, urging her to hang up. What was going on? She needed to talk to Stephen. She'd already tried to call him twice earlier tonight and left messages on the machines at home and at his office. Then she'd called and the line was busy and now he wasn't answering. Why wasn't he home? Was something happening that she should be home for? Something no one had bothered to call her about? Finally the noise of the phone penetrated the swirl of questions in her mind and she disconnected.

What a day! She felt like she'd been in a gigantic paddleball game with herself as the ball and everyone batting her back and forth. That was how it felt, but the perception was wrong. She hadn't been that helpless, had she? Stephen had expected her to fail, to be frustrated and embarrassed. Well, he'd been partly right. She had been frustrated and embarrassed and outrageous and scared and

desperate and furious, but she'd come to Chicago to get something and she'd gotten it. Maybe not easily, and maybe only because she'd had a bit of good luck. Still, she'd told Stephen she was going to come out here and get information about David's father, and she'd done it. And tomorrow she was going to go home, and find him, and bring David back.

Yeah, that probably wouldn't be as simple as she imagined it, either. In her mind, she had a vision of marching up to Dr. Peter Coffin in his New York City apartment, ringing the bell, and demanding that he return her son at once. What if she arrived and Dr. Coffin no longer lived there? Or was there and he wouldn't let her in, refused to talk to her? What if he'd taken David and gone away, gone someplace where no one would find him? What would she do then? Could she get Gallagher to search for him—Gallagher who, like Stephen, thought she was totally off the wall—or would she have to hire a private detective? And how long would that take?

Once again she had an urge to act, and no plan. As a child, she'd hated Monopoly and chess and only tolerated checkers. When she tried to think out a coherent plan, her mind betrayed her by racing off in odd directions. It was one of the ways in which she and Stephen were entirely different. She was all instinct and intuition, he all logic and planning. It used to seem like a good thing, something they admired about each other, but more and more, Stephen pressured her to be more like him, was frustrated with the things about Rachel that made her most herself. How ironic relationships were! I love you because you're you, and now I want to make you ever more like me. She didn't understand it. It would never occur to her to demand that Stephen change. She was never that certain that her own ideas were right.

Someday, when they had David back and things were calm, they'd have to confront these issues. It already seemed like an eternity that David had been gone. Sometimes when she closed her eyes, she had trouble seeing his face. Sometimes it seemed as though he was already fading out of her memory as if someone were erasing him by remote control. Would she wake up someday and find all her memories of David gone, leaving only the scars on her soul?

"It will never happen," she said aloud to the empty room. Not when she could still see Jonah so clearly. She could still smell the sweet baby scent, still feel the warmth of his downy head, still feel the slight solidness of him in her arms. It might have been yesterday that they had laid him, newborn, in her arms. Forget him. Get over it. That's what people always told her. She'd never understood why. Didn't Jonah deserve to be remembered? And who else was there to remember him, that precious, brave little soul whose time on earth had been so short?

It was the same with David. She could still feel his newborn body in her arms, the determined wiggling of his arms and legs. Stephen remembered David as a peaceful baby, but David had been born to escape. Rolling over early, crawling early, cruising the furniture when other babies still sat and stared. At nine months, David had set off on his own across the room, looked back at her, and laughed with glee. So safe, so confident, as long as she was there. Let her disappear from sight, and instantly he would wail. Poor boy. Out of sight for all these weeks. No wonder she'd heard him crying in her head.

She closed her eyes and emptied her mind and waited to see if David's voice would come. Nothing came. His face came back into clear focus but no voice. A queer, pinched, frightened face that was David and yet unlike any way that she had ever seen him. She waited. No. Nothing except anxious questions about what was happening at home and why Stephen wasn't answering. Nothing except a million questions about Dr. Barker's phone call.

Dr. Barker had not been his usual self but even though they'd spoken for several minutes, that was all she knew. Well, she knew he'd called because he had something important—important and upsetting—that he wanted to tell her, but had been unable to make himself deliver the news. That was very unlike Dr. Barker, who she knew from experience usually didn't pull his punches. This mysterious holding back was more frightening than if he'd just gone ahead and told her. All he'd said was that there had been some—what was the word he had used? unusual? disturbing? unexpected?—results to her tests that he needed to discuss, and he didn't want her to fill any prescriptions or take any of the medicines he'd prescribed, except the one for anemia, until they'd had a chance to talk.

Oh, come on, Rachel, she told herself, what's the big mystery? You didn't go in there to get tested for a bladder infection; you went to get tested for AIDS. So if he's got test results that disturb him, it's because you've tested positive, right? What else could it be? Her mind wanted to argue a million other things. And there was always the possibility of a false positive; maybe that's why he wanted to talk to her in his office instead of over the phone, to explain it in detail and then do another test.

Stephen knew Dr. Barker had called, because he'd had to call there first to get her number, so why hadn't Stephen called? Didn't he care? Surely he also had sensed the uneasiness in the doctor's voice? Stephen the professional persuader, the professional manipulator, was keenly attuned to the nuances in other people's voices. And Stephen hated not knowing things. He almost certainly would have tried to get the information himself, and failing that, would have called her here as soon as he'd allowed time for the doctor's call, to find out what the story was. And he hadn't. It must mean something was going on at home. She picked up the phone again and dialed her number.

She got another busy signal. Damn! She needed to know what was happening. She brushed her teeth, put on her nightgown, and got into bed, but she was too restless to sleep. She got up and paced the floor, muttering to herself. Where was he when she needed him? Her imagination played graphic scenes of David's body being found— in a Dumpster, along the roadside, in a ditch, hidden in underbrush, thrust into a culvert, in an abandoned car—each scene peopled with Stephen and Miranda and Gallagher and John Robinson and Carole, complete with appropriately garish lights and sirens and the background chatter of radios, and no one thinking to call her.

Finally she couldn't stand it anymore. Her anxiety level had risen until she could hardly breathe and she was too jittery to stand the confines of the small room. Maybe if she ate something. A cup of tea and a muffin? Probably not. The thought of food made her nauseous. She just needed some air. She pulled on her jeans and a T-shirt, grabbed her coat, and stuck the room key and a few dollars into her pocket. Then she took the elevator to the lobby.

The desk clerk's voice followed her as she headed for the door.

"Excuse me, ma'am. It's hard to get cabs at this time of night. Let me call one for you."

She paused. Half turned. "I'm just going out for a walk."

"I wouldn't advise you to do that, ma'am. Chicago tries hard, but there are a lot of street people around, and some of them are dangerous."

"I won't go far. Just a little walk. I was too restless to sleep. . . ."

"We've got a nice fitness room, ma'am. It's usually closed at this time of night, but I could get security to open it up for you. There's a treadmill. . . ."

"I need to be out in the air," she said, and hurried through the door before he could scare her further. She must project an uncommon air of vulnerability. The whole world seemed determined to look after her whether she wanted it or not. She turned right out the door and headed off down the street in her usual rapid stride, trying to remember the advice she'd read for women walking alone. Look purposeful. Stay on the outside of the sidewalk. Walk in well-lighted areas where there are other people. Well, there weren't any other people and not much light. Six blocks down, she came to the edge of a park. She was half a block along when—country mouse that she was—she realized that parks at night were not the pleasant places they were in the daytime. They were places where street people congregated and slept.

The block ahead wasn't very well lit, either. It was probably time to head back. She had no idea how far she'd come. Her mind had been on Stephen and David, on the mystery of the phone, on Dr. Barker's unusual behavior, on what she would do when she got home. The frantic chugging of her feet had done nothing to diminish the frantic thoughts in her head.

"It's awfully late for you to be out alone like this . . ." a voice behind her said. A black voice, she thought. She hadn't even heard him coming. This was no time to think about the folly of her willful desire to walk. Advice from numerous articles in women's magazines, digested in scattered minutes in doctor's and dentist's waiting rooms, pouring into her head like twin steams of coffee and milk from a vending machine. You only have three seconds to react. Re-

member to breathe. Stop breathing and you're done for. Scream, fight, make noise, do anything that will show your resistance and call attention to yourself. Cooperate, be nice, try to make a human connection, try to talk your assailant out of it. I shall scream and be silent, I shall be aggressive and resist and be nice and cooperative, she thought hysterically. I shall try to breathe when my chest is frozen with fear. I shall split myself in two, with each half behaving differently, and scare him off by my demented behavior.

Screaming felt right. She sucked in a breath and would have screamed, but the man put a hand on her shoulder. "Take it easy, lady. I'm a cop." He had the deep, rumbling voice of an old lion.

She turned, still cautious in case it was a trick, but there he was, tall and massive, with bits of metal and polished leather gleaming even in the faint glow of the street light. "It's awfully late," he repeated. "Could I drive you somewhere?"

"I was just . . . walking," she said. "You scared me."

"Better scared than something worse. Can we take you home?" A patrol car was now sitting at the curb.

"Home is in New York." A stupid, nervous giggle escaped.

"Can we take you somewhere?" he repeated. "Your hotel?"

There was something about him that made her reluctant to argue, aware, even with her inept perceptual skills, that she shouldn't do anything further to irritate him or cause him to question her sanity. Suddenly, she was glad to let someone else take charge. The whole day seemed so unreal, from Mary Poppins psychics to giant rescue cops, with the whole awful business at the clinic sandwiched in the middle. The truth was that right now, much as she might dislike authoritarian figures taking over and telling her what to do, she wasn't doing a very good job of taking care of herself. She did no one any good by getting mugged or murdered on the streets of Chicago.

She wrapped her arms defensively around herself, unable to meet his eye. "I'd be grateful for a lift back to my hotel," she said, and told him where she was staying.

The cop put a hand under her elbow and escorted her to the car. Maybe he thought she was a crazy who might otherwise run

away. Rachel kept her mouth shut and practiced being cooperative. Stephen always told her she couldn't do it, that she lacked the gene for being cooperative. She bent her head and climbed into the car. The driver accelerated and pulled smoothly away from the curb. Into the night, into the unknown, depending on the kindness of strangers, the bleak street she'd been walking whisking past in a surreal rush.

"You were just out for a walk," the big cop said. His tone was as incredulous as if she'd said she was practicing for a jump over the moon. "At this time of night in this part of town?"

"I don't know Chicago very well," she said defensively. Her stomach hurt and there was a buzzing in her head. Was she hungry? She couldn't remember eating dinner. She couldn't remember eating lunch.

"People have to take some responsibility for themselves," the cop said. "We do our best, but we can't do everything, lady. You've gotta help us out, you know. . . ."

"I'm sorry I'm making a nuisance of myself. I wasn't thinking. . . . I've had a lot on my mind—"

"So call a friend or read a book or join a health club or go to a bar. But don't go walking the streets in the middle of the night."

"—ever since my son was kidnapped," she finished.

The blabbing cop fell silent, then said, "Kidnapped? When?"

"Four weeks ago. Almost. In New York." Why was she telling them this? She didn't walk to talk about it.

"What's the story?" the driver asked.

"No story," Rachel said. Suddenly she was almost too weary to speak. "He simply vanished."

"Someone who has it in for you. For you or your husband," the blabbing cop said.

He went on talking, asking questions about the kidnapping, but Rachel didn't hear. There was a faint voice in her head, a voice she would listen to if only this man would shut up. Maybe he'd saved her life and maybe she should be grateful, but what she wanted was for them to hurry up and drop her off, to shut up and go away before she lost the voice.

She felt small and fragile and cold, huddling there on the back-seat, being lectured to like a truant child. The car pulled up to the hotel and the cop got out and opened the door. Her feet felt like giant weights and the rest of her was leaden. "Thanks for bringing me back."

"Next time, be more careful." He climbed into the car and slammed the door. She watched it drive away, then turned and trudged inside. It might be late, but she had to call Stephen. Otherwise, she'd never sleep.

The clerk watched her cross the lobby, and though she didn't look at him, she felt his eyes on her as she waited for the elevator. As the door closed behind her, she could hear someone crying, even though she was alone. She felt a sharp pain in her chest. She closed her eyes and concentrated on her breathing; she seemed to have forgotten how. In and out, she reminded herself. In and out. More sharp pains. And then, shatteringly clear, David's voice, screaming. "Mommy! Mommy! Help me!"

She walked numbly to her room, feeling foolish and ashamed at having gone out and gotten herself into trouble, and frantic with the need to find out what was happening. Without taking off her coat, she picked up the phone and called Stephen. He answered on the first ring.

"Rachel, where in hell have you been? I've been calling. The desk clerk said you'd gone for a walk. People don't go walking around Chicago in the middle of the night." He didn't ask if she was all right. He just said, "You've got to get home as soon as possible. The first plane you can get. There's been a ransom demand for David."

The small desperate cry of David's voice, calling to her, calling for help, tore through her again. "I know," she said. "I know. He's in terrible trouble."

. . . anything possible at the hands of
Time and Chance, except, perhaps, fair play.
—THOMAS HARDY, *The Mayor of Casterbridge*

CHAPTER TWENTY-TWO

Rachel watched Stephen's face as he listened to the caller. He'd had a bad night, she could see. The strain was telling on him. He was missing his usual air of competent authority; he looked beaten down. Beaten down and explosive. Gallagher had the disagreeable look he'd worn so often when he came to interrogate them, a look she now understood was more habit than mood, and Robinson, the only one of them who appeared at all rested, had a strange eagerness on his face. He liked these situations, she thought. He enjoyed the thrill of the chase. Only Miranda looked normal. So normal and unconcerned that Rachel wanted to strangle her.

"Gallagher," she said, plucking at his sleeve. "Has anyone spoken with David yet?"

He raised a finger to his lips and Rachel understood that Stephen was supposed to be alone. That was silly. The kidnapper must know that they'd have the house full of cops. Still, she wasn't going to be the one to spoil the pretense. She sat back down on her stool and reached for the coffee Miranda had just poured. Too fast.

Her shaking hand knocked over the cup and sent a cascade of scalding hot liquid onto her thighs. She jumped up, still without a sound, grabbed a towel, sponged off as much as she could, and fled upstairs, where she could remove her pants without an audience.

She stood in the bathroom, her thighs on fire, and tried to take off her jeans. Her hands were shaking so badly she couldn't undo the button. She fumbled with it, tears streaming down her face, tried to tear them off, but of course, being sturdy denim, they wouldn't budge. A fist banged at the door. "Rachel, are you okay?"

"Stephen. Help me. I can't . . ." she gasped.

The door burst open and Gallagher, not Stephen, rushed in. Grasped the situation instantly. Had her jeans undone and off before she could say a word, and was running cold water into the tub. "Get in and sit down," he ordered. "Stephen's right. You are too helpless to be allowed out. When this goddamned situation's over, I'm going to give you a good talking-to about how to take care of yourself."

"I'm not—" Before she could say any more, the door banged again and Stephen came in. He stared at her, at Gallagher, at the jeans still in Gallagher's hand, turned on his heel, and stalked out again, radiating red-hot anger.

"Stephen, wait . . . it's not . . ." Rachel was talking to an empty room, for Gallagher had followed Stephen out. "Oh shit!" she said, closing her eyes and leaning back. She never used bad language. "Oh shit, shit, shit. Is nothing ever going to go right again?" She'd started referring to her own personal cloud as a joke; she was beginning to believe in it. Maybe it wasn't a cloud. Maybe it was a small tornado that swirled around her, laying all to waste. A one-woman chaos machine.

She lay there and let the rising water soothe her burning legs. She was too exhausted and too much had happened for her to be embarrassed that Gallagher had seen her in her underwear. Gradually, over the course of his investigation, Gallagher was getting to see pretty much all of her, wasn't he? And it was nothing to write home about, either. She smiled at the idea of Gallagher, pen reluctantly in hand like a small boy at camp, writing to his mother about her

breasts and legs. The image coming, for a moment, between her and her humiliation, her embarrassment at being undressed by Gallagher and her shame at the humiliation it caused Stephen.

Gallagher this morning and the Chicago cop last night. The entire official world—and Stephen—thought she needed a keeper. Who knew? Maybe they were right. Maybe she could come to like it. But this was not the time to be thinking about herself, or about Stephen and even Gallagher, despite the raised male voices coming up from downstairs. Today, tomorrow, all the days were about David, until they got him back.

She closed her eyes, lowered her ears beneath the water, and listened to the roar from the tap. David, my darling, are you there? Her heart seemed to skip at the sound of his name, as if the burden of sorrow and waiting, weariness and hunger, was taking its toll and the mechanism was wearing down.

Small and faint, over the roar of the water, she heard a voice. She held her breath and strained to catch the words. It was David's voice, sounding the weary way he did when he was sick or scared. As clearly as if he'd been in the next room, she heard him calling to her to come and get him. Calling to her for help. She opened her eyes, lifted her head, and looked down at her arms. They were covered with giant goose bumps. Not from the cold water. These bumps were her own visceral response to the deep, echoing terror in her son's voice. Goose bumps and a feeling in her chest like it was being slowly crushed by a giant vise.

She stood up and grabbed a towel. Dressed in a long, loose dress that fell free of her burned legs. Pinned back her hair and hurried downstairs. Stephen, Gallagher, Robinson and a couple cops were clustered around the island, their heads together, listening to Gallagher speak. Miranda was loading the dishwasher. She stopped in the doorway and waited for the huddle to break up. Stephen was the first one out, breaking away fast and hurrying toward her, his gaze, when it rested on her, brimming with fury. He would have gone right past without speaking, but Rachel put a hand on his chest and forced him to stop.

"I'm in a hurry, Rachel," he snapped.

"I know. You can spare one minute to tell me what's going on."

"Why don't you ask your friend Gallagher?"

"Because I'm asking you. Have you spoken with him?"

"Of course. That's why I'm in such a hurry. I'm supposed to be at a phone booth in fifteen minutes to take his call."

"I meant David."

"No. They won't let me talk to him."

"What did he say? The kidnapper, I mean?"

"It's on the machine," Stephen said impatiently, pushing her roughly out of his way. "You can listen for yourself."

Rachel watched him go and when she turned, saw that Gallagher and Robinson were both staring at her. It's like we're in a play, she thought. Our lives have become an ongoing performance for other people to watch. People camp out in our house; a near stranger can barge into the bathroom and strip off my clothes, then linger to lecture me on my behavior. No wonder we can't find the words to speak to each other. Whatever seemed difficult when it was just the two of us is that much harder when we have no privacy.

"He didn't mean to be like that; he's just upset," John Robinson said.

"You don't have to explain my husband to me, Mr. Robinson. And just so we're clear about this, as far as I'm concerned, this whole business, this deliberate manipulation, is your fault."

Robinson looked puzzled. "How so?"

"If you hadn't put those damned posters everywhere, the kidnappers wouldn't have gotten stirred up. But if you ask me, these aren't the real kidnappers anyway."

"That was my initial reaction, too," Robinson said.

"But you've changed your mind now, haven't you?" Gallagher asked.

"Maybe . . ."

"What do you mean, maybe? This is textbook kidnapper procedure, toying with the victim, upping the ante. It's just what you'd expect . . ."

"What *you'd* expect," Robinson said.

"I'd like to listen to the call," she said. "May I?" But no one was

paying any attention. Gallagher and Robinson went on arguing while one of the cops made a pot of coffee. "Excuse me," she repeated, "but I'd like to listen to the call."

Still no response. She might as well have been an invisible woman with her volume turned off. Now that they'd paused in their busy morning to explain her husband to her, it was time for the little woman to go away and let them get on with their guy things, as Miranda had done a few minutes ago. She slipped off her loafer, a sturdy, leather-soled item, and slammed it down loudly on the counter. "Excuse me," she said, raising her voice, "but I'd like to listen to the call!"

Everyone turned to stare at her, surprised. "Why?" Gallagher asked.

"So I'll know what's going on. And, as I said to you once before when you were asking one of your tiresome "why's," because I might recognize something about the voice or the words that no one else would."

Gallagher almost smiled. "Not completely helpless," he said. He pressed a button, rewound, and played the message for her, the cocky, taunting voice filling the kitchen. She closed her eyes and listened, not so much to the words—it didn't matter to her what phone booth Stephen should go to or what time he had to be there—as to the voice, its tone, language, inflection. "Could you play it again?" she asked when it was done. Gallagher played it again. Robinson was watching her with gleaming eyes.

"I know who that is," she said.

The change in Gallagher was astonishing. His casual, droopy, waiting pose fell away, and had he been a dog, his ears would have stood up and his tail risen. He fixed his eyes on her, his body taut, his hand extended across the counter as though reaching for her words. His "Who?" boomed out loudly.

"I'm not sure I can remember his name. Jason something . . ." Gallagher's breath exploded with an impatient snort. "Look, it's okay. Even without the name . . . I can find him. I know where he lives. It's . . . he . . . last summer . . ." She was having trouble starting; the impatience made her nervous and she wanted to be clear. If she were the yelling kind, she would have screamed at him to back off.

"Last summer there was a college boy who worked for the lawn care service we use. He always seemed to be the one they sent and he was careless . . . cutting too close to the gardens and mowing down plants, pruning shrubs badly and leaving the prunings lying around, not taking the time with the trimmer to do a decent job on the edges. I spoke with him about it, several times, but it didn't help. He was rude to me. Insolent. We . . . Stephen . . . called the service and complained. They were very nice and assured us that they wouldn't send him here again, but the next time they came to mow, he came again. I watched him closely because of the previous times, and he wasn't any better, so I went out to speak to him about it."

She swallowed hard. Her eyelids dropped, lashes trembling. One delicate hand gripped the other. "I don't like confrontations, but it was necessary. Instead of apologizing or offering to do better, he swore at me. The vilest language . . . and in front of David, too, and then he . . . he . . ." Her voice dropped to almost a whisper. "He grabbed himself and he told me that my problem was that I just needed a good fuck . . . excuse me, those are his words, not mine . . . and he was just the man to do it. I asked him to leave immediately and went inside to call the service. When I came out, he was gone and so were Stephen's golf clubs and all of our tennis rackets."

"Did you call the—" Gallagher began.

"Yes. Of course. I called the police and then I called Stephen and told him what had happened, and he handled it from there. The boy was fired, of course, and the police did find our stuff at his house. Our stuff and lots of other people's stuff as well. The kid was helping himself wherever he went."

"Did you press—" Gallagher began again.

Rachel shook her head. "In the end, we didn't press charges because his father, who was a very nice man, came by and talked to us, apologized for his son, and begged us not to give him a criminal record, we'd ruin his chances for a career, all that stuff. But you've probably got records at the station. Or the landscaping company will remember. Greenscape. Probably Stephen will remember, too. The reason he didn't recognize the voice was that I was the one who was here . . . who kept having to go out and correct him, so I'm the one who heard his voice."

Gallagher picked up the phone. "Wait," Rachel said. "I've got it. Sutton. Jason Sutton. One fifty-three Wolfe Pine Way. His father's name is Harold."

Gallagher gave instructions to the uniformed cop, who hurried out and took off in a blaze of sound and light.

"Do you really think he might have David?" Rachel asked doubtfully. "He didn't strike me as the type to wait this long . . . to have this much patience. He was blunt . . . crude."

Gallagher shrugged. "We'll soon find out."

"You're not going to go rushing over there? Not if he has David . . . David is very scared right now. Whoever has him has become impatient or worried. I think he's being mistreated. I think that they're hurting him. . . ." Her voice broke on the word "hurting," and she turned her face away to give herself a little privacy for her pain.

"Have you heard from him again and failed to tell us?"

Oh, Gallagher, Gallagher, she thought. You can strip me and toss me in a tub full of water. Ogle me in my transparent nightgown. Sneak up and watch me while I work. You want carte blanche to peer into my soul, but we never seem to get any closer, do we? "No, Detective. You know that we share everything with you. The Stark family has no secrets. How could we? You and yours are always with us." She tapped her temple. "In here, Gallagher. I heard him in here."

"Rachel," Robinson broke in. He couldn't bear to be anywhere but center stage. "That's why I sent you Mrs. Proust. To help you with those communications. You really shouldn't have sent her away. . . ."

"I was on my way to the airport!" She felt like she was going to burst if she didn't get off somewhere by herself where she could finish a thought without being interrupted, interrogated, or lectured at, yet she was afraid to leave them alone. Her mind filled with images of Gallagher storming the Suttons' house and David ending up the loser in their macho game. "Are you going over there yourself?"

"First we get things set up. Then we call the house to see if he's there."

"His father works at the post office in Chilton. You could call him there and ask if Jason is home. But how could Jason keep a child hostage for a month at his parents' house?"

"Maybe his parents are away for a month."

"Well, if you're going, I'm going," Rachel declared. "And what about Stephen? He's off on another of their wild goose chases and he doesn't even know that we've identified the kidnapper."

"*If* we've identified the kidnapper."

"Gallagher, excuse me, but when a sweating, leering lout hefts his privates at you and tells you that what you need is a good fuck, the experience sticks in your mind. I know whose voice that is. Think back. I didn't say maybe I know. . . . I said *I know!*"

The phone shrilled into the already tense atmosphere of the kitchen, its harsh tones seeming to hover like garish yellow flashes in the air around them. Rachel looked quizzically at Gallagher, who nodded. "Hello?"

"Oh, so it's the little woman. Well, how the hell are ya?"

"Jason, let me talk to my son," Rachel said.

"Sorry, doll. No can do. He's sleeping."

"David is an early riser. Let me talk to him."

"It's sort of an assisted sleep, if you get my drift. When your old man gets back, tell him we want sixty thousand bucks and we'll be calling back in an hour to tell him where and when. Got that, babe? Oops. We're outta time."

Miranda came in, dressed for work, poured herself some coffee, and carried it to the table.

Before anyone could say anything, the phone rang again. Rachel picked it up with a hand that was visibly shaking, pulled it toward herself cautiously, and murmured her soft hello. "Rachel? It's Dr. Barker. Look, I'm sorry I was such a horse's ass last night. I'm sure I've caused you hours of anxious misery, wondering what I called about and why I wouldn't tell you. It's not like me to be so indecisive, and I apologize. To get straight to the point. Your AIDS test was negative. You're fine. You don't have to worry about that. At the same time, and I know I shouldn't have done this without your permission, but it seemed like such a long shot . . . Rachel . . . I did a pregnancy test. It was positive. You're pregnant."

ANDY HAD A *computer and spent hours playing on it, just like David had done at home. Sometimes the woman would let him go to Andy's house, and they'd go to kids' bulletin boards and talk. Andy's mother mostly wouldn't let them. She thought the boards were dangerous. She was always saying stuff about how kids were lured away from home by bad people. They'd be right in the middle of downloading some cool game and there would be Andy's mom, looking over their shoulders and checking up on what they were doing.*

Andy said he didn't mind. He said he supposed it was better to have a mom who cared than one who didn't. David wanted to say "or better than no mom at all," but he didn't because the woman had told him never to speak about his parents and she'd been very scary when she said it. David didn't even dare mention them to her. Once or twice he'd tried to figure out what it was about her that scared him. He'd decided it wasn't just her anger, though that was very scary; it was her coldness. When he looked at her, he saw that hard, blank face and behind it he saw a hard, cold inside. He thought nothing he could say or do would ever move her or change her mind.

She was cold, and yet she wanted him to like her. No. Wanted him to love her, that was what those stiff hopeful smiles and brusque hugs were about. That and her talk about them being a family. David had tried to be obedient but he couldn't be loving. It was too soon. He was too sad, missed his parents too much. The woman had gradually stopped smiling, and he knew it was all his fault.

The day after the woman beat him, he hadn't gone to school and he hadn't gone fishing, either. He'd been upstairs, trying to unbutton the dirty shirt and fumbling helplessly, his fingers refusing his commands, desperately wanting his mother, when he'd heard footsteps on the stairs. Expecting the woman, he'd tugged violently at the buttons and only succeeded in pulling one off. He'd collapsed on the bed in terror, the pillow over his head, waiting for the angry voice and the first blow. Instead, someone had patted him awkwardly on the shoulder. "Here, I brung you these," the man said. He had some pills in his hand. "You'd better take 'em and get back under them covers." David hadn't been able to find his voice, so he hadn't asked what they were; he'd just taken them and fallen asleep, waking just in time for dinner.

That night, just as the woman was sending him to bed, he had a call from Andy. She let him take it, but she was standing right behind him, so close he could feel her breath on his neck. "Yo, David. Missed you today! You okay? I've got something really cool to show you tomorrow. It's a poster I downloaded. About a missing kid. He's called David. And guess what? Except that his hair is dark and yours is blond, he looks just like you."

David was about to reply when the woman reached past him, broke the connection, and snatched the phone out of his hand. "Get upstairs," she snapped. "And don't let me see you again tonight." He hurried away from her raised hand and scurried up the stairs. As he went, he could hear her voice behind him. "I've got to think what to do now. Got to think . . ."

They brought me bitter news to hear and bitter tears to shed.
—HERACLITUS

CHAPTER TWENTY-THREE

If she lived the Victorian life people were always telling her she belonged in, Rachel would at that moment have descended into a graceful swoon and then taken to her bed with the vapors. Certainly a swoon, with its attendant numbness, would have been preferable to this breathless, painful incredulity. "But it's impossible," she said, forgetting in her shock that she had an audience. "Dr. Barker, I can't be pregnant. It's impossible. There must be some mistake . . . a mix-up . . . someone else's test results. Stephen had a vasectomy after Jonah died . . . after we knew that he . . . that his children might . . . that we couldn't . . . Oh, please, tell me that this is all a mistake!"

"There's no mistake. It was your blood. I can repeat the test, but I'm sure it will tell us the same thing. It explains the exhaustion, the nausea. As for impossible . . . forgive me for asking, Rachel, but has there been anyone else?"

Robinson coughed, and looking around at them, she remembered she had an audience. Remembered and flushed scarlet with mortification. Even Miranda was staring with more interest than sympathy.

"How can you even ask?" Oh, the absurdity of it, that she should be receiving this news before an audience of men she hated and have every word of it recorded.

"Vasectomies do sometimes reverse themselves. . . ."

"Stephen will never believe that . . ." she said, and caught Gallagher's sympathetic look.

"I'm sorry. I . . . we . . . I can't talk about this right now, Dr. Barker," she interrupted. "I'm . . . we're . . . not alone. There's been a ransom demand from David's kidnappers. . . . The phone is tapped. We're being recorded. The kitchen is full of cops. . . ."

"Goddamn!" he exploded. "I'm sorry, Rachel. Come by when you can. I'll make time for you. We'll get this taken care of. Do you want me to talk to Stephen?"

"Right now he's in no position to deal with it. We . . . neither one of us is. Maybe later."

She replaced the receiver and turned to meet Gallagher and Robinson's staring eyes. "It's none of your business, but if you want the rest of the conversation, play the tape. And then, please . . . erase the call. It's not . . . relevant." She looked around for Miranda, but her sister was gone. Moving with the tenuous caution of a tightrope walker, she left the kitchen. She made it as far as the hall before her muscles gave way and she collapsed onto the nearest chair, arms wrapped tightly around her body, her mind a whirl of frantic thoughts.

Oh no. Oh no. Oh no. This could not be happening. Oh, dear God, it mustn't. She had no time for this right now. No. It wasn't that. It wasn't just because of the situation with David. She'd never have time for this. She couldn't seem to catch her breath; her chest, so tight it wouldn't move, didn't expand. Maybe she was going to stop breathing and die. At this moment, death, even a painful one, was preferable to what she faced. She could not lose another child. She simply couldn't bear it.

She put her hands over her closed eyes and pressed, trying to squeeze out the images of her other babies. It didn't work. Her imagination had always been too good, too vivid. She could see them both, feel them both, hear them both. The empty hallway around her echoed with their cries, their gurgles, their laughs.

If she'd wondered before whether God hated her, now she was sure of it. She shook her fist at the ceiling. "Why don't you go try someone who can take it?" she demanded. "Why do you always have to pick on me?" She needed to go and talk to Jonah. That always helped focus her, calm her down. Let her get things off her chest and get her life back in perspective. Only she didn't have the time. Not now. They had to find Jason Sutton, had to find David. And she was overcome by a terrible sickness. To avoid having to pass Robinson and Gallagher, she dashed upstairs. She barely made it.

She marched back into the kitchen, feeling as though her clothes lay in tatters around her and her nakedness was exposed. Her control over her own body was so tenuous, she might fall apart any second. They knew about her; they knew even before Stephen, and how he would hate that. No. No more than she had time to worry about her own feelings did she have time now to worry about Stephen's. "So what are you going to do?" she demanded.

"As soon as we get confirmation that there are men in place around the house, I'm going over there," Gallagher said. "Officer Crimmins will stay here and monitor the phone."

Once again, as if it took cues from their conversation, the phone rang. Gallagher motioned for Rachel to answer it. Behind her, Gallagher's radio came alive with a static sputter and pop and began to speak. She put her finger to her lips, signaling for silence just as he had done to her, and he went out into the hall. She answered with a soft "hello?"

"Lissen, babe. There's a rest stop on the highway going north. Four miles from where you get on. Tell your old man to be there in an hour. With the cash. Sixty grand. Tell him to walk back into the woods. There's a path. It's pretty clear; it's the one that all the faggots use. Someone will meet him there. As soon as we've got the money, we'll call you and tell you where to pick up the kid. None of that friggin' dye and no cops. You got all that?"

"Let's see. Sixty thousand dollars at the rest stop that's six miles up the highway, going north. He's to take the path into the woods and someone will meet him. He should be alone and then you'll call us and tell us where to pick up David?"

"Four miles, babe. Four. Not six. Wouldn't want to get the wrong place, now, would we? Oops. Time's up."

"Wait," she said. "An hour isn't long enough. He hasn't time to get the money. . . ." But she was talking to an empty line.

Gallagher came back in. "It was him," she said. "He's set a time and place to get the money." She moved aside so he could reach the machine, and they all listened to the message together.

Robinson checked his watch. "Guess I'd better get cracking, if we're to have sixty grand in an hour. Tell Stephen I'll meet him back here in forty-five minutes." He hurried out.

"Where is he going to get that much money in half an hour?" Rachel asked.

"Probably has it sitting there in his office. In a safe. He's been waiting for a chance like this for a long time," Gallagher said.

"You don't really think . . ."

"I think he loves this stuff. He's like the guy who drives after fire trucks, only he thrives on personal tragedy."

"But Gallagher . . . he lost his own child."

"So he says."

"What does that mean?"

"He just showed up around here a few years go with his sad story and set up that organization. People just flock to him, to his so-called good cause. The volunteers and the bucks just flow in. I expect he's making a fortune off your situation. . . ."

"Did you ever check and see if he really lost a child?"

"Well, no . . ."

"Then you shouldn't . . ." But Rachel really had no interest in what she'd been about to say or in the conversation generally, so she let her words trail off. She was very tired. She slid onto a stool and rested her head on her arms, the tile counter cool beneath her cheek.

Suddenly Gallagher was there behind her, his large warm hands massaging her shoulders. "I'm sorry, Rachel . . . about the coffee . . . your jeans . . . Stephen . . . I was only thinking about helping you. . . ."

Very un-Gallagher. He sounded truly distressed at having caused trouble.

"Don't worry about it," she murmured. "I know it wasn't . . . I mean, I know you didn't . . . Oh, hell, Gallagher, he'll get over it in a few hundred years. How can any of us be bothered about propriety at a time like this?"

"Your husband treats you like . . ."

She raised her head and put a finger to her lips. "For better or for worse," she said. "So now what? Change in game plan?"

"I've got some calls to make. Got to get some people moving to stake out that rest stop." He lumbered out of the kitchen, a big man, and a tired one. His feet slammed down heavily on the floor, making the paintings on the wall shiver as he passed.

Alone at last, Rachel thought. Alone at last with a head full of thoughts she didn't want to have. She couldn't worry about herself until David was back. Until he was safely at home. She couldn't let herself hope that that time might come very soon. The clock was running. Where was Stephen? Where was Robinson? Would they get back in time?

Maybe she'd better have a cup of tea. Chamomile was supposed to be soothing, or peppermint for a jumpy stomach? She filled the kettle, put it on to heat, got out a cup, took the box of herbal teas from the cupboard.

The door slammed and Stephen came in, his face white, tight, and furious. "The kidnapper said you'd have a message for me," he barked. "If I ever get my hands on that bastard, I'm going to tear him apart." Gallagher came in behind him, lounging quietly against the door frame. Stephen's angry eyes took in the cup, the kettle, the box of tea in her hand. "This is no time for a tea party. What the hell did he say?"

Rachel and Gallagher spoke together. Rachel said, "He wants you to meet him at a rest stop out on the highway . . . with the money. . . ."

Gallagher said, "Your wife listened to the tape. She's identified the voice. . . ."

Stephen made a time-out gesture. "Hold it. Hold it! One at a time." He dropped heavily into a chair. "Gallagher?"

Gallagher explained about Rachel identifying the voice. "Sutton, she says. Jason Sutton. He worked for your landscaper? She had a

couple run-ins with the kid and then he stole some stuff from you? You ended up getting him fired?"

"Hold on! He ended up getting himself fired," Stephen corrected. "No one told him to steal or make lewd propositions to my wife. You think he took David because of that?" He jerked up his sleeve and glared at his watch. "So what are we waiting for? Let's go get him."

"He called to set up a meeting," Gallagher said. He checked his own watch. "He wants you at the first rest stop on the highway going north. You're to bring sixty thousand dollars and take the path into the woods. Someone will meet you there to take the money and then they'll call with instructions about how to pick up David. He said to be there in an hour. That was about fifteen minutes ago."

"Oh sweet Jesus!" Stephen jumped up. "Where am I going to get sixty thousand dollars that fast?"

"Robinson's gone to get it," Rachel said.

"So what do we do until he gets back?" Stephen's feet were dancing with agitation. "Just sit here?"

"Just sit here," Gallagher agreed. He checked his watch again and looked at the kitchen clock for confirmation. "It's not that much longer. Maybe ten, fifteen minutes until you have to leave."

Rachel noticed that Stephen was refusing to look at her. Still mad at her about Gallagher and the jeans incident. She understood that she was the only person he could safely vent his anger at, understood it and also understood the trap it put her in, isolating her from the one person she needed to talk to. He looked so weary and miserable, she longed to go and put her arms around him, but he would only have shaken her off and walked away.

"Yoo hoo," Carole said as she walked into the kitchen carrying a casserole dish. "Well, you guys look glummer than Santa's elves in February. What's happening?"

"The goddamned kidnapper is playing games with us!" Stephen snapped. "I'll be waiting outside." He hurried past her and out the door, slamming it noisily behind him.

"Well, I'll be," Carole drawled, setting her burden down and studying Rachel's face. "Bad, huh? He didn't even stay long enough

for me to describe the merits of this here hot dish I brought you, and it's smack-dab full of ingredients, most of them high in cholesterol, fat, and sodium. Oh well," she shrugged, "when it comes time to eat it, he'll be glad. I've never met a man yet can resist my cooking." She knelt down beside Rachel and gently touched her arm. "Oh, honey, you look positively beat. Last I heard you were whaling the tar out of 'em, out there in Chicago, making those arrogant baby panderers run for their rotten little lives."

In spite of her misery, Rachel had to smile. Carole was like a loopy ray of sunshine. "You make it sound like a lot more fun than it really was. They were scary people, Carole. I can't believe I ever trusted my body to them. Shook me up so much, I didn't sleep last night. Went out for a walk in the dark and scared myself silly. Got a ride back to my hotel and a stern lecture from a cop."

"You never!" Carole exclaimed. "Oh, yeah, I guess you did, didn't you? But you're okay? You didn't get hurt?" Rachel shook her head. "So now what's happening?"

"Stephen's supposed to drop off the money in a few minutes. Then they'll call and tell us where to find David."

Carole seized her hand and squeezed. "You poor thing. Isn't waiting just the worst?" Rachel nodded. "Have you eaten anything? No, of course you haven't. Don't I know just how you are? Wait here and I'll fix you some tea and toast." She patted Rachel's thigh, not missing the responsive wince. "There's something you aren't telling me, isn't there?"

"Dozens of things. Just make the tea, okay?" Rachel handed her the box of teas. "Chamomile or mint. I can't decide."

"Don't you worry. I'm decisive enough for all of us." She narrowed her eyes and studied Rachel. "Mint." She turned away, snapped off the burner, and stuck in some toast.

John Robinson hurried in, carrying a briefcase, followed by Stephen. Gallagher joined them and the three of them went back into their huddle while Gallagher gave Stephen instructions. Carole, doing her best to ignore them, moved quietly around the kitchen, fixing the tea and toast.

Rachel, feeling left out, excluded, and ignored, scrunched down

in her chair and thought worried, confused, irritated thoughts. Foremost among them, though she was ashamed of herself for thinking it, was that this would turn out to be a hoax and they still wouldn't have David back. When the huddle broke up and Stephen headed for the door, carrying the briefcase, she grabbed Gallagher's arm. "Isn't there something I can do?"

"Stay here and answer the phone. Crimmins will be with you." He gestured toward the silent cop in the corner, a man so unobtrusive Rachel had almost forgotten about him.

"Yessirree," Carole told Gallagher's departing back, "we little women will keep the home fires burning and the stew pot hot. We wouldn't want to be involved in anything dangerous, like rescuing our own children. . . ." The door banged shut behind them, and she was talking to empty air.

"Speaking of mothers and children, Rachel, I heard the most extraordinary story yesterday. This mother was out hiking with her son and her son was bitten by a fox. Well, you know what that woman did? She took off after that fox, caught it, and wrung its neck so they could test it to see if it was rabid. Can you imagine doing that? I mean, I can imagine myself doing a little tiptoe dance backwards, trying to get away from the thing, saying, 'nice little foxy' in a dippy, singsongy voice. But catch it and kill it?"

"I can imagine it. When your child is in danger, everything's different, Carole. These past weeks, the number of times I've imagined catching and hurting David's kidnappers . . ."

"Yeah, you're right. I know I've often imagined what I'd do if someone molested one of my kids, and my kids are safe at . . . oh, tell me to shut up, why don't you? How can you stand having a motormouthed show-off like me around? I'm as insensitive as . . . as . . . Stephen."

"Because I love you," Rachel said. "Because you always give me a shoulder to cry on, and listen to my woes, and make me laugh. Because you don't treat me like a fragile looney toon everyone has to tiptoe around." She opened her arms and scooped Carole in, and they rocked, oblivious to the silent Crimmins. The toaster dinged.

"There's the toast. You want butter on it?"

"I don't know. I don't know what I want. I don't know what to do."

"I'll butter it. Wheat toast without butter is like eating shredded wheat straight from the box. Or hay. I've always imagined eating hay as a lot like shredded wheat."

"I've never imagined eating hay."

"Gee, and I always thought you were the one with the creative imagination." Carole picked up the plate and headed toward her. "Oh, honey, look at you. You're crying again. Don't mind me; you know how I blather on. All the tact of a pit bull. I know all this waiting and helplessness must be killing you. You want to talk about it? Sometimes it does help to talk."

"Dr. Barker called this morning. I'm HIV-negative. And I'm pregnant."

"Oh shit!" The plate went tumbling out of Carole's hands, smashing into a pile of crockery and crumbs. "Oh double shit! Stephen's been fixed, right? And you haven't been with anyone else?"

Rachel shook her head. "No one. Most of the time I feel so apathetic, I don't care if I never have sex again, let alone going out and recruiting some stranger . . ."

"They're not usually strangers," Carole commented before she could stop herself.

"I have . . . uh . . . this sounds so crude . . . I have tried to meet his needs . . . not very successfully, I guess, but I've tried. . . ."

"So if it's not Stephen . . ." Carole began.

"It's an immaculate conception," Rachel finished, feeling slightly hysterical.

"Well, I'll be," Carole said, her hands on her hips, surveying the mess she'd made. "We're going to have a job of work convincing Forest Valley that they've got their very own immaculate conception. Soon as I sweep this up, I'll just scoot home and get you a halo. I expect one of mine will fit."

Rachel, laughing through her tears, pulled out a tissue and blew her nose. "I've got to say . . . when all hell breaks loose, it sure is good to have you around."

"Yessirree," Carole said, "I'm so omnicompetent that with a little

help I can even make toast." She proved her point by putting two new slices in the toaster.

"What am I going to do?"

"Drink your tea."

"About the baby? Stephen will insist on an abortion. I doubt he'll even believe it's his."

"And how do you feel about abortion?"

"I'd rather stand in front of an oncoming train."

"Than have another damaged baby?"

"Oh, Carole . . . I don't know. I don't know if I could go through that again, but . . ." She wrapped her arms tightly around her body, as if it might otherwise come apart. She felt like she was coming apart. "There's always the possibility that this one would be all right. . . ."

"Drink your tea," Carole repeated, sliding the cup toward her. "There's time enough to worry about this tomorrow."

. . . hope and dread kept a continual warfare in his breast, alternately
vanquishing one another and starting up afresh to renew the contest.
— HAWTHORNE, "Rappaccini's Daughter"

CHAPTER TWENTY-FOUR

Okay, he was a rotten bastard, Stephen thought. So what? So how was
he supposed to react in the midst of a crisis when some macho cowboy stormed into his bathroom and undressed his wife? With a flutter of his hand and a chorus of thanks? It was hard enough to have
any pride under these circumstances, where he was never alone and
people were always looking over his shoulder, second-guessing him
and telling him what to do. Imagining they knew what he was thinking or feeling when they didn't know a goddamned thing about him.
And what had Rachel done? Nothing. Not one damned thing. She
hadn't protested, just let Gallagher strip off her pants and stick her
in the tub.

No wonder he often felt she needed a keeper, though if she'd
only use her common sense and be more careful, she wouldn't need
rescuing. Not that he had time to worry about Rachel's absurd behavior right now. He had more important things to do. The *most* important thing—getting David back.

A trickle of hot sweat oozed down his spine. Nasty, nervous

sweat. He was flying blind despite having spent most of the last twelve hours in the company of experts. He hated being unprepared; he'd spent a lifetime trying to avoid it. The advice he'd gotten from Robinson amounted to "try not to lose the money." What he'd gotten from Gallagher, who ought to have been his coach in this situation, was crap. Gallagher had only told him to follow the kidnappers' instructions to the letter, to be humble, calm and cooperative at the scene, and not to try any cowboy stuff or heroics. Oh, and to keep his mouth shut. A gopher could have told him that much!

He wasn't naive. He'd long ago given up his childish faith in experts; still, he expected people to know their business, and he didn't have a lot of confidence that these people knew theirs. How could they? It wasn't like kids were snatched on a regular basis in Forest Valley. Yet Gallagher, in particular, had irritated him, and not just because the guy obviously had a hard-on for Rachel—something Rachel wouldn't notice if the guy unzipped and waved his dick in her face. Gallagher, from the beginning, had treated him like a suspect, and even when that faded, the lack of respect remained. He felt like Gallagher had deliberately not prepared him well because Gallagher didn't want him to succeed.

Okay, so he was out here on his own. How was he going to handle this? He tried to remember what he'd learned in the street-smart self-defense course he'd taken a few years back. Well, not so much taken as attended so that Rachel would go. He could remember some stuff about breaking holds, and having only three seconds to react, and about not making eye contact for too long or in too challenging a manner, but that was about all, and what he understood from Gallagher, though this may not have been what the man meant—Gallagher wasn't exactly articulate—was that he should keep an utterly low profile and not try to challenge the person in any way. He didn't intend to. All he cared about was getting David back.

As he turned onto the highway, past the sign where they'd found David's shoe, another thought occurred to him. What if this was all a big hoax and when he got out there, a lone man carrying a lot of money, they were planning to kill him and take the money? Gallagher hadn't mentioned that, nor had he told Stephen how to identify

people at the scene who might be police, or how to signal for help. He just had to trust them and hope they knew what they were doing. Something that didn't come easy at the best of times, since Stephen liked being in charge. Something that was even harder now, with cops he didn't trust and the stakes so high. He wasn't worried about his own safety; he only worried that this would all fall flat and they wouldn't be any closer to getting David back.

He checked his speedometer as he merged into the traffic. Only four miles to go. Four miles. Four minutes. And then he would have done all he could. His eyes were on the road but his mind was on David, picturing David right after he was born, round-faced with funny, round, surprised-looking eyes. Jonah had been a delicate, more intense baby, a mobile mass of arms and legs and eyes all alert and constantly in motion, while David was easygoing. He'd folded up into a perfect, peaceful bundle on Stephen's chest and rested there, content.

Strangely enough, after all his resistance to David's existence, Stephen had felt an immediate bond, a powerful affinity with the tiny boy in his arms. Jonah had scared him when he was first born—the task of caring for such a fragile being had overwhelmed him—and he'd been content to leave it to Rachel, almost in awe of her casual assumption of such responsibility. When Jonah had gotten sick, it had been even harder. All of his hesitation about handling an infant was doubled and tripled when the infant was attached to a tangle of needles and tubes. Every day the intrusive mass seemed to grow as Jonah shrank.

Shoot, he didn't want to remember this. This wasn't the time for his mind to fill with his failure, with his inability to touch his dying son; he didn't want to relive his revulsion as the baby shriveled and died, watching all the while with those terrifyingly wise eyes. For a period after Jonah's death, Stephen had been haunted by that suffering baby face, and by his terrible guilt that he'd been unwilling even to try and soothe his baby's agony. He'd shaken his head, told the nurse he couldn't take it, and walked away. Even now he could see those eyes staring after him and feel the wash of shame.

Through it all, Rachel had been a rock, producing these amaz-

ing reserves of patience, energy, and love for Jonah. He had never once heard her complain, seen her sigh, or felt from her even a shade of regret or doubt or self-pity. She had been like a natural spring, a stream of warmth and affection that just kept flowing as long as it was needed. Steady, gentle-voiced, and smiling for her baby right down to that last second when he had died in her arms. And she had never accused him of not doing his share, or of failing in any way. All the accusations he'd laid on himself, defending himself against what she should have been saying. Should have been feeling. He'd never been able to talk to her about it.

With David it had been different. Right from the start, maybe because he'd made an unconscious decision to make David his, he'd insisted on doing his share. At first Rachel had been surprised, even, he thought, almost jealous, and they'd engaged in an unspoken tug-of-war over possession, but then, as if she'd heaved a sigh of relief, she'd relaxed and let him claim as much of David as he wanted. And he had wanted a lot. He'd wanted to see those first steps, hear those first words, wanted to be there for those special firsts that seemed too often to be reserved to the province of mothers. He'd been there all the way from first tooth to first base stolen.

First base stolen. He'd been rooting for it with his whole body, wondering if David would see the opportunity; wondering if he'd dare to take advantage. David was such an unpredictable combination of courage and shyness, of action and hesitation. When he'd seen his son take off, he'd leaned forward himself, straining toward second as if he could lend support. When David had landed safely and given him that shy, triumphant smile, Stephen had felt a love and pride that rocked him to his soul and scared him to death. He had never imagined loving like that.

In the back of his mind, these past four weeks, was a lurking dread that David was dead, had been dead from the first. It was what logic and experience argued for; it was what generally happened to boys David's age when they were snatched. But he so desperately wanted to be wrong that when Rachel came out with her periodic assertions that she'd sensed David or heard his voice, Stephen had taken some comfort from that. Not said anything to support or

encourage her—the last thing he wanted was a wife who believed in the paranormal and Rachel was already strange enough—but put just enough faith into it to allow himself some hope. There were so many more firsts ahead. David's call had been like water in the desert.

The looming green sign announced REST AREA 1 MI. and Stephen pulled himself back into the present and moved into the exit lane. Behind him, a battered, rust-blotched white van did the same. Cops, he wondered, or robbers? Probably just some poor schmuck who needed to use the rest room.

He brought the Lexus to a smooth and careful stop and got out, pulling his sticky shirt away from his back. He didn't sweat this much when he had a big court argument. The shirt was soaked and he smelled the bitter odor of his own sweat. Immediately an image of David popped into his head, hugging him, then drawing back and asking, in mock-TV style, "Did you forget your deodorant this morning?" Yes, son, he thought, I did. There was nothing on my mind but you.

Moving in a way that was probably stilted by his concern not to appear eager, he crossed the grass, trying not to swing the briefcase, trying not to look as though he, too, found it odd that a man would march purposefully into the woods with a briefcase. He passed the busy toilet facilities with their heavy air of disinfectant and looked around for the path.

The caller had been right; it was hard to miss—a well-worn dirt path leading back into the woods. Just put one foot in front of the other, he told himself. Look around casually, like a normal person would. Don't swing the goddamned briefcase. Don't wrinkle your nose in distaste because the woods smell more like a latrine than the toilets did. He stepped in something nasty and stopped, bracing himself against a tree, to scrape it off his shoe.

"Oh dear! Did you step in something?" Not the voice from the phone. Stephen turned slowly around. A scruffy teenager with a dark, greasy ponytail and a black T-shirt adorned with unprintable phrases smirked at him from behind a tree. "I bet you have something for me," the boy said.

Stephen didn't respond. The kidnapper, following the formula from a TV movie, had given him a password—a pass phrase—that would be spoken by the person he was to give the money to. So far, he hadn't heard it.

"Or maybe I have something for you?" The boy left his tree and edged closer, and now Stephen realized three things. First, that the boy was much younger than he'd first assumed, perhaps fourteen or fifteen; second, that despite the air of deliberate grunge, he was very handsome; and third, that he thought Stephen was there for sex. This was just what he needed. What was he to do, clap his hands and say, "Scoot along little fellow. Go find another pederast to play with?"

"I'm not here to play," he muttered harshly as the boy took a step closer. Despite his revulsion, he couldn't help thinking that this was someone's child . . . a child not much older than David.

The boy shrugged and turned away, leather jacket creaking. "Your loss, man," he said softly, and edged back into the trees. In seconds, he'd disappeared from sight.

Stephen picked up the briefcase and went on. On his left, slightly visible through the trees, was the highway. On his right, also barely visible, a fence separated the highway from the rest of the woods. He wondered how far he was supposed to go. His experience with the kidnappers so far made it perfectly possible that he could walk for hours and no one would show up while they left another teasing message for him at home. But he'd only been here about ten minutes. Too soon to give up yet.

He was plunging through the woods like he was in a cross-country race. Taking a deep breath, he let it out slowly as he decreased his pace, trying to look nonchalant, trying not to swing the briefcase. "Hey! Zorro!" a voice hissed out from behind him. He wheeled around. It was the boy in the leather jacket again, holding out his hand. "I think you do have something for me?" Stephen hadn't even heard him approach.

"Are you a part of this sick conspiracy, too?" He hadn't meant to say it; it just popped out.

The boy stared at him blankly. "Guy gave me fifty bucks to pick up something." His eyes dropped to the briefcase. "I suppose that's

it?" He held out his hand. "So, hand it over, Zorro. I've got people to meet."

"People?" Stephen said.

"Come on, will ya?" the boy said sullenly, no longer interested in flirting.

"Wait a minute. What happens next?" Stephen asked.

The boy's shiny, heavily lashed eyes swept him from head to toe and then he gave a deliberately sexual thrust of his pelvis. "Oh, I'm just the messenger," he said. "Go home and wait for a call."

"My son," Stephen said, fighting to keep his voice neutral. "Is he okay?"

"I'm just the messenger," the boy repeated, holding out his hand toward the briefcase. "You gonna give me that or you gonna fuck around?"

"You know what's in here?" Stephen asked.

"Shit no," the boy said. "Don't care, either. Come on, give it here." He made little summoning motions with his hands.

Stephen tossed the briefcase. It landed heavily at the boy's feet. The boy retreated a step and smiled. "You're not angry, are you?"

"You'd better get out of here if you don't want to find out."

The boy picked up the briefcase in one hand. With the other, he made a graceful, flinging gesture. "Oh, I just love it when you're angry." Smirking, he backed away into the woods. "And don't try to follow me or you won't get that call."

It didn't matter, Stephen knew. He didn't need to follow. There was a neat little transmitter in the briefcase. As long as the money stayed in the case, it would continue to tell the police where it was. He turned and headed back toward his car, trembling now with the aftermath of anxiety and the effort of curbing his desire to beat the crap out of the kid. God! Imagine if it was your kid that grew up into . . . into that! Now all he could do was wait and waiting was not one of the things he did best.

As he unlocked his car, a man leaned out of the rust-eaten van beside him. "Buddy, you got a match? My lighter's busted."

Stephen shook his head. "Got a lighter, though." He pushed it in as the man came around, cigarette bobbing between his lips. When it popped, he held it out the window.

"Cobbs, state police," the man said as he took the lighter. "How'd it go in there?"

"Scruffy teenage kid. Black hair. Ponytail. Leather jacket. Knew the password. Said they'd paid him fifty bucks to do the pickup."

Cobbs nodded. "We'll take it from here. Hopefully he'll lead us to his buddies. You go on home now and wait for the call."

Stephen nodded and started the engine with shaking hands. It all felt so unsatisfying, like craving a big dinner and getting dry crackers and clear broth. Numbly, he got back on the highway, got off at the next exit, and took back roads home, his mind filled with images of David. If this didn't get resolved soon, he was going to explode.

He'd been so excited last night, thinking that something was finally happening. He'd expected to get caught up in it, to be swept along on a tide of activity until they struck some kind of deal and retrieved David. It hadn't been like that at all. Mostly, it had involved waiting. Endless, exhausting waiting. Waiting and hoping and not knowing. Not being able to get a handle on anything. When he got back, he'd ask Robinson how he'd stood it, what he'd done with himself during the waits, the silences. Stephen didn't know how much longer he could go on feeling like a time bomb.

In the kitchen, he found Rachel, Carole, and the man Gallagher had called Crimmins. Rachel's eyes flew to his face as he entered, and stayed there, asking a thousand unspoken questions. She was wearing something soft and loose, he noticed. Her hair needed washing and her feet were bare. He shrugged, irritated. "Not much to report," he said. "I met a kid in the woods and gave him the briefcase. He told me to come home and wait for a phone call. I guess they haven't called?"

The disappointment in her eyes was as tangible as a blow. "He didn't tell you where to find . . ."

"No, goddammit, he didn't," he yelled, not meaning to. "He didn't tell me a goddamned thing except to come home and wait. I'm sick of waiting." He crossed to the basement door and pulled it open. "I'll be downstairs. Call me if anything happens."

"Stephen . . . there's something . . . I need to talk to you. . . ." Rachel said.

His hopes shot up. "About David?" She shook her head. "Then it can wait!" He hurried out, slamming the door behind him.

Rachel met Carole's sympathetic gaze. "It's all right," she whispered. "I have terrible timing. He's got a lot on his mind."

Loud music sneaked around the closed door and the floor shook with the powerful rhythm of drums. "I guess the natives are restless," Carole said, doing a little soft shoe around the kitchen.

"Don't be too hard on him," Rachel said. "He's just trying not to explode."

"And what about you? I suppose how you feel in all this doesn't matter?"

"It's not that it doesn't matter. We just have a different kind of relationship. . . . We're both very independent. . . . We each . . ." Her voice trembled and broke. She swallowed and went on, "we each have our separate ways of coping. . . ."

"If you can call this coping . . ."

The door burst open and Gallagher stormed into the kitchen. "We lost him, the rotten little bastard! He slipped the money into his jacket, went out to the highway, and was gone before we could react."

"Gone? What do you mean gone?" Rachel cried. "And what about the house, Sutton's house? Did you look there?"

The basement door flew open and Stephen, red-faced and sweaty, rushed in. "Well? What? Did you get him?"

Gallagher shook his head. "Lost him."

Robinson, who'd come in behind him, gave a visceral moan. "You lost my money?"

"Fuck the money," Stephen said. "What about my son?"

"We went to the Suttons' house. His mother said she hasn't seen him in over a week. She thought he was up in Connecticut visiting a friend. We called the friend, but he hasn't seen Sutton for weeks." Gallagher spread his hands helplessly. "We'll keep looking."

But Stephen wasn't finished. "What do you mean, you lost him? How could you lose him?"

Gallagher shrugged. "We didn't expect him to ditch the transmitter that quickly. . . ."

"What kind of Mickey Mouse operation are you running, Gallagher? Didn't you have any sort of contingency plan?"

"We had a guy in the woods," Gallagher said defensively. "Following. Kid went out to the highway and was picked up. . . ."

"So why didn't you pick them up? Or follow them? Did you get the license number at least?" Gallagher shook his head. Said nothing. "What do you think this is? Some sort of prize give-away program?" Stephen exploded. "You aren't enforcing litter control ordinances here. This is about my son's life. . . ." He was choking on his anger, drowning in it. He could hardly speak.

Gallagher looked down at his shoes, sturdy brown, carefully polished, with thick rubber soles to cushion the impact of his bulk against the earth. "It wasn't our show," he said finally. "The state cops said they'd handle it." He shrugged. "They didn't."

"So what do we do now? What happens next?" Robinson demanded.

"We're working on it," Gallagher said slowly.

Rachel picked up her purse and headed for the door. "I'm going out," she announced. "Carole, will you come?"

Stephen stepped in front of her. "At a time like this? Where are you going?"

"To find David."

"You should be here, Rachel," Gallagher said.

"Oh, let her go. Let her play avenging angel. At least it will keep her out of our hair," Stephen said, stepping aside.

"Stephen, it's not like that. . . . I . . ." Rachel said. "I have an idea. . . ."

"Spare us," he said. "And at least put on some fucking shoes first." He turned his back and walked away.

Oh yet we trust that somehow good
Will be the final goal of ill.
—TENNYSON, "In Memoriam"

CHAPTER TWENTY-FIVE

"Rachel, wait!" Carole called, hurrying after her, scooping up a pair of shoes that sat near the door. They met by the car, where Carole reached out and took the car keys from Rachel's trembling hand, trading them for the shoes. "Wherever you're going, you'd better let me drive. You're in no shape to . . ."

Rachel surrendered herself to Carole's ministrations. Carole was right. She was in no shape to do anything. She was so tired, she could barely stand. "I won't argue with you." She got into the passenger seat and waited until Carole was behind the wheel. "We're going to Chilton. To the post office."

Carole's face was a mass of questions, but all she said was, "Check. Chilton. Post office," and backed smoothly down the driveway.

"How do you do that?" Rachel asked.

"Do what?"

"Back up like that?"

Carole shrugged. "I never thought about it. I guess it just comes naturally. Am I allowed to ask questions?"

"Of course. Why not?"

"I wasn't sure, that's all. There's a sort of fragile determination about you today. . . ."

"Fragile determination? Don't tell me you've joined the ranks of those who think I'm irretrievably strange?"

"Have a little faith, will you? There are just times when people are so upset that they don't want to talk, that's all. I thought this might be one of them."

"We're going to Chilton to talk to Jason Sutton's father."

"You really think he'll be there?"

"Why not?"

"Because if the police were looking for my son and/or searching my house in connection with a kidnapping, I'd be at home, or with my lawyer, and not at work. And seriously, Rach, before we drive all over hell and gone looking for this guy to ask him questions, don't you think the police have already asked everything you might ask?"

"I guess you're right," Rachel agreed, feeling deflated. "But let's go anyway. I can't stand being cooped up there any longer."

"I know what you mean. The testosterone levels are so high, I felt like I was getting hair on my chest."

"I wish I had half your wit," Rachel sighed.

"And I wish I had your height, your eyes, and your thighs."

"There's nothing wrong with your thighs. . . ."

"Thanks. You have no idea how hard I work to batter them into submission. Given their way, they'd fill the earth. I was fine until I had kids, and then it was like some malevolent fairy came at night and packed the fat around my hips and thighs. Protection in case of famine, I suppose. But I guess I shouldn't talk about pregnancy, huh?"

"No." They drove in silence through the morning gloom. It was another gray day threatening rain, the air chilly and heavy, the emerging greens muted by the misty air. "You know the way?" Rachel asked.

"Sure. Isn't Chilton where I've had to go for the last five years to get exactly the right leotard and tights for Susan's recitals? When she told me she wanted to give up dance lessons, I gave her the appropriate maternal speech about not being a quitter and the importance of having a few unique skills, then locked myself in the bathroom and jumped for joy."

"No one could ever rationally choose to become a mother. Not if they knew what they were getting into . . . except . . ." Rachel began, getting sucked into a normal conversation before she reflected on her own situation. "No one . . ." She trailed off into silence. "Maybe we could talk about the weather."

"Gloomy," Carole said. "Damp. Unpleasant. Think it'll rain?"

"I do."

"I've got my eye on a new raincoat at Treasures. A mere two hundred and fifty dollars. Ron will have a fit if I buy it. I already own two perfectly good raincoats. Perfectly good if you overlook the fact that one of them is too short to cover any of my skirts and the other has a permanent stain down one sleeve from an errant cup of cocoa. The prices at Treasures are so ridiculous, but you should see this coat. A kind of shimmery silvery blue-green. Perfectly plain, except it has a hood and two long scarflike things that drape very gracefully down the front."

"So what's stopping you?"

"The fact that last month I bought a perfectly beautiful sweater at Treasures and the month before that it was a pair of black silk velvet pants. At least they were on sale. No one is thinking about going to parties in February, so I got them for a song."

"I didn't know you could sing."

"Sweetie, I had the best voice in my entire church choir. Loudest, too. The director was always putting her finger to her lips and glaring at me. I was so eager to show off, it never occurred to me that I might be discouraging the people around me." She shrugged defiantly. "It still doesn't. My momma was always after me not to hide my light under a bushel. She was real proud of me. But it seems like everyone else is always wanting me to be tamped down. Wanting me to hold back and give the other kids a chance."

"You've never talked about this before," Rachel said.

"It's just the kind of selfish person that I am," Carole said, "that thinking about you—and I've been thinking about you a lot, Rach, trying to imagine how it must be for you—anyway, thinking about you makes me think about myself. About how people always want us to be someone other than who we are."

"People who have opinions about how we act, how we dress, how we're supposed to feel, who we are," Rachel said. "It's funny how we spend all our time shut up here in the suburbs where there's an unspoken social code about how we're to behave. Maybe it's just something we impose on ourselves, but I always figure that the only men I can know . . . the only men I can talk to . . . are other people's husbands or my son's teachers and coaches. That nothing else would be acceptable."

"It wouldn't be," Carole said. "Look how livid Stephen gets about Gallagher the hunk. As though you'd ever be interested in someone like that. As though you weren't totally devoted to your husband and your son. I don't know. It's like we're still living in the fifties." Carole flipped on her blinker and swooped deftly across the path of an oncoming behemoth. "Even Ronald the phlegmatic has his moments of jealousy. Last year when I was trying to get Tommy's baseball coach to open his eyes and pay attention to his players as individuals, I must have had five or six phone calls back and forth with the guy, and one night I found Ron pacing in the living room—the dark living room, mind you—all in a snorting lather, and when I asked him why—naive me, I thought it was some immense tax problem—he finally mutters that it's me and that guy.

"And I am so dense that I say, 'What guy?' He says the guy I'm always talking to on the phone, and honestly, Rach, it was all I could do to keep from laughing in his face. I mean, you remember the guy? Little, squatty banty rooster of a fellow, always spitting and hiking up his pants? The kind who thinks his athletic cup holds the crown jewels? Ron could at least have given me credit for a little taste."

"You are so bad," Rachel said.

"Aren't I just." She pulled into a spot right in front, cutting off a guy in a shiny red Cherokee who flipped her the bird, and jammed the car into park. "Did you see what that guy did? Women get no slack anymore, do they? Want me to come in with you?"

Rachel shook her head. "He's kind of shy. I'm afraid the two of us would be more than he could handle."

"More than most men could handle," Carole said, calmly pulling

a battered paperback out of her bag. "*The Brothers Karamazov*. I've been reading it for seven months and I still haven't gotten to the good parts."

Rachel shook her head as she went up the steps into the redbrick building. At the counter she asked quietly if Mr. Sutton was available and got an angry look. When they weren't shooting each other, postal employees could be very protective of their coworkers. "I'm not with the police," she said.

"I'll see if he's around," the young man said grudgingly, and sauntered off, two gold rings in each ear twinkling in the overbright fluorescent light.

Behind her, Rachel heard an exasperated sigh and turned to see the next woman in line glaring at her. "If you want to conduct personal business, maybe you shouldn't do it during service hours when the rest of us have things we need to get done."

"I'm sorry," Rachel said, meeting the glittering eyes. "I'm just trying to find my son, who has been kidnapped." She pointed to the bulletin board, where one of David's ubiquitous pictures hung. "That's him. David. He's been missing for four weeks. I guess my anxiety makes me forget about other people's pressing worries." She dropped her own eyes to the package the woman was holding, taking in the address. "I suppose finding a missing child isn't as important as a return to L.L. Bean." She turned away, glancing back over her shoulder in time to see the woman, her cheeks flaming, disappearing out the door.

Her mother would have been shocked, but Rachel didn't feel one bit sorry. The world was increasingly peopled by those who felt that their every need, desire, or whim should take precedence over everyone else's. People on their way to coffee with friends refused to yield to ambulances and fire trucks because they didn't want to be inconvenienced. Returning unwanted merchandise was more important than finding a wanted child.

The earringed young man was back. "If you'll go around the back, he'll meet you on the loading platform. And you'd better not be a cop or a goddamned reporter."

"I'm not." She went around the building and found Mr. Sutton,

looking emotionally tattered, waiting for her apprehensively. When he saw who she was, he flinched.

"I don't know where he is, Mrs. Stark. I already told the police. He doesn't keep us informed of his comings and goings these days. About the only contact we have with him is when he wants some money." He sank down on a plastic mail bin, his head in his hands. "I'm not trying to hide him. Not when he's involved in something like this. You've got to believe me."

Rachel turned another bin over and sat down beside him. "I do believe you, Mr. Sutton. But with my son involved in this, too, I've got to do everything I can. I know the police already asked you this, but can you think of any place your son might go?"

He shook his head, a small, round, balding head with a fringe of curly gray hair. Exactly on the top was a flesh-colored Band-Aid that didn't at all match the pale skin around it. When he looked up, Rachel saw weariness and discouragement in his face. Jason Sutton might be scum in her eyes, but he was still this man's son. God, but life was complicated.

"What about relatives?" He shook his head. "Friends?" Another shake. "What about summer cottages belonging to friends or family, places he might have been familiar with?"

"No. I'm sorry. I went over all this with the police. . . ."

"Hunting camps?"

He started to shake his head again, then hesitated. "I don't know," he said. "My wife's cousins have a place up in the mountains. A place they used to take Jason to when he was a kid, hunting, fishing, camping out. I don't think they use it anymore, but I don't know. I didn't think about them. They've gotten very strange over the years. Extremely religious. We don't have much contact with them anymore. It got . . . uncomfortable. . . . I suppose he might have gone there. . . ."

The look on his face said he hoped he was wrong. "I don't know. The wife . . . she's going to be mighty upset that I told you this. They may be odd, but they're family. You know what I mean?" She nodded. "Do I have to tell this to the police?"

She reached out and patted his shoulder. "That's okay, Mr.

Sutton. I'll tell them. But you need to show me how to find them . . . uh . . . the place." She pulled a notebook from her purse and took careful notes as he explained how to find the camp. It didn't sound easy, but Mr. Sutton was meticulous, and she was sure the police would do fine with the directions. Finally she stood up, ignoring the stinging of her singed thighs as her dress rubbed against them. "I'd better get back and give this information to Detective Gallagher."

"Is he that red-haired bastard?" Sutton burst out. "Excuse me, ma'am. I'm forgetting my manners."

Rachel nodded. "Yes, he's that red-haired bastard. He doesn't exactly inspire manners, does he."

Sutton almost smiled. A quick little motion that fell away as fast as it had come, leaving him looking sadder than ever. "I don't know whether to wish you luck or not, but I hope you get your son back." Shoulders slumped with worry, he turned and went back inside.

"Home, Jeeves," Rachel said, getting back in the car. "You get to the good parts yet?"

Carole sighed. "Maybe it's just me, but I'm not sure this book has any good parts."

"I think you've got to take it as an organic whole," Rachel said.

"What the hell does that mean?"

"Beats me. I heard someone say it once."

"Leaving lit crit aside, did you learn anything?"

"Maybe."

"Maybe? What the heck does that mean? He only spoke Urdu? He told you to consult a psychic?"

"He came up with a possible location. But I'd not putting any hope on it. Wait . . . that didn't sound quite right. Never mind. I don't think this Sutton kid has David anyway. I never really have. But Stephen has such high hopes. And it is possible."

Her voice dropped so low, it was barely audible. "He's not an easy person to live with. He expects . . . never mind . . . when I'm feeling somehow . . . beaten down . . . by the way I can't please him . . . I think about how he is with David. What an extraordinary father he is . . . his capacity for loving, his patience. Sometimes I'm envious,

jealous . . . frustrated that he can't . . . won't do it for me. But I see, Carole, I know . . . that he has it in him . . . and I hope . . ." She raised her voice. "Listen to me. Nattering on about myself, about what I want, like some self-pitying princess . . . when this is no time for me."

She sighed. "I guess I've got to let this thing play out a little longer, but tomorrow I'm going down to the city to find David's father. And I'm a whole lot more hopeful about that."

Carole reached over and patted her hand. "You've gotta have hope."

"It sounds like a show tune," Rachel said, snatching her hand away.

"What's the matter?"

"The matter? Only that my whole life is in shambles and I can only burble along with this false cheerfulness for so long before I trip over reality. That's all."

"Reality sucks," Carole said, then put an embarrassed hand to her lips. "Oops, here I am trying to get the kids to stop using that word and then I go and use it myself."

"Yeah," Rachel agreed, "reality sucks until you consider the alternatives." She waited impatiently as Carole nosed the car up the drive, between the scattered vehicles, and into a spot behind Gallagher's anonymous gray car. Clutching her notebook, she jumped out and hurried inside to report.

"Honey," she heard Carole's voice behind her. "Just don't be surprised if they aren't proud of you."

"Ain't that the truth?" she thought, as she entered the crowded kitchen and they all turned to stare at her.

"Jesus Christ!" Gallagher exploded. "Why the hell didn't he tell me about this? We could have saved ourselves a couple of hours."

Rachel ran a tired hand over her eyes. Poor Mr. Sutton. She knew what an overbearing bully Gallagher could be. It was no wonder the poor man hadn't been able to think clearly when he was being questioned. "You scare people," she said. "You bully us and interrogate us and stare at us with your suspicious eyes until we can't think anymore." She stopped. No sense wasting precious time trying to explain.

"What difference does it make?" she asked wearily. "You know it now. Go do something with it."

Gallagher didn't like that. "If you'd just stay out of this and let us do our job . . ."

"We wouldn't have any leads at all," Stephen said, putting a protective arm around Rachel's shoulders. "Would we?"

"I don't know what to say. . . ." Gallagher began.

Stephen dropped his arm and wheeled around to face him. "You might try 'thank you.' "

And be these juggling fiends no more believ'd
That palter with us in a double sense;
That keep the word of promise to our ear
And break it to our hope.

—SHAKESPEARE, *Macbeth*

CHAPTER TWENTY-SIX

Stephen crossed the room and led Rachel to a chair. "Good job, Rach," he said. "Now maybe we'll get somewhere." He smoothed back the hair that had fallen into her face. "You look beat. Did you get any sleep last night?"

She thought about that, couldn't quite remember. "I don't know. I don't think so."

"What about breakfast?"

"Carole made me some toast."

"Would you like something else? Some soup? A sandwich? Miranda made a pretty decent casserole last night." Was it only last night, he thought? It seemed like weeks had gone by since he'd picked up that message on the machine.

"No tofu?" she said hopefully.

"No tofu. No strange grains. Want some?" She nodded and he rose to fix her a plate. Carole peeked in, mouthed a good-bye, and left.

As he turned from putting the dish in the microwave, Stephen

looked at Rachel on her chair, seeming so small and fragile and lost. She appeared so ineffectual and disorganized, but none of them could match her for determination. It was one of the things about her that he'd forgotten, that undercurrent of steely determination. He'd seen it and admired it in her, back when they were young in New York and Rachel had had to struggle to get people to take her seriously, but their dull, predictable suburban lifestyle didn't require it.

The microwave beeped. Stephen took the dish out, set it on the counter, and got out some silverware. "You want tea?" he asked. Rachel looked at him, surprised, he thought, and nodded as she moved from the chair to a stool high enough to reach the counter island comfortably.

Around them, Gallagher and his men bustled around, spoke into phones, and conferred with their heads together, getting ready to go and hunt for Jason Sutton. "We'll call you as soon as we know something," Gallagher said, heading for the door.

"Wait!" Rachel's exclamation was loud enough, compelling enough, to bring Gallagher to a temporary halt.

"What now?" he asked, sullen as a teenager.

"Take Stephen with you. One of us should be there . . . in case . . . in case you find David."

Stephen wanted to go but he didn't want to leave her. It was odd, because in the morning he'd been so angry at her, so determined to punish her, that walking out and leaving her behind would have pleased him, but something in him had changed. "Rachel, I can stay. I don't mind. . . ."

She raised her wonderful, tear-filled eyes from a determined contemplation of the food. "You have to go. If he's there . . . if he's . . . he'll need you, Stephen."

"Are you sure?"

She smiled. Tremulous, wavering, but a smile. "That he'll need you? You're his father, Stephen; there's nothing in his world more reassuring than you."

He put a hand over hers. "Except you."

"Go on, Stephen, before Gallagher goes without you. I wouldn't put it past him. He's already so irritated with us."

"Okay, Skee. Keep the home fires burning. I'll be back as soon as I can. With our son!"

The day had been awful from that first unsatisfying meeting with the twisted boy at the rest stop until the moment when the police had battered down the door of the hunting camp, dragging out a terrified Jason Sutton, and Stephen had stepped past them into the camp, ignoring their warnings not to touch anything, to search for David.

Their voices, trying to get him to leave the place, to stop touching things, had been nothing more than background noise. He had shut them out as he searched, looking in every nook and cranny, even places that were impossibly small. A small nine-year-old doesn't take up much space. He'd shaken off the hands that tried to stop him, resisted the arms that pulled him away, until there was no place left to search. He'd picked up a shovel and was starting to dig up the yard when Gallagher finally got his attention by shouting in his face.

David wasn't there. Had never been there. The whole thing had just been a scam. A trick. Sutton, suffering from the effects of too much TV and too little discipline, had seen a chance to make some easy money and get some vicious revenge on the Starks, and taken advantage of it. A confession he readily spilled when confronted with hard-faced cops with drawn guns. A confession that Stephen, standing at the edge of the crowd, shimmering with disappointment after his search of the empty camp, felt as a series of barely endurable body blows.

He'd almost kept his self-control. He'd made it through most of the confession. It wasn't until Sutton, turning his face toward Stephen and whining, in his scared, little-boy voice, had said, "It was all that bitch's fault. She made me lose my job, nearly got me a criminal record, and then my dad said I'd have to work for my tuition if I wanted to stay in school. I mean, she screwed up my whole life and all because I told the old bitch what she needed was a good fuck!"

As Gallagher started to remind Sutton of his Miranda rights for a second time, something in Stephen snapped. Engulfed in a wave of black rage, he lunged forward, his hands outstretched, reaching for Sutton's throat. He got close enough to smell the slimeball's sweat, got close enough to feel the sweat-slick flesh between his fingers,

got close enough to compress that neck and watch the fear in Sutton's disbelieving eyes. He got close enough to feel the pulse in Sutton's throat, the fragility of the windpipe, the stark terror in those standing tendons. Close enough to the driving power of his own murderous rage to be grateful later to the two burly cops who grabbed his arms and pried him loose, pinning him firmly between them as he writhed and fought and struggled to get free, determined to reach Sutton again and finish what he'd started.

All the while, as they hauled him back through the crowd, they murmured quiet warnings and admonitions in a way that told him they wished they could let him go so he could pound the crap out of the kid, that they wished they could do it themselves. Finally he subsided, panting, and let them lead him away.

He sat in Gallagher's car and watched the crowd of cops and technicians working the scene. Scene was the word. He watched them put Sutton in a car, just like on TV, complete with the handcuffs and the careful hand on Sutton's head to keep him from bumping as he got into the car. The blare of voices and the flare of lights in the dying afternoon were as remote, as unrelated, as actions on a screen. He had believed he would be coming back with David. Been so sure of it. He huddled in the car, eviscerated, gutted, hollow. All the hopes, reassurances, and lifelines of love that he had prepared and brought for David twisting in the cold wind like tattered laundry. He had no idea what to do next, no energy to do it even if he had an idea.

After what seemed like a few lifetimes spent recovering from the decimation of hope and the debilitating aftermath of rage, he began to think about Rachel, waiting at home for the good news that wouldn't come. No, he thought, Rachel wasn't expecting good news. She might be hoping for it—like him, a parent with a stolen child lives on hope—but she wasn't expecting it. From the first, Rachel had thought that this would be a hoax. That was something, maybe: that she would be wounded, too, but not as destroyed as he was. His arms ached, he realized, not from the tension or the search or the digging, but from emptiness.

No. He'd go home and tell her the news. She would flinch, like

she'd been hit, and they would sit together and feel their sorrow, but by morning, Rachel would be packing her bag and announcing that she was going to New York to find David's biological father. And what would he be doing? He knew the answer to that, too. By morning, he would be making a list of things to talk to John Robinson about when he called Robinson from the office.

Yes. Tomorrow their lives would go on. Not their normal lives, the lives they'd lived before David disappeared, but their new, pinched, aching, inquisitive lives. Roller-coaster lives, full of the uphill climbs of anticipation and hope and stomach-knotting downhill slides into despair and agony. Lives where they held themselves apart, fearful that a show of sympathy would make them crumble, distract them from their tasks, where their feelings flashed and flamed and expired like lightning arcs, there for a moment of connection and then gone into the darkness that surrounded them. A dense, private darkness that no amount of illumination could dispel.

He had gone out believing that he would be bringing back his son. That note of expectant triumph echoed hollowly through the house as he and Rachel sat on the couch, alone for once, and comforted each other. Later, when some of the rage and disappointment had retreated, when he'd gotten beyond his consuming desire to dismember Jason Sutton, and through the awful moment when he'd returned to the house and seen the brightness fade from her face, he'd sat with Rachel beside him, glad he'd taken those earlier moments to reconnect, glad he had the memory of her face, so filled with trust and hope and love as she had sent him off to rescue their son. Later, when they sat amid the bitter ashes of their hopes and faced another day without David.

"Can you believe it? He was actually surprised that I was angry. I wish I'd killed him, Rach," he said. "I wish I'd had another minute with my hands around that miserable little prick's neck. I wish I could have squeezed until his eyes popped out."

She put a hand on his knee. "I know. I wish I'd been there. I would have helped."

D AVID WAS FEELING *better, having spent a successful afternoon down at the brook. He'd managed to catch three trout that the man said were keepers. The man had caught four. Wonderful, wiggly, fighting creatures with beautiful speckled designs on their sides. His mother would have wanted to draw them. The man had cleaned them and now the woman was frying the fish for their dinner. The man usually didn't have anything to do with him. When he wasn't doing chores, which was most of the time, the man sat in the window and stared out. He coughed a lot and walked with a shuffle that pained David to watch. He wished the man were happier or would talk to him more, because even though he was quiet, David sensed that he was kind. The man didn't scare him, didn't seem angry. He seemed like a kind of lonely person who liked boys.*

David had been surprised when the man offered to take him fishing. Together they'd gone out behind the barn and dug worms, and then taken the sandwiches the woman had made and gone down a path through the woods to the brook. The man said it was called Pettengill Brook and wanted to know if David had even gone fishing before. He had, a few times, but only in a lake or at the ocean. This was different. It was real peaceful. They sat in the sun on a big rock that stuck out into the water, and the man showed him how to spot the deep pools where the fish liked to hide, and how to cast his line so he would land there. The first time his pole tip had bent under the weight of a strike, the man had been almost as excited as he was.

After fishing, David had helped with the chores—as much as his aching body would allow—mucking out the barn and working in the garden, then helped the man get the cows in for milking. There was a hired hand, a man called Will who had bad teeth and a sly and furtive way, but he didn't always show up for work. Then the woman would mutter things about no-account drunks, and what could you expect from people who came from such poor stock and had no principles, and the man and the woman would have to do the chores themselves.

When they came in from the barn, the woman told him to go wash up for dinner. While he was splashing in the small bathroom off the kitchen, he heard the phone ring, and he could tell from the change in the woman's voice that something was wrong. She snapped at him all through dinner, so that he lost his appetite for the trout, even though the man very kindly tried to teach him how to eat it without getting all the bones, and she sent him to bed immediately after, even though it was only seven. That night, as he lay in bed listening to the rise and fall of conversation downstairs, David decided that as soon as he could, he was going to run away. Feeling happier than he had since the van had stopped beside him, David began to plan his escape.

And sore surprised them all.
—ROBERT BURNS, "John Barleycorn"

CHAPTER TWENTY-SEVEN

The next day dawned bright and sunny, a cruel irony, Rachel thought, given the state of their spirits. She ignored the fresh brightness as she waved good-bye to Stephen and climbed onto the train.

The most amazing thing was that Stephen hadn't even objected. When she'd announced, cautiously, defiantly, that she had to go to the city, he'd just nodded and said, "I know. And I have to talk with John Robinson." And then she'd nodded and said she knew. It was all so odd, she didn't know what to make of it. Their relationship had somehow changed without either of them saying a word . . . changed in ways that words never seemed to be able to do, and now they were in this together. Well, nearly together.

Actually, she didn't think of their current situation so much a change as a phase, another mercurial phase in their unsettled lives, where things might change at any minute. There was still Rachel's secret, her terrible secret, which she hadn't shared with him. She crossed her arms over her stomach, over the tiny life growing there. Fate was being cruel to her, creating a new life when one so precious

to her hung in the balance. She imagined some malevolent being, watching her and thinking, "Oh well, Rachel keeps losing 'em, we'd better give her another." Soon she'd have to face the facts, have the tests, almost certainly end this life. But not now. This wasn't the time for those discussions. Not the time to be worrying about what Stephen would say.

Wasn't she entitled to make her own decisions? And then she wondered, who assigns entitlements, anyway? She recalled a recent telephone conversation. No, conversation dignified it too much. A recent telephone solicitation, in which a woman who was trying to sell her an expensive new vacuum cleaner had demanded: "Are you an authorized decision maker?" The woman had meant could Rachel spend money without her husband's permission, but Rachel had found the question profound.

Last night hadn't been the right time to tell Stephen, and this morning he'd been tight-lipped and silent, wrapped up in his own thoughts as he drove her to the train. Then he'd rushed off to work before she could say anything. Rushed off to work to meet with John Robinson and plot the next phase of their campaign, a campaign that had something to do with reemphasizing the gray van and the missing shoe. Both she and Stephen shared a sense of urgency now. Stephen didn't hear David in his head, as she did, but he was close enough to David to sense the danger.

The rumbling of the wheels had a soporific effect and Rachel's head was nodding loosely against the seat in minutes. It wasn't surprising, after two nights without sleep, that she should be exhausted, but she hadn't even felt tired until she found herself nodding off. Oh well. It would be good to rest her body. She'd need strength for what she had to do, strength and courage, and a wisdom she was ever surer she didn't possess. She was going to find David's father; she was going to get David back.

She emerged from the station, feeling bleary rather than refreshed by her nap, and caught a cab, giving the driver the address she had for David's father. Not that she really expected to find him. Doctors went to work during the day. But she had to go there. If necessary, she'd stay all day and be there waiting for him when he

came home. Maybe while she was waiting, she might sense David's presence.

The cab let her off in front of Peter Coffin's building. A plain, tidy grayish building with a small portico extending toward the sidewalk and a bored-looking doorman in the lobby. The doorman straightened when she came in and waited expectantly.

"Coffin," she said. "Peter Coffin. Is he in?"

The doorman gave her a funny look and shook his head. "No, ma'am."

"Can you tell me when he'll be back?"

The doorman swallowed. "I don't know if he'll be coming back."

"Is he on a trip?" Rachel demanded. The man shook his head. "He does live here?"

He hesitated. "I'm sorry, ma'am. I'm not at liberty to give out information about our tenants."

"But I've got to see him," Rachel said, feeling like a black abyss was opening in front of her. She had to find Peter Coffin. "It's urgent. It's an emergency."

The man's look said that he couldn't imagine how her emergency had any importance under the circumstances, only Rachel had no idea what those circumstances might be. Maybe this man was part of the conspiracy. Maybe he'd been told someone might show up looking for David, and he was to stonewall if they did.

"Look," she said. "I'm sure you're supposed to protect your tenants, but this is terribly important. I need to see him about his child. His child and mine."

That did it. Now the man was looking at her like she was a Martian. Like she couldn't have said something more absurd if she'd said "His elephant." In the silence between them, the anxious beating of her heart roared in her ears like a gigantic pump, drowning out the street sounds. She watched him pluck a few bits of lint from the sleeve of his uniform, nervously finger the earrings in his ear. Finally the man said, "Would you like me to ring his roommate?" Rachel nodded and waited while the man made the connection and spoke quietly into the phone, listened, stared at her, and said something she couldn't hear.

"He's sorry," the man told her, "but Mr. Bourget isn't up to see-ing anyone right now."

She wasn't going to let him send her away. "Tell him I've got to see him, that I've got to see Mr. Coffin. Tell him it's urgent. Tell him it's about Mr. Coffin's son." She watched and waited while her mes-sage was delivered, watched the incredulous look on the man's face, imagining the same look of the face on the other end.

Finally the man hung up the phone. "He's coming down. You can wait over there on that couch." The annoyed shake of his head said as clearly as words how much she was inconveniencing everyone.

Rachel went as directed and sat on the couch. It seemed like she waited a long time. Maybe the building had slow elevators. Maybe Mr. Bourget wasn't coming down; maybe they were planning to ig-nore her, hoping that eventually she'd go away. She wasn't going to go away.

Finally an elevator opened and a man came into the lobby, look-ing anxious. He went to the doorman and conferred, and the door-man pointed at Rachel. She rose and went to meet him.

The man was slight, delicate, beautiful. The kind of person who normally moves quickly, energetically, a graceful progression nearly on tiptoe, though today his steps were leaden and slow. His dark brown eyes ought to have been shiny and alive, but they were dead and dull, lusterless, with deep circles below them. A man who looked like Rachel felt. "I'm Gabe," he said. "Gabriel Bourget. Peter's room-mate. Is this some kind of sick joke?"

Rachel brushed away her instinctive urge to comfort him—she didn't even know why he needed comforting—and stood her ground. "I'm looking for my son," she said. "My son David. Peter Coffin is his father. I thought he might be here."

"You thought who might be here," he asked coldly, "Peter or your son?"

"My son."

Something flared in Gabe's eyes. Anger. And mocking. "Peter Coffin, Dr. Peter Coffin, is gay. He's never had a girlfriend. He's never slept with you, lady, and everyone knows that. So you can just

take your sick scheme to extort money from a dying man and get the hell out of here before I call the police." He turned on his heel, a dancer's turn, and stalked back to the elevators.

Rachel followed him. "Wait. Gabe . . . Mr. Bourget . . . please, just listen to me. I never said I'd slept with him. I said he'd fathered my son. Please. I just need to see him, to talk with him. This isn't about money. . . ." She plucked at his sleeve, trying to get him to turn and look at her. "My son is missing. I'm just trying to find my son. Maybe he has some idea . . ."

"He's sick," Gabe said without turning. "He's dying. He doesn't have the energy for a madwoman's wild goose chases. He has problems enough of his own."

Rachel wouldn't give up. Maybe Coffin had David stashed somewhere. Maybe he had taken David and hadn't even told his lover. Maybe they were in this together and Gabe was just a very good actor. The only way she could know was to see Peter Coffin herself. Now she was glad the elevators were slow. "Maybe . . . if he is dying . . . maybe he'd like to know that he has a son. Maybe he'd like to see his son's picture and hear about him. Maybe he'd like to know that a part of him is going on. Did you ever consider that?" If they were hiding David, this wouldn't work, but if only Coffin was involved, maybe Gabe could be persuaded. Maybe he'd let her see Coffin. "Just let me come up and talk to him."

It didn't work. "He's not here," Gabe said in a way that told her he resented his roommate not being able to be at home. "He's in the hospital and the last thing he needs right now is this malarkey. He needs peace and quiet and love. He does not need you coming in and stirring things up." The elevator doors finally opened, Gabe stepped in, still with his back to her, and was gone.

Rachel turned and walked out of the building, ignoring the doorman's curious stare as it followed her out. She wasn't defeated yet. She needed a phone book and a phone and when she found them, she might have been the only citizen left on the planet, completely oblivious to the swirl of humanity that flowed around her. Rachel just sat, methodically running down the column of hospitals and calling them until she finally found the one where Peter Coffin was a patient. At least his roommate hadn't been lying about that.

She wrote down the address and hailed a cab, getting one almost instantly, a miracle in the middle of a busy New York day. The weather continued to be perfect and the people they passed were allowing themselves to look as cheerful and optimistic as New Yorkers ever allowed themselves to look. She was feeling neither cheerful nor optimistic but only grim and determined. Determined to find this man and make him tell her where her son—their son—was.

The hospital smelled of chemicals and fear, the whole feeble spread of damaged humanity limping, drifting, or being wheeled through the corridors. Inside there was no trace of the lovely day. The place had the airless, overbright sameness of all hospitals. It could be June or January, midmorning or midnight, and it would seem the same. Like she was attached to a bungee cord, Rachel felt herself being drawn back into those days when Jonah was dying, into those days when she'd lived at the hospital.

"My home away from home," she said aloud, and a man passing turned to stare at her. Don't do odd things, Rachel, she reminded herself. Don't broadcast your peculiarity.

She stopped at the information desk and got directions to Peter Coffin's room. On the floor, the nurse at the desk demanded to know if she was family, and Rachel hesitated before saying yes. She hated to lie, then decided that being the mother of someone's child, even though their connection was not the traditional one, gave her some sort of relative connection. At the nurse's direction, she changed into sterile clothes before entering the room.

Feeling like she'd come to the end of a long journey, she pushed open the door and went in. Across the room was a man in a bed, surrounded by a welter of tubing and machines. He looked shrunken and diminished, the arms that lay listlessly on the blankets reduced to mere sticks with baggy, wrinkled skin mottled with purple splotches. He looked over at her with David's eyes. She looked at the bed and she saw Jonah dying and she saw David alive and Rachel was unable to speak. She could only stand and stare as her throat closed and tears ran down her face.

"I don't know you," he said.

"I'm Rachel," she said. "I'm searching for my son."

"Peter," he said. "And I lost my mother a long time ago. You

won't find your son in here. There's no one here but me. Is your son a patient?"

"No," she said softly.

"Can you come closer? My eyes aren't what they used to be and I don't hear that well, either."

Slowly, she crossed the room, pulled a chair close to his bed, and sat down. "Is your son a patient?" he asked again.

She shook her head. "No. He's not a patient."

"Oh, he's just visiting a patient, then. How old is he?"

"David? He's nine."

"He's only nine and he's wandering around the hospital alone? That's not a good idea. . . ."

"He's not in the hospital."

"I don't understand," the man said weakly. "Then what are you doing here?"

"Looking for my son."

"But you said he's not here." He ended with a spasm of coughing that racked his body and left him panting, eyes closed, exhausted.

Rachel looked down at her hands, not knowing what to say. This wasn't what she'd expected at all. She'd come to New York to track down David's kidnapper and make him return her son and here she was sitting beside a gentle, dying man with David's eyes. What she wanted to do was take his hand and comfort him.

When she looked up, his eyes were open and he was staring at her. "You came here looking for me?" Rachel nodded. "Why?"

"I thought you'd taken him."

"Taken your son?"

She nodded. "You don't have my son? You didn't take David?"

His head moved on the pillow, the attenuated "no" of an exhausted man. "Why do you think I took your son?"

She looked down at her hands again. "It's a long story. . . ."

He gave her a faint smile. "I'm not going anywhere. . . ."

"When we heard about the AIDS, I thought immediately that it must have been you . . . that you were the only person with a reason to take him. I thought that if only I could find you, I would find David. And now I've found you and you don't have him?" She

stopped, stared searchingly into his face. "Are you telling me the truth? You really don't have him?"

He shrugged, a small gesture, limited by his weakened muscles, his diminished frame. "I'm afraid not."

Rachel felt despair settle around her like the folds of a heavy cloak. "Then I've come to a dead end."

"I know what you mean," he said.

She didn't respond. She felt hopeless and mean and stupid. She could hear Stephen's voice crowing in her ear, asking how she could be so certain, telling her that she was being foolish. And yet all along she'd been so sure. "And Gabe doesn't have him?"

He tried for a smile and failed. "The last thing Gabe would want is a child. Gabe is like a streak of quicksilver, or a glorious sunset, but he doesn't do too well with helplessness and dependency. For better or for worse, so long as it's not too bad."

Impulsively, she reached out and put a hand over his. It was so cold. Without thinking, she pulled the blanket up from the foot of his bed and tucked it around him. "Maybe I could make you a cup of tea?" The hospital must have a kitchen, if she could only find it.

"I don't remember your name," he said.

"Rachel."

"Rachel," he repeated. "You haven't told me . . ."

"I will. Did you want tea?"

"If you're going to mother me, I'd rather have cocoa."

She got up, annoyed to find her legs were shaky. "I'll get you some."

"I'm not a pederast, if that's what you're thinking. Neither is Gabe." He said it with a weary resignation, as though at another time in his life he would have argued with her but now he was too tired to bother.

"It never crossed my mind."

"Then why would you think . . ."

She looked across at the face that was so like David's, looked into David's eyes, so genuinely curious. "Because you're the only person I could think of with a reason for taking him . . . and I had to believe that whoever took him did it because they wanted him."

"I don't understand," he said. "You're not making sense. Why would I want to steal your child?"

"Because you're his father," she said. "Because he's your son. He's your posterity."

He shook his head. "You've made a mistake. You've got the wrong person, you know. I've never met you before. We've never had a relationship. I'm not the father of your child. . . ."

Rachel dug through her purse for the pictures as she answered. "It's true that we've never met, that we've never had a relationship, but you are the father of my child . . . of my son, David." She took out David's school picture and handed it to him.

He took the picture in a shaking hand and studied it. "Could you hand me my glasses? They're right there on the table. I've always hated them. My one vanity, I guess, though it's a little late for vanity now, isn't it?" He handed the picture back. "Nice-looking boy, isn't he?"

Instead of answering, she handed him more pictures, pulling them from her purse like clowns from a circus car until the bed was littered with Davids.

"What makes you think he's mine?"

"You were a sperm donor. At a clinic in Chicago. A few weeks ago the clinic notified us that you were HIV-positive and we should all be tested. . . ."

"They were never supposed to release my name. . . ."

"I know. They didn't. Wouldn't. I went there. I begged, I pleaded. I made a huge scene. . . . It's the most slipshod operation you've ever seen. As a doctor and as a donor, you would be horrified. They don't care about people; they only care about their profit. I'm sure they went on using untested sperm long after they knew they should be testing. . . ." She didn't know why she was telling him this. She didn't really care.

He closed his eyes and turned away from her. "I can't be concerned about that now. I did what I could. . . . I notified them . . . told them to tell all their patients. . . ."

"When did you do that?" She didn't want to talk about this. She wanted to talk about David.

"A year ago, maybe longer."

"Why did you wait so long? You must have known, with your high-risk lifestyle . . . you must have known you were at risk back when you were a donor. The gay community knew about the sex transmission factor long before the mainstream press. . . ." The words just came pouring out. She hadn't meant to lecture him, wasn't even sure where this was coming from.

He opened his eyes. "You want to know something funny . . . ironic funny, not ha-ha funny? I didn't get AIDS because I'm gay. I got it because I'm a doctor. I'm one of those rare cases of transmission through an accidental needle stick. I didn't even have a sex life back then, gay or straight. The closest I came was ejaculating into a test tube. I was too busy learning to be the best so I could save the world." He picked up one of the pictures and studied it. "His name is David?" She nodded. "And he's nine?"

"He's nine."

"Will you fix me that cocoa and then tell me about him?"

'Tis hard to settle order once again.
There is confusion worse than death,
Trouble on trouble, pain on pain . . .
—TENNYSON, "The Lotos-Eaters"

CHAPTER TWENTY-EIGHT

A successful law practice, like a successful garden, needs a lot of attention. Regular personal attention. Stephen knew that and he forced himself to go through the motions necessary to keep the wheels spinning, but his heart wasn't in it. For years, ever since he'd passed the bar and gotten his first job, the law had been his life. Now it seemed so insignificant compared to the truly important things. He was reminded of something Rachel had said once—that having a child really put all the rest of life's formerly vital trivia in perspective. So he was finally getting perspective. All it had taken was the loss of his only child.

In the corner of his office, a gleaming wooden baseball bat leaned against the bookcase. A special bat he'd ordered as a surprise for David. It had arrived yesterday and his secretary, unthinking as usual, had unpacked it and laid it on his desk, probably supposing it would be a pleasing beginning to his day. It hurt so much when he came in and saw it that she might as well have whacked him in the stomach with it. He had to keep hoping that someday soon he'd be putting it into David's hands. Unable to stand the sight of it, he carried it across the room and shoved it in a closet.

At noon, he gratefully put his work aside for his meeting with John Robinson. Robinson's conduct yesterday, his avid focus on the lost money rather than on the lost child, had put Stephen off, but on reflection, Stephen had decided to view the man as just another tool, a device he could use to aid his search. He didn't have to like Robinson; he didn't even have to trust him. All he had to do was use him. It was heartless, calculating, and refreshingly straightforward.

He'd barely let Robinson get settled before he made his first suggestion. "We need to use some of that money for a reward," he said. They had, after all, gotten the money back when they picked up Sutton.

Robinson tented his hands and leaned back, a cautious look on his face. "I don't know," he said slowly. "What did you have in mind?"

"One of two things," Stephen said briskly. "A reward for someone who found the other shoe . . . or saw David buying new shoes. After all, he had to have gone into the shoe store with only one shoe . . . or no shoes at all if he threw the second one out. Or, similarly, a reward for anyone who has seen him. His picture is everywhere, it's true, but there are lots of people whose memories are stirred by the promise of money. . . ."

"Not always accurately . . ."

"Something is better than nothing . . ." Stephen reminded him. How strange that their roles should now be reversed. When he'd first sat with Robinson, in the study at home, it had felt like Robinson was peering into his soul and studying his secrets. Now he felt like it was Robinson who was holding back, and he, Stephen, who was doing the manipulating. "How much do you think is reasonable?"

"Are we using your money?" Robinson asked.

"I thought people gave you money specifically to use to find lost children?"

Robinson gave him a sharp look. "We have high expenses. All that equipment . . ."

"Let's not worry about the details," Stephen said. "For now, let's just plan this thing. You're the expert. How do you think we should do this?"

Few people can resist an appeal to their expertise, and Robinson was no exception. He immediately began outlining a campaign to

publicize the little boy with the missing shoe, quickly sketching out a flyer on a piece of paper that began: "Will this Cinderella story have a happy ending? It's up to you." "It's catchy," Robinson said. "We might be able to grab some serious media attention with this, even if it isn't a fresh story. I like it."

Stephen nodded. "It's brilliant."

Robinson was so caught up in the idea, he grabbed the sheet and headed for the door. "I'll get to work on this right away. We might even be able to get something on the news tonight." He hesitated. "Did Rachel tell you about Mrs. Proust? Norah Proust?"

"Mrs. Proust? No. Who's she?"

"A psychic. I sent her to talk to Rachel, but it wasn't a good time. I'd like her to come back and have them spend some time together. . . ."

Stephen shook his head. The suggestion was ridiculous. "I don't think so. I try not to encourage that kind of thing. Rachel is very fragile emotionally. I don't want to do anything that might—"

"I can appreciate your hesitation," Robinson interrupted, "I'm a skeptic myself. But sometimes, when you haven't got a lot to go on, a psychic can help. Especially where you have someone as sensitive as Rachel. All Mrs. Proust will do is help Rachel to focus, help her connect with David. And maybe, between the two of them, they can get him to give them some information about where he is."

"You actually believe in this stuff."

Robinson shrugged. "I've seen it work. I've seen it when it was a complete waste of time. Let's just say that I'm willing to do whatever I have to do to try and find the child. I should think you would be, too."

In one quick speech, Robinson had turned the tables again, and Stephen was on the defensive; he was the one being manipulated. "I don't suppose it can do any harm. . . ."

"Great. I'll call her and see if she can go over now."

"Rachel isn't home."

"When will she be available? Norah's pretty flexible."

"I don't know." Robinson gave him one of those looks that

Stephen hated. "She's gone down to the city." Robinson still stared, impassive, and Stephen found himself saying, defensively, "She went to find David's biological father."

"And you didn't go."

"I didn't want to meet him. It's a dead end anyway. I'm sure of that, though no one can convince Rachel of anything she . . ." He stopped. This was none of Robinson's business. "We're wasting time here. Shouldn't you be getting that stuff out?"

"What if Rachel's right?"

"She's not. The guy's a doctor. He's not going to risk his career, his life, for a child. . . ."

"You would."

"It's different. He's my son. . . ." Stephen stopped, seeing the other side of that argument. He didn't want to discuss this anymore. "I've got a lot of work to do. . . ." Robinson nodded, and Stephen, feeling defensive, said, "Besides, there's no way he could have found out about David. They promise anonymity both ways. . . ."

"Yeah," Robinson said, "tight as Fort Knox. Look how hard it was for Rachel to get the information. Call me when she gets back and I'll send Norah over." He turned on his heel and left.

Looking down, Stephen realized he was systematically shredding the memo he'd just worked on for an hour. He got out the tape and put it back together, then gave it to Charlotte without bothering to reread it. These days, everything sounded like mumbo jumbo to him anyway, even his own words. He did a few routine things, things he could do without concentration, and then turned his chair so he could see out the window. Spring in all her glory was happening without him. Without them.

Before he'd had a child, no one could have told him that it would affect his life like this. He'd expected it would be one more thing to manage; he'd never expected how much David had animated their lives. This morning, up before Rachel in the cool, gray dawn, he'd listened to the creaking of the old house and felt its emptiness. Felt the unaccustomed quiet, the unwanted privacy. He'd gone into David's room, sat at David's desk, and though he'd never admit this to Robinson or even to Rachel, he'd tried to reach David

himself. Tried to empty his mind and in a place filled with reminders, had tried to reach out across an unknown space and touch his son.

Nothing had happened except that his feet had gotten cold and he'd gotten a cramp in his leg. He'd found a map that David and Tommy had made to the location of a secret treasure—a treasure he believed was a stash of Tootsie Rolls and Skittles—and the sight of the childish drawing and David's handwriting had made him cry. He was still crying when Rachel came quietly in and pulled his head against her soft, firm stomach, gently smoothing his hair as she might have done with David, and murmuring comforting words.

She'd reached into the pocket of her robe and pulled something out, putting it carefully into his hand. "Look what I found," she said.

He'd looked down at the small, greenish metal object in his hand. Megrim. David's guardian dragon. "We will find him, won't we?" he said.

Rachel put her own tear-slick face next to his. "Yes, we will," she'd said. "Yes. We will." Then, before leaving the room, she'd said, "One thing I still don't understand. Why would he go with someone without the password?"

"Maybe he forgot. He's only nine."

Rachel shook her head. "David is your son," she said. "Stubborn as a mule. He would have waited until doomsday before going without the password."

"Maybe they forced him into the car. Maybe he had no choice."

"That must be it," she'd said, and left to get ready to go to the city.

Now, sitting in his office staring out the window, Stephen wondered about that. Was there any way someone could have learned the password? Were there other things they'd overlooked? Things they hadn't considered? People they hadn't talked to? Was there someone else out there nursing a secret grudge, like Sutton? He supposed all parents in his situation did this, endlessly reviewing the data, looking for another clue, a missing key, a ray of hope. He turned away from the window and went back to work.

THE DAY AFTER *the fishing, when David came down for breakfast, the woman was standing at the stove, slamming the pans around violently. She gave him a strange look when he came in. He tried to cross quietly to the table, not meeting her eye, but as he passed her, she sighed and slammed a pan down so loudly he cringed. "You're having eggs this morning," she snapped, and he nodded, even though he hated her eggs, which were slimy and half-cooked, and even though he didn't feel like eating. He'd never been able to eat when he was scared. Ever since she'd hit him, he'd been more scared of her than ever. He'd been scared every minute, even though it had been better when he was fishing with the man. Most of the time his stomach hurt.*

Maybe it would be better at school. Maybe he could talk to one of the teachers. Not his own teacher—she was abrupt and impatient and didn't like to listen to any of them—but the other fourth-grade teacher had a sweet face and she'd smiled at him kindly a few times. He'd certainly heard often enough that children with problems at home should talk with their teachers. Maybe she'd help him. Maybe she could find his grandmother or his aunt Miranda and he could go home. The possibility of a plan, the idea of escape, made him feel better, and he reached for his milk, drank it, and stood up. "I don't need the eggs. I'm not hungry anyway. I'd better go or I'll miss the bus."

"You're not going to school," the woman said.

"I'm okay. I feel fine today," he said. He still had bruises on his face, as

well as elsewhere, and it still hurt when he moved, but it wasn't bad, and he wanted to be able to show those bruises to someone. He didn't want her to keep him home until everything had faded.

"Don't talk back to me!" the woman said, slamming the frying pan into another pot. "I won't have it, do you hear?"

"No, ma'am. Yes, ma'am." David's heart had jumped to his throat, choking him. It was getting late. Almost time for the bus. If he ran, he could still make it. "I'll miss the bus," he repeated, his hand on the doorknob. "I don't want to miss any more school."

"You'll do as you're told. Now take your hand off that knob and get back upstairs. I need to think and I can't do that with you hanging around."

"Please let me go to school. I'm going to get so far behind. . . ." He looked over to where the man sat, hoping maybe the man would help him, but the man wasn't there.

"You'll mind me or you'll get yourself another beating, do you hear? Now get upstairs before I make you." Her face was mean and angry, and he scampered away before she could slam the pans again or raise a fist.

Upstairs in his room, he lay on his bed, pillow to his face to stifle the sobs. His parents wouldn't have sent this woman. Even in desperation, they wouldn't have chosen someone so mean. He was surer than ever that the woman was lying to him. He didn't know why, but he couldn't believe that they would have done this to him. His parents loved him, wanted him to be happy, while it seemed like this woman hated him. And he had no idea why.

After a while he stopped crying and began to think about escape.

No themes are so human as those that reflect for us, out of
the confusion of life, the close connection of bliss and bale,
of the things that help with the things that hurt. . . .
—HENRY JAMES, *What Maisie Knew*

CHAPTER TWENTY-NINE

The nurse led Rachel to the kitchen, showed her where the cocoa
and cups were stored, and left her alone. Mechanically, since making
food for others was something she was used to doing, Rachel fixed
two cups of cocoa. Three, actually, since she spilled the first one.
Only her body was in the little kitchen, though; her thoughts were
back in the grim hospital room, her feelings spread out on the bed
like David's pictures. She was stunned by what she'd found. Peter
Coffin's ravaged face filled her mind, mingled with images of David.

She'd always thought that David looked like her. Everyone said
so. People always commented on it, and looking into his face, that's
what she'd seen. She'd never wondered about his father as some
people might have, never seen someone on the street and specu-
lated. To her, Stephen had always been David's father; the donor had
been just a mechanical convenience. But now that mechanical convenience had a face, a voice, a reality. Having seen Peter, she could
see how much her son resembled his biological father.

She didn't want to see it. It seemed to her a betrayal of Stephen.

It seemed wicked, a series of perceptions she shouldn't even let enter her mind. But hers was an artist's mind, a mind attuned to noticing the details, and all the details were there for her to see. The many things that made the man, that had passed down through his genes. It wasn't just the eyes. It was the square shoulders, visible even under covers, visible even though his body was so emaciated. And the shape of his head, longish, squarish, with a high forehead. The squared-away, competent look of him. The blunt-fingered, capable hands. She pictured those hands wrapped around a baseball bat and the pain that swept through her made her weak.

It all made her head swim with thoughts she'd never expected. She'd never wanted to know this man who had fathered her child, let alone care about him. She'd come here with a single purpose—to get her son back. The man she'd come after was a villain, a remorseless child snatcher. She'd never expect to meet a person. Never expected to come face-to-face with the blunt fact of David's conception. Had Stephen anticipated this when he'd opposed her coming? When he'd tried to get her to abandon her plans? She didn't know. Sometimes, though she rarely admitted it, he was far wiser than she was.

She leaned against the wall for support, her arms wrapped tightly around herself to hold back the pain. So what if the man she'd found was troubled, lonely, and dying? It wasn't her problem. Her only concern was finding David. But when she looked at the man in that hospital bed, she saw David and all her focus got derailed. Peter Coffin was dying in the prime of his life. She had no way of knowing whether David would even live to see the prime of his. It was strangely like being forced to watch David die, and it was an experience, an agony, that she had willfully sought.

Rachel felt like she had burst through the wall of her own staid, cramped, agonizing life and found herself in the midst of someone else's nightmare, a nightmare parallel to, yet different from, her own. There was her reality; there was Peter Coffin's reality, and now there was a new reality that mixed up the two. And on top of that, there were her memories.

Being in a hospital brought back all the awfulness of Jonah's death. In the midst of this juxtaposition of awfulness, of the dead,

the missing, and the dying, of the certainty and uncertainty of death, she felt herself utterly lost and helpless. For days she'd gone forth with a mission, with a plan, determined to find her son, convinced she was going somewhere. Her search, her crusade, had kept her focused, kept her moving. Now her momentum had deserted her. It was as though she'd opened a door and found herself staring out into the enormous void. She no longer knew where to look, where to go. Disconcerted by her failure, exhausted by this last dead end, she felt, really felt, viscerally experienced the meaning of the word "hopeless."

She grabbed a handful of napkins and pressed them against her mouth to drown her sobs, dabbing at her streaming eyes. She was leaning against the wall for support, but her legs wouldn't hold her, and gradually, as she sobbed, she slid down the wall until she was sitting on the floor of the tiny kitchen.

The nurse, hurrying in to get something, stopped in surprise at finding her still there. "You're visiting Dr. Coffin, aren't you?" she said. Rachel nodded. The nurse squatted down until her head was almost level with Rachel's. She reached out a hand and patted her shoulder. "I know how you feel. It just breaks your heart, doesn't it?"

"Is he going to be able to go home?" Rachel asked.

"He could go home if he had people to look after him. A lot of our patients do. He'll probably go to a hospice from here. Unless he gets a lot better. We do see it sometimes. Some of these guys have such determination. . . ."

Rachel got up, wiped her eyes, and blew her nose, staring at the abandoned cups. "I'm supposed to be making him cocoa," she said. "I'm not doing very well."

The nurse felt the cups. "It's cold. But you can nuke it. It'll still taste good. Poor Dr. Coffin. It's so sad. He was a wonderful doctor. So good with patients. So good as a patient. Usually doctors make horrible patients, but he never complains. And he's been so lonely. He lies there hoping and watching the door and his friend Gabe hardly ever comes. Are you his sister?"

Rachel shook her head, remembered that she'd claimed to be family, and said, "Cousin. I just found out . . . that he was sick." The last, at least, was the truth.

"Well, good for you," the nurse said, patting her again. "You must be the only family that he's got. It's scary, I know, to see some-one look like that, but if you look beyond that and see the man . . . Anything you can do for him, it's more than he's got now. Just to have someone to talk to—Oops. I'm forgetting. Got a Jell-o emer-gency. Call me if you need anything. I'm Mary." She hurried away.

Rachel was teetering on the edge of an emotional vortex. She wanted to call the nurse back and tell the truth. But what would she say? That she'd never seen the man before in her life but she'd come here to accuse him of kidnapping? Come to demand her son back? What would be the use? Mary was there to care for patients; she wasn't there to hear Rachel's confession. She didn't care whether Rachel was a cousin or a fireplug, so long as she came and visited a lonely patient.

She blew her nose, reheated the cocoa, and went back to Peter Coffin's room. Gabe was there and he and Peter, intently studying David's pictures, didn't hear her come in.

"Why should you believe her? What makes you think the kid might be yours?" Gabe was saying. "It's just a ploy. Somehow she's heard you're sick and she's trying to cash in on it. . . ."

"Why would she do that?" Coffin asked.

"Why does anyone do anything? Because people are opportunis-tic shits, that's why," Gabe said.

"He could be my son. Look at him."

Gabe grabbed a picture, stared at it, then tossed it down. "Dark hair, dark eyes. Superficial crap. There's probably a million kids out there who look a little like you. You think they're all yours? What the hell does she want, anyway?"

"She says she wants her son back."

"And you're supposed to have taken him?"

"She didn't know about . . . about this. She did come to the apartment, didn't she? Looking for me?"

"So she's a good actress. Of course that's what she would have done, to make it look like she didn't know. . . ."

"Gabe, hush. She's right there listening. . . ."

Gabe turned and glared at her. "So what? She should hear this. She should know what we think of her."

"What you think . . . Gabe . . ." The rest of what he was going to say was drowned out in a spasm of coughing that wracked Coffin's thin frame. Rachel watched as Gabe backed away, a look of distress on his face.

Without thinking, she shoved the cups she was holding onto the nearest surface and sat on the bed beside him, pulling him toward her till his head rested on her shoulder while she patted his back. She muttered the same soothing words she would have said to David, silly little mindless hushing words as she rubbed the heaving back in slow, rhythmic circles until the spasms ceased and his ragged breath gradually grew calm and regular. He didn't try to pull away. Rather, his head nestled into her shoulder, just as David's might have done, and looking sideways at the thin, vulnerable neck and graying dark hair, Rachel felt her tears start again.

It was Gabe, his face tight with anger, who broke the mood. "An angel of mercy, how touching. Just what the hell do you think you're doing here?" he demanded, his compact body vibrating with resentment.

"I told you. I'm trying to find my son."

"And you thought you'd find him here?" he sneered.

Carefully, she helped Peter back onto the pillows, cradling his head the way she'd cradled her babies. Only when he was settled did she stand and face her accuser. "I didn't know . . ." she said helplessly. "I didn't expect . . ." She couldn't say it. She couldn't tell him she hadn't expected Peter to matter.

"I told you!" Gabe roared. "I said he was sick. I told you he hadn't taken your son."

"You could have been lying. The two of you could have been in it together. I had to see for myself."

"Well, now you've seen. There are no kids here, right? We haven't got a cozy little stash of stolen children. So get the hell out and take your pictures with you. He doesn't need this crap."

"Gabriel . . . please . . . don't." The coughing had exhausted Peter. His voice was barely a whisper. His hand moved weakly over the covers, plucking at them anxiously.

"I brought the cocoa," Rachel said. "Sorry I took so long. You'd better drink it before it gets cold again."

She moved forward to help him, but Gabe made a belligerent sound and the look in his eye was so fierce, she backed away. "We don't need you," he said. "We don't want you here. Why don't you go back where you came from. Go find some other dying man and try your tricks on him." He very deliberately turned his back on her and stared out the window.

With shaking hands, she started gathering up the pictures. Coffin was silent but there was a pleading look in his eyes. He didn't want her to go, she thought, but he didn't have the strength to argue. Rachel slipped one picture under a fold in the blanket and silently mouthed a promise to return. Then, in a regular tone of voice, she said good-bye and left the room.

She found Mary at the nurse's station, her head bent over a notebook. Rachel cleared her throat. "Excuse me?"

Mary looked up. "Oh, hi. How is he?"

"He was coughing. . . . He . . ."

"I know. Exhausted."

"Uh . . . Gabe is there. . . . He . . . he didn't want me around . . . but . . ." Rachel didn't know how to explain what she wanted.

"I know. He's difficult, isn't he? He's so scared of being left alone. It comes out as anger. Don't take it personally. He's mad at all of us. And he's mad at himself, because he can't take it. He can't face what's happening." She shook her head. "People expect too much of themselves. They don't know how to be forgiving. He can't deal with the ugliness of illness and death and so he thinks he's a failure. He can't see that Peter understands and still loves him. I just wish they could talk to each other, but they don't. They sit there in silence and feel inadequate because they can't comfort each other."

She brushed back a stray curl and tucked it behind her ear. "Listen to me. You'd think I had all the answers, wouldn't you? And here I am not letting you get a word in. . . ." She looked at Rachel expectantly.

"Is there somewhere I could wait . . . until he leaves?"

"Gabe? Sure. Down this hall. There's a waiting area past the elevators. I'll come find you when he's gone." She checked her watch. "It won't be much longer. He never stays long."

Rachel followed her directions and found herself an ugly orange chair in a quiet corner. It was the Israel Rabinowitz memorial waiting area. Hospitals' practice of having plaques on everything amused her. She couldn't imagine an elevator named after herself or Stephen. Wouldn't want anyone sitting on the Rachel Stark sofa or putting their tired feet up on a Rachel Stark chair. Wouldn't want an ocean of other people's tears dripping onto the Rachel Stark upholstery.

When Jonah had been dying and the hospital had been her home, she'd had some moments, roaming the corridors in a state of exhaustion and simmering grief, when she'd burst out laughing, imagining the things she could have named after her. Memorial bed pans. Memorial IV poles. Imagined the sign: IN CASE OF EMERGENCY, BREAK THE RACHEL STARK MEMORIAL GLASS ENCLOSURE AND PULL THE FIRE ALARM. Or given the tears she'd shed, the Rachel Stark memorial sprinkler system.

They'd never done anything to memorialize Jonah, other than his gravestone. If they had, it would have had to be something bright and shining, something to make people smile. She'd envisioned a huge apple, a gleaming, metallic red, with a worm that peeped out from time to time. Like her life. Only lately, it seemed like she couldn't see the apple for the worm.

She looked at her watch. Three-thirty. David would just be getting home from school. Instinctively, she half rose, ready to rush home, already planning a snack, before the reality she now lived with reasserted itself. David didn't come home anymore. He was gone. Several times in the last few weeks she'd forgotten. Stopped her work, gone to the kitchen, and started to put out his snack. It still amazed her, since she'd lived more than twice as long without children as she had with them, how completely her children had become the punctuation marks of her life. No day since David had vanished had felt normal or right. She put her head down on her arm and closed her eyes.

She was looking up at a ceiling. A dingy, yellowed, cracked ceiling with a single fixture, a milky glass globe shaped like an overturned bowl, hanging from a slightly fraying cord. The light wasn't

on and because the shade was pulled, the room was dim. Her eyes traveled across the ceiling, down the wall to the top of a door, and then down the door frame to a knob, a skinny, hard knob made from some shiny brown material. She didn't know why the knob was so important but as she watched, it got closer and closer and finally a hand reached out, grabbed it, and turned. The knob turned but the door didn't open. The hand on the knob grew frantic, scrabbling at it, rattling it, pulling futilely, and finally a desperate voice cried out, "Please! Please! Let me out!" And she knew the hand and the voice were David's.

She had to get out of here. Now. Get home and find out what was happening. She jumped up, grabbed her purse, and hurried down the hall. Pushed the button for the elevators. Grabbed a breath. Pushed it again. "Come on!" she said. "Come on!"

"Oh, there you are," Mary said. "Gabe's gone and you can come back now."

"I can't stay," Rachel said quickly as the down indicator chimed and turned red.

Mary gave her a hard look. "Then at least come and say good-bye. He's expecting you. And he's had enough disappointments."

Like a chastened child, Rachel followed her down the hall and into Peter's room. He lay against the pillows looking pale and gaunt and utterly drained. His eyes opened when he heard her step and she saw that he was crying. "Gabe's gone." It sounded like he meant gone for good rather than gone for the day, but Rachel didn't know.

"I'm sorry," she said, looking at the floor. "He was awfully mad at me."

"He doesn't like anything he doesn't understand. Change scares him. And things just keep changing." His eyes closed. "You've been crying, too," he said. "Why?"

"I was seeing a room . . . the room he's in . . . through David's eyes. They've locked him in and he's very frightened." Her breath whistled out softly. "You have no idea how awful it is to be so helpless . . . to know he's in danger and I can't get to him. I don't know where he is."

"I have some idea, after all these years watching parents, spouses, lovers, friends . . . seeing how helpless they feel when they can't fix it, can't help someone they love. . . ." He stopped. "No. Forget I said that. I've seen it, I've sympathized with it, but I've never felt it myself. Forgive me. I was being arrogant. . . ."

He gave her a self-deprecating smile. "Do you and David have ESP?" She nodded. "My father and I used to have some of that . . . to be able to communicate without speaking. My mother hated it. I think she felt left out, but also, it scared her. And anything that varied from her normal was wrong."

"Is your father still alive?"

He shook his head. "I don't think so. I don't know."

"Don't know?" she echoed.

"I haven't heard from them in years. I went through this phase . . . this naive phase, I realize now . . . when I believed in total honesty. I was excited about my life, what I was doing as a physician, and I wanted to share it with them. I told them everything about myself. You know how it is . . . more detail than anybody wants . . . it just came burbling out. About medical school and what it was like learning to be a doctor, about volunteering at a hospice, about donating sperm so people who couldn't otherwise have kids would be able to. So when I began to suspect I might be gay, I told them that, too. They weren't very comfortable with it, and then I got pretty militant about who I was and what I was, and being with them got to be increasingly unpleasant. Eventually we decided on a mutual parting of the ways."

He shrugged. "No big deal, really. Not so different from what a lot of people go through with their families. I'd only been seeing them on holidays anyway, Christmas, Thanksgiving, Fourth of July. I couldn't go visit them if I brought my lover, and they wouldn't visit me if I lived with my lover. There were tears on her part and silence on his when we were together, and Gabe resented being rejected and eventually it was down to a few phone calls and then a few cards and notes. Then they wrote that they were moving and never sent a new address. I just let it go."

"Do they know you're sick?"

"I wouldn't know how to tell them."

"Do you miss them?"

"I guess I miss my dad a little, but I think he's dead."

"You think?"

"The ESP," he said, sounding embarrassed. "About two years ago, I felt this terrible pain near my heart. I thought I might be having a heart attack. . . . They run in my family. . . . A lot of the men die young. . . ."

"It didn't say that on your health profile," Rachel said accusingly.

"I didn't know it then. It's not the kind of thing you pay attention to, growing up. I never would have known it, I suppose, only it was one of the things my mom threw up at me when I was trying to tell her about . . . about being gay. That the knowledge could kill my father, and didn't I know that that ran in the family? That's how she told me. Anyway, while I was having this awful pain, suddenly I saw my father's face, and I realized it was his pain, and that he was trying to say something to me. He was trying to tell me that he loved me. And then his eyes closed and he went away and I've never sensed him since. So I think he must be gone."

"You didn't even try to reach him?"

He smiled at her. "Of course I did. I rushed to the phone and called. The number was disconnected and the operator didn't have a new one. I supposed I could have hired detectives or something, but I didn't bother. It was too late and anyway I wasn't that keen on finding my mother. No matter what they say about the bonds between parents and children, my mother and I didn't have them. We were like oil and water from the first. Maybe she loved me, in her own way, but she didn't believe in showing it. My bond was with my dad. What about you and David?"

"He's a lot like his father . . . like my husband, Stephen. They're both neat and deliberate and impatient when they don't get things their way. But we're close here." She tapped her forehead. "Stephen doesn't like me to talk about it. Partly because he can't stand things that don't have a rational explanation—he finds a lot of things about me odd—and partly because he's jealous. He's very sensitive about David not being his."

Peter had picked up David's picture and was looking at it. "But he's a good father?"

"He's a great father."

Peter looked at her searchingly. "The two of you couldn't have children of your own?"

Rachel lowered her eyes, instinctively folded her hands over her stomach. "We had a child . . . Jonah. He died when he was an infant."

"Something hereditary," he said. "And now you're pregnant again?"

It was eerie, and Rachel took a step backward. "What did you say?"

"You're pregnant." He ducked his head, embarrassed. "It's an instinct I have. You didn't know?"

She lowered her eyes. "I knew."

"Another donor?" he said.

Not even her mind was private anymore. The idea scared her. "I have to go," Rachel said. "I can't talk about this. I have to get home." She turned and ran from the room.

His voice trailed her down the hall, a cry of desperation that halted her flight. "Rachel, wait. Please. Come back."

Cautiously she went as far as the door and peered in, refusing to get any closer. "Will you come again? Come and tell me more about David?"

"I don't know," she said.

"Will you at least let me know how to reach you?"

"Maybe I'll call you," she said. "I don't want you to call me." She turned away, but the anguish in his voice stopped her again.

"You can't do this to me, Rachel, burst in like this . . . tell me I have a son . . . show me his pictures . . . tell me he's missing . . . that he's in danger . . . and then waltz out again like nothing you've said or done has anything to do with me. Like I'm nothing . . . a wall to lean against. A toilet to use and flush and walk away from. Please. Rachel . . ."

She turned and ran down the hall, crammed herself into an elevator that was closing, and was carried away from the pitiful,

accusing voice. All the way home on the train, the click of the wheels seemed to be repeating "hateful, hateful, hateful." She was hateful. Single-minded, and determined, and so intent on finding her son, it didn't matter who she hurt in the process. Determined to find him and with no place left to look. No compassion left for anyone else. Hateful. Hateful. Hateful. And hopeless. She turned her face to the window and cried.

Never say that marriage has more of joy than pain.
—EURIPIDES, *Alcestis*

CHAPTER THIRTY

Stephen's day had seemed endless. He wondered if this was how life would be from now on, a test of his endurance with nothing to look forward to, nothing to go home to. There was Rachel, of course, but along with the camaraderie of being in this together, there was the flip side, that they each reminded each other most clearly and immediately of their loss. It wasn't something you could prepare for or that anyone could tell you about, this state of having had the center snatched out of your life. Learning to live with chronic uncertainty, learning to cherish your hopes while constantly protecting yourself from hurt. At one point, he'd taken the bat from the closet and held it in his arms, racked with the fear that he might never get to put it into David's hands.

Just before he left, John Robinson called, a triumphant note in his voice, and told him to be sure and watch the news. In response to Stephen's questions, he would only say that they'd been successful in placing their Cinderella story and Stephen was going to be impressed; they were going to get results.

Anticipation put the final crack in his self-control, and all the edginess, all the anxiety, all the tension he'd been building up came leaking out, spreading over him like a slow poison, or like an insidious rash, until he itched from head to toe with the physical urge to do something, to affect something, to make something happen. By the time he got out of the car, having driven home with all the insane aggression of a madman, he was tingling with a restlessness that nearly overpowered him. He felt like a pressure cooker ready to explode.

He found Miranda in the kitchen, staring warily at a large steak. "Red meat?" he said. "What's happened to you?"

"I thought we all needed it. Is there gas in the grill?"

"Plenty. I just filled it," he said, stirred by a desire to touch her, by the desire to do something physical to release some of his tension. "You want a drink?"

"I could use one." Reading his mind, she moved around to the other side of the counter and busied herself with some potatoes at the sink. "You two won't have to put up with me much longer. I've found a place. . . ."

"It hasn't been that hard . . ." he said, coming back with her bourbon, holding himself back with an effort. "Soda or just rocks?"

Her eyes rested deliberately on the front of his slacks. "It's been hard too often. It's not fair to Rachel."

He dropped in some ice, watched the golden brown liquid swirl around, and handed her the glass. "You never complained." His throat was tight, his voice hoarse.

"Where's Rachel?" she asked, putting potatoes in the oven, bending over provocatively.

"She went to the city. She should be back anytime now."

"The city? Why?"

"Boy, you are out of it, aren't you? She went to find David's father."

"You're David's father." She bent low over the tomato she was slicing, showing him her breasts.

"Sperm donor," he said, putting down his glass, staring at her breasts, bouncing gently beneath her T-shirt as she worked. He wanted to touch them, grab them, peel back her T-shirt and take her

nipples between his teeth. He was wound so tightly, he could feel his muscles jumping under his skin. Just this once more? He needed it, needed the relief. What could be the harm?

He turned away, looking at his reflection in the glass sliders. He grimaced, not liking what he saw there. He knew exactly what the harm was. It was like a slap in the face to Rachel, who valued fidelity, considered it a requisite part of love. The harm? He would be deliberately driving another wedge between himself and Rachel, when they both needed to do their damnedest now to keep each other strong. To preserve a relationship so David would have something to come home to.

"Stevie, are you okay?" she asked, leaning against him suggestively.

"Miranda, stop it," he said, stepping back. "We can't. We've stopped. We weren't going to do this anymore. . . ."

She gave him an arch look. "The last of the red-hot lovers has suddenly decided to reform?"

"I have."

"Excuse me, Stevie, but I could have sworn that five minutes ago you were standing there with your tongue hanging out . . . or something hanging . . . uh . . . sticking out. Was I wrong?" She ran a practiced hand across his pants. "No," she said, answering her own question. "I wasn't wrong. So what's happened? My crazy sister finally got you pussy-whipped?"

He retreated until the island was between them. "Don't talk about Rachel that way."

But Miranda wasn't ready to give up. "I'm sorry, Stevie. I don't understand. A few minutes ago you were ready to lay me down on the kitchen floor and bang away and now suddenly you're hiding on the far side of the island, prim as a choirboy."

"Oh shit, Miranda, cut me a little slack, will you? I'm sorry if I led you on. It's just that today . . . tonight . . . I'm feeling so . . . God! I shouldn't have to explain. . . . I feel like a goddamned volcano right now. I just really . . . for a minute there . . . needed something to . . . ." Trying to explain that explosive need for relief made him incoherent. It wasn't about sex. It was about loss and anxiety and lack of control and everything that was happening to him.

Miranda came around, wrapped her arms around his neck, and

tried to pull his mouth down to hers. "I'm always here for you, Ste-vie. You know that. . . ."

The front door slammed, followed by quick steps, and Rachel came in as they quickly jumped apart. "Don't mind me," she said. "Just carry on as if I wasn't here." She dropped her bag and coat on a chair and climbed wearily onto a stool. "Only get me a drink first, okay?"

"Hard day?" Stephen said. "Bourbon?"

"A hard-day bourbon would be great. Is that a steak, Miranda? What's come over you?"

"That's what he said, too. Jeez, you guys are like Siamese twins." She flounced back behind the island. "I'm celebrating my new condo. And I thought we all needed it."

"We all need something, that's for sure. I think what I need is summary execution. I'm turning into the world's meanest person," Rachel said.

Stephen raised his eyebrows but he didn't say anything. He wasn't ready to hear Rachel's story. Her face was enough. She always wore her thoughts on her face and now she was wearing dejected, discouraged, and depressed, broadcasting failure. He hadn't put much faith in her mission but right now he couldn't stand the thought of any more disappointments. If he couldn't hear good news, he wanted no news. Or someone else's news. He waved a hand at the blinking answering machine and the silent TV screen. "Which shall it be, ladies? Messages or the news?"

"Let's watch the news, get all worked up, and shoot the answer-ing machine," Rachel said, taking the drink Stephen offered with an attempt at a smile.

He snapped on the TV and they all stared, riveted, as a graphic of a red high-top sneaker filled the screen and the announcer, in a throaty voice-over, said, "Is this a modern-day Cinderella story? Will there be a new development in the case of a missing Forest Valley boy? The answer may be up to you. That story next on *Newsline Tonight*."

He turned to Rachel and gave a thumbs-up sign. "Great. When Robinson puts his mind to something, he can really make it happen. Wait till you see this. . . ."

She shrugged. "It's nothing new. . . ." She looked worried.

"It's the Cinderella thing, Rach. It's brilliant." She just stared at him, shoulders slumped, looking like she'd lost her last friend. "Don't give me that look," he said, feeling defensive. "We had to do something. . . ."

She nodded. "You're right. We do. David's situation is changing. They've got him locked in a room. I don't think he was locked up before. He's so scared, Stephen. He was scared before. . . . He's been scared all along, but this is different. This is gut scared. This is someone's-going-to-hurt-me scared."

Suddenly she put her drink down on the counter. "Oh, what am I doing? I can't drink this. I'm—"

"That reminds me," he interrupted. "Robinson wants you to talk to that woman . . . the psychic. What's her name? Proust?"

"Not tonight. I'm too tired to even think about it. Besides, I thought you didn't believe. . . ."

"What does it matter what I believe? We've got to do anything we can. . . ."

"Tomorrow," Rachel began. "I'll call . . ."

"Shssh!" He hissed. "Listen. . . . Here it is."

A perfectly coiffed, pleasant-faced blond woman appeared on the screen. She was sitting at a desk. Behind her, on the wall, were enormous posters intermingling photographs of David with gigantic red shoes. Across the screen in front of her was an 800 telephone number. She smiled at them, an earnest, caring smile. "Good evening. In an interesting new twist on the Cinderella story, today the Lost Child Foundation and a national shoe company have joined together in an intensive effort to locate clues to the disappearance of nine-year-old David Stark, son of Stephen and Rachel Stark of Forest Valley, New York." The screen switched to a picture of Rachel and Stephen standing on their front steps, talking with reporters.

"David disappeared four weeks ago while riding his bicycle home from school. Last week, a man collecting bottles discovered this shoe"—a close-up of David's shoe, zooming in to focus in on the faint initials scribbled on the sole—"later identified by his mother as belonging to David, beside the northbound highway entrance ramp." The camera came back to the woman's face. "A ransom

demand earlier this week turned out to be a hoax. The perpetrators have been arrested and this shoe remains the only clue to David's disappearance."

The woman smiled again and looked to her right. "Joining me tonight in the studio are John Robinson, executive director of the Lost Child Foundation, himself the father of an abducted child, and James Dawson, president of Fleet Foot Shoes. Good evening." Robinson and Dawson entered, shook hands, and took their seats, each carefully tugging up his pants legs to avoid bagging knees.

Rachel slid off her stool. "I can't watch. You can tell me about it."

Stephen turned, furious at the interruption. "You should be watching this!" The stool fell with a crash as she headed for the door. "Oh, do what you want! Just be quiet about it." He leaned forward, riveted. Robinson seemed to have found a way to offer a reward without spending his own money. A brilliant stroke, getting a national company involved.

"I'll go check on her," Miranda offered.

He put a restraining hand on her leg. "Stay. This is important!"

The woman smiled at the camera. "If you're just joining us, I'm Donna Newman and with me in the studio are John Robinson from the Lost Child Foundation and James Dawson, president of Fleet Foot Shoes. We're here tonight to ask for your help in locating a missing nine-year-old boy, David Stark, who was abducted four weeks ago while riding his bicycle near his home in Forest Valley. Mr. Robinson, tell us how we can help."

Robinson looked at the camera and to Stephen, who had had plenty of chances to watch and assess him. His eagerness and satisfaction weren't entirely hidden. "Thank you, Donna. I think it would help if I first summarized the facts as we've been able to piece them together. A child is missing and we know very little about his disappearance except the following. On the day or days before David's disappearance, a gray or silver van, make unknown, with one or two people in it was parked near the Forest Valley elementary school. At least one of those people is believed to be a woman. The van had a license plate described as having a bird or animal on it." Behind them, the screen showed a montage of license plates replete with herons, lobsters, whale's tails, and manatees.

"A number of things suggest the abduction was forcible. First, David's brand-new bike, which he was very proud of, was flung carelessly into the dirt by the roadside. Second"—here Robinson looked earnestly into the camera—"like many families with young children who are concerned about strangers, the Starks had a password and David was instructed to never to go with a stranger who didn't know the password. As is the correct procedure in these cases, no one other than the immediate family knew that password. David Stark was a very cautious boy. He wouldn't have gone with a stranger." He swallowed. "But David Stark tried to leave a message for his parents. As his abductors drove toward the highway, he managed to throw out one of his shoes, a shoe with his initials on it. . . ."

Once again the screen filled with the red shoe, zeroed in on the faint initials. Stephen made an involuntary sound, a cry of pain, and closed his eyes. Miranda's hand closed over his and held tight. Behind him, he heard the faint sound of Rachel's bare feet as she returned and righted her stool. Smelled the herbal scent of her shampoo. He didn't resist as she took his other hand. Thus joined, they sat in breathless silence as Robinson finished his plea.

The shoe was replaced by a picture of David, smiling hugely, holding out a large grinning pumpkin. Rachel's grip tightened. "We're here tonight to ask you to help us find this boy: David Stark. Please search your memories and ask yourselves if you've seen this child. At a rest stop? A gas station? In your shoe store? Have you seen a boy with one red shoe? Or no shoes? Have you seen a gray or silver van with a child who looks like David? Is there someone new in your town? In your school? Have you seen someone you didn't think had children buying a pair of size four boy's shoes? Maybe you've seen the other shoe? A single red size four high-top sneaker?" Robinson's voice broke and he turned to the anchorwoman. "Can you . . ."

She reached out and gave his hand a pat. "Thank you, Mr. Robinson. I know our audience out there wants to do everything they can to help. The red shoe that you saw was manufactured right here in America by the Fleet Foot Shoe Corporation. Fleet Foot is offering a generous reward for information leading to David's return. Here to tell you about it is Fleet Foot's president, Mr. James Dawson. Mr. Dawson . . ."

Dawson looked like the kind of guy who'd never had a hair out of place since birth, not since his soft infant hair was brushed by an impeccable nanny with a silver brush. He leaned forward, hands on both knees, and gave the camera a look of sincere concern. "Thank you, Donna. When John Robinson came to us and told us David's story, when he told us that the only lead to a missing child was one of our shoes, everyone at Fleet Foot was deeply moved. What an amazing Cinderella story. Like Prince Charming, all Stephen and Rachel Stark have to go on in searching for their missing child is one of our shoes. When I asked what we could do, Mr. Robinson told us quite frankly that in his experience a reward often brings out information that a simple telling of the facts will not. That it provides the necessary incentive for people to make that one, possibly invaluable phone call. For that reason, Fleet Foot is offering a twenty-five-thousand-dollar reward for information leading to the return of David Stark."

His face faded and David's reappeared, headed by the question: HAVE YOU SEEN THIS CHILD? Beneath the picture was a caption, $25,000 REWARD FOR INFORMATION, and an 800 number. In the background, Donna's voice-over informed them that a staff of volunteers from Fleet Foot Shoe Corporation would be manning the phones at the Lost Child Foundation twenty-four hours a day. David's face was replaced by the shoe, with the question now reading: HAVE YOU SEEN THIS SHOE?

The shoe faded out and Donna and a smooth anchorman were back behind a big news desk. The man looked at the camera, said, "We will be running that number periodically throughout this newscast and during the remainder of the evening. If you think you've seen something, we urge you to call. In other news tonight . . ."

Stephen took his hand out from under Miranda's and shut the set off. The kitchen fell silent. A deep, heavy silence that lingered. The only sound was their breathing. He sat and stared at the dusty screen, wondering. Would anyone call? Would it make any difference? Was there still time? Still hope?

The silence was disturbed by the phone. No one moved. Still in a line, still on their stools, they turned toward the machine and waited.

Breathed through the clicks and beeps. Held their breaths as a woman's crisp, dry tones entered the room. "Rachel, this is Norah Proust. I believe you've begun getting some desperate messages from David. It's critical that we talk. I know you're there. Please pick up the phone."

Stephen looked at Rachel, who was staring in panic. "Go on. Go ahead. Talk to her."

Rachel shook her head. "Stephen, I can't. I'm too tired. What's the hurry anyway? I said I'd do it tomorrow." Across the room, Norah Proust gave up waiting and left her number.

He got off his stool and stood before her, his hands on her shoulders, staring into her face. "Goddammit, Rachel. Can't you just for once do what someone else wants you to do? Can't you try and cooperate with something even if it doesn't fit your own personal schedule? We're all tired. This waiting and not knowing isn't more exhausting for you than for the rest of us. Think about David. He's out there waiting for us to come and rescue him and I don't think he wants to wait until tomorrow because you're tired!"

Rachel, bent like a beaten dog, slipped across the room and picked up the phone.

I have thee not, and yet I see thee still.
Art thou not, fatal vision, sensible
to feeling as to sight?

—SHAKESPEARE, *Macbeth*

CHAPTER THIRTY-ONE

"Now, I know this isn't easy for you," Norah Proust said.

Rachel, resting on the couch with a blinding headache and a feeling of exhaustion so heavy, she felt like she was being flattened by a blanket of lead, thought Norah Proust was seriously understating the facts, but she was too tired to do anything other than what she was told. Stephen had told her to cooperate and that's what she was trying to do. It wasn't easy. There was nothing warm and fuzzy about Norah Proust and despite her token reassurances, it felt a lot more like a trip to the dentist than a chance to relax and open her mind.

"When you communicate with David, do you normally see things through his eyes? Can you see what he is seeing?" Norah asked. She had her hand lightly over Rachel's, the way you might touch a sleeping child. The skin on her hand was rough.

"It's not that detailed. Sometimes I can hear his voice. Sometimes we're just thinking about the same things—"

"You never see the world through his eyes?" Norah interrupted, not letting her finish.

Rachel considered. She liked her responses to be precise. Questionnaires with spaces to fill in for always, sometimes, never, didn't work for her. She needed to qualify and explain her answers. "Before he disappeared, never. Since then, once or twice. Once, right after he was taken, I saw a road. And today I saw a room. I saw his hand on the doorknob."

"Does he know where he is?"

"No. I don't think so. David doesn't pay attention to things like that."

"He must know where he is, at least the house, the physical surroundings, even if he doesn't know the name of the town," Norah said with the exaggerated patience she might use with a child. "Can you get him to tell you?"

The calm voice and the demanding questions irritated Rachel. "I don't know," she snapped, pulling her hand away. "It's just something that happens to me. I don't make it happen. I can't summon him when I want to chat. . . . I don't just beam myself into his head at will."

Norah Proust laid a cool, bony hand on her arm. "Stay calm for me, please," she instructed. "We're not doing this for you . . . because it's something you want to do. We both know that. We're doing this for David. Now, I may be able to help you. There are no guarantees, of course. Maybe I can. But only if you will listen to me and try to cooperate."

Rachel, feeling like a chastened, sulky child, nodded. "My head hurts."

"Then take a break. Take some aspirin or something. . . ."

"I can't," Rachel said, thinking that she'd expected a psychic to be sort of dreamy and mystical instead of like the second-grade teacher she'd hated. Her first impression had been wrong. This wasn't Mary Poppins; this was the Wicked Witch of the West. If Norah Proust was truly psychic, she'd understand why Rachel couldn't take medicine. "You said on the phone that you sensed my messages from David were getting more urgent. What did you mean by that?"

"I think we'd better concentrate on you, Rachel. You're our primary source of communication. I don't want to taint that with my own perceptions."

"How would knowing what you've sensed taint anything? I should think sharing information would help."

"All right," Norah said, ignoring the question. "What we need to do is teach you to focus your communication and see if we can learn more about where David is being held. First, I want you to think back to that first time, when you got glimpses of where he was, and tell me what you saw."

"I had a dentist like you once," Rachel said. "If I said it hurt, he'd just go right on drilling." Norah Proust raised her eyebrows, but she didn't reply.

Rachel sighed as she closed her eyes and tried to call back the memory. She didn't think this was going to work. She'd never been able to make it happen. She tried to relax her mind and let it drift, uncomfortably aware of Norah's hand on her arm. It was almost as though there were a faint tingle where their skin met. At first, it was like she was feeling her way down a cobwebby hall, but suddenly everything cleared and she had the picture sharply in her mind. "A road," she said. "A country road. No houses. No sidewalks. Bumpy and patched. Spring still much earlier than here but the same kinds of trees. More scrubby little bushes, I think. A stone wall."

"Does it look like any place you've ever been?"

Without opening her eyes, she shrugged. "It looks like every place. Like New England. You know. New Hampshire. Vermont. Maybe not as hilly as Vermont; I don't know."

"All right. What else do you see?"

"Fields. Fields beyond the wall that are just turning green."

"You're doing fine. Just fine. Do you see any cars?" Rachel shook her head. "What about people?" Shook her head again. "Anything else? What about buildings?"

As though she were watching a movie inside her head, she squinted, peering deeper into the scene, letting her artist's eye bring things into focus. "Up the road, on the right. There's a driveway."

The grip on her arm tightened. "Can you go down that driveway?"

"I'll try." Like a camera with a telephoto lens, she zoomed in and tried to look down the driveway. "I see a red barn," she said. "It needs paint. I think it's a real barn. I mean a working barn." She

stopped talking as she realized what she was seeing. Parked in front of the barn was a silver van. She was only seeing it in her head, in her imagination. She couldn't even know for sure that she was seeing through David's eyes and not imagining what she thought she ought to see. Still, she was stunned and more than a little frightened by what was happening.

"I see the van," she whispered.

"Good. Can you see the license plate? Can you read it?"

This must be what it was like to be hypnotized, this surreal sense of putting yourself into someone else's hands and letting them direct your mind. She tried to cooperate but her mind wouldn't go any farther down the drive; it wouldn't let her look at the plate. Instead, her eyes flew upward, watching with delight the graceful soar of a large bird as it rose, startled, from the bushes and climbed steadily higher. As she watched it soaring, she realized that she was seeing through David's eyes, feeling David's delight in natural things. The delight she'd taught him. David had no interest in the license plate and a genuine fear of the van. "He won't let me see it. He doesn't want to get any closer," she said.

"No," Norah Proust said, releasing the tight grip on her arm. "I don't suppose he does. Would you like me to fix you some tea?" Rachel shook her head, too drained to sit up and sip. "Do you mind if I fix myself some?"

"No. Of course not. There's all kinds in the cupboard by the—"

"I brought my own."

She might look motherly, but her style was anything but, Rachel thought. "How much of this do we try to do at one time?" she asked.

Norah looked at her watch. "Not much more than another hour, I don't think. I know. I know. You're tired," she said as if she'd read Rachel's mind. "But time is of the essence, I'm afraid. I can't reach David like you can, but I've been sensing some very disturbing things. Have you heard from him today?"

"Please," Rachel said. "Go make yourself some tea. I need to be alone for a few minutes. . . ."

"Of course." Norah got up and glided out of the room. Rachel stared after her, at the closed door, and tried to sort out what it was

that bothered her about Norah Proust. Mostly that Norah wouldn't answer her questions, wouldn't share her own perceptions.

Her thoughts were interrupted by the door banging into the wall. She and Stephen were the only ones who didn't bang the doors. It was a practiced skill. "Sorry," Norah said. "Before we start again I need some favorite toy of David's."

Like a search dog, Rachel thought. Give her something to sniff with that sharp little nose and she'll be off and running. "Is Stephen in the kitchen?" she asked. Norah nodded. "Ask him to help you find Megrim."

"Megrim?"

"His guardian dragon," Rachel said, choking on the words.

Norah Proust looked skeptical. "I need something he plays with," she said. "Something he's attached to. . . ."

"Megrim," Rachel insisted. "I know what I'm talking about. He's my son. . . ."

"I didn't mean to . . ."

"Yes, you did. I'll go get him myself." She swung her feet off the couch as Norah grabbed her arm.

"I'll do it. You need to stay here and relax. You're supposed to stay focused."

"Oh, I'm plenty focused. But I don't see how anyone could be relaxed around you. . . ."

"I can't help you if we're going to quarrel . . ." Norah said.

"Quarrel." It was the perfect word, wasn't it, from the Wicked Witch of the West. She probably used the word "admonish," too. "I'm not trying to be quarrelsome," Rachel said. "Just please don't argue with me about everything. I'm not a ninny, you know. I only ask questions when I need to understand the process." Norah just sighed and left the room.

"Are we having fun yet?" Rachel asked the silence around her. Wearily, she closed her eyes and waited for the woman's return. Gradually she became aware of a sharp pain, a pain in her lower abdomen that frightened her. Was it the baby? Was she losing it before she'd even had time to think about what to do? No, it wasn't that sort of pain. It was a familiar pain, though. Yes. Now she knew. It was the

pain of needing to go to the bathroom. The pain of waiting too long with no relief in sight. And it wasn't her pain. It was David's.

She could see him now, leaning against the wall, his hands pressed against his body, doing the little foot-hopping dance. It brought a smile to her face, a smile that faded as she realized what was happening. He was locked in. Locked in for heaven knew how long and they wouldn't let him out. "It's all right, sweetie," she thought. "If they won't let you out, just find an old glass or cup, or even a metal box, and use that. You don't have to wait. This is no time to be polite." As if he'd heard her, she saw a startled look on his face and then he began to look around the room for a container, moving in a slow, hesitant way like a little old man.

Only four weeks and he was so changed. Thin, worried, fearful. "Oh, David, my darling," she said aloud. "What have they done to you?" He turned toward her and she looked into his eyes. Eyes filled with terror. "Oh, darling. Tell me where you are and I'll come get you. I'll come right now. Please, sweetheart, where are you?" Involuntarily, her arms reached out.

He opened his mouth to speak just as Norah Proust came in, banging the door again. Rachel jumped and David was gone.

Rachel sat up, her eyes flying open, and glared. "He was just about to tell me something and you have to go and make all that noise. Can't you come through a door without banging?" Norah was clutching Megrim, the small verdigris dragon, in one hand. "Here. Give me that. . . ."

"I think it would be better if I—"

"I don't give a flying fuck what you think," Rachel said. "I'm sick to death of what other people think I should do. I'm sick to death of having someone interrupt me every single time I get close to David. I'm sick of people spending their time thinking I'm weird because I can sense David and then treating me like I'm some sort of electric drill that can be operated at will to bore into David's mind. I told you. It doesn't work like that." She held out her hand for the dragon.

Norah Proust put her hand behind her back, glaring at her. "Rachel, you've got to get a grip on yourself. I can't help you if you

insist on behaving like this. I know you're frustrated, but abusing other people won't help."

Rachel stood up, still holding out her hand. The force of her anger made her tremble. The outstretched hand was unsteady. "Give me the dragon. . . ."

"No," Norah Proust said. "I'd like you to lie back down and concentrate, but if you won't, I'm going to try to reach him myself. To do that, I shall need the dragon. . . ."

"I told you!" Rachel exploded. "It doesn't work like that. I can't just summon him at will. . . ."

"You can learn," the other woman said flatly. "You're just an undisciplined person."

Rachel grabbed her arm and tried to force her to relinquish the toy. "Give me that!" she yelled.

The door banged again. Stephen standing there, hands on his hips, his face furious. "Just what the hell is going on here? Rachel, what's come over you? Mrs. Proust is trying to help us and you're acting like a two-year-old!"

"She won't give me the dragon," Rachel said.

"I'm afraid your wife is not cooperating," Norah Proust said.

"Please, Rachel," Stephen said, not giving her a chance to explain, willing, as usual, to expect the worst of her, "can't you just this once try and cooperate?"

"But I was . . ." Rachel sputtered. "I was with David . . . in that room. . . . He was about to tell me something and then this woman—" she pointed a shaky finger at Norah—"came banging and clattering in and scared him away!" She paused for breath, knew he wasn't listening to her. "What the hell do you care, anyway, Stephen? You never believed in this stuff when I talked about it and now here you are bellowing at me to cooperate with some gestapo psychic because your precious John Robinson sent her? If she's so special . . . and if you suddenly believe in this crap, why don't the two of you go somewhere else in the house, set up your own little mental shortwave radio to David, and leave me alone?"

"She's overwrought," Norah Proust said. "Maybe we should leave her alone for a few minutes. Let her compose herself . . ."

"No," Stephen said. "No. We haven't got time. . . . She's got to understand that she's not the center of the universe, that sometimes she has to cooperate, conform her conduct for the good of others. . . ."

"Thank you, Stephen," Rachel said. "I appreciate your efforts to infantalize and trivialize me in front of others. Maybe that works on other people but it doesn't work with me. If the two of you won't leave me alone, I guess I'll have to leave you alone. . . ." She strode toward the door. As she passed him, Stephen put a hand on her arm to stop her. She looked down at the hand and up into his face. "We're supposed to be in this together," she said. "Remember? It's not your problem and it's not my problem. It's our problem. Insulting me and treating me like an idiot won't help. Now, please let go of my arm."

He stared back at her, his face flushed with anger, and didn't drop his hand. "Listen to me, Rachel. . . . You've got to . . ."

She was nearly choking on her anger, but she understood his double dilemma. He was as afraid for David as she was and he hated to lose face before an outsider. "Stephen, Stephen, you listen to me for a change. I need to be by myself for a while, to see if I can get back in touch with him. I can't do it with an audience. I can't do it with noise and voices and people coming and going." She shifted her eyes to Norah Proust, who hovered a few feet away, her face as angry as Stephen's, still clutching the little dragon. "Maybe it might have worked with a different sort of person, but I don't work well when I'm being bullied, and she's a bully."

Stephen dropped his hand. "Do what you want. You always do anyway." He turned and walked away.

"Rachel, please," Norah Proust said. "I know we can make this work. . . . You just have to tell me what you're seeing. . . ." Ignoring her, Rachel turned and went upstairs.

She'd barely closed the bedroom door behind her when she realized that she was very cold. She put on socks and her warmest sweater, but it didn't help at all. She got into bed, snuggling under the covers, but that didn't warm her up and after a few minutes, huddled up in a small ball, she realized that tears were pouring down

her face. At first she thought it was what had happened downstairs, but soon realized that she was thinking of Peter Coffin, of the horrible way she'd left him.

Everywhere she turned, she was reminded that she was a wretched human being. By the memory of Peter Coffin's ravaged face. By Stephen's words. By Norah Proust. And most of all, by the fact that she couldn't do the one thing she cared about doing: save her son. She curled into a tighter ball, closed her eyes, and wished she were dead.

Someone was breathing. The cautious, quiet breathing of a person trying to eavesdrop without being detected. She was aware that the breathing was inside her, and along with it, she felt the sensation of a hard, cold floor beneath her. She was with David again. He was lying on the floor, his ear pressed desperately hard to the metal grillwork of a register. Distant voices reverberated faintly through the metal, the words indistinct. Together she and David took a breath, held it, and listened. Heard a woman say, ". . . no other choice with all this publicity. We're going to have to get rid of him." The man's fainter response was indistinguishable.

A wave of fear, intense as an electric shock, ran through her body as it ran through David's. "Oh, sweetie," she thought. "Please just give me a clue to where you are and I will come. Please, David, tell me. Where are you?"

The bedroom door banged open as Miranda came in with a pot of tea. Rachel sat up in bed and screamed out an explosion of all her rage and frustration. Miranda dropped the tray. Stephen came running to see what had happened. She turned to the two of them, standing there and staring at her. "They're getting ready to kill him," she said. "They're getting ready to kill him and I'm never going to have a chance to find out where he is because . . ." She spoke with a voice choked by sobs and tears were running unchecked down her face. ". . . because every time I get close to him, every time he might be able to tell me something, one of you comes clopping and banging in and scares him away." As she spoke, she was pulling on her shoes. "I've got to get out of here. Away from all of you, if I'm ever going to have a chance to save him."

She wrapped an elastic around her hair as she charged toward the door, intending to walk right through them all if necessary.

Suddenly Miranda broke her silence and collapsed against the wall, her hands over her face. "It's all my fault," she sobbed. "It's all my fault. The whole thing. If I hadn't babbled on to that couple about the password, they never could have taken him. He never would have gone with them, and he'd still be here with us."

With ruin upon ruin, rout on rout,
confusion worse confounded.

      —MILTON, *Paradise Lost*

CHAPTER THIRTY-TWO

A silence as dense as a fog bank filled the room, disturbed only by Miranda's sobs. As dense and as chilly, freezing them into a stunned tableau. Stephen was by the door, a hand up on the jamb, leaning in. Without the wall's support, he thought he might have collapsed from astonishment. Miranda hunched before him, her back to him, her face buried in her hands. Rachel stood by the bed, one hand to her chest like a Victorian dowager, her face shocked and terrible. Finally Stephen had to speak; he had to know what his sister-in-law's irrational confession meant. Despite their intimacy, he felt no compassion. "Miranda, what on earth are you talking about?"

"There must be a connection," she said without taking her hands from her face, so that her voice was muffled and indistinct. "I didn't mean to. Honestly I didn't. It was just conversation. I never for a moment thought . . . I never even made the connection until just now."

"What are you talking about?" he repeated. "What conversation? What connection?"

"That older couple. Rachel, you remember. I told you about

them. They had me show them houses all over town. Said they were planning on moving here with their daughter and her child, so they were interested in the schools. I was really hopeful about them . . . had a couple different clients right on the edges of their chairs, expecting an offer. And then one day I had an appointment with them and they never showed up. Never called. Checked out of their motel and just up and disappeared. I was pissed, but I didn't think much about it, except that they were being extremely rude. But customers can be like that sometimes. Incredibly inconsiderate, like my time isn't worth anything. I mean, I showed them just about every inch of this town and then they split without a word. But now, looking back on it, I remember that they drove a van. . . ."

Stephen's forte was the perfectly formed question and the precise eliciting of information, but the facility failed him now. He knew he'd spent too much of the last four weeks angry and he knew that for the most part that anger was counterproductive. A cool head was more successful—he'd been training himself for years to keep a cool head—but this was too much. Miranda's tardy announcement hit him with a double whammy of astonishment and fury. "Dammit, Miranda, will you get to the point and stop whining about being a mistreated realtor? What's this stuff about the password? We don't care how many properties they looked at." He had to stop. The pressure of his overwhelming anger left him breathless.

"Maybe it's not such a big deal," she said.

"Well, we can't know that until we have some idea what you're talking about, can we?"

"Well, I . . . uh . . . we were having this conversation about kids . . . you know . . . about how dangerous the world is these days . . . and about ways to keep kids safe. It was when I was showing them the schools . . . and I was telling them about how you guys had a password with David. And then the woman asked me something like what sort of password was it. . . ."

"Are you saying that you told two strangers what our password was?" He couldn't help himself. He shouted the question at her. Miranda flinched and sidled away.

"Come on, Stevie, calm down," she said. "I didn't mean any

harm. I mean, I didn't see how telling two strangers about the password, strangers who'd never meet him, could do any harm. It just
was part of the story, you know?"

"You gave our password to strangers?" he thundered, "and you
didn't think it could do any harm? Why in hell do you think we had a
password, because we liked the sound of the word 'rutabaga'?"

"I never—"

But he cut her off. "And you've been sitting on that information
for four weeks? It never occurred to you that there might be a connection? Haven't you paid any attention to what's been going on
around here?" He was ready to dismember his sister-in-law, and from
the look on her face, Rachel wouldn't do anything to stop him.

"Calm down, Stevie," Miranda repeated. "It may not have anything to do with what happened. . . ."

She tried to back out of the room, but he grabbed her arm and
pulled her back in. "Calm down! Miranda, you've got to be kidding.
You gave the kidnappers the key they needed to steal David and you
want me to act like it's no big deal? How brainless can you be?" He
swallowed, fumbled for some internal control, squelched his desire
to strangle her. "What kind of van was it?"

"I'm not stupid, Stephen. . . ."

Maybe he wouldn't squelch the urge. He could feel his hands
twitching. "What kind of a van, dammit? Did you even notice?"

"Silver," she said sulkily. "That kind you see around everywhere."

"Jesus Christ," he exploded. "This is stupidity beyond belief!
Where have you been living for the last month, on Mars? We've been
talking endlessly about the password and the silver van and two people, one of them a woman, lurking outside David's school, and it
never occurred to you until now that you might know something?"
He gripped her arms tighter and shook her furiously. "How could
you be so dumb?"

"Stephen, don't hurt her," Rachel said. "We need her information. I'm going to call Gallagher." In her voice there wasn't a shred
of desire to protect Miranda.

He dropped his hands to his sides and stood, panting, staring at
Miranda. Disbelief nearly outweighed his anger. On her face, instead

of the contrition and embarrassment he should have found there, instead of the shock and dismay that should have resulted from her discovery that she'd carelessly withheld vital information, that she'd delivered up the nephew she loved to kidnappers, he found the sulky anger of an aggrieved lover, the incredulity of a woman who expects better from a man she's screwed. "Get a grip," he snapped. "This isn't personal. This isn't about you and me. It's about David. Don't you see, Miranda, this is a matter of life and death."

Rachel, hanging up the phone, said, "They'll find him and send him right over. I only hope it's not too late." Her big, compelling eyes were fixed on her sister. "They're talking about getting rid of him, Miranda. Your nice couple. The kidnappers. Now that things have gotten tense, with all of Stephen's beloved publicity, they're scared. They've locked him up and they're discussing what to do with him. Maybe you didn't mean any harm, with your unchecked, insipid babble, but you sure as hell have caused it!"

"You don't know that it was me! Maybe I never should have said anything," Miranda muttered, kicking at a broken teacup.

"Oh, get off your high horse." He wanted to hit that sullen face more than he'd ever wanted anything. Through clenched teeth, he said, "You're not a kid anymore. You have to take some responsibility for what you do. Why did you wait so long? Don't you care what happens to David?" She shrugged and turned her back on him.

He couldn't stand being in the same room with her any longer. "I'll go downstairs and wait for Gallagher." He pushed past her and stumbled down the stairs. Halfway down he thought of another question and turned and shouted back at her, "Where were they from?"

"She said New Hampshire. That's the address they gave. But I don't think the van had New Hampshire plates."

"What plates did it have?"

She shrugged. "I didn't notice, other than that they weren't green and white and New Hampshire's are. But won't the motel know? They have to give that information, don't they?" She stuck out her foot and started grinding the handle of the broken cup.

"Stop that!" Rachel said. "I like that cup. I can fix it if you don't destroy it completely."

"Don't yell at me," Miranda snapped, and kicked the piece across the room. "It was an innocent mistake."

Stephen turned his back on her. How incompetent could a person be? All these important pieces of information and she hadn't noticed anything. She'd paid so little attention, she'd failed to make these vital connections, and now she was sulking like a scolded child. He knew Miranda wasn't a genius, but he'd never before considered that she might be truly stupid. What else besides stupidity could explain her lapses? Unless she was an accessory herself, and then she never would have confessed. Unless she'd been overcome by guilt? No, it couldn't be that. She simply wasn't a good enough actress. The only thing that made sense was stupidity. Self-involved, blindered stupidity.

At least she'd be able to describe the couple. And someone at the motel, or maybe one of the home owners, might remember what the license plate was. God, what a day it had been. He felt like he'd been on the world's biggest and longest roller-coaster ride. He helped himself to enough Scotch to float a small ship, threw in a token ice cube, and went into the living room, starting the drink with the eagerness of a thirsty dog. Desperate for the numbing relief.

Megrim was sitting on the coffee table, left behind by Norah Proust after Rachel had rejected her and she'd departed in a huff. He picked it up and held it on his palm, admiring the delicacy of the work. Megrim was an elegant little thing. He remembered Rachel reporting that it had cost far too much but was so fine neither she nor David had been able to resist. It was fine. As he sat staring at it, the image of David bursting into the room, fresh from the store, to show it off, appeared. He saw David's bright eyes, the triumphant grin, the small, competent hand with dirty fingernails. He shuddered, unable to face the thought that followed—that he might never see that face alive again.

Rachel's words rang in his head, words he'd ignored while his focus was on Miranda. "They're talking about getting rid of him . . ." she'd said. Talking about getting rid of him. Talking about getting rid of him. Talking about getting rid of him. Each repetition hit him like a booted foot. They were running out of time.

Had the kidnappers correctly judged that Miranda wouldn't make the connection or had they simply not cared? Maybe they hadn't thought about it. Maybe they weren't particularly sophisticated. But they'd come here and they'd taken David away and no one had noticed them. Had they, as Rachel insisted, specifically targeted David, or were they just opportunistic, using the password to take him because Miranda had so conveniently provided it? He wished somewhere in this mess there would occasionally be answers instead of only questions. He wished he could close his eyes and wake up and this would all be a bad dream. He was grown-up enough to know that wishing won't make it so. He had to be cold, rational, and adult.

He closed his eyes and tried to master his rage, his confusion, his incredulity. He focused on his breathing until the pain subsided and he could breathe normally again. Then he got himself a yellow legal pad and started writing down his questions.

D AVID LAY ON *his stomach on the floor, his ear pressed against the cold, hard grate of the register. He'd discovered, in the weeks he'd been here, that sounds from downstairs traveled up to his room through the heating duct. If he listened very carefully, he could sometimes understand what they were saying. The man and the woman were down in the kitchen, he could tell, but their voices were faint. All he could hear was sound, not words. And then, more clearly, the woman's voice, raised, angry as she always seemed to be lately: ". . . don't see that we've got much choice. We've got to get rid of him. . . ." Her voice dropped away and he couldn't hear anymore. He didn't think she meant to take him back.*

Outside, the endless gray was deepening into a darker gray night. He wasn't sure how many hours he'd been locked in, only that it was many. There was no clock in his room and his watch was lying on the sink in the bathroom. The bathroom. It was just across the hall but he couldn't get to it. At first that hadn't mattered much; what had bothered him had been the fact that he was locked in. But as the hours had passed, and he'd exhausted himself by banging on the door and begging to be let out, his interest in the bathroom had increased as his need for it had become more obvious.

At one point, he thought he'd had a brilliant solution—open the window and just pee out. He'd felt a spark of amusement at that idea and it had been followed by the thought that once he had the window open, maybe he'd just go through it and keep on going. That had really cheered him up. He'd felt

almost happy for a moment, as he pulled back the curtains and undid the lock. But then he'd pushed and pulled and tugged until his knuckles were bleeding and his fingertips were raw but there was nothing he could do. The window was nailed shut.

He got into the bed, wrapped the covers around him, and covered his head with the pillow. He felt very small and helpless. He wanted his mother. He wanted his father. He wanted someone to come and fix it. He'd tried to be a big boy and to be good and cooperative because he'd thought it was what his parents wanted him to do, but he no longer thought that. He didn't believe that his mother and father, who loved him and wanted to make his world good and safe, would have picked these people. The people had lied to him. He didn't know how they'd gotten the password; all he knew was that it hadn't been from his parents.

He wiggled restlessly under the covers. He needed to use the bathroom. Finally he went to the door and yelled to them, telling them they had to let him out. No one answered. He grabbed the knob and jiggled it, first gently and then as hard as he could. Then he started pounding on the door and yelling. Yelling until his throat hurt and his voice was rough and raspy. He had his legs twisted together, but he wasn't going to be able to last much longer.

Even though he knew she couldn't hear him, he called, "Mommy, Mommy, help me!"

In his head, it felt like he was getting an answer. "It's all right, sweetie. If they won't let you out, just find an old glass or cup," she said, "or even a metal box, and use that. You don't have to wait. This is no time to be polite."

"Mommy, please. Please come and get me. They're going to get rid of me," he thought, and again it was like she was answering him.

"Oh, darling. Tell me where you—" Then she was gone. He couldn't feel her with him anymore. He tried for a while to get that comforting feeling back, but it wouldn't come. After a while, he got up and prowled the room, looking for a jar. He found one in the closet with pennies in it. He knew the woman would be mad, but he no longer cared what she thought. He dumped out the pennies and used the jar, wrinkling his nose at the smell. He put it in the rear of the closet, under some old blankets, hoping he wouldn't have to use it again. Then he lay back down on the floor and listened.

Where there is no vision, the people perish.
—PROVERBS 29:18

CHAPTER THIRTY-THREE

Stephen felt better with Gallagher there. That was certainly a feeling he'd never expected to have. He'd learned to be philosophical about winning and losing and about the foibles of his fellow men, but inside he was a grudge carrier. He didn't let it poison him; he looked for creative ways to get revenge. Gallagher's behavior had given him a place of honor on the grudge list and this probably wouldn't affect that; still, Stephen was glad to have someone else question Miranda. He knew her too well, owed her a little too much, and was far too angry to bring the necessary single-mindedness to the job.

"Saw Robinson's little Cinderella story on the news tonight," Gallagher said. "You've got to give the guy credit sometimes. He sure knows how to work the media. You get any hot tips yet?" His face was impassive but his manner said "I doubt it." His clothes carried the smell of old pizza, and a small tomato smudge in the corner of his mouth suggested he'd left his meal in a hurry.

Stephen shrugged, determined not to get sucked into the man's game. "Robinson hasn't called."

"He won't," Gallagher said. "If there's glory to be had, he'll take it for himself. Wait and see." He looked around the empty room. "So where's our star witness?"

"In her room, sulking. I'll get her."

"That would be nice." Gallagher settled himself on the couch and crossed his legs. "I guess she won't be serving coffee, then?"

Stephen was about to suggest that Rachel could make some, but checked the impulse. They weren't there to wait on Gallagher. He was there to do the job he should have been doing all along— interviewing a witness. "I guess not," he said.

She came out of her room with a tight face and her chin held high, sailing past him with stiff shoulders and not a glance in his direction. He watched her backside, swaying gently under a short, pleated skirt, as she went down the hall. Her costume was teenage ingenue—white blouse, dark sweater, plaid skirt. She might have been coming in from field hockey. Good luck, he thought. In his experience, Gallagher wasn't inclined to cut women any slack no matter how cute they were. He followed more slowly to give Gallagher time to get started, knowing that if Gallagher gave her a hard time, she was going to be looking to him for help.

"Dream on," he muttered under his breath. "The extent of my charity is that I haven't strangled you."

He met Rachel at the bottom of the stairs and instinctively put out an arm, pulling her close. She looked up at him, and, as often happened when she did that, he felt he was seeing her eyes for the first time, her oddly light, luminous eyes. Troubled eyes. "I didn't get to ask you about your day," he said.

"It hasn't exactly been an uneventful evening. Anyway there's not much to tell. My day was a bust. The guy is a doctor about our age who got AIDS from a needle stick and now he's lying there in the hospital lonely and dying. And naturally I did everything I could to brighten up his day, marching in there and accusing him of kidnapping a child he knew nothing about. Showed him David's pictures, made a personal connection, got him thinking about the fact that he'd fathered a child who was in serious danger, and then walked out on him while he begged me to stay."

"Are you sure?"

"Of what? That he didn't know about David? Yes. That is, I suppose in a general way, having donated sperm, he was aware of the possibility of children, but I don't think he'd ever considered the reality of them."

He nodded. "I'm sorry about forcing you to . . . about Ms. Proust. I was only thinking it would help. . . ."

"Just like me and that poor guy in the city. You had to be pretty desperate to suggest a psychic. I realize that. We're both pretty desperate or neither of us would be behaving this way. You had no way of knowing that she'd turn out to be like a bad second-grade teacher, bullying and controlling. I don't know. Maybe if she'd been gentler, less directive, she might have helped. It seemed to be working a little bit, at first, if only she hadn't kept butting in. It was like trying to watch a movie when people keep talking."

She shrugged. "I don't know. She did say she'd been getting a sense from David that he was in danger, but then she wouldn't tell me exactly what the message was. You know, what he was saying to her. It reminded me of that time I tried to see a shrink . . . a psychiatrist . . . to talk about Jonah, and whenever I'd ask a question about the process she'd want to turn it into a discussion of why I asked the question. I asked the question because I wanted to know the answer. It was the same way with Norah Proust."

She sat down on the stairs and pulled him down beside her. "Let's not go in yet. Let her experience the pleasure of a Gallagher inquisition on her own." Stephen sat down beside her and put his head on her chest, listening to the purr of her voice vibrating through her skin.

"Maybe I expected too much," he said.

"I do think people tend to expect too much from psychics," she said. "According to what I've read, it's more a matter of impressions and general information. They don't exactly come up with surnames and—"

"Why doesn't Robinson call?" he interrupted, his thoughts jumping to the next subject on his mind. "If this turns out to be a dead end, too, I don't know what we'll do. Watching the news tonight, it seemed so clear . . . so simple." He picked up his head and

ran a hand through his hair. Greasy. He needed a shower. "Surely someone must have noticed something!"

She put up a hand and touched his face, her fingers cool and gentle. "Maybe he's too busy to call. Maybe they're getting lots of calls."

He didn't tell her what Gallagher had suggested about Robinson. She didn't need any more bad news or, if Gallagher was wrong, any more reasons to be critical of Robinson. He only said, "But Gallagher hasn't heard anything. . . ."

She put a finger over his lips. "We don't know that. It's too soon to get discouraged. Any more discouraged, I mean."

She pulled her hand back and ran it through her own hair. She looked old and worn, the circles under her eyes large and black, like the artificial smudges on a football player. "Maybe they're going to do an update at eleven or something. Anyway, we've got Miranda. Even though she's my own sister and I ought to know her by now, I still couldn't believe . . . can't believe . . . How oblivious can a person be?" Her voice trembled with anger.

"Based on Miranda, I'd say very."

"It just doesn't make sense," she said.

"Does any of this make sense? Could you have imagined a month ago that you'd be running off to Chicago, playing dramatic scenes at a fertility clinic? Or going to New York to track down a sperm donor? Could I have imagined that I'd be spending hours in dingy phone booths waiting for calls from a kidnapper? Of course not. No one ever expects something like this to happen. . . ."

"But we did. That's why we had the password. The password that . . . that my idiot sister volunteered to the very stranger who wanted to make it happen! If you don't kill her after this, I'm going to. She presents a clear danger to the human race!"

He put his arm around her and pulled her against him. "She didn't mean to, Rachel. . . ."

She flung her head back and stared up at him. "Don't you dare defend her!"

"Quietly, Rach. She'll hear you," he said.

"I don't care!" she said. "I don't care at all. After all the misery she's caused us, nothing's bad enough. . . ."

"She's not the one who took David, remember."

"As if I could forget. But who were they? And why did they take him? Why him?"

He looked at the closed door. A barrier to knowledge. Angry as he was at Miranda, he couldn't stand not knowing what was happening. "Let's go in and see what she has to say. And try to keep our tempers." It was easy enough for him to caution Rachel. The harder question was whether he could keep his own temper. He stood up, took her hand, and pulled her to her feet. He could tell she didn't want to go.

"I don't know if I can stand it . . . listening to her. . . . I don't know if I can keep my temper, Stephen. . . ."

"Just think of her as a source of information. Hate her as much as you want but remember, all we care about is her information." Rachel nodded. Without further conversation, they went into the living room and settled themselves quietly in chairs.

It hadn't been more than a few minutes, but Miranda had already reached the tearful stage. She was staring at Gallagher with swimming, reproachful eyes. His response was impassive as ever. At least, Stephen thought with satisfaction, the man applied the same standard to everyone. No one was treated well.

"Now, Miranda," Gallagher was saying in a voice that dripped sarcasm, "do you remember our conversation shortly after David's disappearance?"

Miranda dropped her eyes to her lap and nodded.

"I said, do you remember it?"

She raised her eyes, chin trembling, and gave him an angry look. "Yes. I remember it."

"So you'll recall that at that time I asked if you knew anything which might shed some light on David's disappearance?"

She nodded but he waited for a verbal response. She hesitated and then spat out a grudging confirmation.

"And do you recall your response at that time?"

Miranda was silent, staring at her fingers. Finally she said, "I didn't think I knew anything."

"And you've changed your mind?"

"Yes."

"What made you change your mind?"

"It just . . . it just popped into it . . . tonight. Maybe it was that program on the news. . . ."

"Thought you might get yourself a nice reward?" he suggested.

"Of course not! That's a disgusting idea. . . . I don't have to sit here and listen to—"

"You know what I think is a disgusting idea?" he interrupted. "I think it's disgusting that you have information about your nephew's kidnappers . . . that you gave them the password they needed to snatch him . . . and you couldn't be bothered to remember it or share it with anyone else. I think it's disgusting that you've watched your sister and brother-in-law in agony over the loss of their son and it never occurred to you to search your memory and see if you could help. . . ."

"I already told you. I didn't think it was important; I didn't make the connection. Anyway, I have been helping. . . ."

"Some meals. A few cups of coffee." He practically spat out the words. "Miranda, you've seen the kidnappers. . . ."

"You don't know that. . . ."

"Oh, sure I know that and so do you. You've talked to them, driven them around, probably told them all about David and Rachel and Stephen. . . ."

Stephen felt for the first time that Gallagher cared about David. Cared about what had happened. Cared about getting him back. He reached out and took Rachel's hand. She grabbed back and squeezed without taking her eyes off her sister's face.

"Go ahead," Gallagher said. "Tell us about them."

Miranda shrugged. "Ordinary."

"How much time do you figure you spent with them?" he asked.

"Hours," she said. "Hours and hours. I must have showed them every—"

"And all you can remember is that they were ordinary? Maybe it would help if I asked you more specific questions?" She nodded.

"All right," Gallagher said. "How many of them were there?"

"Two. I already told you. . . ."

"About how old would you say she was?"

"Old."

"Old fifties, old sixties, old seventies? As old as your mother and father?"

"Yes."

"Yes, as old as your mother and father? Sixties?" She nodded. "Both of them? They were the same age?"

"No."

"No? One of them was younger?" She shook her head. "Older?" She nodded.

Stephen squeezed Rachel's hand tighter, trying to keep from getting up and hitting his sister-in-law. He shifted restlessly in his chair and sighed. Gallagher turned and shot him a warning look.

"Much older?"

Miranda shrugged. "I'm not much good at guessing how old people are."

"But you had an impression that he was older. What gave you that impression?"

"The fact that he looked older," she said. Gallagher only waited silently, watching her. Finally she gave an irritated twitch of her shoulders. "He wasn't very well. He moved more slowly, like he'd been sick or something. Once or twice he didn't even bother to get out of the car. He seemed depressed. She did most of the talking and sometimes when he tried to talk she'd give him these looks like he'd better shut up if he knew what was good for him. She was pretty mean. Mean and controlling. But you have to understand, I deal with a lot of people who aren't the world's most pleasant, in my line of work. I've learned to ignore it. It's the only way. . . ."

Gallagher practically rolled his eyes. "Would you recognize them if you saw them again?" She nodded. "And if I had an artist come and work with you, could you describe them any better than you have to me?"

After a silence, she gave up a very grudging "maybe."

"Where were they from?"

"I think she said New Hampshire, but that wasn't what their license plate was."

"What was it?"

Miranda studied her feet. "I can't remember."

"Try a little harder," he suggested.

"It had something on it."

"One of those conservation plates?" he suggested.

"No. I don't know. I don't remember. Are we done yet? I'm sick of this."

"What color was it?"

"Who knows."

"Did the man or the woman have any sort of regional accent that you could detect?"

"No."

"Any limps, scars, or other unusual physical characteristics?"

"No."

"What did the woman look like?"

Miranda scowled. "Plain. Grouchy. Her wrinkles were mostly frown lines. I remember thinking that she must be no picnic to live with. Opinionated. She was always saying stuff like "If people just minded their own business" or "Folks these days just lack gumption." I especially noticed the word "gumption" because hardly anyone talks like that anymore. She had iron gray hair, short, recently cut. Didn't wear makeup except for lipstick. Simple clothes. Not expensive but not cheap. Dull, boxy, boring."

She fumbled with a lock of hair, twisting it around her finger. "Wait. He did have a physical characteristic that I noticed. Not like a limp or anything, just a funny way of bobbing his head while he was walking. I remember thinking that it reminded me of a bird, the way their heads bob? And his hair was all gray, a nice, silvery gray, and thick. A guy who might have been handsome when he was younger, but he's had a long sad life and basically given up. Yeah, that's it. That's how he struck me—like someone who has given up."

"Tall? Short? Medium sized?" Gallagher asked.

"He was tall, thin, stooped. And he had very big feet. She was . . ." Miranda hesitated. "She was big, but not in a way that seemed heavy. Just big. The impression I got was of someone who had been strong and athletic and was just beginning to experience the first, irritating

limitations of old age, like her progress was no longer effortless and she expected it to be? She'd get out of breath, following me around, and then she'd give these little exasperated sighs. At first, I thought it was me. I suppose part of the problem was that she was always asking questions while she rushed around."

"Questions about what?"

"Well, I told you about that. About the town and the schools and whether there were a lot of children and was it a good place to raise children? Was there a library? Were there sports? Nothing unusual. Anyone moving to town with children wants to know those things."

"But she didn't have children."

"No, but she said that their daughter . . . except she said her daughter, was going to be living with them. That's why they wanted a bigger house and a town with good schools. Which, of course, we do have here."

"Can you describe the conversation in which you told them the password?"

"You make me sound like such a jerk," she said. Gallagher didn't respond. "Oh, I don't know. We drove past a couple of kids on their bikes and she asked something like did we worry a lot about our kids being safe around here. I think I said something like it was a very safe community, there had never been an incident that I knew of, but that some parents, like Rachel and Stephen, were still very careful. She asked what did I mean by that and I told her about them having a password. She said what sort of a password, and I said it was something completely ridiculous, that it had to be something no one would guess and that wouldn't come up in ordinary conversation."

She fumbled in her pocket for a tissue, wiped her nose, and continued. "She said like what, like 'eggplant'? And I laughed and said that was pretty darn close, really. It was 'rutabaga.' "

Stephen felt Rachel's hand tighten in his, saw her lean forward in her chair toward her sister, a deadly look on her face. Rachel's restless foot shot out and hit the coffee table with a thud. Miranda jumped and looked at her. Their eyes met and held until Miranda finally ducked her head and looked away.

"You ruthless, despicable little worm," Rachel said. Her eyes glit-

tered wildly and he could practically see the heat of her anger. Had he and Gallagher not been there, he wasn't sure Miranda would have been safe. "You traded away my child's life to help you sell a house. You screw my husband when my back is turned. . . ."

"At least I'm not pregnant when my husband has had a vasectomy," Miranda spat back. "I guess I'm not the only one around here who isn't perfect. . . ."

Stephen sat staring at his wife in the stunned silence that followed. "Rachel, what is she talking about?"

"Me," Rachel said. "I'm pregnant. I don't know how it happened, but the baby can only be yours. . . ."

He didn't wait for her to finish. It was finally all more than he could take. "I can't stay here," he said. He went upstairs and got his wallet and his keys, and left.

The jaws of darkness do devour it up:
So quick bright things come to confusion.
—SHAKESPEARE, *A Midsummer Night's Dream*

CHAPTER THIRTY-FOUR

Rachel stared at her sister and understood for the first time the meaning of the expression "Scales fell from his eyes." She had had many reasons to resent Miranda and Miranda's treatment of her over the years and had always found excuses. Even the adultery she had blamed primarily on Stephen. But this wrongful and unnecessary revelation, this vicious violation of her privacy, had been a deliberate attempt on her sister's part to deflect the blame and the focus from herself. Miranda was so self-centered, she couldn't see that this was only about finding David. She couldn't see beyond the determined attempt to force her to plumb her depths and bring up all possible valuable knowledge to the underlying purpose, to the necessity to know everything. She saw it only as a personal attack.

Rachel was sick of this, sick of everything. After a month in an emotional rock tumbler, she was battered and bruised to her soul and there was no respite, no relief. She needed to get away from people for a while. "I'm going to get some air," she said.

Gallagher got up, as though he was going to walk her to the door. "It's all right," she said. "I'm okay. Really."

"Going to the cemetery is more like it," Miranda said. "Gonna go squat over your baby's grave and moan about your tragic lot in life. It's time you got over it, you know. Lots of people lose children . . . and most of them don't have great husbands like—"

"I don't expect many of them have sisters who are accessories to the crime, though, do you?" Rachel interrupted. She thought of Stephen's muttered desire to strangle Miranda and thought she might save him the trouble and do it herself. She took a step or two forward, feeling the desire flow down into her hands, and then Gallagher stepped between them.

"You aren't helping," he said. "Come on." He took Rachel by the arm and led her firmly out of the room, closing the door behind him. "I know how you feel. I'd like to strangle her myself. But as you can see, getting mad at her and yelling at her isn't productive. She just gets more and more defensive and difficult to deal with. I had her on a roll for a few minutes there and I think I can do that again, but not if you hang over her threatening to tear her hair out."

"I know. I'm sorry. I just can't believe . . ." Rachel spread her hands wide in a gesture of disbelief. She didn't know what to say. "There's nothing to say, is there?"

He shrugged. "There's little about human nature that surprises me anymore." His eyes dropped to her chest. He blushed and Rachel felt her own face grow hot. "I guess you hadn't told your husband that you're pregnant?"

"I tried a few times, but it hasn't exactly been a time for personal conversation. We're . . . we've been . . . the timing just hasn't been right. I knew he wouldn't take it well, that he wouldn't believe me, that it would require some delicacy. This isn't how I would have chosen to deliver the news." She almost smiled as she contemplated the absurdity of her situation. "I guess when one thing goes wrong, everything else follows. The timing could hardly have been worse. What the hell, when your life is already in the toilet, what difference does it make if someone flushes?"

"Don't give up now, Rachel," he said. "This is when you need your faith most."

"When my sister turns out to have been an accessory, my husband walks out on me because I'm pregnant, I spent my day in New York accusing an innocent dying man of kidnapping, and the real kidnappers are trying to figure out how to kill my son, where, exactly, am I supposed to look for hope?"

Gallagher laid his hand flat on his chest. "Here," he said. He touched his head. "And here."

"You can still surprise me," she said.

"Back to work," he said, not meeting her gaze, and let himself into the living room again, closing the door carefully behind him. He, at least, had learned how to use the doors.

She got a heavy sweater and a flashlight and walked through the woods to the back gate of the cemetery. "Good thing I'm not superstitious, isn't it?" she remarked to a passing tree. It was a mild night, the air smelling earthy and damp, and alive with the passionate cries of lovelorn frogs. The ground underfoot was damp and spongy, and she moved through the night as silently as a ghost. The gate, which ought to have been locked, was not, and swung open for her with only a slightly disagreeable screech of rusty metal.

She felt a sense of urgency that she didn't understand and something else, if not fear, then uneasiness, until she reached the familiar corner and knelt by her baby's grave. The narcissus, illuminated by the flashlight's beam, seemed to be bending their delicate heads toward the ground, and the air was full of their perfume. "It's all gone to hell, baby," she said as she settled herself on the ground by his side. "All gone to hell. I didn't see how it could get much worse, but it gets worse every day. You wouldn't believe how mean I've become."

A stray gust of wind flew by, chilling the back of her neck and rustling some of last year's leaves that had piled up against an adjacent stone. She looked around cautiously, shining the light in a big circle around her. A mist was rising from the damp earth, and it seemed like she was surrounded by shadowy forms. "Not that I'm superstitious or anything," she said, "I'm just not used to being here at

night. I always used to tell David, when he had bad dreams, that all the same things are there at night that are there in the day. There isn't anything different, nothing new or scary. But it feels different. I guess if you're blind you get used to it. Do you and the ghosts want to hear what's been happening?"

She realized that she was talking in a loud voice, and lowered it. "Your daddy and I have tried to be good people, baby, even if all of this is making us more horrid by the day. We never did anything to deserve this. But that's stupid, isn't it? It's stupid to assume that there's a logic to life, or a fairness. If there were, you'd still be with us. Tall and handsome and wise, instead of frozen forever as a tiny, wide-eyed baby. Did I ever tell you that joke about God and Job? Probably a dozen times, right? We're at that point now where all I have to do is give the punch line, aren't we."

She laughed, a small bitter laugh, and patted the damp ground. "Yeah, you remember. Finally Job recounts all the woes that have been visited upon him, and he says, 'Why me, God? Why me? Why have you done all this to me?' And the heavens open and a huge ray of light, a powerful, searching beam of light illuminates poor, miserable Job, and God answers 'Because you piss me off.' I guess if we were religious, that would be blasphemy, wouldn't it?"

She was crying now, but she didn't care. That was why she came here, because it was a place free of everyone's expectations. She'd been doing her best not to cry. Doing her best not to come here, to conform to people's notions of what was normal. Self-control was what everyone expected of her and she'd done her best. But it was sad, goddammit! It was sad to lose a child, wrenchingly sad to have another kidnapped, and ironically, cruelly sad, to be pregnant with another at such a time, knowing that she'd probably have to lose it as well.

"Your daddy thinks that he's the one with all the trouble, given that on top of all he's had to suffer, now he's got a wife who's pregnant by somebody else, and this time he wasn't even consulted. God! As if I had any interest in having an affair. Even at those times when I was dying to be understood or pining to be admired and supported, or even just listened to, I never thought for a second about having

sex with someone else. I like a simpler life, not one that's more complicated. You'd think he'd understand that, wouldn't you, after all these years? But I think he doesn't even notice me, most of the time, and when he does, he sees me through the lens of his own experience. He thinks he knows everything already so he never has to ask; he never has to pay attention. Is it so much to ask, really, to be seen as I am?"

She wiped her wet face on her sleeve. She had failed the mom test again. No tissues in her pocket, and now she was talking to Jonah about sex when he was forever stuck in infancy. It was time to get serious here. She hadn't come here to talk to Jonah; she had come here to think about David. To assimilate her experience with Norah Proust, trying to find the silver lining in that dark cloud, and to move on, here where she might be undisturbed. She vaguely recalled a character in *Winnie-the-Pooh* having a thinking spot. This was hers.

Out there, it was all too confusing. They made her feel like a Ping-Pong ball these days. First she was a nut and a head case because she could connect with David and she was not supposed to do it or talk about it. Then suddenly she was surrounded by people who wanted her to turn it on and off like a water tap. And then, every time she did get it going, someone barged in and interrupted.

She had to admit that for a little while it had worked. She could see things through his eyes, something she hadn't been able to do before. Tonight she had seen the place where he was, but when she tried to get close, David wouldn't let her. She wiped her eyes again. Was he trying to protect her, or was it just because he was so scared himself, scared of looking at the things that were instrumental in taking him away? She sighed. She was so tired.

She sat silently for a minute, heavy with despair. The darkness was almost complete except for the lights of a few distant houses glowing faintly through the mist. Jonah's tiny, worried little face hovered in her mind. Then it was David's face, sometimes alone and sometimes mixed up with that of Peter Coffin. The dead face, the living face, the dying face. From somewhere nearby she heard the sharp, frightened squeal of a small animal. First a series of short,

sharp cries, then a longer, single cry, and then silence. The pain she'd felt back in her room, the pain of David's fear, came back.

He was lying on his stomach on the floor, and she was with him, holding her breath just as he held his, and listening to the faint voices, her body, like his, rigid with fear. Together they heard the woman's voice: ". . . and then dump him in the well up by the old cellar hole. He wasn't here long enough for anyone to care much, and if they ask, we can say he went back home."

She felt his fear, shared his panic as he rose and went to the door, rattled the knob again, tried the locked window, and then crouched, desolate, in a corner of the room, his hands against his face to hide the sobs. A stab of agony ran through her, piercing and terrible. The pain doubled her over and her scream split the night, echoing eerily through the empty graveyard.

She couldn't stand it! David was in her head and he was inside her and she couldn't do anything to help him! All she knew was that he was on a farm in Maine. And that simply wasn't enough.

And then Rachel, halfway to her feet and busily dusting the dirt off her hands, stopped in midcrouch. "Oh my God!" she said. "Oh my. He's in Maine! Somehow, he's told me. Somehow I knew. I know!" Excitement exploded within her, driving back for a moment the looming horror of David's situation that gnawed at her like Promethean vultures. She had to go home. Tell Gallagher. Get it on the air. It was something. Something. She stumbled down the hill, her flashlight veering wildly through the night as she ran, stumbled, fell to her knees, dropped the flashlight, found it again, got up, and ran on.

He seems so near, and yet so far.
—TENNYSON, "In Memoriam"

CHAPTER THIRTY-FIVE

The house was dark and both Gallagher's and Miranda's cars were gone. All the doors were locked. Miranda's doing, no doubt, deliberate and mean. Rachel had to scrabble around in the dark to find the spare key to let herself in. She stepped into the silent house and fumbled for a light switch. Even lit, the place looked strange, as though she had never really seen it before. To her heightened and overtaxed senses, the air felt heavy and oppressive. It was as though all the emotions of the past four weeks were still swirling around the rooms.

She grabbed the phone and called the police station, got the now familiar-sounding chronically bored policeman, and left a message for Gallagher to call, stressing that it was urgent. She never got the sense that the man believed her. Maybe everyone who called the police station thought their business was urgent. Urgent cats in trees, urgent branches rubbing up against windows. Urgent neighbors who insisted on putting out their trash at 5 A.M., each as important, or unimportant, as urgent parents with missing children.

It was ten-thirty. She was considering turning on the TV to see if

there had been any response to Robinson's earlier program when she realized that her new information needed to be broadcast. Her first thought had been to share it with Gallagher, who would probably be skeptical but might be responsive, but Robinson offered an even more immediate opportunity. Robinson wouldn't care how she'd gotten it—he was the one who had sent a psychic to her—and he might be able to get it onto the eleven o'clock news if she could only reach him in time. Stephen had scribbled the 800 number by the phone and she immediately dialed it.

"Lost Child Foundation, this is Rick."

"This is Rachel Stark. I need to speak with Mr. Robinson."

"Mr. Robinson's tied up at the moment. Is it something about the missing child?" The voice sounded terribly young.

"This is the missing child's mother," she said. "Please find Mr. Robinson for me."

"As I said, Mr. Robinson is unavailable. You may share your information with me if you'd like."

He wasn't listening, she realized. He was merely acting as a conduit. An automaton. A robot. But if he wasn't listening, who knew what he might have heard and discounted. She hoped all the volunteers weren't like this. She swallowed hard to force down the choking panic. "What's your name?" she asked.

"Rick, ma'am."

"Okay, Rick, are you listening to me?"

"Of course I am, ma'am."

"Who did I say I was?"

"I'm afraid I didn't get your name, ma'am."

Rachel thought she might explode. She wasn't a physical person, nor a violent one, but it was good for this boy Rick that they weren't in the same room. Was nothing ever going to work? Would nothing ever again be simple? "Rick, I am David Stark's mother. You know. David Stark. The missing child. I have some important information for John Robinson and I need to get it to him before the eleven o'clock news."

She seemed to have at least half penetrated the fog. "I'm afraid Mr. Robinson isn't here, ma'am. He's at the TV studio. . . ."

"Does someone there have that number?" she interrupted.

"I'll ask." She heard him shouting, "I've got the missing boy's mother on the phone. Does anyone have a number where she can reach Mr. Robinson?" There was a long silence while she listened to his noisy breathing against the background of phones and commotion, her heart ticking off the seconds. She tried to still her panic and stay functional while her mind was full of David's terror and farmhouse wells. Then Rick was back. "I've got a number you can try, ma'am." He read it to her, repeated it, and she thanked him. She disconnected and dialed the new number.

A brisk voice answered with something she didn't understand. "This is Rachel Stark," she said, speaking slowly and carefully. "The mother of the missing child, David? I need to speak with John Robinson from the Lost Child Foundation and I understand that he's there."

"Yes, he's here, but I don't think I'll be able to reach him, Mrs. Stark," the voice said. "I believe he's about to go on the air."

"Tell him it's an emergency," she said. "An emergency. A new development. Tell him it's a matter of life and death." There was a stunned silence on the other end and then the voice promised to try. Rachel was put on hold listening to a radio station that was playing Eric Clapton's song for his dead son. She bit her lip hard, trying not to scream, and the hot salty blood mingled with her hot salty tears. It seemed an eternity as she stood there, panting like a spent runner, her stomach heaving, her message hovering like an enormous lump in her throat. Would he bother to come to the phone even for a message as urgent as hers, or would he prance onto the air for his moment of glory, missing the vital bit?

She couldn't break the connection and the song went on and on, raking her vulnerable soul with bared claws. She already knew far too much about tears for lost children. She had to hope he would come, but didn't dare trust it, just as she didn't trust Robinson. And so she stood there, trying not to listen, until finally there was the scuffling of the phone being lifted and a brisk, self-important voice barked "Robinson." Not "Hello, Rachel." No acknowledgment of her at all.

"John? Rachel Stark. Just two things but they're very important. First, I still don't know where he is, but I know he's in Maine. . . ."

"That fits," he interrupted.

"Fits?"

"We had a call. Someone was sure they'd seen him at a rest stop in New Hampshire . . . that little tip of New Hampshire that extends down toward the coast. . . ."

"John, listen to me. The other thing is that they're getting ready to kill him. He's on a farm somewhere. A farm with a dilapidated red barn. A working farm. And they're talking about putting him in an old well." Her voice broke then and she couldn't go on. "I . . . don't . . . know . . ." Her words were spaced by sobs. Now, when she desperately needed to speak, her throat had closed and the words wouldn't come. ". . . what to . . . do. If they . . . know . . . we're close . . . won't they . . . move faster? But . . . how else . . ."

"You're right, Rachel," he said. "Getting the word out is our only chance. I'll do it right away. I've got to go now. They're starting, but I'll call you as soon as I'm through, I promise. Will you be okay?"

"Don't worry . . . about . . . me." Then she remembered about Miranda. "John? Wait! Another thing. There's a witness. Gallagher has a description of them. Of the couple who took David. Get him on the air." She didn't wait for him to speak but disconnected, meaning to force him to go and act. She didn't want sympathy. She wanted action. She wanted to scream in a voice that would shake the whole nation, "WHERE IS MY SON? SAVE MY SON!"

She grabbed the remote and switched the TV on, staring, riveted, at the screen as the immaculate announcers reminded them of the earlier broadcast and informed them that John Robinson and Mr. Fleet Foot would be joining them on the eleven o'clock news. Now the minutes seemed to move with all the stately slowness of a procession. She washed her face and hands. Made tea. Wiped the counters. Put in a load of laundry. Checked the answering machine but there were no new messages. Went outside to look for Stephen's car. Called him on the car phone and got no answer.

She climbed up on a stool and watched the commercials, chewing on a fingernail. But she couldn't sit still, so she paced the kitchen, waiting. Finally, with fanfare and graphics, it was time for the news. There were a few brisk minutes of domestic murders, accidents, and fires, and then Robinson and Dawson were introduced.

Again it was Robinson who spoke first, but what he had to say surprised her.

He looked at the camera and said, in a trembling voice, "Somewhere in the state of Maine tonight, a terrified young boy may be only hours, or even minutes, away from death. A death that only you can prevent."

Just like a true crime show, she thought, and realized, with one of the jolts that seemed to shake her so often these days, that she *was* in the middle of a true crime. That David's abduction was true. That what was being done to all of them was a crime. She stared at the screen as the woman anchor smiled—how could she smile?—and announced that they would be right back with the details after a commercial break. If it was only a matter of minutes, why were they being wasted on cars and fast food? Because tragedy sells.

She stared unseeing at the parade of products, thinking that Stephen should be here. This was no night for them to be apart. Where was he? Where would he go? She couldn't quite imagine Stephen checking into a motel. For all his independence, he was a homebody. He didn't like the impersonality of hotels. He always complained that when he traveled he couldn't sleep. But where else would he go? He didn't have a best friend. The closest thing to that was Ron, Carole's husband, and they weren't that close. But would he storm out of their house, abandoning her in the midst of this crisis in their lives, only to take refuge in the home of her best friend? Yes, she could imagine it. It would never occur to Stephen that Carole's loyalty might make the situation awkward. As his affair, or whatever it was, with Miranda so clearly demonstrated, Stephen didn't understand about the boundaries of friendship and loyalty.

Neither did Miranda, who had probably fled to her new residence. Or her new boyfriend's residence. Or any other uninhabited residence in town, for that matter. Miranda carried the keys to the kingdom. But Rachel didn't think that Stephen would be with Miranda. His interest in her was only physical. He wouldn't be turning to her for consolation. Especially not tonight, when he wanted to kill her. If it wasn't already over, it had now come to a dramatic end.

She picked up the phone and was about to call Carole when the

immaculate woman with a well-modulated voice—they all sounded alike to Rachel, like clones of one another—introduced John Robinson, reminded her audience of the quest and the reward offered earlier in the evening, and Robinson began to speak again.

"Earlier this evening, we appeared on a newscast and asked for your help. As a result of that request, callers have reported a trail of sightings leading from David's hometown in New York to a rest area in New Hampshire, but no farther. However, a psychic who works frequently with police departments nationally in locating missing children, who volunteered her services to the Lost Child Foundation, reports that she believes the child is somewhere in Maine. She's with us tonight to talk a little about that. . . ."

The camera switched to Norah Proust, looking considerably less witchlike in a stylish suit, striding across the set to shake hands with Robinson, Dawson, and the anchorwoman. She slipped into a chair, grimaced at the camera, and folded her hands neatly in her lap. Then, in response to Robinson's questions, she presented a brief account of her experiences in helping to find missing children and began to describe the scene Rachel had reported to her earlier in the evening. She concluded by reporting that she had received a strong sense that David was in immediate and serious danger and that she kept getting visions of water or wells along with strong images of fear from the kidnapped child.

"You bitch!" Rachel yelled, jumping to her feet and shaking her fist at the smug face. "You didn't come here to help us. You came here to steal information to enhance your reputation. You came here to pick my brain so that you could go on TV and look like a professional psychic." She recalled Gallagher's animosity toward Robinson, his cynical assessment that Robinson would do anything to keep himself and his organization in the limelight. "This is sick!" she said. "Sick. Goddammit, Stephen. This was your doing. If it gets David killed instead of rescued, I'm never going to forgive you!"

She picked up the phone and called Carole. "Are you watching the news?"

"Umm-hmm." In that murmur, Rachel read hesitation.

"Is Stephen there?" Silence, then affirmation. "Put him on,

Carole. It's important." She waited an eternity, unable to distinguish any words from the mumble of voices in the background.

Finally Carole came back. "He won't talk to you."

"I see. Then will you please tell him that that stuff about David being in Maine, and the well, all those things Norah Proust was just saying . . . tell him those came from me. Tell him that I called the station a few minutes ago and told all that to Robinson. Carole, did he say why he's in this snit? Because Miranda told him I'm pregnant. If you're any kind of a friend of mine, you'll tell him he can't stay there tonight. Tell him you don't approve of men who get their wives pregnant and then walk out on them in times of crisis. Tell him he belongs at home, and if he won't come home he should go to a motel."

She was about to hang up when she thought of one more thing she wanted to say. "Tell him David overheard them talking about putting him in the well—tell him that's what I just saw—and ask him how he'd like to sit all alone in a dark, empty house with that knowledge in his head." She put down the phone without waiting for Carole's response. It wasn't nice; she was mad at Stephen, not Carole, but adversity, she kept discovering, didn't make her kind.

She was too restless to sit and watch the screen. As she was picking up the remote, Gallagher came on, looking hot and sweaty and uncomfortable. Gallagher was a man who wanted to be doing, not talking about things. He looked like he was being led to his execution. Poor man, Rachel thought. She never would have imagined feeling sorry for Gallagher, but she did. The smiling anchorwoman introduced him and Gallagher managed to present, without holding Miranda up for public ridicule, the fact that a witness had come forward with a description of the kidnappers. Gallagher then displayed a pair of rough sketches, describing them as quickly produced by a police artist, for the audience to see.

Rachel was surprised that they looked like anybody, but it appeared that once they'd gone away and left Gallagher alone with Miranda, he'd managed to get her to cough up quite a decent set of descriptions. Rachel was sure she'd never seen them, yet they were adequate to allow someone who had to respond.

She squeezed her eyes shut and kept them shut. She couldn't

look at this anymore. It was so dreadfully tantalizing, with all the immediacy and drama that TV loves. But would it do any good? Could anything happen in time? Did people in Maine even have access to all this stuff? Would they be watching? Or was it only local and only people in New York would go to bed discussing how awful it was? Pondering the legitimacy of psychic assistance. Wondering if the poor child would be rescued, or what the headline would be in the morning. KIDNAPPED NEW YORK BOY DIES IN MAINE WELL or DAVID STARK ALIVE AFTER DRAMATIC RESCUE.

She was full of a sense of impending disaster. She got off the stool, stamped her foot, and screamed. It made no difference. Not when she was feeling both her own fear and David's. Was filled with it, sick with it. It writhed through her like a live thing; nothing but a final resolution would relieve the pressure. This was a race to the finish and there were no time-outs. There would be no respite until she saw David again, alive or dead.

She was standing in her own kitchen, eyes squeezed shut, gripping the edge of the counter for support, but under her cheek she could feel the hard, unyielding grid of the register under David's face; she could smell the stale, acrid scent of urine from the closet, and she could feel the hot tears of despair and terror as they ran down her son's face while he listened to his death being discussed. She could see it, she could feel it, it was as real as if she was in the room. Yet there was nothing she could do.

I am a man more sinn'd
against than sinning.
—SHAKESPEARE, *King Lear*

CHAPTER THIRTY-SIX

"Her heart is breaking with the knowledge that they're planning to kill your son and you're sitting here drinking a beer and sulking because you accidentally got the girl pregnant," Carole said. "In my eyes, that doesn't make you much of a man."

Stephen knew Carole could be blunt, but this was taking it to a new level. "It's not my baby," he said, pretending to concentrate on the screen. It was hard to feign an interest in Pizza Hut.

"Well it sure as shit ain't an immaculate conception and Rachel's not the cheatin' kind." This time even Ron turned around to stare at her.

"Everyone's the cheating kind, given the right opportunity," Stephen said.

"Judging by your own personal standards, I can see how you might think that. But Rachel isn't you. She's cautious and reserved and private. And conservative and faithful. But even if she'd been sleeping around, that wouldn't make her any worse than you and she's never thrown you out or walked out on you, has she?"

"I'm not pregnant." Carole just didn't understand. Fooling around was one thing. It wasn't important. It was precisely because Rachel wouldn't fool around that he was upset. Because if she'd gotten involved enough to sleep with someone, it was serious. Maybe another time he could have coped—maybe—but not now. Not when he needed all his energy for David.

"Given your track record, it's a darned good thing men can't get pregnant, isn't it?"

"Carole!" Ron said. "Is this really necessary?"

"Necessary? I don't know the answer to that, Ron. Is any communication between members of the species necessary? Jesus, honey. This isn't a spreadsheet analysis or an occasion upon which we ought to consult Miss Manners. This is a case in which your buddy here has walked out on his wife in the midst of the biggest crisis anyone we know will ever face because he's got this wrongheaded notion that his wife has cheated on him . . . when everyone knows that he's been cheating on her with her own sister in her own house. I mean honestly, isn't this a case of the pot calling the kettle black?"

"Carole, get a grip, will you? He's our guest. . . ."

Carole glared at her husband with a face as red as her hair. "He may be your guest but he sure ain't mine. I don't entertain bottom-dwelling scum suckers."

Stephen got to his feet. "You just don't understand, Carole. . . . Imagine how you'd feel if your sister suddenly blurted out to Ron that you were pregnant, when Ron couldn't father a—"

"If Ron's mistress had the audacity to try and tell him anything about me that was my own private business to share with him, I'd take her head off and hand it back to her as I booted her out of the house!"

"It was information I was entitled to have. . . ." He was feeling very sorry for Ron, married to this harridan.

"Well, I don't know about your almighty entitlements, Stevie, but I do know about your obligations. And right now, they're to be at home with your wife, giving what support you can. By the way, she asked me to tell you that those things the psychic said, about where David is and about the well? Those are all things she called and told

Robinson just before the show. So, knowing Rachel like I do—like we both do, whether we think this ESP stuff is just something that happens or whether we think it's pretty weird shit—I imagine she's feeling whatever David's feeling, which has got to be pretty damn bad, don't you think, given that the folks who've snatched him are talking about killing him by dumping him down a well?"

No, Carole didn't understand. She expected him to be benevolent and resilient, to put the insult Rachel had handed him aside as if it didn't matter. Right now, he *wanted* Rachel to feel bad.

Carole gave a decisive shake of her head. "And if you aren't planning on going home and lending your support, you'd better not plan on going home anymore. Because if this all goes bad and she's facing it alone . . . you won't be wanted at home anymore anyway. Some things are just plain irreparable. You can't walk out on your spouse during a major crisis because you've got some wrongheaded notions about infidelity and then hope to walk back in and find things all warm and fuzzy." She rubbed her hands together and then dusted them on her thighs, like she was getting rid of crumbs. "Yessiree, you blow this one and it's gonna be time to hit the road, Jack. . . ."

"Oh, put a cork in it, Carole." He got up and went into the kitchen, where she was standing with her hands on her hips, glaring at him. "You don't know what you're talking about," he said. "This isn't your business. You just don't understand. . . ."

"You're right about that, Stevie," she said, turning her back on him. "I don't understand. I don't understand what ever possessed me to tell your wife that I thought you were attractive." She picked up her purse and keys. "I don't understand how you can have such a monumental ego that you refuse to believe a woman who has never lied to you. I don't understand how you can put your own wounded pride before love for your son. More important, I don't understand why I'm wasting my time trying to talk sense to a jerk like you when my best friend is all alone on what may be the worst night of her life." She headed for the door, calling back over her shoulder, "I want you gone when I get back. I mean that, Ron. I want him gone!" And then she was gone herself, leaving the two of them staring after her.

"Whew! Is she often like that?" Stephen looked over at Ron, who was staring fixedly at a car that appeared to be driving on clouds.

"She's right, you know," Ron said.

"You have to say that. She's your wife. You've got to live with her. . . ."

"My point exactly," Ron said.

Stephen picked up his jacket, checked in the pocket for his keys, and left without another word. Jesus! Wasn't life hard enough without being lectured by that little feminist twit? He'd always sort of admired Carole's outspokenness, until now. Now he was glad he was married to a nice quiet woman like Rachel. Well, he had been glad. He couldn't imagine Rachel with another man. Shit! Nothing made any sense anymore. He kicked the tire on his car and it hurt like hell. He'd forgotten he was wearing running shoes.

The mist was turning into a light rain. He sure wasn't going to stand out here all night and wonder what to do while he got cold and wet and his clothes were all at home. All hell was breaking loose. He needed to be where he could be in contact with what was happening. Maybe he should go to the Lost Child Foundation and see what was happening. That was a good idea. Be right there on the scene as the information came in.

Feeling better now that he had a plan, he jumped in the car and backed out of the driveway. Backed without looking, without turning on his lights, straight into the path of an oncoming car. The thud of the collision smashed his head into the window, which cracked into a spiderweb, and left him sitting there, dazed and confused, as an enormous man in a security guard's uniform opened the door, grabbed him by the front of his shirt, and hauled him out of the car.

"Just what in the Sam Hill did you think you were doing?" the man demanded, his eyes blazing. "Where were your lights, man? Don't you know it's the middle of the fuckin' night?"

Stephen, feeling the nausea and shock following his adrenaline surge, could only mutter "sick" as he leaned forward and vomited on the ground, just missing the man's shoe. The big hands released him as the man backed up, muttering a stream of expletives. Stephen ran

a distracted hand through his hair and it came away wet. He looked down at it. In the dim light from his open car door, he saw his palm was red. As he stared at it, an image of David's lifeless body being pulled from a well exploded in his brain like Technicolor fireworks. "I was . . . wasn't . . . I'm." He was about to say he was sorry, but he'd been a lawyer too long, knew too well never to admit to fault, even when he was at fault.

What was he doing? Where was he going? He tried to remember, overcome by the stupidity of what he'd just done, trying to think his way around that searing image. He shook his head to clear it, but that only made things worse. Staring at him over the supine body he could see Rachel's eyes. Rachel's eyes boring into him, lost, desperate, abandoned, scared.

"I was . . . going . . . going home to Rachel," he said finally. "My wife, Rachel. She's home alone. We've lost . . . our child's been . . . David may be . . ." He swallowed, trying to get a grip on himself, but words kept tumbling out. "Did you watch the news tonight?" The man nodded, looking as confused as Stephen felt. Carefully keeping his distance in case Stephen was truly crazy. "You see that stuff about the child . . . the kidnapped child?" Another nod. The man's face was only partially illuminated by the undamaged headlight of his car. "My son," Stephen said. "The kidnapped child. My son. They're going to kill him." He ran a hand through his hair again. Winced. Picked out a piece of glass.

"What's going on out here?" Ron asked, hurrying down the driveway with a bouncing flashlight in his hand that he proceeded to aim right into Stephen's eyes. "Steve? Jeez, man, you've got blood all over your face. Are you okay?"

"This idiot just backed out in front of my car!" the security guard complained. "Just backed right out with no lights on. I didn't even have time to hit the brakes. You got a phone so we can call the cops? Shit! I'm gonna be late for work. Why couldn't you have watched where you were going, buddy? Sheesh! I lose my job and I'm gonna sue you for every nickel you've got. I know my rights. . . ."

Stephen fumbled his wallet out of his pocket, wondering if his

brain was damaged. His appendages didn't quite seem to be work-ing. He teased out a card and handed it to the man. "Here. Let's just skip the cops, okay? Get an estimate and send it to me, and I'll pay to get it fixed. Pay for a rental, too. I haven't got time to wait for the cops."

The man took the card and looked at it doubtfully. "I dunno," he said, his eyes narrowing suspiciously. "Is this some kind of trick? Like I take this card and let you drive away and I never see you again. How do I even know this is you?" He held out the card, trying to give it back. "Let's just share the information we're supposed to share and wait for the cops."

"Jesus, man!" Stephen said. "I'm trying to do you a favor here. I said I'd pay, didn't I?"

"And all that stuff about some kid being kidnapped. What's that got to do with anything? You ain't got a kid in that car."

"Please," Stephen said. "I've got to go. Just send me the bill. . . . Look, you want to see my license? Do I have to prove I'm me? Is that it?"

"Hey, Steve, you can't do this," Ron interrupted. "This is what in-surance is for."

"I haven't got time," he said. "I've got to get home. Home to Rachel. Home to find out what's happening."

"Not in this thing you aren't," the guard said. "Rear wheel's bent. You can't drive it."

"You see, Steve," Ron said. "We've gotta call the cops. Your vehi-cle may be totaled. The frame may be busted . . . and if so, you're talking maybe thirty-plus thousand dollars here."

His brain was too full of other things to argue. He threw up his hands in a gesture of defeat. "Okay, okay, so call them. Just make it quick. I've got to get home. . . ."

"And I've got to get to work. . . ."

Ron leaned into the car and manipulated the buttons on the car phone. When he pulled his head out, he looked frustrated. "Big night for accidents, cop says. They don't know when they're gonna get here. You guys wanna come in and have some coffee or some-thing? Maybe you'd like to call work?"

The security guard shrugged. "I dunno. Maybe if I call it might help to keep me from getting fired."

"Can't hurt," Ron said. "Coming, Steve?"

Stephen shook his head and instantly regretted it. He could practically feel his brain slosh. He felt awful. "I'll stay here," he said. "Don't feel much like walking right now."

"Hey, are you okay, man?" Ron asked. "I mean, should I call an ambulance or something?"

He ran his hand through his hair again, and it hurt again. Boy, he was a slow learner tonight. "No ambulance. You want to call someone, call Rachel, explain what happened, and tell her I'll be there as soon as I can. And tell her not to worry. I'm okay. You'll have to give me a ride over. . . ."

Ron's look was astonished but he had the grace to keep his mouth shut. "Sure thing. Right away, just as soon as the cops have come and gone," he agreed, and retreated up the driveway, followed by the guard, leaving Stephen alone.

He sat down on the edge of the seat, feet on the ground, and sank his head into his hands, feeling like the rug had been pulled out from under him. Indecisive. Disoriented. Not himself. The accident itself was a big blur. Stupid, and he didn't do stupid things. All that was clear was his need to get home. It was strange, but while the accident had left him generally dazed and confused, with respect to Rachel it seemed to have actually jarred some sense into him. Literally. He hardly understood it himself. One minute he was filled with righteous indignation and offended male pride and the next minute he could see so clearly that he'd been a horse's ass or worse.

With David in such trouble, nothing else mattered. He closed his eyes and groaned. What an ass he'd been. He belonged at home with Rachel. Screw up, go astray, wander, curse, muddle, or philander, he was always on his way home to Rachel. He'd always been on his way home. Because bitch as he might, she remained the touchstone of his existence. The center of his life. When it seemed like everything was falling apart, she was all that remained to keep him sane, to keep him connected, to remind him what mattered. Complain though he might, it was through her eyes that he saw the good things in his life,

the good that he did, the good that he was. For all his determination to make things happen and to get David back, she had been the one who had actually produced results, and she had been the one who had kept hope alive, for both of them, during the last four grim weeks. Of course he was going home to Rachel. Where else would he have gone?

O, that a man might know
The end of this day's business, ere it come.
—SHAKESPEARE, *Julius Caesar*

CHAPTER THIRTY-SEVEN

Carole had come, bitched and soothed, sympathized, fed her, hugged her, and departed, and Rachel had finally fled from the television, from the anchorwoman's modulated perfection, John Robinson's smarmy smugness, and Norah Proust's false prophecy and taken refuge in her workroom. It was the one place in the house that belonged entirely to her and tonight the only place that felt safe. The rest of the house echoed with David's absence.

She climbed up on her stool, seized a pen, and started drawing hearts. Not cute little valentine hearts, nor fistlike anatomically correct hearts with ugly, tubular protrusions. She drew jigsaw-puzzle hearts. Valentine hearts covered with the jagged lines of puzzle pieces, first fit together and then broken apart and scattered across the page. It was how she felt, like her heart was cut into dozens of jagged, scattered pieces. The hand wielding the pen jabbed so wildly at the paper that her flying elbow knocked a jar of pencils and the phone on the floor. She picked up the pencils, put the jar and the phone back on the corner of the worktable, and laid her head down on the drawings, her tears blurring the bold lines.

She was still there when Stephen came in, bent over her work-table, drawing endless pictures of the kidnappers and David and Peter Coffin and Jonah, all of them vivid and hasty and smudged with tears. It wasn't something she could have explained to anyone, only something she had to do. Drawing David, even though the pictures showed his fear and his despair, made him seem closer.

She looked up in surprise when Stephen appeared in the doorway holding a bloody towel against the side of his head. He was deathly pale and seemed confused. The pen dropped from her fingers. "Stephen . . . oh . . . what on earth? You're hurt."

"I was in an accident, Rach. Ron tried to call. He said it rang and rang but no one answered."

"But I was here the whole time. I never heard a phone. . . ." She was off her stool, across the room, and had her arm around him before she'd finished speaking. "Come straight upstairs and lie down. You look terrible. Did you see a doctor? I could call Dr. Barker. . . ."

He leaned into her, making a small sound that might have been disagreement, but he didn't say anything, only wrapped his free arm around her and pulled her close. Rachel didn't try to move away. She felt no urge to. Her instinct, as always, was to soothe things, to fix them, to make the hurt go away. What she couldn't do for her son, she'd try to do for her husband.

Yes, he had been a jerk earlier, but what was the point of staying mad? Under the circumstances, they were naturally subject to insane mood swings and irrational behavior, both trying to find a place to put the hurt they couldn't contain. The only appropriate response was patience and forgiveness. Besides, Carole, during her brief drive-by shouting, had been mad enough for both of them. Rachel had never seen her friend so mad nor had she heard many of the terms that Carole had used to describe Stephen—unprintable, colorful, and delivered with all the panache of a pro.

"Come on," she urged, trying to lead him to the door.

But Stephen wasn't ready to be put to bed. He stumbled past her to the worktable and stared down at the drawings she'd been doing, so she went back and stood beside him. "They help to pass the time," she said. "I was going crazy, sitting here waiting."

He'd picked up the drawing of David on the floor, his ear to the

register. "This is . . . it's awful, Rachel." The shock of it froze his face
and strangled his voice. "This is what you're seeing?"

She nodded, her neck stiff and her head heavy, reluctant to admit to the obvious. Drawing was such a natural language for her, she
sometimes forgot the power of pictures, the fact that while others
struggled for words, she struggled to translate the visions. She'd
never meant these to be seen. "I never thought to draw it before.
Things were never so clear. . . . I wish . . . I almost wish . . . that they
weren't now. It hurts so much."

"He's so scared!" Words gouged out of his soul. His hand, with
the drawing, slowly dropped to his side like it was too heavy to hold.
"There's been no news?"

She shook her head. "Nothing. I keep thinking that someone
will call. That something must be happening and they haven't bothered to tell us. There's no one more directly involved but we're the
last to know. It's like science fiction. The night the earth stood still. I
feel as if I've been holding my breath for hours."

"No one has called? Not Gallagher? Not even Robinson?" He
looked like he might cry, but mired in her own anger and bitterness,
she had no comfort to give him. She who only minutes before had
seen herself as the comforter.

"Especially not him. Robinson and his crew have had what they
wanted from us," she said. "That Norah Proust! What a charlatan. I
never did feel like she gave a damn about David. Now I understand."

"We could call them," he said.

"We could. When I spoke to him at the station, John Robinson
said he'd call me as soon as he was done with the show. That was an
hour ago." She looked at her watch. "More."

Stephen crossed to the visitor's chair and sat down. "The truth is
that no one gives a damn about David except us. Yet I can't believe,
after that broadcast, that no one has called with any information. No
one?"

"They could be getting hundreds of calls and we wouldn't
know. . . ."

"Maybe we should go over there."

She sank back onto her stool, feeling like she was being pressed
down by a heavy weight. "Maybe we should." The thought of the

noise and people and commotion horrified her. She'd rather be almost anywhere. But it was their link to David. Looking over at him,
pale, bloody, and exhausted, she could see that Stephen felt the
same way. He usually needed to be where the action was, but tonight
he, too, felt intimidated, felt reluctant to leave their refuge, was worn
out from the struggle.

"There won't be any privacy there," he said.

She got up and crossed the room, kneeling on the floor by his
feet, and put her head in his lap. He tangled a hand in her hair and
let it rest there. "I don't feel very hopeful anymore," she whispered.

"I know. I feel it, too," he said. "I've always relied on your
faith. . . ."

"I don't know where it went. I was so certain we'd get him back,
that it was just a matter of figuring it out . . . and now we know
so much, he's so much more with us, and yet I feel him slipping
away . . . like I'm in that well myself and the water is closing over my
head."

"Rachel!" His voice was broken, tragic. "Please. Stop. I can't listen to this! Just let me hope . . . as long as . . . ." His voice died away
without uttering the words he couldn't say. He reached out and
switched off the light. "Too bright in here." They sat together in the
darkness, listening to the sounds of the house around them.

"We'll have to go away for Christmas," she whispered. "I could
never do another Christmas in this house . . . without him. Or we'll
move. This house . . . every room . . . it's so full of him. . . . Listen!
Hear the way the floor creaks? I'll never hear that without imagining
that he's creeping down the stairs." Somewhere a door banged and
she jumped. "You see! He'll always be here. Oh, Stephen, how will
we stand it?"

He massaged her head with his hands, running strands of her
hair through his fingers. "We can't give up, Rach. Not yet. Not now.
This is when he needs us most, when he needs our faith that he'll be
all right. . . ."

"I don't have any faith anymore," she said. "I can't . . . I
haven't . . . I don't . . . I don't know what to do. There's this huge,
hollow emptiness in me."

"We can't give up!" He shouted it, the words reverberating in the

small room. "Come on." He urged her to her feet. "We'll go up to his room and sit there. Maybe that will help." Now he spoke with the voice of a weary old man. The hand that tugged at her was shaking.

"Help what? Help how? They're going to kill him Stephen. After all these weeks, we're so close to him and it's too late!" She didn't know how to make him understand this sudden loss of faith. How could she explain it when she couldn't even understand it herself? Like an engine out of gas, her enduring hope had just chugged to a stop.

He grabbed her by the shoulders and shook her. A gentle shake, not rough, the way he sometimes was. Like her, he was weary. "Rachel, stop it! We don't know it's too late!"

"I know it!"

Her words were like the cry of a wounded animal. Stephen sank back into his chair. "Then at least let me still hope," he whispered. "Let me still hope."

They sat in the silence. In the darkness. Wrapped in their despair. Suddenly, Rachel whispered, "The phones. The phone hasn't rung at all. Robinson didn't call. Gallagher didn't call. No one from the Lost Child Foundation called. It doesn't make any sense."

She got up. Switched on a light, picked up the phone. "Stephen, look! Oh no! I can't believe I did this." She held out the phone so he could see. The device on the bottom was set to "no ring." "It must have happened when I knocked it off the table . . . so anyone who tried to call . . ."

He shook his head. Carefully, because it hurt like hell, astonished that anything more could surprise him. "Then maybe there are messages . . . on the machine . . . other messages besides mine . . . if you didn't answer. . . ." He made no move toward the door.

Rachel nodded as she adjusted the phone so it would ring, and set it gingerly on the table. "We should go and see. . . ." But her sense of urgency seemed to have deserted her. She crossed the room and sat down beside his chair again. She felt too weary to move. In a minute she would get up and go. They would both get up and go.

Silence wrapped around them again. Occasional rain splattered on the windows. The old house creaked and sighed. Rachel leaned

against Stephen's knee and listened to her watch tick. Listened to her heart beat. Listened to Stephen breathe, just as she had knelt so many times, listening to her children breathe.

Into that silence, the ringing of the phone shot through both of them like an electric shock. Rachel stumbled across the room and grabbed the receiver. Pulled it cautiously to her ear, afraid to hear the news it was bringing. "Hello?"

"Rachel?" A voice as weak and exhausted as her own.

"Yes?" She didn't want to talk to someone so discouraged. It could only be bad news.

"It's Peter. Peter Coffin. I've been trying to reach you but they wouldn't give me your number . . . the ones who are answering the phones." He paused, gasping. "I know who has David. I hope it's not too late."

"Your parents," she said, suddenly knowing this was so. She winced as Stephen turned on the overhead light, felt him lean in against her shoulder.

"My parents. Today Gabe told me that my mother had called several months back, and he'd yelled at her for neglecting me when I had AIDS and I was dying. I guess she decided to . . ."

"But you don't know where they are. . . ." she interrupted.

"I've found them. When it didn't matter, I didn't try very hard. I didn't care about seeing her when I believed my father was dead. There was no reason to expose myself to that raging hatred. But tonight on the news, when I saw the picture . . . I knew it was them . . . my mother . . . and my father. That he was still alive. And that she was making him do this. I located a cousin. Got an address. . . ."

The ticking of her watch seemed to be getting louder. Irrationally, she said, "Why did you wait so long to call, Peter? . . . Every second is precious!" Behind her, she could hear Stephen's voice, demanding to know what was happening. She pinched her ear shut to close out the distraction. "Peter, why did you wait?" Foolish, because she didn't even know if he had waited. Holding her breath as she waited for his answer.

"I didn't wait. I called the Maine State Police. And the Lost Child Foundation. That 800 number. But then I knew I needed to call you,

too, in case no one else did. They wouldn't give me your number, so
it took a while. I couldn't remember your name, but Mary, my nurse
did, and then, the first few times I called, no one answered."

"Where is he?" she asked, and he told her. "We've got to go
there. We've got to go right now."

She would have hung up and raced to her car, but he stopped her,
his voice desperate. "Wait! Will you take me with you? David doesn't
need to know who I am. . . . I just . . . I just need to be there . . . to see
that everything is all right." His voice dropped, faded, came back
again. She could tell he was at the limit of his strength. "I think he'll
do the right thing . . . but then . . . he let himself be talked into
this. . . ."

"Yes. Come. We can talk about this on the way," she said. "Give
me your number. We'll call you as soon as things are arranged."

She scribbled the number on one of the pictures. Looking down
at it, suddenly she could see the resemblances among David, Peter,
and the old man. Resemblances she'd been too numb to notice.
Now they seemed so clear. "Stephen," she said, looking into his impatient face, "we've got to charter a plane and fly to Maine. Peter's
coming with us. Peter Coffin. He knows where David is."

It was part of the strangeness of the night, of their strange affinity, that Stephen didn't argue. He asked for the information he
needed, picked up the phone, and started making arrangements. In
a few minutes he told her, "Call him back and tell him to meet us at
the airport in an hour." And Rachel, unworldly as she was, knew
which airport and exactly what to do.

When they tried Gallagher and Robinson, both were, as they expected, already gone. Only Gallagher had left a message on the
phone. "Damn Robinson," Stephen said. "He never called."

"Yes," Rachel agreed. "For something like this, he deserves to be
damned."

She got a warm sweater, gathered up the fleecy cover from David's
bed, and tucked Megrim into her pocket. Stephen washed the blood
off his face and changed his shirt. And they were heading for the
door. Toward her car. On their way. Praying with every breath, with
every step, that they were not too late.

She felt a new surge of energy and maybe the rekindling of something like hope. "He didn't try very hard to reach us," she said. "Gallagher could have sent a car. . . ."

As they opened the door, a sheet of paper fluttered to the ground. Stephen picked it up, gingerly, wary of more bad news. "From Gallagher," he said. "We're supposed to call him."

"Assholes!" Rachel exploded. "A note in the door? This is so wrong. We're being treated as inconsequential here. Robinson and that witch woman are probably already on their way, so that they can be on the scene if . . . when . . . David is found. Them, but not us! I want to say jerks, idiots, assholes, but none of those words are strong enough for the kind of manipulation that's been going on. I hate them all!"

"Selfish, Machiavellian thieves," he suggested, initiating a word game they sometimes played. He sounded almost gay.

"Scheming, duplicitous interlopers," she said.

"Dishonorable, interfering impostors."

"Iniquitous, interfering impostors."

"Dishonorable, duplicitous dastards."

She laughed and at the sound of it recognized that it was something she hadn't done for a long time. "I like that one best," she said. "I think I need new wipers."

"Not tonight you don't."

"As long as we make it to the airport. All these things are doing is smearing the stuff around."

They drove on in silence—an endless silence punctuated by the *tunk* of the wipers—peering through the tunnel that their headlights made in the mist, staring down that narrow lane of light, their minds in another place. Rachel was a timid driver, but she pushed the car just as fast as she dared, hoping nothing came at them out of the fog. It was too late for cyclists and joggers but there were still deer.

"It's just up ahead, I think. On the right," he said, startling her. She stomped on the brake and then accelerated, bringing a groan from him.

"What?" she said.

"My head. It hurts when you jerk it around like that."

"Were you really in an accident or did Carole whack you with her cast-iron frying pan? Is that how you really got wounded?"

"The only wounds I suffered at her hands were a million turkey pecks to the soul. She sure doesn't mince words."

"I often wish I could do that."

"I'm so grateful that you can't," he said. "I like you peaceful and quiet. It's very comforting."

"I don't think I've been very comforting lately," she said.

"I don't think either one of us has been."

"What if we get there and he's—"

"Shsssh!" he said. "We're not going to—"

"I'm sorry. I forgot. A momentary lapse. We'll talk about something else. Do you remember our first date?" She steered the Volvo cautiously into the turn and stared ahead up the unlit road. Here it wasn't foggy and the rain was falling harder. She peered through the silvery needles of rain. No houses, no signs, not even a mailbox, just a ribbon of shiny black rising steeply uphill. "Are you sure this is it?"

"We've got another mile or so. It's just a tiny airfield. You can't expect big signs or anything. I'll keep an eye out. About the date. Yes, of course I remember it. We met in a bar. You were with that redheaded bastard. He was abusing you. I told him to leave. Then I asked for your number. You wouldn't give it to me but you took mine, and later you called me up. Right?"

"I guess," she said, peering distractedly into the darkness. "Oh, there it is. I wonder if Peter will be able to find it."

"He'd better. We don't have time to wait."

She glanced in her rearview mirror. "There's a car behind me."

"Probably him. Slow down. Put your blinker on; it's just up there. See the road?"

They bumped down a rutted road that ended abruptly at a small building. A tattered wind sock flew from a pole beside it. In what appeared to be the middle of a field, lights were on and they could see two men moving around a small plane. "Your chariot, madam," Stephen said.

Another car pulled along side and parked. A woman got out of the driver's door and walked around to help her passenger. Rachel

recognized the nurse from the hospital, Mary, and was surprised. She opened her door, walked around to where Peter was leaning weakly on the woman's arm, and waited for Stephen to join them. "Peter Coffin, my husband, Stephen Stark." The men shook hands, everyone too exhausted, too focused on the reason they were there to bother with any pissing contests. Not that Peter Coffin seemed the type for posturing, even when he was healthy. Then Peter introduced the nurse.

"This is my keeper, Mary. She insisted that I couldn't come alone," he said, "and she wouldn't let me take a taxi."

"I told him he shouldn't leave the hospital," she said grimly. "A lot of good that did. Doctors don't listen to nurses like they should."

"We haven't got time to . . ." Stephen began. He stopped, looking from Coffin to the plane. "Can you walk that far?"

Peter smiled. In the light from the single floodlight that lit the lot where they were standing, Rachel saw that his eyes had a bright, unnatural glitter. "With a little help from my friends." Leaning heavily on his companion, he started off across the field. Stephen and Rachel followed.

The knot in Rachel's chest was so big, it felt like she was moving a boulder every time she took a breath. By the time they reached the plane, she was hanging as heavily from Stephen's arm as Peter was from Mary's. Peter and Mary got into the plane. Stephen helped her in, the pilot turned and spoke to them all briefly, and then they bumped down the runway and lifted into the sky, the roar of the engine surrounding them so entirely, it was like being inside it.

Stephen's hand, when she touched it, was icy. It closed around hers like a drowning person grasping a lifeline. She returned the pressure. Her other hand was in her pocket, wrapped tightly around Megrim. Then she released the dragon, reached back, and took Peter's hand. It was thin and dry and felt as fragile as a bird in hers.

Sitting in the dark roar of the cabin, holding hands with Stephen and Peter, she reflected on her relationship with them, the bizarre yet so fundamental way in which they were all involved. As she connected them now, through her hands, she connected them through her body, through David. How odd it was, and yet how true, the ways

in which they were all linked. She was the mother of their child; these men were the fathers of her son. Stephen, whose son had died, the emotional father, and Peter, dying himself, the biological. In the eternal chain of fathers and sons, she was central yet superfluous, the conduit through which they both flowed toward the future. But tonight, the fathers went forth for different reasons: Stephen went as a father to seek a son; Peter, as a son to seek his father.

She squeezed their hands and felt the pressure returned. With the pressure, she felt a surge of hope, all of their hope, running out from them toward the future, toward David, in his grave danger, who was all of their posterity. Peter's labored breathing, audible even over the engine noise, marked the cadence for all of them. They were all exhausted, at the end of their tethers, gasping for breath, grasping for hope, wishing their way through the dark, wet night toward David.

THE VOICES DOWNSTAIRS *faded to a whisper and then to nothing at all. David, exhausted from fear and hunger and weeping, fell asleep where he lay, his cheek still pressed against the register. What woke him was the sound of the key in the door, the sharp rattle of metal on metal and then the hard, solid snap of the lock as it released. He pushed himself up on his arms, still dazed and aching from his hours on the hard floor. The first pale gray light was showing at the window. His stomach hurt terribly, rumbling as it hit him with sharp pains.*

The door opened with a spill of harsh yellow light and the man and woman came into the room. He looked up at them, confused by sleep, scared by the strangeness of the woman's face. In her hands she held a brown burlap sack. The man carried coiled rope.

"David," she said, "there's danger again and we've got to move you. We're going to put you in this sack so no one will know it's you. If you cooperate, we won't have to be rough and we won't hurt you, but if we must, we'll force you to cooperate. I don't think you'd like that, would you?" Her voice was distant and matter-of-fact and reminded him of the way the vet had sounded, telling him and his mother that their injured kitten couldn't be saved and would have to be put to sleep.

He pushed himself to his feet, looking past her at the door, wondering if he could dodge past them and get out. The woman watched his eyes and followed their gaze. "We can't let you escape," she said. She turned and locked the door, and David's heart sank.

He looked at the man but the man wouldn't meet his eye and stared in-stead at the rope. "Come over here, David," she said. "You know you can't get away. You might as well cooperate."

His eyes darted around the room. Was there anything he could use as a weapon? He was only nine, and not a particularly big nine, either. But he was a brave nine, and he wasn't going to let them stuff him in a sack and drop him down a well without a fight. As his mom often said, when they were having discussions about what to do in difficult situations—reality lessons, she called them—he didn't have anything to lose by trying.

The key was still in the door. Maybe if he could distract them somehow? There were ski poles in the closet, poles with nice sharp points on the end. He'd used them a few times as imaginary swords, or lances, or spears when he'd played up here alone. He took two cautious steps backward, ducked into the closet, and grabbed a pole. He came out swinging, saw the surprise on the woman's face, swung the pole at her head. She ducked, and as he swung again, she grabbed the pole in her two big hands, gave a tremendous jerk, and David flew forward, right into her arms.

"That's quite enough of that, you little brat," she said roughly, twisting one of his arms backward and forcing him onto his knees. She held him down with one of her own knees as she twisted something around his wrists.

"You're lying about moving me," he yelled. "You're going to drown me. You're going to put me in that sack and drop me in a well." He didn't want to cry, but he couldn't help it. He wanted his mother and he was so scared, it was choking him. "You're liars. Liars. Liars. And I hate you!"

"Father, tear off a piece of that duct tape and hand it over so I can shut him up. I'm not listening to any more of this."

David twisted his head aside and looked up at the old man, who was fumbling with a roll of silver tape. The man had sometimes acted like his friend; he'd been kind. He thought he could see a tear on the man's cheek, but there was a tearing sound and the man handed over a strip of tape. The woman grabbed his chin, twisted his head sideways, and slapped the tape over his mouth. "Better give me another, longer one," she said. "Long enough to wrap around his head."

Through lips sealed with sticky, terrible-tasting tape, David felt a scream rise, try to escape, and stick in his mouth, filling it, backing into his throat, choking him. He could hear small, terrified noises that he knew were his own.

There was another ripping sound. She grabbed his chin again, slapped on another piece of tape, wrapped it tightly around his hair, and released him. "Breathe through your nose," she said.

She held out her hand for the rope, bent down, and began to tie his feet. There was nothing more he could do to help himself. He closed his eyes and cried for his mother.

And down the long and silent street,
The dawn, with silver-sandaled feet,
Crept like a frightened girl.

—WILDE, "The Harlot's House"

CHAPTER THIRTY-EIGHT

The first light fingers of dawn were prying the lid off the night when the little plane dropped out of the sky and coasted to a stop at the Bangor airport. Having spent the whole tense time with his knees practically in his ears, Stephen heaved an audible sigh of relief. Airplane seats were not designed for people. A police car ablaze with lights was there to meet them. As they unfolded themselves from the cramped seats and climbed down the steps, Stephen saw the door open and a tall man in uniform got out. He hurried over, hand outstretched. "Stephen Stark," he said, shaking the trooper's hand. "Is there any news?"

The trooper identified himself as Scott Hawes and then waited for the rest of them to come up before he answered. He held out his hand as Stephen introduced Rachel, and Stephen saw him hesitate as Peter Coffin and Mary were introduced. "Coffin?" he repeated.

"Yes. I'm the one who called you about the boy. About my . . ." There was a slight pause, a tremor in his voice, as he said, ". . . parents."

Coffin's emaciated condition did not escape the trooper's notice. "We could continue this in the car," he suggested.

"Can you take four?" Stephen asked. The trooper nodded. They followed him to the car and got in, moving with economy and a shared sense of urgency. Stephen helped the others into the backseat and then got in himself. "Have you found them?"

"Not exactly."

Stephen thought his heart skipped. He heard Rachel's sharp inhalation from the rear. He didn't have to look back to know her face. "What are you trying to tell us?"

"We found the farmhouse all right," Hawes said. "But there was no one there."

His spirits sank even lower. "Deserted?"

"Oh no. Someone's been living there right along. That's what the neighbors say. And the livestock are well cared for. Food in the refrigerator's fresh. And we found where they'd been keeping the boy. They'd even enrolled him in school, though he hasn't been there for a few days. . . ."

"Their cars are gone?" Rachel interrupted impatiently.

"Nope. Cars are there, clothes are there, cows are there. Just no people."

"So what are you guys doing?" Stephen asked.

"Watching the house, waiting to see if anyone shows up. Soon as it gets a little lighter, they'll start searching the woods."

"They've gone to put him down the well," Rachel moaned. "Tied him up and dropped him down the well."

"Well?" Hawes asked. "That psychic lady said something about a well. . . ."

"She's no more a psychic than I am," Stephen said. He looked back and saw that Rachel and Peter Coffin were holding hands. He felt a twinge, tried to evaluate it, and quickly abandoned it, confused by the enormity of the problem. Nothing in his life had been stranger than tonight. He'd been through so many mood changes, he felt like an emotional rainbow. A chameleon. He resented Coffin's tie to David, yet without Coffin there would have been no David. Yet without Coffin, there would have been no kidnapping. Yet

without Coffin, they wouldn't be here, still with a hope of rescuing him. The ins and outs and incredible connections layered in his mind like an Escher drawing. Everything circled back on itself, merged, was itself and something else.

He liked things clear, liked to impose his own order on things. Mentally, he pushed himself away from his confusion and sought for something he could control. "You're taking us there?" he said.

"Yes."

"How long?"

"Twenty minutes."

"So long?" Rachel said.

"Can't you go any faster?" he asked.

"No."

"Twenty minutes from here or from the airport?"

"Airport."

Silence fell on the car. They each sat with their own thoughts as the car hurried through the dawning day, over the speed limit but below the limit of their urgency. Gradually the ghostly shapes along the roadside formed themselves into trees, houses, and walls, the big expanses of gray into fields. Stephen distracted himself by falling back on his childhood practice of counting telephone poles. Suddenly Rachel said, "Oh!" like a person struck with an unexpected blow.

Hawes hit the brake.

"Don't slow down," Stephen said. "Don't slow down. What is it, Rachel?"

"Something's happening," she said.

"Something good?" he asked impatiently. "Something bad? What?"

She was quiet. He looked back and saw she had her eyes closed and her fingertips pressed to her forehead. "Bad," she said finally. Then, "Wait!" Hawes hit the brake again.

"Don't slow down," they all said.

Stephen thought he heard Hawes mutter "Car full of nuts" under his breath.

"What is it, Rach?"

"I don't know . . . I . . . he . . . something dreadful has happened,

I think. I can't tell, exactly. I'm not seeing anything, only feeling this smothering sense of dread. No sound. No pictures. Just fear. Smothering . . . he's . . . wait!"

Stephen was ignoring the road now, looking back at her. Saw the grimace of pain as she seized Coffin's hand and squeezed. He held out his own and she took it. There was a peculiar sensation of energy, as though she were electrically charged. He closed his eyes and held on. "What?" he said.

"Inside something. A blanket, maybe. He's all wrapped up, muffled. He's too afraid to even think."

"Trooper, how much longer?" he said.

"Maybe five."

"Stephen, stop asking. You're going to make yourself crazy."

"Could I get any crazier?"

The nurse looked at her watch. "Medication time," she said as easily as if she'd just sailed through a hospital door instead of being cramped in a speeding car with three frantic people. She opened a bag, took out a thermos, poured some water, and handed the cup to Peter. Then she shook out pills and extended them on a flat palm toward him.

"You know I hate this," Coffin said.

She nodded. "I do. You'd hate things more if you didn't take them."

Stephen watched the skeletal hand around the glass, the skinny throat working, averting his eyes when the other man passed the glass back, leaned his head against the seat, and closed his eyes, exhausted by the mere act of swallowing some pills. He realized that Coffin's presence represented an enormous act of will and that only determination was now driving the ravaged body. Embarrassed at his staring, he looked away and met the nurse's eyes. Grave gray eyes. She gave a faint nod to acknowledge what he'd seen. It said better than words her understanding that her patient might be dying but this was business he had to settle first.

"Here we are," Hawes announced, pulling into a driveway already jammed with official vehicles.

Stephen got out, opened the back door, and helped Peter Coffin

to his feet. The nurse came around and gave him her arm. Stephen offered his own arm to Rachel, and looking like a ragtag Victorian promenade, they marched slowly forward through the crowd until they came to the person who seemed to be in charge.

In the group surrounding him, Stephen was not surprised to find John Robinson, Norah Proust, and Gallagher. He reserved his gaze for Robinson, ignoring the others. "You might have tried to reach us, John. He's not your child." He turned his back on Robinson's explanation and stuck out his hand to the man in charge. "Stephen Stark," he said. "David's father. This is my wife, Rachel. And this is Peter Coffin, the kidnappers' son. He's the one who called you about the location. . . ."

Suddenly they were surrounded by police. Stephen had a claustrophobic moment when he wanted to break loose and run but he managed it, and they began to tell their version of the story. Someone found a chair for Peter, and they listened as the lieutenant in charge explained the situation. It was much as they'd heard in the car. The empty house, signs of recent occupation, signs of David, neighbors' confirmation that David had been there. The man in charge, called Deaver, explained it briskly, succinctly, in an almost perfunctory manner.

Stephen noticed a group of men heading toward the woods behind the barn. "Where are they going?"

"To search the woods," Deaver said. "We've been waiting for some light."

"What about the well?" Rachel asked. "Is that where they're going? To the well?"

"That woman over there, the one who claims to be a psychic, keeps talking about a well, but she's got no idea where it is, and as far as we know, as far as the neighbors know, there is no old well on this property."

Stephen rubbed his cold fingers together to warm them, wishing he'd worn a warmer jacket. It was almost June and felt like November. "There's a well," he said, and turned to Rachel. "Do you know anything about the well, Rach?"

She looked nervously at the cop in charge and then down at the

ground. "All I know is that there is one, somewhere." She pointed at the searchers who were spreading out into a line and heading into the woods. "Can we go with them?"

Deaver shook his head. "I don't think that would be a good idea."

"Why not?" Stephen asked.

"We might need you for something."

"Like what?"

"Identifying a b—" Deaver stopped, but not in time. "Hey, what's with the two of them?"

Stephen looked around. Peter Coffin and Rachel, hand in hand like Hansel and Gretel, were walking slowly toward the woods. As he watched, Norah Proust detached herself from a group, ran after them, and plucked at Rachel's arm. Rachel's response happened so fast, he could hardly see what was happening. One minute, Norah was standing there pulling at Rachel's sleeve, the next minute she was lying on the ground in a heap, staring and rubbing her jaw, and Rachel and Peter were already walking away.

"Following a trail of crumbs," he said, and started after them.

ALL HE COULD *see now were the pinpoints of light coming through the burlap. He was inside the bag, its rough fabric scraping harshly across his face, the dusty smell choking him. He couldn't cough because of the tape, and several times he thought he was going to choke as he huddled in the bag, jostled around as the old man and woman carried him. He could hear the grunts of the woman and the man's labored breathing as they went.*

Suddenly one end dropped and hit the ground, and David spilled halfway out into the murky dawn, his head and shoulders unceremoniously dumped into cold wet leaves. He looked anxiously from one to the other. Was this it? Were they at the well? Terror swelled within him like one of those toys that grows in water, filling him until it pushed out all other feelings. Neither the man nor the woman looked at him. They were staring at each other.

"I can't do it," the man said.

"You don't have to carry him," she said. "I can drag him. We're nearly there."

"I don't mean that. I can't kill the boy," the man said. "He's my grandson. He's all we've got left to leave behind now, with Peter gone. If we didn't want to care for him, we never should have taken him. If we don't want him, let's just give him back."

"I'd no idea he'd be so much trouble. So stubborn, so cold, so unloving," the woman answered. "He's just more of his father's bad seed. You can see it

by looking at him. Far better that it should just die out. As for giving him back, how could we?"

"We could just do it. Just say we did wrong and give him back."

"Don't be such a fool," she said. "You think they'd pat us on the back and say thanks and leave it at that? We'd go to prison for the rest of our lives."

"He's a good boy," the man said. "And there are people who love him. . . ."

"Peter was a good boy, and we were people who loved him . . . and then everything went wrong. There was a taint there, that overtook him, made him a sinner. . . ."

"I don't know that you ever did love Peter."

"Of course I did. He was my son. Anyway, what difference does that make now? I'm cold. You're cold. Let's just get this done with and go home."

"You make it sound like a simple chore. He's a human being. . . ."

"So am I. And I don't intend to spend the rest of my days in a prison somewhere."

"If we kill him, we'll deserve it."

"If we kill him, no one will ever know. Listen, Father, this is no time for second thoughts. We're already up to our ears in this. You wanted to change your mind, you should have done that before. It's too late."

David wiggled the rest of the way out of the sack and tried to slither away across the leaves. It was almost impossible and made a lot of noise. The woman gave him a weary look. "Don't waste your time," she said. "You'll just wear yourself out and then we'll put you back in the sack."

Behind the tape, he tried to scream at her, tried to tell her that they couldn't kill him; his mother and father needed him to come home. The woman came and put a foot on his back, pressing him down into the leaves. "Be quiet," she said. He closed his eyes and lay still, trying to breathe through the leaves that were matted against his face. "Come on, Father. We're almost done. Take his other leg and help me out." She grabbed his leg and started dragging him.

His shirt came untucked and rucked up so that his bare skin was exposed. Branches scraped his stomach and raked his face. He was smothered by wet, slimy leaves that clung to his cheeks and his nose, choking him with the scent of rot and damp. He turned his head sideways and made one last effort, trying to jerk his legs out of their grasp.

"Here we are," the woman said. "Help me shove this cover off." They dropped his feet. He heard grunts and the scrape of wood on stone. "There. That's wide enough. Plenty of room. He's not very big."

David felt her hands on his body, pulling him up. "Come on, Father," she snapped. "Help me."

The man's "no" echoed through the woods, so startling that the woman let David drop.

"I already told you. It's too late for some misguided attack of conscience," she hissed. "Let's get this over with."

"No," the old man repeated. "I won't. I can't. He's a good boy, Mother. I agreed to take him because you were going to raise him. Going to have another chance to do it right. I didn't help you steal Peter's son so we could throw him down a well. . . ."

"Don't ever use that name in front of me again! Peter is dead to me, you hear? Dead and gone." She was panting like some big animal. When she spoke again, her voice was tight with fury. It barely sounded human. "Are you going to help me or not?"

Once again the old man's firm "no" echoed through the woods.

David lay on the ground by their feet, staring up at their angry faces. Maybe, if he could just get his body going, he could roll away and they wouldn't notice. He was gathering his energy when the woman bent, suddenly, and snatched up a heavy stick lying near his head. He heard the crunch of feet, a whirring, like the sound of a branch rushing through the air. He stared with horror, unable to move, as the big branch arced through the air above him. "Mom, Dad, help me!" he thought as it connected with a jarring thud.

At the door of life, by the gate of breath,
There are worse things waiting for men than death.
—SWINBURNE, "The Triumph of Time"

CHAPTER THIRTY-NINE

Their departure had been brave enough, but Rachel knew that Peter wouldn't be able to go far without help. It hadn't been a planned departure; rather, they had been drawn toward the woods together by something in each of their minds. Rachel to her son, Peter to his father. Before long, Stephen and Mary had joined them, Stephen putting his strong arm around Peter without a word, and the four of them had forged ahead, oblivious to anything that might have been going on around them, ignoring the calling voices behind them.

"He's alive," Rachel said. There was a gleam in her eye that hadn't been there before. A gleam in her eye and a confidence in her step that inspired Stephen as well. Behind them were footsteps, dulled by the mat of rotten leaves, and Deaver caught up with them. "This is foolish," he said. "You don't know these woods and you aren't dressed for searching. Besides which, this man is sick. He's in no shape to be undertaking . . ."

"We haven't any choice," Rachel interrupted. "David's out here in these woods somewhere. We've got to find him."

"That's what all those men are for . . . trained officers . . . you don't need to . . ." Deaver began.

They walked on, ignoring him. He muttered an undeleted expletive. "I thought you said you were the boy's mother?" Deaver said.

"I am the boy's mother," Rachel agreed. She supposed he was confused because she'd walked off hand in hand with Peter instead of with Stephen, but she had no time now to help him out. This was life and death, not chitchat. "I'm his mother and I'm going to find him. You can come along if you want, but please don't keep talking at us. It's distracting."

"What in heaven's name am I distracting you from? You're just tramping through the goddamned woods, lady."

Rachel put a finger to her lips. "Shssh!" Deaver fell silent, staring at her with troubled eyes while she stopped and listened to sounds that only she could hear. "This way," she directed, pointing right. To the right lay a boggy lowland dotted with tussocks of grass, live and dying trees, and the decaying trunks of fallen trees. Where the land rose slightly, there were remnants of an old stone wall. "Along the wall."

"Wait a minute," Deaver said, "Don't tell me you're another one of those goddamned psychics."

"I'm not *another* anything," Rachel said. "Just a mother searching for her child. And please don't try to tell me I should let professionals do it. We've already been through that bullshit."

They started walking again, but Peter was slowing down, gasping. Finally he stopped. "I can't . . . do it . . . any more."

"Then we'll carry you," Stephen said.

"I'll wait here with him," Mary offered.

"No. We'll slow down," Rachel said. "We're nearly there, anyway."

"Nearly where?" Deaver growled.

"Aren't you supposed to be back there coordinating the search for our missing son?" Stephen asked, tension making him mean.

"I *am* coordinating the search for your son," Deaver snapped, waving what looked like a portable phone. "While I'm following four civilian lunatics through Haley's Swamp to be sure they don't get lost. One missing person is enough."

"More than enough," Rachel said. "Let's go, then." She plunged
ahead, ignoring the water that filled her shoes, the branches that
tore at her clothes, stung her face, tangled in her hair, following
an internal compass she didn't dare question, driven by a mission
she didn't doubt. The others followed more slowly, helping Peter
through hard spots. Always behind her, like a hound at her heels,
came his labored breathing. When she looked back, she saw him
there, dead white, sweaty, and terrible, but she also caught the determined look in his eye. It would do no good to suggest that he go
back. For him, no less than for Stephen and herself, this was something he must do. Must do or die trying.

Rachel hoped no one would die this day, and it was that hope,
the hope in her heart that had risen and fallen like a moon tide over
these many weeks, that kept her cold feet moving. That drove her
fast and faster along the rough, wet path. "Hold on, David. I'm coming," she thought. "We're coming. We're coming as fast as we can."
She tried to listen for an answer, but there was noise all around her
and a rush of blood in her head that drowned out sound. She didn't
dare stop.

The wall began to climb uphill and then the land gradually leveled out. Her foot slipped on a rock and she twisted her ankle, the
pain making her gasp out loud. From behind her, Stephen called,
"What is it, Rachel?"

"It's nothing," she called over her shoulder. "Just twisted my
ankle."

Deaver and Stephen had made a chair with their hands, to carry
Peter up the hill, and the three of them had fallen far behind.
Rachel paused where the land leveled and peered ahead while Mary
knelt beside her and gently probed the ankle.

She looked down at Mary, who shook her head. "It's gonna
hurt."

David's cry for help exploded in her head. "Oh my God!" she
said. "We've got to hurry. Something's happening." She took off at a
hobbling run, ignoring the questions they were yelling at her. Ignoring the pain in her foot and the pain in her side, she ran until she
was so out of breath, she had to wrap her arms around herself to

contain the burning in her chest, ran until her breathing was a loud, animal grunt. And even then she didn't stop, but slowed so that the others caught up. It was much brighter now and far ahead she could just see what looked like a patch of blue.

"Over there," she gasped, pointing. "Something blue that's moving. Do you see it?"

Deaver pulled binoculars off his belt and peered intently ahead. "Just one person," he said. "Woman, I think. Struggling with something."

He handed the binoculars to Stephen and began speaking into his radio. Stephen passed them to Peter. Peter put them up to his eyes, steadying them as best he could with two shaking hands, and stared for a long time. Finally he handed them back to Deaver, nodding. "It's my mother," he said. He sat down on the stone wall, his head dropping into his hands. "I've come this far, but I don't know if I can . . ."

There was a crackle and splutter as Deaver instructed his men. Rachel tugged at Stephen's hand. "Come on," she whispered, "we can't wait for them." Hand in hand, the two of them began walking forward. Slowly. Then faster. Then faster, Rachel breaking into a run, pulling Stephen after her. Still holding hands, they were racing through the woods toward the bobbing woman, a rush barely slowed by Rachel's limping gait.

They burst out of the woods into a small clearing, where they could finally see the blue figure clearly. She had David in her arms, his feet already poised over the well.

"Don't!" Rachel's scream filled the clearing. "Stop! Don't do it! Let him go!"

The woman turned, her crazy eyes not even seeming to see them. "Peter's bad seed," she said. "I told him. I told Father we had to get rid of it, but he wouldn't listen. People don't like to listen to me. They don't like it that I'm right. But I am. I am. I've always been able to see evil when others couldn't. Evil and immorality and perversions. It's not normal to sell your seed in a test tube, you know." She turned away from them, muttering something they couldn't hear.

"Please don't hurt my son!" Stephen's words burst out, thick with agony and fear. The woman showed no sign of having heard.

As one, they sprang forward. Stephen seized the woman, who let go of David with a laugh. Rachel hadn't seen the man in dark clothes lying on the ground. She tripped over him and fell to her knees. David, released from the woman's grasp, slipped into the well. "No!" Rachel screamed. She clambered to her feet, rushed past Stephen and the struggling woman. She hadn't come this far, gotten this close, only to lose him now. With a strength born of terror, she shoved off the cover, an ear-splitting rasp of wood on stone, and bent her head to look.

At first, with her body blocking most of the light, she could see nothing but darkness in the narrow shaft. Gradually, as her eyes adjusted, she saw something white about five feet below. She took a breath, forcing back her terror of dark, narrow spaces, and leaned in as far as she could. The whiteness resolved into David's bound hands, caught on a piece of pipe, his body swaying below in the darkness. "David . . ." The name echoed eerily, distorted and too loud. She saw the white hands jump, lowered her voice to a whisper. "Darling, don't move. Daddy and I are here. We'll get you out." She reached down toward him. David. Her son. Their son. It wasn't too late. But she couldn't reach.

She stood up. Saw Stephen still struggling with the woman. "Forget her, Stephen," she called. "David needs help."

Stephen flung the flailing woman away from him and rushed to her side, peering into the gloom.

"There," Rachel whispered. "Down there. His hands are caught on that pipe."

Stephen stood on tiptoe and bent as far as he could, reaching into the darkness. "I can't reach him."

"You can hold my feet and lower me down," she said. The fear of going down there was paralyzing. Her chest was tight and she was cold all over. But there was David, hanging, almost literally, by a thread. This was no time to be squeamish. There were noises as other people arrived. It didn't matter. Her world was very small right now—just the three of them. Everything else rolled off her like rain

off glass. "Come on," she urged. "Hurry. We don't know how long that pipe may hold."

"Maybe someone else . . ." he began. "You know you're afraid of—"

"It's narrow," she said, hearing in her own voice the choked, thin sounds of fear. "No one else is small enough. . . ."

He shook his head. "Never mind. Okay. I'll hold your legs. Ready?" She swung up onto the edge of the well, turned onto her stomach, and stuck her head into the well. She felt his hands on her ankles. "Here you go."

The temperature dropped as she was lowered into the dark. Where her shirt rode up, she could feel the rough, slimy stone against her stomach. She heard the echo of her breath and also, she thought, the echo of her heart. Lower and lower, her body blotting out most of the light, Stephen's grip agonizing on her swollen ankle. She reached out and felt around the edges, cringing at the cold, slippery walls. Where was he? Had he slipped? Frantic, she forced her hands to move faster. Searching, searching until at last she touched David's cold, limp hands.

"Lower," she called, forgetting to whisper. The word reverberated and boomed around her. She felt David's hands jerk and slip off the pipe, caught the rope in her own hands and held on, though even her son's slight weight nearly wrenched it from her grasp. Her arms felt like they were being pulled from their sockets, and she knew it must be the same for poor David. She hung there, swaying now at the end of Stephen's grasp, with David swaying at the end of hers, like a long, awkward human rope, bound tenuously together in their love and terror.

She took a deep breath, steeling herself against the sensory assault her own words would bring, and called, "I've got him! Pull us up."

Suddenly it seemed like there were a dozen hands on her feet and legs. It felt like she was flying backward up the well shaft and back into openness, air, and light. Hands reached out and took David from her as other hands set her back on her feet. Her shaking legs gave way and she was sitting on the damp ground, surrounded by people talking at her.

Maybe they weren't speaking English. She couldn't understand a thing they said. She was remembering the time, as a child, when she'd crawled into a culvert on a dare and gotten stuck there, waiting for what seemed like an eternity in the cold, echoing darkness, while icy water ran along her stomach and the corrugated ribs pressed into her back, while her friend ran for help. Her father had to pull her out by her feet. She'd tell David about it. Maybe it would make him feel better if she made it sound like an adventure. She didn't need to tell him about the terror that had clutched her then and come back so vividly now. He'd had enough of terror and fear and captivity.

She looked around, but he wasn't in sight. People were bending over a figure on the ground. She rose, took a few limping steps, but that brought her close enough to see long legs in muddy work pants and gray hair. The old man. Peter's father. His figure so still on the ground, Peter bent over him, the limp, age-spotted hand between his own two skeletal hands, Mary by his side.

But where was David? And where was Stephen? Why had they left her? "Where is my son?" she asked. A cacophony of words burst out around her. They were still speaking in foreign tongues, but she followed a pointing hand to another knot of people. Even from the back, she recognized Gallagher.

David. She tore her way through the uniformed crowd, pounding on the unyielding backs, trying to get to her son, all the while calling to him, "David! David! Are you alive?" She couldn't get through, couldn't get to him. Panic bubbled up, expanded until it filled her chest, choking her, and then, as she beat on yet another shoulder and uttered her cries in another deaf ear, David's voice exploded in her head.

"Mom. Mom, are you there? Where's my mom?"

"I'm here, my darling. Mom's right here." Gallagher's arm shot out and pulled the man away and she burst through to her son's side. The others might have been ghosts, they mattered so little.

David lay, pale and silent, on a pile of coats, clutching Stephen's hand. His mouth was bloody and his face raw where they had pulled off the tape, but when Rachel appeared, the wounded mouth spread in a wide grin. Tears pouring down her face, Rachel knelt and pulled

her poor, battered boy onto her lap, wrapping her arms tightly around him. Stephen, beside her, wrapped his arms around both of them, pressing his wet face against hers. "You're not dead," David said. "I was so scared. They were going to put me in the well. He tried to stop her and she hit him with a log." Snuggling into the warm space between their bodies, he started to cry.

The beating of her heart was so loud, Rachel could hear nothing else. She saw Stephen's lips moving and shook her head. There was no room now for anything but David. No room for words, not even room for Peter's sorrow. David was safe, finally safe. At long last back in their arms. All his fear and pain and loneliness vented in the sobs that shook his small body as she and Stephen rained kisses down on his soft, dark head.

Then, from the mass huddled around the old man, she heard a great sob she knew was Peter's. Over the thudding of her heart, she heard Peter's voice, on the phone, and remembered what he'd said. "I hope he'll do the right thing. I think he will. . . ." The old man had tried to do the right thing. Perhaps lost his life trying. Peter and the old man. Rachel and Stephen and David. Parents and children. All strangely linked together by a series of fateful decisions. She'd never imagined anyone other than themselves involved in David's conception, yet the ripples from that decision had spread out and touched other lives, and bounced back to touch hers again.

"No one ever imagines this," she said aloud. "No one could."

She raised her tear-filled eyes and looked at Stephen over David's head. He was crying, too. He stretched his arms and pulled her closer. Too close. Too tight. David, between them, wiggled and said, "Hey!" Stephen loosened his grasp and they both bent again to David's head, their faces touching, Stephen's rough and stubbly against her own. It would take a long time to repair the damage, she knew, but still she felt like she was in the middle of a miracle. Even with so much wrong and so much unresolved, everything was going to be all right.

About the Author

KATHARINE CLARK was an assistant attorney general in Augusta, Maine, before moving to Massachusetts to marry, later working in public interest law and general private practice. She retired to raise her children and to write. Currently the president of the New England Chapter of Sisters in Crime, she lives in Concord, Massachusetts.